Rails to a River

RAILS
TO A
RIVER

. . . a long awakening

A NOVEL

Jim H. Ainsworth

FIRST EDITION

This is a work of fiction. All the characters, names, incidents,
organizations, and dialogue in this novel are either the products
of the author's imagination or are used fictionally.

ISBN 978-0-9904628-1-1

Library of Congress Control Number: 2014919260

Design by Vivian Freeman, *Yellow Rose Typesetting*

Printed in the United States of America

Season of Harvest Publications
2403 CR 4208
Campbell, Texas 75422

In memory of

DR. FRED TARPLEY,
the pied piper of writers—professor, mentor,
encourager, editor, advisor, friend.

A final goodbye. You made all things seem possible.

What booklovers are saying about Jim Ainsworth's writing:

Jim Ainsworth has a great writing style, and his use of the metaphor and simile is exceptional. His characters are truly realistic—no super heroes— just folks living their lives the best they can with all the ups and downs of humanity. Listen for the music; search for the flow.

—Ken Ryan

Jim Ainsworth cuts his characters from traditional American cloth— a little Huck Finn, a little Nick Adams, a little Holden Caulfield... a little John Wayne, a little Marlon Brando, a little James Dean.

—Professor Charles Bailey

Ainsworth makes you think... he makes you hurt right along with the characters... and that makes the characters more real, more interesting, and leaves one with an ache inside for them.

—Mary Miller

Ainsworth is a gifted writer who displays great skill with language, descriptions and dialogue. I'm hooked and cannot stop reading his work.

—Barbara Brown

Jim's talent as a storyteller is remarkable.

—Bobbie Purdy

I felt I was experiencing the events myself as I laughed, cried, and feared for the complex characters. They are so fascinating that a broad spectrum of readers will enjoy them.

—Loretta Kibler

I thought it would be impossible for Jim to write another book that lived up to the standard he set with his Rivers trilogy, but I was wrong. Ainsworth makes you feel the music.

—J. A. Cross

Jim H. Ainsworth is my favorite author/bar none.

—Charlotte Hilliard

Ainsworth is a masterful storyteller.

—Jerry Gervers

Rails to a River

ACKNOWLEDGEMENTS

Thanks to early readers Barbara Brown, Dr. Stephen Turner,
Dr. Larry Anderson, Trice Lawrence, Jan Bartley, Janet Currin.

ONE

1971

TEE JESSUP WEAVES HIS WAY DOWN ONE OF THE CONCRETE
canyons of downtown Dallas, his cheap double knit summer sport coat
suspended with a middle finger over his right shoulder. His breath comes
hard and fast as he tries to put distance between himself and work. He
stops at an abandoned shoeshine stand wedged between the back doors of
a dying shoe repair shop and a hamburger joint, both scheduled for dem-
olition as relics of a bygone era. The tiny buildings appear as refuse tossed
out the windows of the multi-story steel, brick, glass and stone fortresses
that tower over them.

Tee expects to find shade and a brief respite from human contact
between the buildings. He puts his hated Florsheim wingtips on the foot-
rests, throws his coat over an arm rest, leans back in the seat, and loosens
his tie. Only fools wear coats and ties in stifling heat and humidity. The
hands of the Fidelity Union Tower clock show a minute past ten, and the
LTV Tower thermometer red line is already over ninety. If the forecast is
right, it will pass a hundred by noon on the way to one-ten. The bar across

1

the street looks like a cool oasis but will not open till three. Even if it were open, Tee knew he could not find solace there. He had tried.

His heartbeats slow as he takes a series of deep breaths. Being outside is better, but he still feels trapped by the tall buildings and streets where the sun is seldom seen but always felt. When his breathing becomes normal, he walks to a nearby telephone booth, deposits three quarters, and waits for the old man's voice to come over the wires. They talk until the quarters run out. It still surprises him that a lapsed Protestant has turned to a Catholic Priest for counseling, mentoring, and friendship. But Father Robert Messenger is the only one who understands, the only one who knows the whole story.

The priest knows what brought Tee from the arid and clean air of the High Plains to the humid and stifling air of downtown Dallas; from a place of unlimited vistas to a place where he only sees steel and concrete; from the euphoria a man feels horseback to the suffocation he feels trapped in an elevator or cubicle.

But not even Father Bob can explain why Tee was spared, why it seems as if he has been plucked by some malevolent force from a life he understood and loved and set down into this suit-and-tie existence, into what one of his college professors called the corporate culture. The old priest could not explain why two events, sixty-seven days apart, five hundred miles apart, shattered Tee's hopes, rudely maneuvered his life down a road he does not wish to travel, toward a place he does not want to be.

And Father Bob cannot explain the dreams, the ones that begin with deafening clashes of metal against metal, ear-piercing screams, and swirling liquids that mix with blood in colors so bright they make his eyes hurt. He cannot explain the voice that sounds like wind might sound if it had a human voice, the voice that beckons Tee to the place where it happened.

When the dream takes him there, he feels like an interloper on ground that has given him birth and nourished his life for almost two decades, but the cold, dry, thin Texas Panhandle air recognizes him with a whistled greeting. The sun's rays spread across the bluestem grass revealing hoof marks left by cattle and horses in the prairie sod. The departing sun throws shadows across the prairie before he sees them.

They come from the west, as if spawned by the sinking sun. The two boys ride nearly identical palomino horses, the only color raised on the ranch. Tee recognizes the matching wool blanket coats made by their mother in brilliant colors so that her sons can be seen from a long distance. She has knitted bright orange wool neck scarves to cover their ears under their black hats. The boys stop at the crossing, dismount like grown men, and let their reins drop to the ground. The horses stand patiently as they were trained to do. Each brother places a penny on a rail.

The nine-year-old stands on the crossties and looks down the tracks while his ten-year-old brother puts an ear to one of the rails. The rail pulses and hums a few minutes before the train's whistle pierces the clear air. The boys remount, lift their hats to the engineer, sit calmly in their saddles as the train passes, wave to the brakeman as the caboose departs, then ride to the middle of the still warm tracks. The oldest holds on to a long saddle string and picks up his flattened penny without dismounting while the younger dismounts to retrieve his. Copper trophies in their pockets, the boys ride west until the sun takes them back.

The dream has come unbidden so many times that Tee can bring it to mind at will. He looks down the street to the parking garage where his car sits on the roof, dreads touching door handles scorched by the sun. He briefly considers driving away, but replaying the dream has calmed him. He pulls his tie snug, puts on his coat, and begins retracing his steps. He remembers to stand straight, willing away the slight stoop from an imaginary weight on his shoulders. The limp is barely noticeable as he walks back to face his new life.

Two

1963

FEW THINGS RATTLED CONCHO, BUT HIS SENSE OF SMELL TOLD him something was different, and he did not like it. He could not see the tiny trail of gasoline left by the pickup as it changed from intermittent drops to a steady stream. The short-barreled, gentle-eyed blond sorrel that both Jessup brothers roped from looked over the front of the open-top trailer at his young charges like an attentive parent. But wind noise kept the boys from hearing the dog-like growls coming from the horse's throat, and they paid no attention to his unusual headshakes.

The setting sun rained down on the faded black hood of the '57 Chevy pickup, reflected off the windshield and into the eyes of John Theodore Jessup and his wife, Winona. Sons Jubal and Tee sat in the pickup bed with their backs to the cab and to the sun, deep down in their hats to keep the wind from taking them. The brothers tried to talk over the road noise and wind about the next rodeo and about the girls they had seen at this one. Jubal, the older, had a wide, thick trunk, a broad face, and his father's serious, ice-blue eyes. Younger brother Tee was wide-shouldered but rail thin with an angular, hollow-cheeked face, dark chestnut hair, and brown eyes. Nothing marked them as brothers unless one heard their almost identical voices. Winona referred to her sons as her Greek gods of the prairie. Jubal was her Adonis and Tee was her Apollo.

John Theodore was always addressed as John T. The taciturn ranch manager known for keeping his head when others panicked hummed a few bars of "Hey, Good Lookin'" between the retelling of the day's rodeo events as if Winona had not been in the stands watching Jubal and Tee perform. He could barely contain his uncommon exhilaration and knew that it would have to be tucked away in the warm recesses of his mind as soon as they reached home. Their sons had taken first and second in calf roping. Tee, just out of high school, had held the fastest time until the last roper—his older brother. Jubal, a year older and making a name for himself as a top hand, shaved a tenth of a second off his brother's run.

People commonly said, "Tee's good all right, but we're all gonna read about Jubal Jessup someday." Tee was good, but Jubal, well, Jubal was almost inhuman good. Tee had to work at what seemed to come natural to his older brother.

But the boys paid little attention to the competition between them, to what people said. They were best friends and each knew that the key to their roping wins was Concho. John T had helped to bring the little colt into the world and knew at once that he was not a breeding prospect but saw something else in him that he could not put to words. And the horse had a way of looking at John T that was unnerving, yet comforting. He offered to buy the colt from Earl Donovan, his boss and owner of Blind River Ranch, a month after he was born. One look at the colt and Earl immediately accepted John T's paltry offer. John T poured four years of his life into making Concho a world class roping horse for his boys.

Not a man to drink away from home, John T had felt obliged to take a few celebratory pulls from a bottle of Jim Beam as the rodeo progressed. His friends had encouraged and toasted him each time a competitor missed and his boys caught. He had honed humility to an art form, never boasted but had every right to celebrate sons who had bested grown men in a man's rodeo as well as a horse that stuck his tail in the dirt and held the line tight while Jubal and Tee flanked their calves and took two wraps and a hooey to stop the clock. The half empty bottle now lay in its customary spot under the pickup seat and would likely stay there until the next rodeo.

He stopped humming the Hank Williams song and slowed on boasting to the only person he could, Winona, allowing his subconscious to travel the road he could have driven blindfolded. Mere proximity to the Texas Panhandle ranch where he had worked and lived most of his life replaced his euphoria with the burden of heavy responsibility and chores to be done before bedtime.

By the time he reached the dirt road leading to the ranch, the light from the sun had faded and a warm afterglow had settled on John T, a happiness and fulfillment he had seldom felt in his forty-four years, years filled mostly with hard work and sacrifice. Though his boys were fulfilling his own life-long dreams, his senses tingled with the feeling of reward and accomplishment he had felt watching his sons execute the things he had taught them on the horse he had selected and trained. He smiled at Winona and saw she was radiant, too. Black hair pulled back and braided in a pony tail emphasized her soft dusky skin and black eyes that lapsed between serenity and flashing. The sound of the approaching train was so familiar to their ears that they took no more note of it than the lowing of cattle that lulled them to sleep most nights.

John T had taken his foot off the accelerator and barely noticed the engine coughing as he coasted to within a few yards of the railroad tracks he had crossed thousands of times. The Fort Worth and Denver railway, the Denver Road, ran from Fort Worth through Wichita Falls, Childress, Amarillo, Dalhart, to Texline, where it connected with the Colorado and Southern. The pickup's engine stalled as the front tires crossed the tracks. The truck had enough momentum to carry the back tires across. Only the back of the trailer was left hanging over the west rail. When the truck stopped, John T realized the train had been coming for a few minutes and it was on them by the time the whistle blew. He pushed Winona toward her door. "Get out!" He flung open his door and screamed at his boys to jump out of the bed as the train struck the back of the trailer. Jubal's head lay on the seat of the boys' shared saddle while Tee had taken the dry side of the saddle blanket for his pillow. Both were asleep.

The train moved the trailer with the same ease Concho might have used to swat a horse fly. The pin that attached the trailer to the pickup's

7

bumper finally sheared but not before it had lifted the truck enough to throw both boys out of the bed. A back tire burst as the truck fell back just as the boys were thrown free. A support bar John T had added to the trailer for stability hung on the train long enough to drag the trailer a few yards beside the track before being ripped off. Sparks flew from the rails as the trailer was dragged and train brakes applied. When it finally gave way, the trailer lay on its side in the ditch beside the rails, wheels slowly spinning like the hands of a clock gone haywire.

John T saw Winona standing, saw his boys thrown free of the wreckage to land only a few feet away. He had seen them get in worse wrecks working cattle. He was heading for the trailer and Concho when he heard Winona scream his name.

The brothers had landed only a few feet apart. Tee's eyes were closed, and he was bleeding from deep cuts on one arm. The other arm and one leg were bent in ways God had not intended. There were no marks on Jubal, his athletic body in repose as if taking a peaceful rest. But his blue eyes were locked open, the flashing mischief gone.

John Theodore and Winona Jessup had seen their share of death and dying, broken bones, blood and guts. It was part of ranch life. But the air seemed to go out of them as they dropped to their knees, John T beside his dead son and Winona beside the one who had survived, their warm glows replaced with cold, shivering terror. Their breathing changed to ragged gasps for air that seemed insufficient and suddenly, terribly foul.

Concho's scream awakened them from their stupor. John T tried to ignore the horse's squeals as he used his Case knife to slice open one leg of Tee's jeans. He broke a shovel handle to use as a splint for Tee's arm and gathered sanitary napkins from a vet bag he carried behind the seat to pad the compound fracture. He cut a jagged hole big enough to put his hand in and ripped the shirt's long sleeve away. He placed the napkins next to his son's arm and wrapped the handle next to them with adhesive tape while Winona worked on the leg. She discovered blood on the back of Tee's head and was dabbing at it with the hem of her dress when John T handed her another padded napkin. She folded a saddle pad for a pillow.

Winona was focused, oblivious to Concho's screams as she applied pressure to stop the bleeding on the cut arm, but John T wanted to cover his ears and swallowed hard to keep from screaming himself. They took turns touching fingers to Tee's neck, checking his pulse. Not satisfied, Winona placed an ear next to his chest and nodded at her husband. Splint in place on Tee, John T sat in the dirt beside Jubal, closed his son's eyes, and held them with his thumbs. Winona sat beside Tee and let go the tears she had been holding.

They were surprised to see the train's engineer, brakeman, and conductor watching them minister to Tee. The engineer's arms dangled like useless appendages; his hands shook. The brakeman sobbed unashamedly. The wide-eyed conductor finally spoke. "My Lord. Never seen anything like this."

The engineer's voice quivered. "I tried to stop. Swear I did."

John T wrapped a red kerchief over his son's eyelids and looked toward his pickup. His voice was a few decibels above normal. "I'm sure you did. It's my fault. From the smell, I lost all my gas. Ran out a split second too soon. The boys and I could've pushed it across if we had a minute more." His raw, raspy voice begged to have that minute back.

Winona looked up at the conductor. "Did you call for help?"

"I radioed it in, but they said we're a good fifty miles from an ambulance or a hospital. Anything we can do?"

John T pointed a hand toward the front of the train. "You can move that train out of this crossing. Ambulance can't reach us without crossing the tracks."

"We're supposed to wait for the railroad to send an investigator out. We can carry him between the cars. There'll be a stretcher."

John T stood and looked at the man with slanted, red eyes. "You want to take up that precious time for some damn rule? Take a chance on dropping my boy?" He walked to his truck and pulled his .30-30 from the rack behind the seat. He kept the gun on his shoulder as he looked toward his horse, then back at the rail men. "You're probably right about the stretcher, but that ambulance will have other things we'll need close at hand. They need to cross the tracks here."

The conductor and engineer nodded at the same time. "We'll move it. You want us to help with that horse?"

John T shook his head. "My job to do. I'll tend to it." He took long strides toward the horse and trailer as the trainmen departed to both ends and the middle of the train. They watched from the train as it began to

9

move. An involuntary, painful hum escaped John T's throat as he walked. Concho stopped squealing when he smelled the man he trusted approaching. He looked up beseechingly at John T with one terror and pain-filled eye. The horse had tried to jump over the top and broke a leg. The useless leg lay trapped under the trailer. John T rubbed the horse's velvet muzzle, placed a palm between his eyes. "I'm sorry, Conch." He levered a shell into the chamber, put the gun's barrel under Concho's ear and pulled the trigger. One small grunt, a release of air, and the horse's pain was over.

John T felt as if he had put the rifle under his own chin. Not a man to express strong emotions, he breathed deeply, put a thumb over each eye as if to staunch the pain, sat down and leaned against his horse's belly and wept. As he breathed in short gasps, a low grunting noise came unbidden from his throat. He had been raised to view horses as useful work animals that occasionally brought pleasure to their owners. He liked most all of them, but he loved Concho.

From her sitting vigil by her son, Winona heard the shot and watched her husband fade with the last rays of light from the sun as he slumped beside his dead horse. She wrapped both arms around her knees as if protecting herself from any further agony and rocked back and forth, whining with pain.

Half an hour later, a young Army medic home on leave and filling in on Sunday for the regular mortician, stepped out from the glare of the flashing lights of the funeral home ambulance. He frowned, then nodded, made some adjustments, and motioned for John T to help lift Tee onto a stretcher. Winona crawled into the hearse doing double duty as an ambulance with her surviving son and locked eyes with her husband. There was not room for all the equipment and both sons. John T stayed with Jubal. The medic looked toward the dead horse and the dead boy, closed the doors, and drove away.

John T watched until the ambulance was out of sight before he bent double with pain. The boys' hats, John T's toolbox, and a five-gallon can of gas lay scattered. As he tenderly placed both hats on the pickup seat, he saw the bottle of Jim Beam lying against the accelerator pedal. He picked up the bottle and threw it as far as he could. *Why did I start across that track when I knew the train was coming? I smelled the gas but ignored it.* He put the spare on the Chevy and rolled the flat tire into the ditch, hoping to never see it again, then unfolded two saddle blankets and laid them in the pickup bed.

He wept as he picked up his son and held him in his arms for the first time since Jubal had been a toddler, trying to squeeze life back into his lungs, beats into his heart. He carefully placed his body on the blankets and his head on the saddle seat. Using a trouble light he kept in his toolbox, he primed the carburetor and got the engine to run for a minute before it died. He traced the line until he found the tiny crack and wrapped it with electrical tape from his toolbox. He shook the five-gallon can of gas that might have saved their lives. There was enough to get to the funeral home—more than enough to have crossed the rails. Deadness settled over John T, a protection from madness that allowed him to function without feeling. The sounds of sirens arriving too late seemed to come from the cauldrons of hell bringing more vengeance and fury to his already-tortured soul. John T did not wait.

THREE

JOHN T ABANDONED HIS PACK-A-DAY CAMEL HABIT AFTER THE funeral. He shaved and bathed only when Winona reminded him. His wiry black hair turned mostly white in less than a month, and he dropped from his usual one-eighty to a buck-sixty. His voice caused shivers of revulsion to travel down his spine, so he used it only to give essential instructions to ranch hands. He had worked on the ranch so long that his duties could be performed almost without conscious thought. Ranch hands stared and whispered about the ranch manager's strange behavior but never dared to discuss it with him.

John T figured he had only so many words in him, and he saved them all for his son. Every day after work, he passed Winona on Route 66 on her way back from nursing Tee in his Amarillo hospital bed. Tee's arm, leg, and head injuries were slowly healing, but he had not opened his eyes, had not spoken. Winona stayed with him during the day, and John T stayed until midnight each night.

Every night, John T stood by the boy's bed and told stories to his son.

13

He had decided to start from the day of Tee's birth and recount every story he could recall about his son's life. Something told him that by the time he reached the day of the train wreck, Tee would wake up. The process took thirty days. When John T reached the events of the last day of Jubal's life, he found himself reliving some of the joy he felt at the rodeo, the satisfying glow he felt on the way home. But the sound of the train whistle in his head washed away the glow and brought back the agony. John T, who had never cried in front of his son, broke into sobs. "It's my fault, Tee. I took several pulls from a bottle of Jim Beam that day. It must have dulled me. I knew the train was coming but just kept on going across the track, thinking I had plenty of time. If I hadn't welded that brace on the trailer, the train might not have caught it and we might have got by with a little damage. It's my fault your brother's dead, and you can't wake up."

When Tee did not respond, John T stopped talking to his comatose son. To keep his brain from going to deadly places, he massaged and flexed the boy's arms and legs to try and keep Tee's ropy muscles toned. When he resumed talking, his words were scattered and sometimes incoherent, as if he were talking to himself rather than his son. "Jubal was the first-born, and I admit I was disappointed when he took more after my daddy's Irish people than me." John T ran his hand through Tee's thick, dark hair. You took more after me, so you got the name."

John T began kneeling by the side of the bed each night, looking out the hospital window into the darkness, trying to see the God he had ignored for too long. He clasped his hands and spoke to him, sometimes silently, and sometimes in a soft whisper. He begged for forgiveness for whatever sins had caused this tragedy to befall his family, his sons. He was clumsy at first, inarticulate, confused, unfamiliar with this Deity who had taken one son and seemed poised to take another. But gradually, he thought he did feel a Presence, and occasionally, heard a voice. But the voice did not answer his questions.

The hospital and the room started to smother John T eventually, and he broke out in hives when he started from home each day. Tee's doctor told him he had the onset of shingles. The visits had become torturous as each day shaved away a little hope. Doctors and nurses now looked at him and Winona with sad expressions that said there was no hope.

Winona met a priest as he was leaving the room next to Tee's. Though she was not Catholic, she found his presence comforting, his words reassuring. At his invitation, she began lighting a candle and saying a prayer for her son in the sanctuary of his church each evening before going home. The ritual gave her a few minutes of precious peace. After John T went out on the ranch each morning, she sat on the ground and stared at the sun. Her grandfather had been a Choctaw Shaman and had told Winona he believed she also had his gift—that a dream after middle age would tell her if she did. She had paid little attention to what the old man said. Until now. Her father had disdained Choctaw beliefs and ignored his father, had never understood how he qualified as a Holy Man.

She did remember the Choctaw worshipped the sun and believed four was a holy number: four directions, four seasons, four elements, and four parts to the family. Now, their family was three. The dream her grandfather had spoken of now haunted her each night. And with each recurrence, it became clearer. She began to plan.

FOUR

SIXTY-SEVEN DAYS INTO TEE'S LONG SLEEP, JOHN T AND WINONA stood at the foot of his bed as a prematurely gray doctor dressed like a ranch hand went through his usual procedure of probing and prodding Tee Jessup's non-responsive body. He tried not to shake his head, tried to keep his expression neutral.

Winona watched the doctor; John T watched his son. "What are the chances he will ever wake up?" The sound of her husband's voice startled Winona. She knew the use of his vocal cords brought pain to John T, that the sound of his own voice made his skin crawl with renewed revulsion for the person he had come to despise.

The young doctor, surprise on his face, stared intently at John T. It was the first time he had heard the man speak. "We just don't know. I've studied case histories. Comatose patients have awakened after months, even years. But we're going to have to consider a long-term facility of some kind soon."

Winona knew what the doctor was going to say. It had been revealed to her in the dreams. The time had come. She took her husband's hand and led him out of the hospital to their truck. She sat on the tailgate and studied the morning sun a few minutes, then motioned for John T to get in and drive. They drove east with no words passing between them. After an hour, Winona signaled her husband to pull off the road and stop. She walked away from the truck and stretched her hands to the sun and faced the four directions. They repeated this ritual every hour. John T never questioned her. Never spoke.

By the time the sun had traveled its path across the sky and headed for the western horizon, they were in Pushmataha County, Oklahoma, beside her grandfather's grave. Winona had never seen it before, but the dream had told her how to find it. She made her usual prayer to the sun, took some dirt from the grave and tossed a small amount in each of the four directions. John T felt a small kindling of the fire she used to inspire in him as he watched her appear to regress into the beautiful, dark, vibrant woman he had married. She wordlessly pointed south when they returned to the old truck.

It was no-moon dark when she signaled John T to stop in the middle of a rattling bridge with high banisters an hour and a half south of the grave. The bridge sat at a sharp curve and spanned a creek wider and deeper than some rivers. Winona took John T's hand and held it. The late call of a bobwhite quail interrupted the usual night sounds of tree frogs and bullfrogs croaking on the bank of a nearby pond, as if the bird were sending a warning. Their stomachs complained, their heads dizzy, their thoughts cloudy from lack of nourishment. Neither had eaten in two full days.

Winona felt she owed her husband an explanation he had not requested. "You do not know this place. My grandfather lived in that bottomland over there. My father was born there. My grandfather was killed there by other members of his tribe because they believed he had used spiritual powers to do them harm. This creek was out for several days after the killing, so my grandmother and her sons had to bury him in their yard. He stayed there for many years until my father moved him to the grave we just visited."

John T felt like a stranger, an intruder in this strange country. The air was heavy, the sounds and smells of night unfamiliar. He was used to unobstructed vision across the prairie he loved and felt confined by the trees that blocked his view. Winona laid a large envelope on the seat between them. They sat quietly holding hands until they heard the distant sound of a train whistle.

The train track crisscrossed its way across the creek on the way to them. Winona knew it would emerge from a blind curve only a few yards north of where their pickup was parked, knew where it was coming from, where it was going, and how fast it would be moving when it crossed the trestle. When they felt the ground vibrate with the approaching train, they left the truck and waited out of sight below the trestle. The train's light moved back and forth as it filtered through the woods. Winona felt it searching for them, felt its magnetic pull.

As the train regained its speed, she asked for forgiveness from the engineer, forgiveness from God as she again faced each direction and supplicated with her arms and a low chant. John T took her hand in his and joined her on her knees as Winona prayed a fervent prayer in a language he did not understand. He stood when she did, watched her make the sign of the cross, and stepped on the crossties between the rails with her as the train began to rattle the trestle. They embraced, faced away from the train, and were swept away.

Tee Jessup's eyes opened with the morning sun.

———•❖•———

In 1829...Choctaw chiefs who sat on the national council
passed a law empowering anyone who found the glowing
entrails that dark shamans left behind while they flew
about through the night, to put the shaman to death.
—*Shaminism: An Encyclopedia
of World Beliefs, Practices and Culture.*

FIVE

TEE FELT NUMB WHEN HE AWAKENED, COULD NOT REMEMBER where he was or what had happened to him. He was afraid to try to move, worried he might not be able to. Then he felt something unfamiliar, became aware of blood coursing through his body, awakening and warming his organs, alerting the magnificent and mysterious engine of life force that his conscious brain was back in control. His skin started to tingle and itch from the top of his head to the ends of his fingers and toes. He retreated from consciousness again, then awakened feeling suspended, floating in a confined space, surrounded by murky liquid, comforted by the sound of a beating heart. Then he heard his mother's voice, a mellifluous sound from far away. He began to feel a deep sense of comfort and serenity, the influence of a familiar, invisible force taking control of the temple that housed his soul, healing it.

Blinking lights and beeps startled him, tubes and wires snaked from private regions of his body to machines he did not recognize. He threw back the sheet that covered him and felt a sense of violation and shame for having

21

allowed his body to be so breached. A cast on one suspended leg made his whole body seem heavy. He traveled the rest of the room with his gaze, saw his saddle in the corner with a rope coiled and tied with saddle strings, his black hat hanging from the horn. He smiled. His mother's work, no doubt.

His eyes were still open when a young nurse entered the room just after daylight. He lifted himself on one elbow. "Where am I?" Tee put a hand to his throat. The voice was not his own. The timbre reminded him of the moaning sound the wind made as it traveled through the attics and barn halls of long-abandoned buildings on the ranch.

The nurse bolted from the room. Tee tried to pull at the lines and hoses attached to him, but his hands would not cooperate with his brain. She returned with the cowboy doctor who had examined Tee the day before. The doctor stared in amazement. "Well, you finally woke up."

Tee looked at the young doctor as he clumsily pulled at the sheet. "Where am I and who are you?"

"You're in a hospital in Amarillo. My name is Dr. Stuart Bozeman. Who are you?"

"I'm Tee Jessup. Where are my parents? My brother?" His irritability grew as the doctor grilled him with questions he considered absurd. What year is it? Who is president? *What the hell?*

Tee gained control over his movements, examined the cast, the gauze. Desperation crept into his voice. "I need to go home. Unhook me from all this." As the doctor put a firm hand on his shoulder and filled in the blanks of that terrible day, Tee began to remember the few seconds after the collision. "That can't be right. Nobody was hurt. I remember seeing my parents standing by the truck, Jubal thrown out right beside me. He's taken worse falls from plenty of horses."

His injured arm and leg began to hurt, and the leg grew hot inside the cast as the doctor explained what had happened to his brother. "Traumatic brain injury. He did not suffer."

When Tee looked into the young nurse's heart-broken eyes, his eyes filled. "Jubal was killed? How long ago? Was there a funeral?" He wiped his nose with a tissue and sat up straighter. "I need to see my parents. Did you call them and tell them I'm awake?"

The doctor pressed a hand against Tee's chest. "Son, you've been in a coma for almost ten weeks. Good thing you're strong and healthy, or you might not have even survived a very bad concussion that shocked your brain stem. Your arm is pretty much back to normal, and that leg can come out of the cast now that you're awake."

Tee could not comprehend he had slept for weeks, that his brother had rested in a lonesome grave all that time. Red-eyed and shaking, he pointed at his throat. "What's wrong with my voice?"

"There was some disturbance of the vocal cords when we had to put a tube down your throat and leave it there."

Tee spoke to the nurse. "Please get my parents. Now."

She put her palms up as if supplicating to a higher power. "I called them first thing. Someone has been calling every hour since I found you awake this morning. I don't understand it. Your mother is always here by this time. Both were here yesterday morning, but your father didn't return last night like he always does." She patted his hand. "They take turns staying with you."

As the events of the train collision emerged from the shadows of his mind and coalesced, Tee determined to get out of the hospital and find his parents. On the second day, he tested his broken leg with crutches. The doctor cautioned about a lifetime of limping if he pushed himself too far.

He maintained his composure during the day and confined his hysterical weeping to the quiet of the night. He was weeping in the dark when he heard the door to his room open. Expecting a nurse, he watched though tiny slits as the light in the hall outlined a large, stooped figure clad in dark garments. The big man came into the room and approached his bed in the darkness.

Tee recognized the trappings of a priest. *Was the man going to administer last rites?* "I'm not dying, and I'm not Catholic."

The priest stepped back. "Didn't think you would be awake. Yes, I know both those things about you, Tee."

Tee doubled his pillow to lift his head and examined the priest and the man who lurked in the doorway. The lurker was wearing a badge. He turned back to the priest, his face barely discernible in the dim light. "Figured you might be in the wrong room. How do you know my name?"

"I knew your mother. She came to my church every day to light a candle for you, and we prayed together for your recovery. She was a fine woman, but I'm afraid she placed a terrible burden on my shoulders."

Tee noticed the past tense. "Go on."

"My name is Robert Messenger. My parishioners call me Father Bob. Your family's truck was found on a rural creek bridge about five hundred miles east of here. Near a little town in Northeast Texas called Riverby. "Do you know it?"

Tee shook his head. "Never been there, but I think I remember my mother saying my grandfather was born near there."

The priest turned to the man in uniform and nodded. "That may explain a few things, though I don't know how." The deputy's expression showed only confusion.

Tee sat up in the bed. "Appreciate it if you would stop dragging it out and talk about who you are and how you know me and my family."

The priest caressed the cross hanging on his chest. "I'm afraid both of your parents were killed in a train collision."

"There must be some mistake. It was my brother killed in a train collision, not my parents." Tee used anger to keep away the pain, to deny what he had heard. He felt coldness wash through his veins, a visceral rage he had never felt before. This calamity could not be happening to him. It was not right. His body, his mind, and every fiber of his being rebelled against it. Two orderlies and the priest held him while a nurse put the needle in his arm.

Six

THE PRIEST WAS SITTING IN A CHAIR BESIDE TEE'S BED WHEN HE awakened from his drug-induced sleep. His presence brought back Tee's fury and fright. "You said my mother laid a terrible burden on your shoulders. What was that?"

Long gray eyebrows drooping from their thickness almost covered the priest's despondent brown eyes. Hair curled over his collar and hair in his nose and ears suffered from the same neglect. "Your parents' pickup was left on a dirt road beside the rails where they were killed. An envelope was left in the seat with my name and phone number on it. Law enforcement contacted me."

Tee reached for his crutches and stepped off the bed. "Let me see it."

The priest put his hands on his knees and slowly shook his head. "It's safe. I am not to show it to you until you leave this hospital and carry out a few of your mother's wishes. Please understand that I am following her instructions. Allow me to tell you what happened and possibly you can explain something I do not pretend to understand."

"It's my mother you're talking about. I have a right to know what happened to her and why. I don't believe she trusted you with something she wouldn't tell me. Already told you we're not even Catholic."

The old man shifted his weight in the chair and ran fingers through his thick, gray hair. "I understand your concern, and believe me; I am as perplexed as you are. Although I believe your mother and father committed a mortal sin against God, I am bound by conscience to carry out their request to me."

Tee's face flushed. "What sin against God?"

"Suicide." The word escaped from the priest's throat like an exorcised demon.

Tee hobbled over to the only other chair in the room. "They wouldn't. My parents are strong people. Nothing scared my daddy, and Mother never gave up on anything."

The priest made the sign of the cross and faced Tee. "Though I believe they were wrong, I am convinced they thought they were doing it as an act of courage, of sacrifice, not out of fear, weakness or hopelessness. Do you know about your mother's Choctaw heritage?"

Tee shook his head. "Some. Why?"

"We can go over this in detail when you're back on your feet. The doctors told me not to disturb you any more than necessary. You face a risk of going back into a coma."

Tee tried to mask the fear those words struck in his heart. "Not telling me is about the worst thing you could do to me now."

The priest scooted his chair closer to Tee's and extended his hand. Tee felt a bond forming between them as he took the warm, callused hand.

"Your mother's grandfather was apparently a Choctaw Holy Man. I have done some library research on the tribe's religion, but I remain mostly ignorant of their beliefs."

Tee leaned forward. "Just tell me what instructions she left."

"I'm sorry. I can't do that without an explanation of why. Her grandfather told her that she had the same gift of holiness he possessed, that she would have a dream sometime after middle age to confirm it."

The priest rose to look through the window. "After your brother was killed, she began having the dream. I cautioned her that the dreams were just symptoms of stress after the train accident, to ignore them. But they were very real to her."

Father Bob sat again. "Her letter to me says the dreams told her if she and your father sacrificed their lives at a certain time and place and in a certain way, you would awaken to live out your life. The instructions were specific."

Tee's mind raced, sorting through this strange story, a story that could not possibly describe something his mother would believe or do. She was not superstitious. The nearest church was thirty miles away from the ranch, but she took her sons often. She prayed. She never mentioned adherence to any Choctaw beliefs.

"Mama was smart, read all the time. And she was never superstitious."

Father Bob nodded, hung his head. "I only knew her for a short time, but that much was evident. She knew a lot about the Bible as well as Greek mythology, said you and your brother were her Greek gods. But the dream was real to her."

"There should be a funeral. When did they die?"

The priest nodded. "Four nights ago. Your mother knew the religious...as well as the physical implications of what they were doing. She left specific instructions. You can imagine the devastation to their physical bodies. Their ashes have already been scattered on your brother's grave. A marker has been ordered. She asked that it be done as quickly as possible."

Tee needed something physical to touch, some remembrance of his parents. He hated to ask the question. "Were they in the pickup?"

"No, it was not involved in the...accident. The deputy who was with me here the other night delivered it to me. It's parked on the church parking lot, waiting for you."

The room seemed to become a prison. "I need to get on out to the ranch, talk to Ford Donovan, my daddy's boss."

The priest pressed a card into Tee's hand. "That is my contact information. Your mother said you would want to go home first. I will need at least a week to carry out some of your mother's requests. Contact me when you're ready."

SEVEN

DRESSED IN THE STARCHED AND PRESSED WRANGLERS, BLUE pearl-snap shirt, and black Resistol hat his mother had left, Tee walked out of his hospital room. His limp was barely noticeable as he walked down the corridor carrying his saddle and the suitcase of clothes Winona had packed. His already thin body now resembled a wavy slice of bacon, and he stooped like he was carrying something heavier than a saddle on his shoulders. From a distance, he looked and moved like an old man.

Staff lined up to say goodbye. Several offered to help with the saddle, but he insisted on carrying it. A tearful young nurse who had grown fond of Tee walked beside him with a spiral notebook filled with the names of friends who had visited while he was in a coma. The list of his parents' friends and his own seemed like strangers, part of a past life.

Father Bob was waiting beside the pickup when Tee stepped outside. The unfamiliar sun struck him with all of its force, and he had to lower his gaze as he threw the saddle into the pickup bed. The priest was full of instructions, but the words barely registered with Tee. He avoided his probing stare, took the keys, and drove away.

Less than an hour later, he stopped beside the Denver Road rails at the crossing where his brother was killed. The events of that day were fairly clear in his mind, though he was unsure if he remembered the wreck or had reconstructed it from the repeated questions he had asked the train conductor when he visited Tee in the hospital. He crossed the rails and parked.

Tee walked beside the tracks until he found signs where the trailer had trapped Concho. He squatted and propped one elbow on his better leg, imagined the terrible squeals of pain and terror. He could not experience what his brother and his horse had, but felt a compelling need to experience some type of punishment. He had been spared and needed to know why.

He walked back to the approximate spot where his brother had landed, kneeled, and ran his hand through the weeds and dirt. Sunlight reflected off shards of a whiskey bottle in the ditch a few yards away. Tee walked toward the broken glass and saw the flat tire and wheel where his father had left it. It was hot to the touch, but he picked it up and threw it into the bed beside his saddle. He leaned against a fender until the sadness and terror of it all started to overwhelm him.

He drove six miles on ranch property and stopped at a cattle guard that marked the entrance to Blind River Ranch headquarters. The road on the other side of the cattle guard seemed to lead nowhere, so seldom traveled it resembled a river wash more than a road. A small stone entrance had been constructed several yards off the road with a faded sign that read Blind River. Earl Donovan, the original owner of the ranch, had wanted the sign and stone entrance away from the road for reasons he carried with him to his grave.

Tee felt like an intruder as he crossed the cattle guard and headed toward the only home he had ever known. A mile down the dusty road, he entered a curve where tall Leyland cypress trees stood as sentinels against the ever-present wind and blowing sand, announcing the entrance to the oasis that was ranch headquarters. The Donovans' low-slung, ranch style private residence stood in its usual regality, surrounded by a stone fence and shaded by evergreens. Tee had kept the grounds clean for several years but had not bothered to really examine the Donovan house. He and Jubal were not allowed inside the big house without John T or Winona or one of the Donovans. Today, he stopped to look with fresh eyes and realized why first-time visitors to the ranch always marveled at the big structure that seemed to rise out of native rock.

A guest house sat behind the main house, a cypress cabin with a metal roof where Earl had often deposited the royalty of American oil when they visited. The cabin was furnished with rustic, comfortable western furniture and a library that included first editions as well as an eclectic selection of hardbacks ranging from Zane Grey and Louis L'Amour westerns to the classics of literature.

The ranch manager's house where Tee had grown up sat across the road from the guest house. Earl left his estate built from oil, horses, cattle, and real estate to his son, Ford. Taxes, legal and administrative expenses took almost half, but Ford was still left with about forty million. The ink was barely dry on the paperwork when he bought a six hundred-acre ranch in the bluegrass of Kentucky. When he wasn't traveling abroad or following his thoroughbreds to race tracks, he preferred to stay at the Kentucky ranch. Blind River reeked with Earl Donovan's touch, and Ford did not like to stand in his father's long shadow.

The ranch manager's brick house where John T and Winona had raised their two sons would have made a fine impression without the owner's house to dwarf it. Tee parked the truck in its usual spot beside the rust-red pipe fence that enclosed the dirt yard. It was not unusual for headquarters to appear abandoned during the early afternoon, and Tee soaked up the solitude. He wandered through the horse barn and bunkhouse, tried to hear the voices of Jubal and John T. After an hour, he screwed up the courage to knock on the door he had never had to knock on before. He was shocked when it opened almost immediately.

Sarah Ledbetter had teased and sprayed her dishwater blonde hair into an immovable bouffant that seemed to make her wide blue eyes bigger and accent her ivory skin. Jubal had said she had bedroom eyes, hinting he knew that from experience. Even with a nose red from a cold, no makeup, and her perpetual look of sadness, Tee found her demurely attractive. She projected fragility and vulnerability that seemed to cry out for protection. The apron seemed out of place on her. Tee detected a sympathetic smile behind the tissue she held to her nose. He had grown unaccustomed to the use of his vocal cords, afraid the creature that had invaded his mind, voice and body since the accident might say something offensive.

He cleared his throat. "Sorry to bother you. I had word the rest of my stuff was here." The voice he heard seemed to emanate from some foreign presence.

He couldn't help but look past Sarah to the living room where millions of words and sounds of laughter had flowed easily among his parents, his brother, and himself. Sarah looked as if she might cry. "Tee, you look…older, somehow. I am so sorry about what happened." Once the dam cracked, words poured out. "I hate being here in your house, but Ford insisted we go ahead and move in. He said it looked like you might not be coming home, and even if you did, you weren't old enough to take your daddy's job. Then we heard you were…coming home, I mean."

She blew her nose and looked at her bare feet. "Oh, God, that sounded awful, didn't it? I must look awful, too."

A mixture of anger at his parents, pity, and self-loathing kept Tee from smiling. He had spent much of his youth denying the message his shiny eyes seemed to convey—a message he was about to cry. "You look fine. Your daddy around? I wanted to see him if I could." Cutt Ledbetter, Sarah's father, had been John T's best friend and top hand for more than a decade.

"I saw a dust cloud coming up Chinook Road a few minutes ago. That's probably him." She looked over his head toward the Donovan house. "Don't hold it against him, Tee. John T told Ford that Daddy was the best man to take his place. He had to do what Ford said. Ford can tell you. I expect he's with Daddy."

"Ford's here?"

"Been here almost a week."

"Still bringing a different woman every time?"

The question seemed to shock Sarah, and Tee wished he had not asked it. She seemed near to tears of sorrow for his predicament, so he walked to the end of the porch and looked around the corner of the house. He saw the dust cloud, knew they were coming from Chinook, knew several minutes would pass before the pickup emerged from the dust. John T and Earl had segregated the almost 200,000-acre ranch into four parts and named the north ranch Chinook. Each ranch had a small two-bedroom house where a ranch foreman and his family lived. Cutt, Maggie, and Sarah had lived on the Chinook. Tee leaned against a corner porch post and watched the rooster tail of dust come closer.

Maggie, Sarah's mother, stepped outside and spoke to Sarah. "Where did you get off to?"

Sarah nodded toward Tee and Maggie put a hand on her throat. She had the same expression of angst her daughter did. "Why, Tee. How wonderful to see you. Would you like to come inside for something cold to drink?"

Tee walked nearer. Maggie, an older version of her daughter, wore a housecoat over her gown, had gone several days without washing her limp and thin gray hair. She seemed to have aged ten years since he last saw her and appeared too fragile for him to hug. Sarah and her mother never seemed suited to the sometimes harsh life on a Texas ranch, though both had lived their lives in the area. At social and school functions, they appeared delicate as fine china, misfits. Maggie eventually almost stopped being seen outside Chinook headquarters. Cutt made excuses for her, said she was sick.

Tee wondered how a man as tough as Cutt Ledbetter lived with these two porcelain dolls. "No, thanks. I came to pick up my stuff and say hello to Cutt. And to you, of course."

Maggie put the other hand to her throat and looked shyly down as if afraid to stare at her own feet. Her voice was faint. "Well, he should be here any minute."

Tee barely glanced toward the door as Maggie went back inside. "You already out of college?"

"Just a junior."

"Then why aren't you there?"

"I took off a semester. Mama needs me here. She's been sick a lot."

Tee could not accept that he had lost an entire summer, a rodeo season. His brain always returned to early June, the day it had stopped. Sarah's close proximity made him nervous, too. She had always seemed to occupy a world foreign to him. "Sorry to hear your mama is still sick." He pointed a fist at the dust cloud. "You don't have to entertain me. I'll just sit out here and wait for Cutt."

She turned her back to him if dismissed. "I do have a pie in the oven."

She had the door almost closed when he called after her. "Where's Iffy?" Tee and Jubal had bottle-fed a young black colt that had lost his mother; named him Iffy because he seemed unlikely to survive; kept him in the yard.

Sarah rubbed her hands on her apron. "I figured you knew. Iffy did fine. Your daddy and mama sold him...along with all the other things."

EIGHT

A SMALL TRICKLE OF SWEAT RAN DOWN TEE'S BACK AS HE watched the Blind River Ranch white truck John T had used for ranch business emerge from the dust and stop behind his own. Cuttsell Ledbetter seemed to appear out of the dust cloud made by the truck before it stopped rolling. Cuttsell was a burly man with red hair flecked on the ends with a color that resembled West Texas sand. He approached Tee with one of his big paws extended and a warm smile.

"Cuttsell Ledbetter." Tee ignored the smell of whiskey, accepted the hand, and the boy and man engaged in their usual struggle to see who could squeeze hardest. The big man always let the boy win.

"You're one of the few people I let call me that." Cuttsell was his mother's maiden name, but everyone knew him as Cutt. "You're a sight for sore eyes. Came to see you in that damned hospital, but they said you likely never knew I was there."

Tee put a finger to his temple as if that explained everything. Ford stood back a respectable distance while Tee and Cutt talked. Earl Donovan's son was ten years older than Tee, and he and Jubal had always looked on the young man's money, looks, and charm with a mixture of envy and admiration. They seldom saw him away from the ranch, but when they did, he was usually in the company of a beautiful woman. He was an excellent rider, taught by professionals, but John T had said he would never be a true horseman. Said he didn't have the temperament for it.

As he approached Tee for a handshake, Ford had the look of a French aristocrat who spent a lot of time lying on the beach. His olive skin was mahogany dark and his curly hair looked shiny, as if it were wet or treated with some type of oil. The effect made his widow's peak more conspicuous. Tee was not used to seeing a man's socks or ankles, and Ford had abandoned his boots for tan loafers that looked like house shoes and socks that looked more like women's hose. Loose-fitting black slacks and a shiny red pullover shirt had replaced his Wranglers and piped-yoke custom-made shirts. Tee saw dread in his face as Ford's handshake went limp.

Ford tugged his earlobe like Earl Donovan had. "Cutt and I were just saying things will never be the same around here without John T and Winona."

A slight tic at the corner of Tee's mouth. "Or Jubal."

Ford jerked his head toward the guesthouse. "Welcome to stay the night if you like."

"Appreciate it."

Ford turned away and headed for his house and Tee turned back to Cutt. "They said my stuff was out here. Okay if I pick it up?"

"Sure. I got something else that belongs to you in the house." Cutt went inside and returned with a saddle stand that John T had made. "I see you got your saddle in the back. Your daddy left this here because he made it on Blind River time. You know how John T was."

Tee picked up the stand and carefully put it in the pickup bed. "Think Ford will be okay with me taking it?"

"It was your daddy's, and now it's yours. You'll stay for supper, of course. Sarah's frying some buffalo steaks. Maggie's under the weather again."

"Guess I'll go on down the road if I could get my stuff." Tee was not ready to have supper at his mother's table with another family.

Cutt winced as he pointed toward the bunkhouse. "Maggie helped your mama pack up everything and store it in the bunkhouse."

When they finished loading the two duffel bags and two footlockers, the pickup bed contained all of Tee Jessup's worldly goods. Tee winced when he noticed the bent bumper. It took both men to pull open the bent tailgate. "Guess the whole truck is bent out of shape."

Cutt nodded. "Probably just the bed."

Tee sat on the open tailgate. "Suppose they sold our cows and horses, too."

Cutt stared toward the range where the Donovans had allowed the Jessups to keep forty-two head of mixed breed cattle and seven horses that were mostly ranch culls. He sat beside Tee. "Sold, Tee. Every last one. Your mama and daddy sold everything they had, even the furniture in the house that was theirs and the clothes in the closets. Ford bought the furniture. You ain't got the money?"

"Mama made plans with a Catholic priest in Amarillo for me to go to college. Paid for it in advance. You think I can get that back?"

"I don't know, Tee. Your mama had her heart set on you going. Said there was something in you that even you didn't know was there. Don't you remember her talking about it all the time?"

Tee remembered but never took her seriously. "In one ear and out the other, I guess."

"And it wasn't just your mama. John T told me more than once you ought to do better than working on a ranch like him."

"He never mentioned it to me." Tee felt a hollow feeling in his stomach when he considered his father thought him unsuited for ranch work.

"He looked at it different than Winona. Said you would decide one day on your own that college was a good idea for you. Winona had no such notion. Said you would have to be dragged kicking and screaming and she was prepared to do the dragging."

"Never done anything but cowboy, Cutt. You know that. Never wanted to do anything but maybe have my own ranch one day. College ain't in the cards for me."

"She intended for you to go, Tee. If I know Winona, she set things up so you won't have much choice if you don't want to waste the money."

"How about I work out here, stay in the bunkhouse until next spring? Then I might feel different about things."

Cutt looked away, and the lines in his forehead deepened. "I figured you might ask. You got the makings of a top hand, so I asked Ford. He says Winona made him promise to never hire you."

Tee made the same clicking sound he used when he wanted a horse to pick up the pace or when he heard bad news and could think of no words to express his pain. It had become his way of groaning, something picked up from John T. "She made him promise not to hire me? How did she know I was ever going to wake up? Did you or Ford know they were going to die?"

Cutt held up both palms as if pushing the thought away. "No, no. None of us had any idea about their plans. We would have tried to stop it."

"So what did you think they were planning when they sold everything and moved out?"

Cutt looked down at his boots. "I didn't know what to think. John T clammed up after the accident. Didn't confide in anybody, didn't even talk unless he had to. Your mama told Maggie they didn't know how long you were gonna need to be in a hospital of some kind. We just figured they had to turn it all into cash."

"Can't help but wonder what would have happened to me if I had stayed in the coma with no family around."

"John T brushed off my questions about you or their plans. Maggie and me figured they were moving to Amarillo to be closer to you. That they could both find work there. God as my witness, Tee, I never wanted to take your daddy's job like this. I would have been happy to work for him the rest of my days."

Tee walked away a few feet. "I'm in a fix, Cutt. If I can't work here, can you get me on at another ranch?"

Cutt seemed to feel a sharp stab of pain as he rose from the tailgate. "I can, as a matter of fact. The cowboy fraternity is pretty close knit. I got contacts at the XIT, the Sixes and Lambshead, but are you sure? You'll have to start at the bottom. Provide your own horse, ride fences, maybe live in a line shack three or four months during the winter. It's a hard life and not what they wanted for you. I can hear Winona's voice warning me right now not to do it."

Tee got behind the wheel and closed the door. "Guess I'll go over to the college and see if I can get a refund. At least enough to buy a horse."

Cutt leaned in through the passenger window. "Speakin' of horses, me and your daddy buried Concho down by the blind curve in the river. Drug a big rock over his grave. Thought you would want to know."

Tee looked longingly toward the river where he hunted as a boy but did not reply. He heard the sound of a train whistle and wondered if he imagined it. In his dreams, a train whistle was followed by screeching brakes and a metal against metal collision, a horse's squeal of pain, and his mother's scream.

Cutt stubbed the toe of his boot against a pickup tire. "Maybe you can take some ranch management courses at that college, get on the rodeo team."

Tee looked straight ahead as if he were trying to consume the ranch he loved, carry it away in his bloodstream. "Not likely with a bunged-up arm and leg. Don't even know if they have a rodeo team. Tell Maggie and Sarah I said goodbye."

Tee waited in the parking lot of Father Bob's church until people stopped coming out and the priest's green Plymouth was the only car in the lot. He found the rectory door open and sat across from his desk. Father Bob put a hand on his shoulder when he arrived a few minutes later, felt the tension in Tee's body. "Collect your belongings?"

"I did."

Father Bob sat behind a mahogany desk that had seen better days. The old desk groaned when he clasped his hands and placed them on top as if in pain from having seen and heard so much human tragedy.

Tee leaned forward. "What now? You gonna show me Mother's letter?"

"In due time and in accordance with her instructions. Your next step is to visit the college at Canyon and see the dean of admissions."

"The semester has already started. Won't I have to wait till spring?"

"Only been going for a few days. You can catch up. The dean and I have a tutor for you if you need it. Arrangements have been made for your room, board, books, and tuition. The dean of admissions will be expecting you."

"Don't I get any say-so in this? I don't want to go to college. I might hire a lawyer to get the money back."

"Your mother said you would resist. It's true you might hire a lawyer and get the money she provided for you, but I suspect there would be little left after you paid his fees."

The priest came around the desk and sat next to Tee. "Understand I do not condone what they did, but your parents literally died for you. They sold all their worldly possessions to provide for your future. Would you deny them their most fervent desire?"

Tee looked away and composed himself. "Say I do go. Where do I stay between semesters? What about spending money, clothes, gas for the truck?"

"You can stay on campus between semesters or with friends or relatives. If the campus closes for a holiday or any reason, I can put you up here. As for spending money, your mother felt you should get a part-time job. She made inquiries at the college, I know. If there is an emergency, you can come to see me."

"Why would I come to see you?"

"Because I have access to most of the money. She left behind a safe deposit key and written authorization. She didn't trust the college longer than one semester. There is some money for emergencies, but your parents wanted it conserved to maybe give you a start after college."

"Did my mother tell you what I ought to major in, too?"

"She said your major field of study would choose you, not the other way around. I didn't understand, but those are her words."

NINE

AS FATHER BOB HAD PROMISED, A TUTOR AND LIVING QUAR-
ters were arranged for Tee on the college ranch. Winona had been
there, too. The little caretaker shack sat alone on the ranch, the
burned remains of a barn nearby. Ed Pickard, the ranch manager, a
Slim Pickens look-alike who went by Slim, explained his ranch duties
and showed him the shack. "You'll have to work a little on some of the
plumbing every once in a while, but we can probably get you the parts.
Seems like a mighty lonesome place for a boy like yourself to live."

It was lonesome, but Tee found succor in the quiet. Winona must have
known about the headaches and nightmares that might come. Tee soon
learned the signs—headache in the afternoon followed by screaming, sweating nightmares at night. He was glad nobody could hear his screams when
the normally soothing sounds of a train whistle and the rattling of a trestle
magnified to ear-piercing noise and the screams of Jubal, Winona, John T
and finally, Concho. A malevolent presence always hovered in the dreams,
coming and going, lurking, fading from obscurity to clarity. Tee could not

describe the presence, even to himself, only that it was clad in black. Probably something from a book he had read or a story he had been told.

He also dreamed about roping. He threw his loop, pitched his slack, dismounted, ran down the line, flanked, and tied in slow motion. Encouraged by Slim, Tee tried calf roping again from a college horse. But the injuries and time off had added a second to his time, and the loss of Concho a second more. He could not afford his own horse and trailer. Roping without Jubal or Concho and getting beat by what had once been less talented ropers seemed wrong, and just being in the arena saddled him with crippling depression for days afterward.

He treated his college experience as due punishment, trudging through the days and nights as he imagined a monk might function inside a monastery. Tee's silence and the sad, piercing, hurt look in his eyes, his slight stoop, led other students to treat him more like an odd teacher or parent than a peer. Classroom work was a duty forced upon him, but he tackled his college ranch duties as if he had something to prove to his father.

He listened for a voice, waited for a sign that would tell him his course of study had been chosen for him. When none came, he listened to professors who tried to counsel him, but eventually chose courses and professors he thought would be the easiest and would provide the most direct route to a degree, a job, and the right to whatever blood money might remain from the sale of his parents' property. He was determined to replace everything they had sold, especially the livestock, to atone for his survival.

Sarah returned to college, but he seldom saw her on campus. He had gained almost a full year on her when Slim knocked on Tee's door with Sarah in tow. Her eyes and cheeks were red from crying.

The shock at seeing her at his little shack left him wordless for a few seconds. "What's wrong?"

"Mother died last night." She sounded more angry than grief-stricken.

"She died? How?"

"That damn ranch stole everything she held dear, then finally killed her."

Tee looked toward Slim with a question, but Slim shook his head and walked away. "How?"

"Daddy said she just didn't wake up this morning. Doctors are calling it a heart attack, but Mother died from sadness."

"Sadness? I'm so sorry. What can I do?"

"You can drive me back there." Sarah collapsed in his arms. The physical contact confused him. He could not remember ever touching her before.

Tee tried to gently question Sarah on the way to the ranch about dying from sadness, but Sarah said only that she was always tired, and doctors could not find out why. Maggie had been a source of mild curiosity for Tee and Jubal and the subject of whispered, disguised conversations between John T and Winona. She and Winona had been close friends.

The ranch yard was filled with pickups. Tee stopped in front and waited for Sarah to get out and go inside. "I'll park and find you later."

She stared straight ahead, as if she could not bear to look at the house filled with people. "No. You have to go in with me. I can't face all those people alone."

Tee parked by the bunkhouse, and they walked together to the front door. Cutt wordlessly embraced his daughter and ushered her inside. Loud talk and laughter reduced to whispers as all eyes focused on her. One of the ranch wives finally approached. Her hug brought a flurry of mother hens, clucking in unison. When Sarah looked as if she might faint from all the attention, the solicitous women led her to her mother's rocking chair.

Tee stayed by the door as the women led her away. He pushed his head against the door facing and worried he might be more likely to faint than Sarah. His family had been alive the last time he was in this house. He sensed his mother's presence so strongly he searched the room for her. The house had the same furniture, right down to the wall hangings. Only the family photos were different. He opened the door and backed out, looking for a place to be sick.

He trotted to the horse barn and went inside a stall. Cutt was waiting when he stepped out, a cold beer in each hand. "We didn't consider your feelings in this thing, Tee. I apologize for that. Must have been tough to go in there."

Tee took a long swig, washed out his mouth, and spit it out. "I'm the one who needs to apologize. You lost your wife."

Cutt pointed to two metal chairs he and John T used to sit in when they shared a glass or two of good whiskey. "Let's sit a spell." He leaned his chair back against a stall. "I lost Maggie a long time ago. Can't say exactly when or why, but she went away in every respect except breathing when Sarah was just a kid. She had been a faithful churchgoer, but just stopped going to church one Sunday. Never went back; not to Mass, not to Confession."

Cutt looked away, warding off tears. "She didn't give up her rosary beads, though. Rubbed on 'em night and day." He looked directly into Tee's eyes. "I expect it was as hard on Sarah as it was on me."

"What happened to her?"

"Don't know. She was plain miserable. Took her to doctors in Amarillo, even one in Dallas."

"Psychiatrists?"

"Two psychologists over the years. She wouldn't ever speak to a psychiatrist. So we did head doctors and body doctors. I think the sadness just finally took her. I knew she was fragile when I married her, but I sorta liked that, I guess. Guess there's something in me has to have something to protect."

Tee didn't know what to say. He had heard Winona speak sympathetically about Maggie, but he never understood how serious things were. "Nothing happened to make her sad?"

"I'm not a shrink, but I've had a long time to try and figure that. She was raised on a little wheat and milo farm a few miles south of here. Her parents lost the farm when she was little, and things were hard after that. Her daddy turned to drinking, and I think he could get pretty mean when he tied one on. Maggie never told me about the meanness until both her parents were dead."

"I never knew that. Did Mother and Daddy know?"

"Maggie told Winona things she wouldn't tell me, I expect. But I don't know for sure."

Tee put his hands on his knees, dropped his head, and stared at the dirt between his boots. "I've had a long time to think about what they did, but I can't get it right in my head. Do you think they just went out their minds with grief?"

Cutt took a ragged breath. "Wish to God I could answer that. I just know they were never the same after that awful thing happened."

The sad conversation, Cutt's sharing of family secrets, made Tee feel more like a man, as if he were filling in for John T. Cutt stood, crushed the beer can, and tossed it into a trash can by the barn door. "Well, I hear you're doing well at college. Still got your heart set on being a rancher, or did you decide your mama was right?"

The abrupt change from talk about Maggie to talk about himself made Tee feel guilty, but Cutt had revealed a family secret, so he decided to reciprocate. "Guess what I learned hasn't hurt, but I still want to ranch. Ford runs around the country watching his thoroughbreds race. That seems like a great life to me." The words had never escaped his lips before. The idea was fanciful and he knew it. John T would have scoffed.

"Racehorses? Not a cattle ranch?"

"I figure cattle, too. Got to have cattle to have a real Texas ranch." He saw thinly veiled sympathy on Cutt's face. "Look, I know it's probably foolish, but Slim Pickard, the guy who runs the college ranch, took me to Raton, New Mexico, last year to see the races. We went out early to watch the workouts."

Tee stood and gestured with both hands. "I tell you, Cutt, the dew was rising from the infield that morning as the sun came up. Watching those jockeys and horses was, well, made me feel like I haven't felt in a long time. And can you imagine what it feels like to see your horse cross that finish line first?"

Cutt's face filled with sympathy. "Maybe that's why they call it the sport of kings."

Tee was embarrassed, wished he hadn't shared his secret dream. "I know it's a dream, a rich man's sport, Daddy always said."

"A ranch of any kind is a dream nowadays, at least a big ranch. Unless you inherit it. Your daddy and me, we're throwbacks. Our way of life is disappearing fast, Tee."

"I've heard daddy say that, but I loved the life we had here, Cutt. Never understood why Daddy and Mother discouraged me when I wanted it for myself. I know I would have to start out working on a big ranch and work my way up, save every dime."

Cutt rested his arms over a horse stall door. "In some ways, it is a good life. You and your family always had a nice house to live in, a pretty new pickup to drive, and always beef on the table and in the freezer. There's big skies and beautiful scenery, good neighbors, the pleasure of riding a good horse you trained yourself. It's a life men who spend their lives in suits and ties in big tall buildings in cities dream of."

"I hear a *but* on the end of that."

"Well, I know you've seen the dirty, hard part—the droughts, the deaths, disease, the danger, the heartbreak. But take John T and Winona. They didn't own the roof over their heads, not even the freezer where they stored their beef. I don't either. They only had that one pickup. The other one belonged to the ranch. Even most of the furniture belonged to the ranch. They had a few cattle and a few horses, but mostly what the Donovans didn't want. I don't know about them, but I could sell everything I own right now and not have enough to build a new house."

"I know all that, but they seemed happy most of the time. It's a great place to raise kids."

"They were a matched pair, and you and Jubal were a matched pair. But take me and Maggie. She was miserable, and we spent the best part of our lives out in that little Chinook cabin, depending on a generator for electricity. No phones. TV reception every once in a while. Cut off from the world. And she wouldn't talk."

"I always liked solitude."

Cutt laughed heartily. "You got your mind made up, don't you, son? Okay. Consider this. Your daddy and me always figured we would spend our days working for a good man like Earl Donovan. Then he drops dead, and we had to work for his spoiled son."

"Never thought of Ford as being that bad."

"Ford means well, I suppose, but he will never fill his daddy's boots, and that bothers him. I might say something that pisses him off tomorrow morning, and he could throw us all out by afternoon. I hate the feeling that a man twenty years my junior has that sort of control over me. Sorta like being a slave. Can you live with that?"

Tee nodded. "I never noticed it much until a year or so ago. Daddy did seem to tense up when Ford came around."

Tee was undeterred. College had taught him a few things, made him more curious. He could stand taking orders until he had his own place. "What choice do I have, Cutt? I know about pie in the sky. I figure to start small, build a little at a time."

"You know much about thoroughbreds?"

"You know I've only fooled with Ford's a little. Daddy always said they were like a bunch of high-headed spoiled kids that would kick your head in first chance they got."

Cutt laughed. "The ones we have here are just out to pasture. Ford keeps the really good prospects up in Kentucky."

"I've read a lot about it. I know that's not as good as doing it, but I thought maybe Ford would let me work a little for him up in Kentucky and get some real experience."

Cutt looked toward the mourners starting to leave the house. "I never had a son, Tee, so John T and Winona sorta let me think I was helping to raise you and Jubal. If I had a son, I hope he would have been like you. Now, guess we better show our face over there and thank these find folks for dropping by."

Tee looked toward the Donovan house as they walked back. "Ford coming to the funeral?"

"I never called him. Figure somebody else did. Guess it will depend on how far he has to come."

The Ledbetters were lapsed Catholics, so Cutt elected to hold only graveside services. He knew the day would be hot, so he chose to begin at sunrise. Tee was there an hour early. He kneeled at the markers for John T, Winona, and Jubal. A young tenor's rendition of "Danny Boy" at a college program had burned into his brain, and he softly repeated it. "And I will hear, though soft your tread above me. And then my grave will warm and sweeter be. For you will bend and tell me that you love me, and I will sleep in peace until you come to me."

Tee whispered "I love you" to the graves and stood as the hearse arrived with Maggie's body, followed by Cutt and Sarah in Cutt's pickup.

Sarah hugged him and Cutt's rough handshake turned into a hug. As the sun rose to reveal the faces of Panhandle friends who came to pay their respects, Tee felt a kinship return that had been lost since his family died. Most of the mourners were at least as old as Cutt and Maggie. Eyes full of fierce determination and persistence looked out from faces colored by the sun and etched with the lines of time and a more or less continuous struggle with Mother Nature. These were Tee's people—his heritage.

Tee had to look away as tears came during the service. He felt guilty for thinking of his parents and brother instead of Maggie. The Donovans' late and somewhat noisy arrival just before the Methodist minister started his prayer annoyed Tee. He could tell from the way Cutt flinched that he felt the same way. Ford was the first to speak to Cutt as the services ended, putting a hand on his shoulder and whispering condolences in his ear. Tee watched Ford work the crowd, shaking hands, telling stories, trading on the reputation and influence his father had spent years cultivating.

As the small crowd dispersed, he felt a hand on his shoulder and turned to see Father Bob Messenger. Tee shook the priest's hand and led him away so they could talk. "Didn't know you knew Maggie."

Father Bob looked toward the small group. "I didn't. But at my age, you look at the daily obituaries to make sure your name is not there. I saw Blind River mentioned in Mrs. Ledbetter's obituary. Took a chance that you might be here." They made small talk about Maggie for a few minutes before the priest pressed a sealed envelope addressed to Tee into his hand.

Tee recognized his mother's flowing script. "Why now?"

"She said to give this to you about the time you were halfway through college."

"Tell me something. Do you believe their sacrifice was what woke me up, gave me life?"

"I only know that your mother believed it and apparently, so did your father. The only thing for sure is they did it for you. What greater love could there be?"

"Then what's my role in this? What do I owe and who do I owe it to?"

"I can't say for sure everything that was in your mother's heart, but I think she would be happy if you were happy. And the way to happiness is through helping others. I think it was Ralph Waldo Emerson who said, 'No man can help another without helping himself'."

"What does that mean for me?"

"It means find something to do that will help your fellow man. God has a purpose for all of us." Tee's face showed doubt and confusion. Father Bob had his own doubts. "May I ask you a question?"

"Go ahead."

"Do you know the significance of the place where it happened? I wonder if it was a special place, maybe holy to her grandfather or to Choctaws in general."

"I looked up newspaper articles in the college library. It might be a place Mother used to talk about. Maybe where some of her folks lived a long time ago. I think she might have taken my brother and me there once. I don't recall much about it, and I got no desire to go back."

The priest nodded. "I understand that."

Tee turned to watch the mourners disperse. "All this stuff about dreams and rituals and Choctaw legends cost me both my parents."

He kept the letter in his coat pocket next to his heart until he was back on campus and alone in his shack.

> Tee,
> I hope by this time you have taken a few steps down the road to forgiveness. I have found few absolutes in this life, but I have never been as certain of anything as I am about the step your father and I are about to take. I dreamed of your awakening as vividly as I have ever seen, touched, or experienced anything in my lifetime. If you are reading this now, my faith has been redeemed. Never forget your father has had to show the greatest faith, however. It was my dream, not his, and he made the supreme sacrifice to show his love for you and for me.
>
> What I have asked of you is onerous for a boy and difficult for the man you have undoubtedly become. I don't expect you to understand what happened or what has been asked of you. Some things cannot be explained, they must be taken on faith. Someday, I pray the reason for all of this will become clear to you. You have a gift, my son. I pray that you find it. I loved you all of our days together and I love you still.
>
> Mother

Winona had left her Bible in one of the footlockers she packed for him, and Tee carefully placed the letter inside. He pulled his only chair out to the small porch, covered himself with a ragged quilt, and stared at the deserted prairie until the sun came up. He tried to understand but could not.

TEN

SARAH NEVER RETURNED TO FINISH HER LAST YEAR AT COLLEGE, electing to stay behind on the ranch she had vowed to escape at the earliest opportunity. She began writing to Tee. He always answered but never initiated contact. There were college girls, of course but most found him too serious. One told him he seemed more like her father than a boyfriend. As he neared graduation, Sarah's letters became more and more romantic. Tee tried to respond in kind but could not summon the words or the feelings.

Near the end of Tee's final semester, Cutt wrote him a letter listing all the reasons why Tee needed to come visit them during the holidays. The final one said simply, "I need to see you." Tee had spent three Christmases alone and did not want to spend another.

Sarah was a good cook, but Tee could not keep Winona's Christmas dinners out of his mind. The sights and sounds of Christmases past in the house crowded out Cutt's serious conversation and made Sarah's words sound prattling. Cutt insisted that he spend the night with them, but Tee knew Sarah had been sleeping in his old bed and he could not bring himself to sleep in his brother's room. He opted for the bunkhouse. Sarah walked out with him when he decided to turn in.

In the middle of the ranch yard under the big mesquite, she stopped and pulled on his shirt sleeve. When he turned to face her, she looked down so that he could not see into her eyes. "You'll be out of school soon. I don't want you going away from here alone. I want to go with you." Her voice was almost inaudible at first, then moved up a few octaves so that the last sentence sounded almost like a desperate plea for help.

He had to restrain himself from stepping back, even running. The loneliness he experienced after losing his family had seemed unbearable at first, but he had endured it so long that solitude had become like a quiet, even necessary companion. He considered himself to be on a mission to fulfill whatever purpose God had for him when He spared his life. The purpose had not been explained to him yet, but he thought it started with replacing what John T and Winona had lost, then owning a ranch even better than Blind River. His clear, unobstructed vision of the road to accomplishing those things did not include taking along a woman. Tee kept everyone at a distance. He couldn't afford to love anyone else for fear of losing them.

His response was clumsy. "You want to go with me?" He tried to make light of it. "What would your daddy say about us going off together?"

She wrung her hands. "Daddy's the one who put me up to it. He wants you for a son-in-law. I thought you knew."

Marrying Sarah had never entered his mind, but Tee admired no man alive as much as he admired Cutt Ledbetter. "Cutt approves of this?"

"Approves? I think he loves you more than he does me. We both want to help you get through this terrible thing."

"So you're proposing because you feel sorry for me?"

"I didn't mean to put it that way. I figured you would never ask, so Daddy said it was up to me. I knew it was a mistake." She turned to walk back inside.

Tee was embarrassed for them both as he reached for her arm. "Where would we live? Ford won't let me work here."

She whirled as if she had been struck. Her voice cracked. "Work here? Why would you even consider that? Didn't you tell me you already had a job offer in Dallas? I want to get away from here."

Tee had already decided to accept the job in Dallas but figured to go there as a single man, live frugally, and save toward a down payment on a small ranch of his own. He figured ten years of suffering might do it. "Who would look after your daddy now that your mama's gone?"

"You know Cutt Ledbetter as well as I do. There's a steady stream of widow women bringing him food day and night. He wants to be rid of me, and those women want me gone." She turned and ran back to the house before he could reply.

In the quiet of the bunkhouse, Tee allowed himself to feel grateful that anyone would want his damaged soul in their lives. He was not whole and might never be again.

<hr />

Sarah and Cutt watched Tee walk across the stage just after the new year to receive his diploma, Cutt as excited as Tee imagined John T and Winona might have been. Cutt waited alone outside the auditorium. Tee shook his hand. "Where's Sarah?"

"Said she had some old classmates she wanted to look up. She'll meet us at the restaurant."

Tee knew that Sarah had few, if any, college friends, so Cutt wanted him alone. Cutt was nervous when they sat down in the restaurant. He reached across and put a hand on Tee's arm. "Sarah tells me she got up the nerve to ask you to marry her."

Tee looked down at the table. "Not sure I'd make a fit husband, Cutt. I'm pretty damaged goods."

"You been hurt bad, that's a fact. I wanted to tell you that if you're not ready or if Sarah is not the girl for you, there will be no hard feelings between you and me."

The thought of having someone along to help him adjust to life in the big city had taken on some appeal for Tee, but marriage scared him. "Appreciate your telling me that, Cutt. But Sarah, she seems so delicate. I'm afraid I couldn't make her happy."

"That's one of the things I wanted to mention. She's a lot like her mother. Some women wouldn't be happy with anything less than a penthouse suite, but Sarah will be satisfied with a lot less. But like Maggie, she craves security. She wants a suit-and-tie man. To be totally honest, if you still have your heart set on being a rancher, she might not be a good choice."

Tee was not a suit-and-tie man and didn't want to be one. But something about the way Cutt expressed his feelings touched him. He made up his mind.

They were married two weeks later by a roving cowboy preacher, an old friend of Cutt's, in the living room where Tee had grown up. Ford attended the wedding, tugging his earlobe, squinting, and checking his watch. A bejeweled beauty with long, thick blonde hair and shiny blue eyes hung on his arm. Her green dress covered her from neck to floor, but clung in the right places. Ford introduced Hope to Tee as his new wife.

Tee's surprise showed. "Congratulations. Looks like we're both married men now."

"That invitation to stay the night in the guest house is still open."

"What invitation?"

"Offered it to Sarah. She turned me down flat."

Tee turned to look for Sarah. When he turned back, Ford had turned to talk to another guest. Hope lightly touched his arm. "Can't blame a girl for not wanting to spend her wedding night in her front yard."

Tee had been nervous all night, but he found her smile and gentle admonition comforting. "Guess not." Hope was clearly not the arm candy Ford usually sported around the ranch. As she turned to follow Ford outside, Cutt broke out the bourbon, and Cutt's widows unveiled their desserts.

When Tee and Sarah said their goodbyes and stepped outside, the ranch yard and buildings were covered with a light blanket of snow. Flakes were still falling. The wedding guests went back inside when the wind swirled, blowing snowflakes onto the porch. Tee was pleased he had covered their luggage with a tarp. The newlyweds climbed into his pickup, but Tee did not start it. He felt a rush of emotion he had not felt during the ceremony. He stepped into the yard where he had ridden his first colt and his first bicycle. The snow made for silence interrupted only with the occasional light gust of wind. He could hear his boyhood shouts of joy and those of his brother and parents.

Sarah stepped out of the truck and stood beside him; the memories flooded, and he could not speak. In the flattering moonlight, they seemed a handsome couple. Being in control after Maggie died had agreed with Sarah. Doing ranch cooking and cleaning and caring for baby calves had toned her muscles and given her pale skin a healthier glow. She had scaled back her makeup and let her hair go wild and free. On Tee's arm, she seemed more confident. Her mother's death seemed to have released her from the mutual dependency both had always displayed.

Tee's face seemed to have been formed by a novice sculptor. His cheeks were even more hollowed, and he was still rail thin. Ranch work at the college had broadened his shoulders, but he still walked with a slight stoop that made him look like an invisible feed sack was on his shoulders. He wore his hair a little longer, and the end of each strand now looked singed, like a horse's flax mane. From a distance, one would think he was becoming prematurely gray, older than his years. The expression in his eyes still held sadness and tragedy that usually marked much older men.

Tee drew in deep breaths; let his memory run down the paths where he and Jubal had trailed behind John T and Winona and the older ranch hands, to the spot where they had killed a mother rattlesnake and several babies, and the place where two young brothers had brought a runaway bull down with two ropes.

"Well." It was the only word he could muster as snowflakes started to collect on his shoulders and hair.

Sarah squeezed his arm. "Well, what?"

Tee looked into her eyes and did not see what he felt. That was expecting too much. "Just thinking of the roundups and breakfasts we had on all the sub-ranches and here at headquarters. Supper was good after a day's work, but it's the breakfasts I remember most. Wish I had known how good this life was when I had it."

"The one we're going to now will be much better. You wait and see."

Tee heard the familiar imaginary train whistle as they drove out of the yard. He stopped at the railroad crossing, stepped out, and placed a penny on a rail.

<hr>

The bellboy smiled and winked at Tee as he closed the curtains in their second floor room at the Holiday Inn in Amarillo. Sarah demurely peeked through the curtains at the parking lot below. They sensed each other's apprehension. Tee took her into his arms and chuckled as he whispered into her ear. "You'll be the first one to see me in pajamas. I bought my first pair."

Sarah put both hands on his chest. "I bought a new nightgown. Not too sexy, I guess."

"Get into it and we'll see."

He expected a see-through short nightie when she emerged from the bathroom, but her new gown was a black floor-length and definitely not see-through. He couldn't even see her bare feet, but he decided she had chosen wisely. When he emerged from the bathroom in his new dark blue pajamas, Sarah sat on the side of the bed running wooden rosary beads through her fingers. She had turned out the lights, but he could see her lips moving in what he assumed was a prayer. She stiffened when he sat down beside her. He put his arm around her and pulled her head to his shoulder. They stayed in that position until Tee reached for her hand and lifted her up.

They stood beside the bed, locked in a tight embrace. He bent to pull up her gown but she pulled his hand back up and put both hands firmly against his chest again, as if she were pushing him away. He sensed she was afraid of him. "You nervous?"

She nodded. "Sorry. Let's turn out all the lights."

The only light came from the bathroom door, and Tee wanted it left on but acceded to her wishes. When he turned away from the light and his eyes adjusted to the blackness, he saw her gown crumpled in a chair and Sarah under the covers. He peeled off his pajamas and joined her. She trembled when he took her into his arms. "You almost seem afraid of me."

"Course not. Just a little chilled, I guess."

The trembling, discomfiting at first, gradually turned his urgency into gentleness, and Tee found something inside himself he did not know existed. When he returned from the bathroom, the covers were up to her neck and the gown was gone from the chair. As Tee lay beside her, a sudden sense of sadness came over him. There had been no member of his family to attend his wedding.

The next day, they visited Palo Duro Canyon. Both had been there before. Sarah seemed disinterested. Tee knew the history well, but the stories of Comanches, Texas Rangers, longhorn cattle, and Charles Goodnight made him feel once again he belonged to that era, not this one.

He left his new bride asleep the next morning to make his prearranged meeting at the Immaculate Conception Church and the office of Father

Robert Messenger. The priest greeted him warmly. "I am finally coming to terms with the assignment given by your mother. In fact, I now know that God blessed me with this responsibility."

Tee could not suppress a smile when he handed over the diploma. The priest examined it as if it were fragile, sacred parchment. "Economics and finance. Did your course of study choose you like your mother said it would?"

"I suppose it could have. I asked her to speak to me many times, but she never did. Never came to me in any dreams, either. I have no idea what I'm gonna do with that piece of paper, but there it is."

The priest chuckled heartily. "She said you would say that, too." He pulled a folder from a file drawer, pulled out a checkbook, wrote a check, and handed it to Tee.

Tee felt as if his parents were in the room watching. "Eleven hundred and forty-six dollars?"

Father Bob chuckled again. "She planned it closely."

Tee was embarrassed to take the money. "What do I owe you? You went to a lot of trouble for me and my family."

"I have been well paid."

"How about the church?"

"Well paid, also. Take that money with my blessing and your parents' blessing and make yourself a life."

"What about their final arrangements? I thought about that a lot."

Father Bob smiled a sorrowful smile. "They paid in advance."

Tee took the keys to John T's pickup out of his pocket and held the key ring on his index finger. "I bought a car. But I can't quite bring myself to sell Daddy's old pickup to a stranger. She's got a few miles left in her. Would you consider taking it? "

The priest smiled. "I can't accept it as a gift, but you're welcome to leave it here on the church lot."

"It needs driving once in a while."

"I'll use it on church errands."

Tee was relieved. "I'll bring it back after I pick up the car I bought. I'll leave the key under your door mat." Tee shook the priest's hand and walked toward his pickup.

Father Bob followed him. "Tee, I have carried what I first considered a great burden for more than three years. Now, it's necessary to place that burden on your young shoulders. It is with surprising sorrow that I do so."

"Wish I could leave that burden here with the pickup. I feel like I am meant to do something, but still have no idea what that is."

"God says that everyone has a purpose in life. Your mother trusted us to find yours."

Tee stared northwest, toward the Blind River railroad crossing. "Reckon either one is going to ever let me in on it?"

"Your faith is being tested, Tee, but I believe you will rise to the occasion. If you need counsel, you know where to find me."

ELEVEN

URBAN LIVING MADE TEE MISERABLE AT HOME AND AT WORK. He spent the first year of apartment life in Dallas walking the streets every night, trying to see stars obscured by city lights, listening to any voice that might be his family, looking for signs that never came. He thought a house would improve things, but he sat in the backyard of their rented bungalow on weekends, staring at neighbors' fences, trying to see a blocked horizon; trying to figure out a way to explain to himself and his wife why he was unhappy; trying to rid himself of the recurring headaches and nightmares, the roaring in his head and the burning inside. When Sarah heard the first nightmare and described its horror to him, he felt little better than an animal. She made appointments with doctors, but the medicines they prescribed brought nausea and made the nightmares, headaches, and depression worse. Sarah's concern and the doctors' worried looks made him feel like a creature to be pitied or a rabid dog that had to be put down.

Tee tried to hold silent conversations with Winona, John T and Jubal but never knew if they listened, never heard them answer. He asked God if there was a penance to be paid. If so, must he suffer forever to pay it? He decided that his punishment was simply going through the motions of day to day living. He was doomed to be ordinary, even boring. The malevolent force that had taken his family had decided that ordinariness was the sublime punishment for a boy who dreamed of greatness in the rodeo arena. Dullness was the supreme bludgeon for such a boy. He would be beaten with it until he succumbed to eternal sleep, never having achieved anything significant or worthwhile. The spectral, black-robed stalker continued to appear in his thoughts and in his dreams until Sarah told him she was pregnant.

The arrival of his son lifted the aura of tedium as Tee saw himself through the innocent eyes of his child. He was the primary male role model for this uncluttered being. The birth of a child changes the life of any thinking, feeling parent, but this birth was more. The boy made him feel as if he belonged on Earth again, brought a sense of family, worth, purpose, and beauty to what had been a barely tolerable existence. The nightmares and headaches slowed in intensity and frequency, replaced by tranquil dreams. Depression changed to milder episodes of melancholy. The boy filled a void Sarah was unable to fill. The world now seemed to have new possibilities for Tee. And from the moment he saw his son, Tee felt his brother had returned. They named him Jubal.

TWELVE

TEE POURED HIMSELF A CUP OF COFFEE, HIS FOURTH OF THE day, from the silver coffee and tea service on a table next to his desk. A cup-a-day man before, easy access and little else to do drove him to become a pot-a-day man. A private cubicle, a panoramic view of downtown Dallas, and a perennially full coffee urn seemed to leave little to dislike about his banking job. Tee Jessup—Financial Systems Analyst, white letters on brown plastic, slid perfectly into a brass holder affixed next to the cubicle opening. The brass holder was permanently attached, but the sign with his name and title was not. Tee almost enjoyed the feeling of imagined dominion over the ant-like people who walked and drove toy cars twenty-one floors below.

A picture of Sarah on their wedding night at the ranch leaned next to a snapshot of his smiling toddler son. The pictures had their usual calming effect. He turned his swivel chair toward the twenty-first floor window, put his feet on the window sill, and stared across downtown Dallas at Mercantile Bank, idly wondering if the people working there were as bored as he was. The job at Republic National Bank had seemed an answer to his prayers nine months ago, but the good working conditions and pleasant surroundings were poor compensation for mind-numbing boredom.

Nolan Clinton had assigned Tee as the official liaison between the Controller's Division and the two-year-old Information Systems Division. His responsibility was to attend two meetings per week and report on the progress of automating the accounting of the bank. He had attended only a week's ration of meetings when he heard a fellow elevator passenger laugh and refer to the meetings as the Grand Council of Nerds. The luster faded further when the bank president accosted him in the hall and chastised him for not wearing his silver star pin, the bank's logo, on his lapel.

Tee went to two regularly scheduled meetings a week, took copious notes, and wrote good memorandums of everything. He submitted the reports punctually to Nolan, along with suggestions on how to complete the project. Nolan had four other Financial Systems Analysts in his department, and they all met every Friday afternoon. In his first Friday meeting, Nolan reprimanded Tee for wearing a light blue shirt instead of white, but said nothing about Tee's reports.

The Grand Council of Nerds meetings never accomplished anything. Tee's memorandums became more and more caustic until he finally declared the meetings a costly waste of time. When he mistakenly left a copy of that memo on the Xerox machine, it quickly traveled through the bank, and each reading bought Tee an equal portion of new enemies and friends. He learned that those meetings had been occurring for two years and represented job security for the dozen people who attended them.

When the bank's controller got wind of Tee's caustic memo and its unauthorized distribution, he called Clinton in for a dressing down. The normally unflappable and unfailingly professional Nolan Clinton claimed Tee had jeopardized his entire department. In a meeting with Nolan and the bank's assistant controller, Tee agreed to tone down his reports.

With brutal truth no longer available to him, Tee began reporting things that did not happen in the meetings to see if anyone would notice. When nobody did, his reports began to take on more exaggerated qualities of fiction, including a claim that the meeting attendees had formed an enforcement squad to squelch a bank robbery. In another memo, he reported the team had aborted a large bank fraud that threatened the very existence of the Federal Reserve. When nobody questioned him, he knew for certain that nobody was reading his reports.

On the first anniversary of his employment, most of the staff who worked in the bank controller's division showed up at his cubicle with flowers. They clapped when Nolan handed Tee a framed certificate declaring he had been made an officer of the bank. The unearned promotion made things worse for Tee. Another month of tedium and lack of productivity made him feel deeply insecure, as if he could not be trusted to work on a worthwhile project. When he begged Nolan to assign him something meaningful to do, he told Tee nothing could be allowed to interfere with his liaison work. Desperate, Tee wrote a memorandum to the president of the bank detailing the worthless nature of the meetings.

Tee was working on his third cup of coffee the next day when his interoffice phone rang. Nolan's secretary requested his presence down the hall at once. Tee stood and pulled on his coat, observing proper protocol. Coats had to be worn everywhere outside of one's immediate work area. All his fellow analysts knew he was being called on the carpet.

He knocked on the wall of the cubicle of fellow FSA Walt, a computer geek who arrived first every morning and left last at night. Dot-matrix printouts covered Walt's cubicle. He received new stacks of reports each afternoon and pored over them diligently. But he could never get the reports to agree to the handwritten ledgers kept by the accountants across the hall. And the handwritten ledgers took priority. Computer reports were known for inaccuracies and had little credibility. But Walt was undeterred and determined. He kept his head down as Tee passed.

Bruce, an East Texas country boy who wanted to be president of a small town bank, sat in the next cubicle. He and Tee had become friends and shared their frustrations. Bruce nodded, smiled, and gave a thumbs-up as Tee passed.

Tee paused and leaned against the opening to Denny's cubicle. Denny wore a perfectly coiffed and immovable Roffler Sculpture Kut and kept a straight razor in his desk for touchups. A James Bond fanatic, he frequently asked Tee to cover for him while he attended multiple showings of Sean Connery's latest at the Majestic Theater a few blocks from the bank building. Denny worried about getting caught doing nothing or attending movies during business hours, but he reveled in the excitement of getting away with it. He flashed a row of perfect white teeth in an irreverent smile and held up a yellow tablet with "Give 'em Hell" written in black and outlined in red.

Eric, a big gregarious fellow who had to be told most days to tuck in his shirttail and comb his hair, sat in the last cubicle. Two years older than Tee, he loved his bank job for the same reasons that Tee hated it. Eric had a large group of accounting clients on the side and used his cubicle and bank facilities to run a small accounting firm. He had breakfast downtown mid-morning and lunch mid-afternoon, usually with clients. He shook his head when he saw Tee. He had told Tee he was crazy to cause trouble, had given his best advice. If Tee ignored it, that was his lookout. He made a slicing motion across his throat and mouthed, "*Adios.*"

Nolan's corner office had gray sheetrock walls, and Tee sat in a chair against one. He could feel the eyes of the other FSA's trying to bore through their cubicles. Nolan cited bank and corporate policy for a half-hour before launching into the inappropriateness and embarrassing content of Tee's memo to the bank president. He kept his voice even and never lost his professionalism. Tee held a grudging admiration for such controlled civility. "Tee, I am deeply disappointed in your performance but am willing to give you another chance. Sign this report for your personnel file, and we can begin anew."

Tee made his familiar clicking sounds as he read each of his transgressions. The facts were correct but incomplete. Tee's voice was low and calm, but he could not avoid the natural tone some considered ominous. It seemed to strike Nolan like a brisk wind. "Doesn't say that my memo was false. And I don't see anything here about the number of times I have come to you to ask for responsible, real work. And why is the bank okay with wasting time and money?"

"Those meetings are performing a vital function for this financial institution."

"What vital function? Those damn meetings have been going on for nearly three years, and nobody can list a single thing accomplished. I sure know nothing has been done since I started going. If anyone ever has the audacity to suggest we actually take some action, he's overruled. And you're not doing a thing about it."

Tall and handsome with a long face and just-right hair, Nolan leaned back as if he had been struck. His expression turned boyish, as if he were deciding whether to challenge Tee to a fist fight or invite him to have a beer. "Why do you have to carry a chip on your shoulder, Tee? Most men your age would kill for this job. You complain about it and endanger your family's financial future."

Tee looked across the desk, trying to answer the unanswerable. He had asked himself the same thing many times. Nolan straightened his posture and adopted his bank executive expression as he pushed the document toward Tee. "Protocol has to be followed, Tee. Sign and maybe we can start over and put your little *faux pas* behind us."

Tee stared at Nolan until the air in the room seemed to grow clammy and prickly. Then he stood, unhooked his silver star, slid it across Nolan's desk, and walked out. Nolan called after him, but Tee never slowed. His expression was sad and serious as he nodded toward each of his fellow FSAs on the way out. He stopped for a final look inside his cubicle, slid his laminated plastic nameplate out of its holder. His personal belongings had already been taken home, so he carried only a small folder with copies of his memos and his nameplate as he walked out onto the cavernous streets of downtown Dallas, wondering what Jubal would think of his father if he knew he had lost another job.

THIRTEEN

TEE REACHED HIS CAR IN THE DOWNTOWN PARKING LOT early enough to miss rush hour. He thought about stopping to cry in his beer but decided that might make things worse. As he pulled onto their street, he saw a pearl-white El Dorado parked in front of the small house they had rented in Grand Prairie, a city just west of Dallas. He had never seen the Cadillac before, but knew only one person who might drive that type of car. He found Ford Donovan sitting in his rocking chair in his living room with legs crossed in a position to best display his cordovan crocodile boots. Jubal leaped from Ford's lap and ran to his father.

Tee held Jubal with one arm and extended the other for Ford's handshake. "Ford Donovan, as I live and breathe." Both hands had grown soft. Ford had returned to custom western shirts that snuggled against a wide frame that carried forty more pounds that looked to be mostly muscle. The tan smile-pocket pants looked like they were the bottom half of an expensive western suit. Light from the setting sun passed through the sliding glass patio door and reflected off a silver Vogt belt buckle. Rubies outlined the initials FD.

67

Tee suppressed his envy. "Looks like you been working out."

"Joined a club out in Kentucky and the DAC here. Polo keeps me sharp, too." Ford's widow's peak seemed more prominent with his hair combed back. His hair line had receded a little on each side, and he had used something to straighten his curls.

Tee had never seen his old boss away from the Panhandle, a realm where mere mention of the Donovan name engendered automatic respect and sometimes subservience. Tee felt conspicuous and sissy in his cheap black suit, narrow black tie and wingtips that agonized his feet and calves.

"Sorry to drop by without notice, but I was in the area. I have some friends who want to start a polo club in Dallas."

"Where?"

"Place called Willow Bend. Think it's in a suburb. Plano sound right?"

"Yep. All the rich folks are moving that direction. Didn't know you played. How many polo horses do you have?"

"Just four now. You should play with us sometime. You'd be good at it."

"Might be good at tending the horses, but I never played any polo. How did you find us?"

"Cutt talks about you two and the boy all the time. He gave me the address. Been after me to drop in since you got married."

Tee looked around for Sarah. She worked as a secretary at an insurance firm a few blocks from their neighborhood. "Sarah still at work?"

"Cutt told me where she worked, so I dropped by and let her lead me here."

The commode flushed before Sarah appeared in the hall, dressed as she was when she left for work that morning. She was startled to see Tee. "You're home a little early. Everything okay?"

Tee tried to hide it. "Could be worse, could be better."

Sarah sat delicately on the couch. Tee sat in the other rocker, and Jubal stood between his father's open arms and knees. Sarah smoothed her dress and tugged at the hem. The silence was awkward. Her shyness sometimes irritated him.

Tee gestured toward the refrigerator. "Think we might have a beer around here somewhere, maybe even some cheap bourbon."

Ford shook his head. "Sarah already offered. Spirits will be flowing where I'm going, and all I have to do is push an elevator button to get to

68

my room. Why don't you two go with me? Get you a sitter for little Jubal, and we'll make a night of it. I can get you another room so you don't have to drive home."

Tee looked at Sarah, but she stared at the floor. "Not a chance. It ain't exactly been a good day for me, and tomorrow doesn't look much better. Another time."

They made small talk about Blind River and Cutt for an hour or so before walking Ford to his Cadillac. Awkward goodbyes were accompanied by half-hearted invitations to let them know when he was coming again so they could take him out to eat or so that Sarah could cook him a proper meal. Sarah was back inside before Ford was out of sight.

Tee found his wife on the edge of their bed, wringing her hands. "What's wrong with you?

"You said you had a bad day. Do you still have a job?"

Tee knew that his face was always a dead giveaway. The bank had been his fifth job in four years. Three small companies he worked for had simply gone out of business and closed their doors, and he had quit a fourth job with a large defense plant. But the job he left today was one they had both seen as their future. And Sarah's main goal in life was to have a secure present and future. Tee had failed in one of the few requests she made. Keep a job.

He avoided her question, changed into old jeans, and nursed iced tea on the patio as a light mist fell, making him appreciate the metal cover he had installed last summer. The rain calmed him a little. As Sarah sat beside him in jeans and sweater, her face contorted into a near sob. She pressed her fingernails into the palms of her hands. "What happened this time? Didn't think you could put a big bank out of business."

"Very funny. You think those companies folding up were my fault?"

"I didn't say that. But isn't there some way to find out if a company is in trouble before you go to work there? You do have a degree in that sort of thing."

"Nice of Ford to drop by. I thought for a minute he might be coming to offer me a job taking care of his racehorses or working back on the ranch."

Sarah's eyes widened. "Are you serious? Did you get fired from the bank or not?"

"No."

She shivered with relief that lasted only a second.

"I quit." He knew her eyes were filling. They always did. He refused to look. "You know I hated it. Not doing anything for weeks at a time would drive anybody nuts."

"Did any of your friends quit? I'm trying to understand why you're always the one to leave."

Tee did not answer, and they sat in silence as he pondered what fatal flaw kept him from succeeding in the business world. He thought he was meant to be a rancher. "I've never been out of work more than a few days. I'll find something. I always do."

"I would rather not use our savings."

"Me, neither." They had guarded the nest egg left to him by his parents, added to it whenever they had a nickel to spare. The money was not to be spent on things mundane but used only for urgent needs. Tee figured land was the only urgent need, but Sarah wanted a house in a nice suburb.

Tee started a methodical job search through Dallas and Fort Worth papers the next morning and began dialing and mailing resumes. He was getting to be a pro at looking for jobs. Four days later, he garnered an interview for a controller position with Wellstone Industries, a small cabinet manufacturing company on the north side of Dallas. A long commute, but the proposed salary bump was enough to pay for the extra travel, and the controller title would look good on his resume. He parked in front of a small, austere office building of white brick flanked by a warehouse and a manufacturing facility. The company occupied half of a city block in a light industrial district. Easy access, plenty of free parking. Tee hated parking downtown. This might work.

The interview went well, and Saxby Chandler, Wellstone's president, called the next morning to offer him the job. Tee accepted. He might not be able to keep a job, but he needed to prove to Sarah he could still find one.

FOURTEEN

THE IRS AGENT SCARCELY LOOKED UP AS HE TOOK THE CHECK from Tee's sweaty hand as if Tee were an obedient lapdog returning a fetched bone. He always had to stand in the agent's cubicle because the only chair was full of computer printouts—the same printouts every week for the last six weeks. Tee knew they were the same because he had read the first page six consecutive Fridays while he stood like a dog on his hind legs, begging to be patted on the head and sent back to the offices of Wellstone Industries to fetch next week's contribution.

Murderous traffic on the streets outside had delivered enough unwanted sweat to wilt Tee's button-down collar and cause his shirt to cling under his cheap seersucker summer suit. In a rare moment of humor, Sarah had joked it would save money on their cleaning bills, that nobody notices wrinkles in seersucker because it's wrinkled all the time. But Tee noticed. He hated the damn suit and the silly blue flowers on the wide tie she bought to match. Temps near a hundred and almost matching humidity made the misery index high enough outside to increase the crime rate in Dallas. Coats and ties in Texas summers were as sadistic as the pea-brained bureaucrat who made him stand and wait every time Tee brought his Friday check.

He folded his arms and tried to show impatience without expressing it verbally. "Never insult or irritate a man who carries a gun with a caliber higher than his IQ." Saxby Chandler, Tee's boss at Wellstone, repeated that phrase every time he left the plant to deliver their check for withheld payroll taxes to the IRS office in downtown Dallas. But Tee knew that IRS agents who work at desks don't carry weapons. Only Special Agents get to carry weapons. But this guy might as well have been carrying a forty-four magnum. The simpleton could end Tee's livelihood with a phone call and a signature. And Tee had a wife and son to support.

Dexter, the agent, finally stopped shuffling papers long enough to pick up the sheet Tee had prepared listing all employees' weekly salaries and each type of tax withheld. Dexter was about the same age as Tee, but desk-work had produced a forty-inch waistline that seemed unmatched with his narrow shoulders. Tee had already done all of the work, but Dexter methodically checked each employee's gross salary amount, withheld taxes, and the net for all thirty-four employees against payroll withholding charts.

He looked up and gave a condescending smile when he checked the salary number beside Tee's name. Tee knew the smug look meant Dexter made more. The agent needlessly compared the total to the amount of the check Tee had brought. Tee stuck his hands in his pockets to keep from strangling him. Why would he bring him a check that didn't match the paperwork?

"Everything okay?" If Dexter could make Tee stand there while he did redundant work, Tee could ask a redundant question.

Dexter answered without looking up. "Just let me check your totals." He pulled an antique ten-key adding machine close enough to reach and started punching in numbers with arthritic precision. Tee wanted to rip his hands away and show him how to use it.

He pointed to the adding machine tape he had stapled to the payroll summary this week just as he did every week. "Already added it up."

"I have to check your figures."

"Yep. I guess adding machines do lie every once in a while. Could never figure out how to get one to print errors on those tapes, though."

Tee walked out of the cubicle and strolled down the narrow hall between rows of duplicate cubicles, cracking his knuckles to ease the tension. From the east window, he saw the outline of the silver stars that surrounded the Republic National Bank building, wistfully remembered his old cubicle, the silver tea service, and long, lazy days.

When he returned, Dexter was on the phone with the bank. As the agent exercised his power to make money disappear out of Wellstone's bank account into the government's, he drew himself straighter and seemed to inflate. "I'll make you a copy of the check and your report. I have to keep the original for my files."

"No need. Like I been telling you for six weeks in a row, I always keep a copy. We all done?" Tee handed him a copy of his parking ticket, just as he did every week.

Dexter looked up as if Tee had asked for a personal loan. Tee repeated the same question he asked every time. "Mind stamping that so I don't have to pay?"

With great reluctance, Dexter opened the top side drawer and shuffled through a mound of paper clips, fingernail clippings, government issued ballpoint pens, and loose change.

Tee stared at his laced white bucks, the only item of clothing he wore that he almost liked. If you had to wear shoes instead of boots, these suited him better than black wingtips. "It's in the second drawer. You keep the damn thing in the second drawer. Why do you always look in the top drawer?" Tee's voice had taken on a sense of urgency and his face was dark. He regretted his harsh tone when Dexter rolled back in his chair as if Tee were going to strike him—a distinct possibility. They stared at each other for a few seconds until the agent finally pulled out the stamp and validated the parking ticket.

Tee jerked the ticket out of his hand and waved it under his nose. "You would think that stamping this ticket costs you money out of your own pocket. Fact is, it doesn't cost anybody a damn thing to let me park in the taxpayers' building for an hour every Friday."

The fear in the agent's eyes stroked the fire in Tee's belly. "If you weren't so damn slow, I could park on the street. I drive down here on my own dime because you require it. All this could be done over the phone or at our local bank. Or through the mail. But no, hell, no. You make me come down here and be humiliated every week. You can bet your sweet ass I'm not about to pay to park, too."

In minutes, Tee was down the elevator, in his car, and out of the building that had started to close in on him. He tried to erase the visions of grabbing Dexter by the scruff of the neck and throwing him out a window, tried to ease the roaring in his head and fire in his stomach that had returned of late. He pulled into the parking lot at Wellstone Industries a few minutes before closing time at five. He stopped at Patty's desk outside the president's office. "Saxby in?"

Her response was loud and definite. "No, he is not."

The exaggerated head shake told Tee that she was lying again. She protected her boss as if he were head of a multi-national corporation instead of president of a piss-ant cabinetmaker. Saxby Chandler's inability or unwillingness to communicate with his employees was a major factor in the company's steep and accelerating slide into bankruptcy. And Patty was his enabler. "Anybody with him?"

"Okay, he's in there, Tee, but he gave strict orders not to be disturbed."

"He gives those same damn orders every day at this time so he can crack open the gin." Tee opened the door and walked in.

Saxby Chandler had his feet on the windowsill behind his desk, looking out at a factory that he did not understand. A team of installers was loading kitchen cabinets on a flatbed truck with forklifts. Saxby had just left his twenties, a few years ahead of Tee. Wellstone was a small outfit, but Tee had been impressed that a man of Saxby's age had already advanced to president. Like Tee, Saxby was in over his head.

Saxby had promised to support Tee, show him the ropes, because he was a CPA and had Tee's controller position before he became president. It took Tee about a month to learn Saxby had no more idea of how the company worked than he did. Saxby had bluffed his way into becoming controller much the same as Tee had. When a Nebraska construction company bought Wellstone, he bluffed his way into the president's office. Saxby had convinced Tee that the parent company had the funds and clout to move tiny Wellstone to the next level. But when Tee asked them for cash to pay back taxes to the IRS, they refused and scolded him for letting Wellstone get into such a mess.

Tee noticed a few strands of prematurely gray hair when Saxby turned to face him. He had watched the young president age five years in the nine months Tee had worked for him. Saxby sat the ever-present Beefeater-on-the-rocks-with-a-twist on one of the coasters Patty kept scattered throughout the dark office. He had spent almost twenty-thousand dollars of the company's badly needed money to turn his office into his inner sanctum. Picture-frame paneling, lush carpet, walnut desk, leather chairs, the works—Tee's first sign he had made another mistake. The president of a cabinet manufacturing company did not need a bank president's office. The obvious extravagance hurt morale, too. When Tee discovered that he had hired on with another company with cash flow as well as IRS problems, he had groveled to Nolan Clinton and asked for his old job at the bank, but that bridge had been burned.

Saxby was not pleased to see Tee. His voice was slightly slurred. "Well, if it isn't Tee Jessup, chief bean-counter of Wellstone Industries. Did you get that leech downtown satisfied?"

Tee sat in one of the soft leather front chairs. "I figure to make that trip about two more times, then I won't have to go anymore."

"He turn us loose?" He waved his glass at Tee. "Calls for a celebration. Can I get you one?"

"No thanks on the drink and no, that little weasel did not turn us loose. He'll hang on like a dog on a bone. I think we are the reason for his existence. Still can't figure out what the hell you were thinking when you stopped depositing withheld taxes." Saxby had used employees' withheld payroll taxes to pay vendors, and it took Tee about two months to figure it out. When he did, the money had already been spent. The IRS caught them during a surprise audit seven months into Tee's tenure. They blamed Tee because he was controller. He avoided personal responsibility for the taxes and penalties because he had not been an officer of the company when the withheld taxes were diverted.

Saxby pointed toward the manufacturing facility framed in the window behind him. "Like I told you before, it was either pay vendors or stop making cabinets and shut the place down."

"IRS treats that like theft, you know. Penalty is a hundred percent."

"We been through that before, Tee. I did what I had to do. Stop rubbing it in and tell me what you mean about two more trips downtown."

Tee leaned forward. "I've been telling you for two months that there will be a Friday when we won't make payroll. When that happens, it's over. My guess is we got about two more weeks."

Saxby stirred his gin, ran the lime wedge around the edge of the glass. "Why? We worked out payment schedules with the vendors, got our receivables current."

Tee's reply was loud enough for Patty to hear through the door. "We? I don't remember seeing you in those meetings where I almost got on my hands and knees. I walk out there in the yard with a cashier's check or cash and hand it to the driver every time one arrives with materials. But pretty soon, there won't be any cash. Our order backlog is about gone. And our customers *are* paying on time. But if just one delays payment, we're through."

FIFTEEN

SARAH LIKED HAVING HER HUSBAND WORK AT A BANK, BUT the job at Wellstone suited Tee better at first. It was certainly not in the country, but it was away from downtown and the worst traffic. Riding an elevator and working high in the sky made him claustrophobic. At Wellstone, he could walk out on the yard anytime, stroll through the factory, shoot the bull with installers or shop workers. He ate off a lunch wagon, and there was no official dress code, though he followed Saxby's lead and wore a tie every day. He had made friends out in the factory and felt guilty none of them knew their jobs were in jeopardy.

As Tee prepared for the worst, he kept the brewing trouble at Wellstone a secret from Sarah. This time, he vowed to ride it out, to not resign until he had another job. He could no longer take chances. Sarah and Jubal were having an early supper when he arrived home that night. He gave a perfunctory kiss to Sarah and put a finger under Jubal's chin to tickle him. The boy had grown into his own chair at the table, and his smile was a soothing balm for Tee's still-tortured soul, a recompense of sorts for the loss of everyone he loved. He wanted another child to complete the four parts that Winona said made a family whole, and was disappointed every month when Sarah said, "Not this time."

"No supper for me. I'm going to Fort Worth."

Sarah, still wafer thin, pushed back a plate of food barely touched. "Fort Worth?"

Tee nodded. "Got a meeting downtown at the Petroleum Club."

"What kind of meeting?"

"Job interview."

Panic came into her eyes. "Did you quit your job again?"

"Nope. Just keeping a hook in the water for something better."

"When were you going to tell me about this interview?"

"Wasn't set until this afternoon. The guy I'm interviewing is in from Rhode Island and is only here for one or two nights." Tee hoped that out-of-state reference would please Sarah. Such things tended to impress her.

"But why are you looking for a job?"

"I wasn't exactly looking. I've changed jobs so much I'm on a first name basis with a head-hunting firm. They set it up. Said this company is looking for somebody with my type of my experience."

"Experience? In what? Making companies go broke?" For a shy woman, Sarah sometimes dug deep down and found a way to say something that hurt.

Tee glanced at Jubal to see if he seemed to understand the conversation. Jubal's eyes were wide, sensing the tension. Tee needed to stay calm for him and for the interview. "Look, I know it's probably just a way for them to make a commission, and I know my record on holding jobs is lousy. But I told you before we married I didn't want to be an accountant. I want to ranch."

Sarah stood and hugged him. "I know. But you and I both know ranching is a pipe dream. You have a family now. You need a good steady job with a big company that provides security for us."

On his way to Fort Worth, a sense of desperation settled over Tee. Sarah was right. Ranching was just a dream. He needed a way out, to find a stable job with a stable company. Streetlights twinkled in the caverns of downtown Fort Worth as he was ushered into the fortieth floor dining room of the Petroleum Building.

He followed the white-jacketed headwaiter across the cavernous room to a window table where an untouched amber drink sat in front of a man in his sixties staring out the window. He seemed to be unfolding as he rose to greet Tee, and the unfolding took some time. Though somewhat stooped, the man towered over Tee.

Tee shook the man's hand. "Tee Jessup."

The man held Tee's hand firmly and studied him, looked deeply into his eyes. The eyes that examined Tee were steely, but the expression was kind. When he finally got his hand back, Tee had the feeling the interview was unnecessary, that the man had delved into his brain and now knew everything there was to know about him.

The elderly gentleman gestured toward the chair across from him and finally spoke. "I'm Jacob Locke."

Wary of appearing gluttonous or needy, Tee ordered an economical well-done skirt steak. Jacob left his sirloin strip barely touched but ordered chocolate cheesecake covered in strawberries and dug into it with relish. They made small talk about personal things and the economy until the waiter brought coffee. Tee had barely touched coffee since he left the bank; it brought bad memories. Jacob's cup clinked against the saucer as he uttered his first serious words. "Six jobs in five years. That's quite a record."

Tee relaxed. The thing he feared most was out in the open. The interview was over before it started. He sat a little more upright. "That's right."

"Care to explain that?"

"Don't know if I can. Four companies went under; I quit one because I couldn't get along with my boss, and the bank job made me feel like my brain was in danger of atrophy. I quit it, too." Tee paused and waited for a reaction. Jacob smiled slightly. Tee looked out the window, and it calmed him more. The man was easy to talk to for some reason. "And now, Wellstone is on the verge of bankruptcy. Can't seem to pick a good one."

"You like being an accountant?"

Tee picked up a packet of raw sugar and turned it between his fingers. Nobody had asked him that before. "Can't really say that I do."

"I suppose that explains why you haven't pursued your certificate."

"Certificate?"

"Wouldn't you agree that the CPA is recognized as the pinnacle of the accounting profession?'

"Never expected to stay an accountant very long, I guess."

Jacob folded his napkin and made an almost imperceptible signal to a solicitous, hovering waiter to clear the table. Tee figured the interview was over, but Jacob leaned forward and spoke earnestly. "And yet, my information is that you are well-suited to your chosen profession."

"My mother would have said the profession chose me. Not the other way around." An uncomfortable pause. "You think I'm suited for it? After six jobs?"

"You have shown skill at identifying problems. Of course, many can recognize when something is not working, but only a few can find and implement a solution."

"I never found any solutions that worked."

"You did manage to find a few hidden problems at Wellstone and helped to keep creditors and the IRS at bay for the better part of a year. Did you learn anything in the process?"

Tee wondered how Jacob Locke knew those details. "To be truthful, one of the companies I worked for went under because they simply lost money. Sales were low, expenses were high. But I never figured out why three other companies had reasonable profits but burned through cash. At Wellstone, I think it has something to do with the manufacturing process, but I admit I don't understand how to find out."

Jacob looked out the window again. "My company is considering purchasing a stake in a small company near Fort Worth. They're dropping impressive profits to the bottom line, but struggle with cash flow."

Tee leaned back. "One thing I have learned. Don't go to work for a company with cash flow problems."

Jacob smiled again. "Understood. However, your experience with such problems is what brought us together for this pleasant conversation. We see some value in your past experiences, however unpleasant they may have been for you. It's what separates you from the other candidates. I have two CPAs vying for this job."

Tee wished for a recorder. He wanted Sarah to know that his experience had some value. "Why do you want to buy a company with cash flow problems?"

"They're in the recreation business and so are we. Snowtrack, one of our companies, makes snowmobiles; Harborcraft, the company I am speaking of, makes camper tops and trailers and is expanding into motor homes and mobile homes. We expect to buy them cheaply, and we are value investors. And, as I said, the profits are impressive, and the future looks bright."

Tee swirled the lukewarm coffee in his cup. "Mr. Locke, I feel like I've been walking around with a cloud over my head since I got out of college. My wife wants security. With a little boy to support now, I can't afford to make another mistake."

Jacob Locke scooted back from the table and crossed his legs. "A man who spends his life looking for security rather than adventure and challenge will find neither."

They sat in silence until Locke led the way to the elevator. Tee pushed the down arrow. "What's the name of the company again?"

"Harborcraft. A free spirit named Billy Harbor started it in his garage making pickup camper tops."

"And you say they're making big profits but running out of cash?"

"Yes, and I need to know why. They're close to being ready for a public stock offering that will solve their cash flow problems, and we are prepared to take a stake in that offering."

Tee shook his head, trying to remember terms from his corporate finance class. "Is the stock traded now?"

Jacob shook his head. "All closely held by less than half a dozen people including myself. The paperwork has been filed for the offering, and the audit opinion will be issued soon."

"Would I be working for you?"

"No. Technically, I'm only a shareholder. You'll be on the regular payroll of Harborcraft. But the company owners are lusting after Snowtrack's cash reserves. When I insisted on having my own man inside the company, they readily agreed to my terms."

Tee stepped off the elevator and paused. "Snowtrack is the company that makes snowmobiles?"

"Yes."

"Could I ask how you knew all those details about Wellstone?"

"We had merger talks with their parent company in Omaha. We were close to an arrangement but decided against it at the last minute. Saxby Chandler has almost destroyed the Dallas division."

They waited in the heavy air of Main Street until an attendant brought Jacob's white Oldsmobile around. Tee opened and closed both fists. "When are you going to decide?"

"Are you interested?"

"Yes, sir, I believe I am, but we haven't talked about pay."

Jacob pressed four folded bills into the valet's palm in exchange for his keys and stood beside the open door of the Olds. "You mentioned your mother earlier. We haven't talked too much about your family. Have you rid yourself of the anger and sadness you must have felt at losing your entire family in tragic events?"

The remark stunned Tee. Blood flowed to his face and upper body. "How do you know about that?"

"I make it my business to know as much as I can about any man I consider for any type of business or personal relationship."

The direct nature of Jacob's inquiries and Tee's firm answers had brought a strange sort of boldness to Tee. "I'm not sure that's any of your business."

"If I decide to offer you a job, it's critical to me."

"I'll tell you one thing for sure. I am not an object of pity."

"I can certainly see that, but it doesn't answer my question."

Tee looked up and down Main. "Having a new son has helped."

"I'm prepared to offer you twenty-four thousand a year to start. Review in six months."

Tee's dream ranch had reduced to a small acreage large enough to pasture a couple of horses for himself and Jubal. Four thousand a year salary bump made that seem a little more real. "When would I start?"

"Report to Barry Steadman, VP of finance, Monday week. Give him this card and envelope. The letter inside has all the details of your employment and directions to the Mansfield home office."

Tee looked at the card and envelope. "You knew I was going to accept?"

Jacob Locke sat behind the wheel of his car. "No, but the important question was whether I was going to offer. If you had given weak answers, lied, or made excuses, I wouldn't have considered you."

They shook hands again, and Tee had one final question. "When will I hear from you?"

"Call me at the number on that card when you find out why they're burning cash." He closed the door and drove away. Tee started walking the seven blocks to the cheap parking lot where he had parked his worn out '54 Ford.

Sixteen

EXHAUST FUMES MIXED WITH BURGERS AND FRIES ON THE warm summer breeze as Jacob Locke drove away. Tee had the feeling he had been slapped and embraced. How would he explain to Sarah that he had accepted another job without meeting the people he would be working with at a place he had never seen? One thing gave him comfort. He liked and trusted Jacob Locke. And that thing he said about security versus adventure and challenge made sense.

When Patty would not let him in to see Saxby the next morning, he handed her his resignation letter and headed toward his small, window-less office. He had work to do if he intended to leave things better than he found them. As Tee expected, she scanned the single paragraph and called after him. "Tee. Come back here. He'll want to see you."

She knocked on the door, ushered him in, and placed the letter on Saxby's desk, tapped it with a long fingernail before walking out and closing the door. Tee enjoyed knowing she probably had her ear pressed against it.

He watched Saxby's expression change as he read. "I'll be damned. This is a hell of a time to be abandoning ship, Tee."

"Seems like a real good time to me."

"People in Omaha gonna give me hell about this. I talked them into hiring you, remember. This the thanks I get?"

"Wellstone is not in my future. I doubt it even has a future."

"Who's gonna go downtown every Friday?"

"That's up to you. You're the one got us into that mess."

◆◆◆

Sarah took pride in her cooking, the one thing her mother had passed on to her. "The beef you get at the grocery stores here doesn't compare to the fresh beef we had back home. Same for the vegetables. Things just never taste right."

Three-year-old Jubal finished his meal and took his usual spot on his father's knee as Tee finished his last bite. "Would you like to move back out west?"

She began clearing the table. "There's a lot more important things than fresh beef."

"Like what?"

"Rain, for one thing. Then there's trees, a nice house, shopping close by." Dishes in the sink, she turned to face him. "You've got that look again. Tee, if you quit another job, so help me...."

"I took another job, Sarah. It's over in Mansfield. Pays twenty percent more than I make at Wellstone."

Tears filled her eyes. "Mansfield? You'll be so far away Jubal and I won't feel safe."

Tee traded his worn-out '54 Ford work car for a used '68 black Cougar owned by one of the young cabinet installers at Wellstone who needed the boot to make a house payment. He had always wanted a Mustang, and the Cougar was close enough. A black leather interior and the best sound system he had ever heard inside a car persuaded Tee to overlook the ninety-nine thousand miles on the odometer. The installer left a Tammy Wynette tape in the eight-track and Tee felt good enough on the way home to turn up the volume as Tammy sang "Stand by Your Man" and "D-I-V-O-R-C-E."

Tee's little family made a trial run in the Cougar to the Mansfield offices of Harborcraft the Sunday before he was to start work on Monday. Distress was evident on Sarah's face at the sight of ten mobile homes joined together to form a single long building. "Now you're working in a trailer park?"

An additional home on each end made the office complex appear as a giant C. A six-foot high cyclone fence with a padlocked gate enclosed the ample parking lot. There were no manufacturing facilities in sight. Tee was not thrilled with working in a complex made out of trailer houses, but was happy with the hay meadow next to it and the heavily wooded area behind. Almost like working in the country.

On Monday morning, a '72 black Fleetwood Cadillac caught Tee's attention as he parked on the lot and walked toward what he assumed was the main entrance in the middle of the string of connected trailer houses. The long Fleetwood had a set of longhorns as a hood ornament and a man's photograph on both license plates. *Double Wide* was above the photograph and *Doug* below. Tee paused and chuckled. The car looked like something out of a television situation comedy.

He stood inside a small reception room until a woman about his age with green eyes, dark eyelashes that looked natural, and long ringlets of auburn hair to her shoulders appeared at the opened sliding glass window. She looked familiar and something about her lifted Tee's spirits. "Can I help you?"

"I'm Tee Jessup. I have an appointment with Barry Steadman." He pushed the Jacob Locke letter through the sliding window. She smiled before disappearing with the letter, her white teeth highlighting her freckles. Tee sat in the small reception room with paneled walls that smelled of cheap wood and trailer-house glue until a sixtyish, lean man in a faded western shirt open almost to his belly and worn, soiled Levis sprinkled with sawdust appeared in the doorway. He leaned against the doorframe with his arms crossed and smiled at Tee. "Billy Harbor." The announcement came with a chuckle, as if the man were toying with a mouse.

Tee stood and offered his hand. "Tee Jessup." Billy Harbor's hand was wide and rough, punctuated with bony knots.

Harbor motioned for Tee to follow him. "Old Jacob Locke sent you to spy on us, didn't he?"

"Spy? Think he just wants me to try and help locate some problems."

"You know how to do that?"

"Not really."

"Finally, an honest man."

When they stepped into a narrow, poorly lighted hallway, Harbor looked in both directions as if making up his mind. He turned west, and Tee followed, looking over his shoulder toward the east end of the long cavernous hall. The floors were covered with cheap carpet and moved a little too much, creaked a little too loud, as they walked. Harbor looked inside every office as if he were trying to find an empty one to deposit Tee. Near the end, a few doors before the hall made a ninety to the north, he stopped and gestured for Tee to enter an empty office.

Tee had not been made uneasy by what he had seen so far. The facilities at Wellstone were well worn, in need of paint and had a musty smell that depressed him. These offices appeared new, and the smell of cheap paneling, carpet and glue seemed refreshing by comparison. Tee could see his Cougar from the window and had a view of the coffee pot in a tiny break room across the hall. He sat in the black swivel chair between a particleboard desk with mahogany veneer and matching credenza. The mahogany veneer was worn down to the particleboard on the desk edges. A four-shelf bookcase stood against the outside wall.

Billy Harbor sat in one of the two black side chairs. "You can tell Locke I don't give a damn whether they do the stock offering or not. I got my money."

"I understand you started Harborcraft."

"In my garage."

"I thought you sold it to these other guys."

"I did, but none of these college boys who bought it know a damn thing about making camper tops. They brought me back to run the factory till they can find somebody to make what we sell. I'm charging them through the nose for it, too."

Out of questions and confused, Tee was relieved to see two large men standing in the hall outside his door. Both held coffee cups; one held a cigarette between two fingers. Billy Harbor shoved his way past them. The smoker offered a freckled hand with red hair to Tee. "Barry Steadman. I'm Vice-president of Finance; this is Doug Throckmorton, Sales VP." Barry looked to be in his late thirties and Doug more like mid-forties.

Tee stood and shook the hand. "Tee Jessup." Barry Steadman was about Tee's height but wider and about fifty pounds heavier. Doug Throckmorton was a giant. Tee barely reached across the man's huge paw and could manage no squeeze. He was as tall as Jacob Locke and twice as wide.

Barry chuckled at Tee's expression. "Takes two suits from the big and tall department to cover Doug's frame."

Tee laughed nervously. "Looks like he could hunt bear with a switch." He could feel the floor move as the man entered his office behind Barry.

Barry took the inside seat, and Doug barely squeezed into the one near the door. He used the heels of his hands to shove Tee's desk back. "Call me Doublewide Doug. I've sold more doublewide mobile homes than anybody in America."

"Guess that's your Caddy I saw outside. Never saw anybody's picture on license plates before."

"A man can buy about anything if he's got the cash." Doublewide placed a log-sized arm on Tee's desk blotter. "You ever been in radio?"

"Radio? Guess not."

"You got the voice for it. We might use you in some commercials I been thinking about." The floor creaked again when the man stood. "I'll leave you two number-crunchers to go at it. Somebody has to keep the money coming in so you boys can count it. When we get that fourth plant going out in Gainesville, I'll be throwing money at you boys like shit hittin' the fan."

When Doug took four steps down the hall, Barry leaned forward and had his mouth open to speak when they heard and felt Doug turn around. He filled the door opening. "People look at me the first time they see me and think fat. I ain't fat. You got good shoulders, but you're skinny as a possum been run over and left in the road a week. Tell you what, you drop and give me as many pushups as you can; fifty bucks says I can do one more than your best."

Tee smiled, figuring his chain was being jerked. "One more, huh?" Tee had been lax on most of his exercise but still did pushups most mornings. He knew he was good for fifty, probably as many as seventy-five. He stared up at Doublewide Doug. *No way this four-hundred-pounder can do fifty.* Then he remembered underestimating the strength and agility of a three-hundred-pound high school coach. "Make it on your fingertips, and I might take that bet."

Doug peeled a fifty from a large roll in his front pocket and laid it on the table. "Put your money where your mouth is."

Tee hesitated as he reached for his billfold. He almost never carried more than thirty bucks in cash. He thought he saw Barry relax a little when he hesitated. He pulled a twenty, hid it in his fist, and looked at Doug. "Tell you what. You go first, and I'll do twenty more than you for an even hundred."

Doug picked up the fifty, peeled off a second one, handed the hundred bucks to Barry and walked down the hall. Barry laughed as he stuffed the bills in his pocket. "He bet me a hundred he could get you to do fifty push-ups within ten minutes of meeting you."

Tee felt his face warm. "I get it. Pay me fifty when he loses the best, then collect a hundred from you. I would have fallen for it if I'd had fifty to bet."

"Don't let the Doublewide Doug ruse and the silly Cadillac fool you. It's part of his sales strategy. Makes people remember him. He usually wears a big cowboy hat, too."

"Four-hundred pounds is enough to make a man memorable without calling himself Doublewide."

Barry laughed. "You can see he's sort of sensitive about his weight. More than one of our shop people has felt his wrath for cracking fat jokes."

"I'll try to remember that."

"All the same, he's cunning as a snake, smart as a whip, and probably right about being number one in selling trailer houses. He made deep into six figures in commissions last year. Got a big house over in a swanky neighborhood in Fort Worth, swimming pool, trophy wife, the works."

Tee stood that six-figure number on a visual scale beside his new salary. "You mean he doesn't live in a doublewide?"

Barry laughed. "Says they're made to sell, not to live in."

Tee liked Barry. He was easy to talk to and laughed a lot. "So Barry, tell me what I'm doing here. Where do I start?"

"You start by meeting Lew Wallace, our president. Then we'll all tour the offices and the local plant. I'm not sure what Jacob Locke told you, but I think you need to pay close attention to the plant. We have a cost accounting problem."

Tee's spirits sank. He thought Wellstone had the same problem, and his experience in cost accounting consisted of one college course.

SEVENTEEN

OFFICES WERE BIGGER ON THE EAST END, AND THE NEXT-TO-last one announced that Doublewide Doug resided behind the big door. A twelve-by-fourteen color glossy of Throckmorton in an ornate frame hung below the name. Lew Wallace's office was at the end and ran north and south, spanning the width of the two buildings joined by a hall, like the top of a T. Brushed aluminum letters on a red background spelled President with Lew Wallace in burnished black below.

The room had four vanity walls filled with certificates and awards, shelves filled with athletic trophies, baseballs and bats, footballs and helmets. Lew was an inch or two shorter than Tee, but his balding head sat atop the frame of a body-builder. He tried to crush Tee's hand in the handshake and bounced on the balls of his feet while talking. "Did Mr. Locke explain who owns what?"

"Said you or Barry would explain that. I did a little research, but I'm still not clear on how you came to own Billy Harbor's business or how Jacob Locke fits in."

"Jacob Locke owns the majority interest in a small corporation he formed to buy out Billy Harbor. Billy was a sole proprietor. Locke recruited Throckmorton and me as minority shareholders. We brought in Barry to do the accounting and sold him a few shares." Lew's recitation of events sounded more like a cross between a play-by-play of the last seconds of a close football game and a reading from a literature professor. Lew liked big words.

"I thought Locke was just a minor shareholder looking into investing."

"That's about half right. Got almost nothing in Harborcraft yet. We borrowed money to buy the other plants. But he's considering tapping Snowtrack's big pile of money to buy a bigger stake."

Lew Wallace waited until Tee nodded, then pointed toward his south window. "Let's walk to The Still out back first."

Barry saw the question on Tee's face. "We call it The Still because Billy Harbor is said to have made more than his share of moonshine back there in the day. I'm beginning to think he made his money doing that instead of making camper tops."

They exited through the only south door, walked through a gate in a chain-link fence and followed a winding dirt trail through live oak trees, paper trash, and scrub brush. The factory was less than fifty yards south of the offices, completely surrounded by trees and underbrush except for the paved main entrance from the farm-to-market road on the west. A perfect location for a still. An open door large enough to accommodate trucks and forklifts revealed a crude assembly line where eight men worked with screw guns installing metal skins on camper frames. Billy Harbor sat in a webbed lawn chair leaned against the door frame peeling small curls away from a short two-by-four with a long pocketknife.

Wallace seemed to take great pride in the manufacturing facility as he turned toward Tee. "Ever use a screw gun?"

The building looked like a converted hay barn to Tee. "Can't say as I have."

"I'm thinking of starting a program where all of our executives spend a week out of every month on the factory floor, learning how to manufacture and assemble our products."

Tee nodded as he thought he saw a smirk on Steadman's face. "Sounds good. Don't see any mobile homes."

Lew Wallace bounced. "This is just a pickup camper top facility. We make the mobile homes in Arlington and Grand Prairie. And we've got new operations cranking up in Gainesville, Georgia; Bakersfield, California; and Tulsa, Oklahoma. The plants we bought were in pretty rough shape, but we got 'em cheap. We're in the process of streamlining things."

Jacob Locke had barely mentioned the out-of-state plants, but Tee had done some library research and knew about them. Wallace turned back to the assembly line. "We keep The Still mostly out of sentiment and to keep Billy Harbor busy. It's his first real facility after he left his garage." He said it loud enough for Billy to hear.

"What about the van conversion business in Arlington? Do you do it in the same building as the mobile homes?" Tee wanted to show what he knew.

Wallace seemed impressed that Tee knew about that. "Nope, it's done in a separate little building. It's a small operation that began a lot like Billy's. We bought it for a song." He bounced, obviously relishing the recitation of Harborcraft's past and future. "The Gainesville plant manufactures travel and camper trailers, and the Tulsa plant makes motor homes. We intend to be the leader in recreation vehicles in America in five years."

Wallace's enthusiasm was contagious, and Tee started to feel he had finally made a good decision. It was quitting time when they returned from tours of the Arlington and Grand Prairie facilities. His head swam with talk of plane trips to California and Georgia. Tee was fired up as he walked back down the dark hall to his new office. He needed to sit in it alone for a few minutes, to become acclimated to his new home-away-from-home. The perky redhead who had greeted him that morning stood in the middle of the hall. She walked toward him with her hand extended and spoke barely above a whisper. "I never introduced myself this morning. I'm Esther Shook, receptionist, sometime bookkeeper, sometime secretary around here."

"Guess you already know my name."

"I put a man in your office. Seems upset. Doublewide told me you could take care of him."

"Everybody really call him Doublewide?"

"Gets mad if we don't."

"Who's the guy in my office?"

"I think he's from the IRS."

91

"And you put him in my office? Why?"

"Because that's what Doublewide told me to do."

Tee's last curt conversation with Dexter at the IRS had been bothering him a little since it happened. Insulting an IRS agent who could make your life miserable was borderline stupid, but Tee could not imagine the man following him here. The liability for withheld taxes was Wellstone's, not his. He took a deep breath before he entered the office. But the man sitting in Tee's side chair was not Dexter. Tee thought he saw a bulge at the man's side and a shoulder holster came to mind.

He had learned how to modulate his changed voice to exert authority. "Tee Jessup. What can I do for you?"

The man's face showed distress. "Gene Vinson. The young lady said you were the man I needed to talk to."

"What about?"

"About Billy Harbor threatening to kill me."

EIGHTEEN

GENE VINSON MAY HAVE HAD A GUN UNDER HIS ARM, BUT he was pale, and his fingers drummed nervously on both arms of the chair. Tee sat behind his desk as he tried to absorb everything the man's appearance told him. Razor-cut, perfectly coiffed light brown, thinning hair with a shiny glaze said he had used a hairnet and half a can of hairspray that morning. The vanity gave Tee a tentative sense of comfort. The card the man handed him told Tee that Gene Vinson was, indeed, a Special Agent from the Criminal Investigation Division of the IRS. That meant the bulge could really be a weapon. "Run that by me again."

"Your boss threatened to kill me."

Tee could only remember two things about dealing with IRS special agents. They suspected or knew a crime had been committed, and the person or persons being investigated needed to say as little as possible. Tee nodded. "Go on."

"The IRS has been investigating Mr. Harbor for almost a year. He deals mostly in cash and we believe he has hidden large amounts of income."

93

"You have proof of that?"

"They don't send us out unless there is reasonable certainty of tax evasion or similar criminal activity."

"So he's guilty until proven innocent?" Tee knew that taxpayers dealing with the IRS faced a higher burden than they did in the regular system of justice.

The agent ignored the question. "Harbor's refused to cooperate with our investigations from the beginning. Says he doesn't have any records. Claiming no records is the same as a confession."

Tee knew he should end the conversation and usher the man out of the building, but he was afraid of getting on some IRS hit list. And he was intrigued. "When did he threaten to kill you?'

"Not more than an hour ago."

"So what do you want me to do?"

Vinson leaned forward and patted the bulge under his cheap suit coat. "Look, I've never drawn this weapon and don't ever want to. But I've got a job to do. Thought maybe somebody around here could get him to cooperate. If he opens up his records, then I can call back the regular agents and get as far away from him as I can. That's all I want. I admit the man scares me."

"He doesn't seem the type to kill anybody."

"Ever look into his eyes? Cold as a snake's. He's exactly the type of guy who would kill somebody. And he's probably connected."

"You mean the mob? Seriously?"

The agent leaned forward and whispered. "I got a wife and two kids, and Harbor recited my address from memory."

Tee felt an irrational sense of power drawn from the agent's fear. "Look, I don't work for Mr. Harbor. I have no control or influence over him. Don't see how I can help."

Vinson held up a vertical palm and made chopping motions. The awkwardness of the gestures would have been comical under better circumstances. "I'm not making idle threats, but this could go bad for you and everybody who works here. From this point forward, we're looking at making a major assault on Harbor and everybody he has any type of dealings with. I'm talking major, costly disruption."

"You tell Billy Harbor that?"

"That's when he threatened to kill me."

"Everybody's gone home. How long have we got before you call in the vultures?"

"I don't really know, but not long."

———————◆•◆•◆———————

Billy was waiting for Tee when he stepped out of his Cougar the next morning. "What did you tell that IRS bastard?"

Tee had not slept much. He looked at the skinny, harmless-looking old man with different eyes. "What could I tell him? I don't know diddly about your business."

"What did he tell you?"

"Just that you threatened to kill him. That so?"

"Why hell, no. I might have told him I knew people who could erase him and all his history like he never existed."

Tee chuckled. "Can't imagine anybody seeing that as a threat."

"It's not a threat. I *do* know people like that. Never said I was gonna sic 'em on him, though."

"He took it as a threat, especially when you told him where he lived."

"He was pushing me pretty hard. Wanted him to know I wasn't no pushover. Hell, it ain't hard to find out where he lives. He's listed in the Arlington phone book."

"Still, I don't think threatening an IRS agent is very smart. Especially a special agent."

"If I wanted the asshole dead, he'd already be dead. A man who gives advance warnings is stupid. Him and his cronies been making my life miserable ever since I sold my part of this thing to these college boys."

"Did you pay taxes on the gain from the sale?"

"A damned arm and a leg. That's what got 'em started after me. Said they couldn't figure how a business that ain't never turned a profit could be worth a quarter million dollars."

Tee made a mental note of the price. "And how did you answer that question?"

"The truth. Who's to account for the ignorance of a bunch of wet-be-hind-the-ears college boys. Can't blame me if they paid more than it was worth."

"They're threatening to bring a team in here and confiscate records."

"Hell, I told 'em plenty of times there ain't no damn records here. The dimwits don't seem to understand that was a completely different company than the one you boys got."

"They figure Harborcraft bought you lock, stock, and barrel. Records and all. That's the way it usually works. Did you not turn over any records when Wallace and the others bought you out?"

Billy smiled. "Just what I wanted 'em to see. Jacob Locke knew he wasn't buying the past, he was buying potential. He's the only smart one in that bunch and they lie to him. These old boys here are dumber than fence posts. Except for Throckmorton. That big bastard is slick and crooked as a dog's hind leg. Lew Wallace is a nice fella, but he's a damn mushroom farmer, and Barry Steadman is a Johnny-come-lately ain't figured out how things work yet."

"Mushroom farmer?"

"You know. Stays in the dark all the time." Harbor chuckled. "Hell, he tried to get me to take stock in their damn company instead of cash on the barrelhead. I told him where to shove his shares of stock."

"How did they know what it was worth without records?"

Billy grinned. "Told you I showed 'em all the records they needed to see."

"So, show those records to the IRS and maybe they'll go away."

"Those records would send me to jail for sure."

"You know why they're burning cash?"

"I got a good idea."

"Sounds to me like they used up their cash to buy up a bunch of companies. They don't need me to figure that out."

"That ain't their problem. They got all of those trailer-house outfits to swap their companies for worthless stock in Harborcraft. I'm the only one that got cash. Lew Wallace may be a mushroom farmer, but he can sell ice to an Eskimo. He convinced these thickheads the stock was a mother lode just waiting to be mined."

Tee glanced toward his office window. "I've got to get to work. What are you gonna do about the feds?"

"From the talk I hear, you're Locke's fair-haired boy. That old man thinks you're smart enough to cure what ails this dump, I figure you're smart enough to get the government off my back."

Tee laughed. "I don't recall Mr. Locke saying a thing about helping you out of IRS problems."

"You get them off my back, I'll help you find out why they're burning cash."

"IRS guy says you're connected. What do they call it, a made man? Maybe that's your best bet."

Harbor sneered, made a dismissive gesture with one hand, and walked away.

Nineteen

TEE HUNG HIS COAT ON A RACK IN THE CORNER OF HIS OFFICE and plopped into his desk chair. A stack of perforated computer reports in the middle of his desk reminded him of his days at Wellstone. The reports irritated him. He had not even had time to open the drawers to his desk, and he was already being covered in paperwork. He was cleaning out cigarette butts and ashes from his middle drawer when Barry Steadman appeared at his door. He pointed to the stack. "Those are last quarter's financials. Look 'em over as soon as you can. I apologize that I won't have much time to spend with you today. The auditors are here and giving me grief."

As Tee lifted the first sheet, unexplained dread filled him. He opened the other drawers and found them empty except for a few pencils, some scrap paper, and a coffee cup with stains in the bottom. He was running a finger around the edges of the cup when Barry returned to his door. "Listen, don't do anything to encourage Lew about us going out to the shop and using screw guns. The guys out there on the line don't want us getting in their way."

Tee forced a smile he did not feel. "Maybe they could come up here and do our jobs." The idea seemed appealing to Tee. He envied men with repetitive jobs whose work showed immediate results. Six pages deep into the financials, he was confused and more depressed. He stretched and looked toward the break room. Esther was making a new pot and never took her eyes off the job as Tee walked in with the dirty cup.

He waved the cup in her direction. "Don't know who this belongs to, but I guess they won't mind if I use it." He ran hot water over the cup and washed it, staring at Esther as she poured Maxwell House grounds into a filter.

She turned on the pot and turned toward him. Her voice was soft and low. "You gonna help my daddy with the IRS?"

"Your daddy?"

"Billy Harbor is my daddy, but nobody around here except Double-wide knows it. I'm trusting you because I have to."

"Thought your name was Shook."

"I was married when I was seventeen to a runty little thug named Shook. Daddy ran him off before I turned eighteen."

"So why keep it a secret?"

"Because Lew Wallace would never have hired me if he knew. Daddy told me about the job when it came up."

"Why would he not hire you?"

"Lew likes Daddy in a way, but Daddy stands for everything he detests. And then there's nepotism." She took the cup Tee twirled on his finger and filled it with fresh coffee. "What's with the deep voice? Doesn't seem to suit the rest of you."

She put two fingers over her lips as if she wanted to take the question back. "I mean, I like it, but it seems to belong to somebody much older. Maybe somebody who's smoked a few decades."

"Always had a deep voice, but the cigarette sound probably comes from vocal cord damage done in an accident a long time ago."

"I see. Well, it's nice, distinctive."

"Thanks."

"You gonna help Daddy or not? I'm afraid they'll haul him off to jail, and all of us will lose our jobs."

"Look, Esther, I don't even have my feet wet on the job I was hired to do. Don't see what I can do to help."

"You may not have much choice. " She headed toward Lew Wallace's office at the east end.

Tee caught up, touched her arm. "I'll have to put Barry in the loop if I help him. You and Billy okay with that?"

"If you have to, tell Barry, just not Lew. I'll help you with Daddy's stuff. I'm usually first here in the morning and the last to leave at night."

Tee was leafing through the income statement supporting schedules later that afternoon when Esther returned. "Sorry, I know you're busy, but I need to tell you one more thing. I did Daddy's bookkeeping, as much as he would let me, before he sold out. And there's a shady numbers guy down on Deep Elm in Dallas who got him out of a jam once before."

"Shady? What does that mean?"

"Means he's not afraid to get his hands dirty, among other things."

By quitting time, Tee had made three pages of notes and started a thirteen-column worksheet, trying to segregate all the entities that made up Harborcraft when Barry Steadman walked in followed by a trail of smoke, closed the door, and sat heavily in one of Tee's chairs. He stared blankly at the stack of reports on Tee's desk as if they held some cure to the dark despair on his face. The silence was interrupted only by the deep drags he took off the cigarette he held close enough to his check to risk burn. Tee rose to open his window.

The movement startled Barry. "Goes without saying Jacob Locke told you we got a cash flow problem."

"Yes."

"And that we have a stock offering ready to take care of it?"

"Go on."

"Since you took the job under that condition, you are free to back out, pack up, and leave. I sure won't blame you if you do. Locke won't either."

Barry's bland statement struck a nerve. Tee stood and opened the door to let more smoke out. "Well, Barry, it's like this. I quit my last job to take this one. Don't think they would welcome me back. Just walking away is not as easy as you make it sound. What the hell are you talking about?"

Barry ran the fingers holding his third cigarette through his hair and smoked boiled up. "I've been in meetings with Arthur Andersen all day.

They're giving me grief on the public offering. The way it stands now, it may not happen."

"Is that Arthur Andersen as in one of the big eight CPA firms?" Tee felt his stomach lurch as he realized he had not asked the right questions of Jacob Locke. Having one of the big-eight audit a small company like Harborcraft made Barry's announcement about the stock offering seem more ominous.

"They helped us through the preliminary filings with the SEC. I just assumed they would certify our financials since they basically prepared them."

"So now they're backing out?"

"They're threatening to. They assigned a new partner to the job, and he's holding our feet to the fire. The first guy said a clean opinion would be no problem, that he would take care of it. But this guy, he's threatening and pushy. I think it's a way of collecting more fees, but he's adamant."

Tee looked up as a short, wide man with bristly, gray-streaked hair and eyebrows that grew together leaned against the door frame with a smirk on his face. "Does this mean we're not friends anymore, Barry?"

Barry ground out the cigarette on the bottom of his shoe. "I think you're running a bluff to run up fees. You ain't the only CPA firm in town."

The man kept his smile. "Try getting somebody else to take our leavings after word gets out you were about to do a stock offering with bogus financials."

The man nodded in Tee's direction. "Name's Grady Allison, partner at Arthur Andersen."

Tee returned the nod but did not rise to greet him. He already disliked the man. Arrogance was all over his face and demeanor. Allison looked at Tee as he spoke to Barry. "It takes a lot of billable hours to construct a set of financials that will satisfy the SEC from the pile of crap you guys bought. Hell, those trailer house outfits had worse books than Billy Harbor."

Barry stood and pointed a finger at Grady. "As I recall, a big portion of your last bill ain't been paid yet. Since you seem intent on taking us down, I'll do everything I can to see it's never paid."

Grady took the vacated seat as Barry walked away, stared at Tee's blank walls. "Your certificate should have been hung by now. First thing."

Tee stared out the window, wondering what he would tell Sarah.

Grady's face reddened. "How long have you been here?"

"Not long."

Allison whistled. "Boy, you stepped yourself right into a hornets' nest, didn't you? Didn't you do your homework before you took this job?"

"Maybe you could fill me in."

"It's pretty simple, really. We've been in and out of here for almost six months, pulling together readable financial statements from crap. We got it far enough to do initial filings with the SEC for a stock offering. But doing accounting work ain't the same as doing an audit. Hell, by all rights, we should have walked away. We're not supposed to audit our own work."

"So why didn't you?"

Grady's smile faded. "The previous partner assigned to this job was committed to developing a long term relationship with Jacob Locke."

Tee began taking notes. "Sounds like another way of saying look the other way if the money's right."

Grady stood and stared at Tee's notepad. "I pulled the plug on this thing when I found out we were not present when a physical inventory was taken at the end of the last fiscal period. This company doesn't even know what it owns."

"So why didn't you observe the inventory? You said you were hired more than six months ago. You must have known when the count happened."

"You can bet I'll be getting to the bottom of that." He waved a stubby finger at the walls. "And I know your certificate hasn't been hung because you don't have one."

Tee wanted to go home and play with his son, but knew he couldn't sleep until he found out if he still had a job. He walked down to Steadman's office and found him with his feet on his desk, smoking and looking out the window. The news about the cancelled stock offering and the cash flow problem seemed to be common knowledge, so Tee left the door open. "Explain what's going on."

Barry looked into the corner behind his desk and saw a mouse sitting on its hind legs like a begging dog. "Have you met Bo? He's one of Grady's junior accountants." He took a plastic bowl from his desk drawer and put it on the floor. When he stepped away, the mouse ran to it and worked on the crumbs inside the bowl. Both men stared until the mouse finished. Bo sat on his hind legs again, staring at Barry and Tee in turn, then scurried behind a bookcase.

Tee was astonished. "A tame mouse. He live back there?"

Barry smiled. "He's chewed himself a hole in that wafer-thin paneling and comes and goes as he pleases. Rodents got free rein under these trailer houses."

"So, how long do we have before we run out of cash?"

Steadman shook his head as if to clear cobwebs. "Depends. If Mr. Locke can use his influence to get us a short-term working capital loan, we might survive until the new mobile home plants start positive cash flow." He cleared his throat. "If not, we got about six months, tops."

"This is my seventh job in less than six years, the fifth company to go belly-up. Guess I'm like the kiss of death."

Steadman laughed giddily as if Tee's self-blame released him from his own guilt. "Hell, Tee, you ain't been here long enough to have caused this. Anybody's to blame, it's me and Lew."

Tee slumped in the chair, stretched his feet across the cheap but new flower-design carpet. "What now?"

Barry cleared his throat. "I been thinking. I may try to go over Allison's head to a more senior partner. If we can do the inventory now and get their blessing, we might roll back the numbers to fiscal-year-end and satisfy AA enough to get a clean opinion."

"You think that might work?"

Barry dialed. Tee spoke before the call could go through. "You know about the problem with Billy Harbor and the IRS?"

TWENTY

IT TOOK ALMOST A WEEK AND MANY HEATED ARGUMENTS with Grady Allison and his more senior partners, but Barry Steadman got his provisional delay on the stock offering and an oral agreement to observe a new count and rollback the numbers. Barry summoned Tee to his office on Friday and told him to be in Georgia Saturday morning to set up the inventory and supervise the counting. "I'm on the way to Tulsa, Lew is going to Bakersfield, and the rest of my staff is going to set things up in Arlington and Grand Prairie. We'll do those counts when we get back next week." Barry handed him a stack of inventory forms and sent him to Esther for flight arrangements.

Tee sat in front of Esther's small metal desk in a narrow room between Lew Wallace's and Doublewide Doug's offices. "Barry said you could get me into Gainesville, Georgia, early tomorrow morning."

Esther smiled and handed him a folder. "Already done. Tickets are in there and information on the motel and rent car. Hope you're not used to luxury digs. None of those in Gainesville. I called Buddy Newsome, the plant manager down there, and he suggested one right by the plant."

Tee was grateful. He knew little about arranging travel. "Wish I had somebody as efficient as you are to go with me and help out." He was only half joking. The only inventory he had ever supervised was at Wellstone, and he had never figured out how to conduct it or price the work-in-process.

Both elbows on her desk, hands under her chin, she replaced her smile with a serious, pleading look. "If this big hippo I work for would let me, I'd go in a heartbeat. If you agree to help Daddy with the IRS, I might play sick and sneak down there."

"I asked Barry, and he says we don't have any choice but to try to get the IRS off Billy's back, but I don't see how I can help much with the rush job on this inventory and the stock offering taking up my time."

She handed him another of Gene Vinson's cards. "This guy could make everything all of us are doing a waste of time. Barry and Lew don't understand that. At least call and tell Vinson we're working on it. I'll take you to see the shady guy I know when you get back. Maybe he can come up with something to satisfy the feds."

"Why can't he just do it himself?"

"That explanation would take longer than you have."

Tee looked at the travel folder. "When do I leave?"

"You'll have just enough time to go home, pack, and kiss Sarah and Jubal."

"And how do you know their names?"

"Did you forget I'm jack-of-all-trades around here? That includes personnel. I saw your resume, insurance applications, the works."

Tee barely had time to pack and change out of his suit and tie. Jubal was at a nursery, and Sarah's co-worker said she had stepped out. He left her a note of apology that said he would call from Georgia. He wanted to go by the nursery to tell Jubal goodbye but could not take the chance he might cry.

He called Gene Vinson from the airport and told him he would work with Billy Harbor to organize and provide the IRS with all the information they needed. He needed a couple of weeks to get that done. Vinson seemed relieved and agreed to the delay.

Buddy Newsome was a Georgia country boy who spoke with a soft Southern drawl Tee found comforting. Tee liked him from the moment they shook hands at the fleabag the next morning. He wore khaki pants, roughout boots, and a loose-fitting, faded chambray shirt that had always been a stranger to the heat of an iron. The crooked bill of his gimme cap and the way he wore it cocked back told Tee he had little personal vanity. Tee felt a little overdressed in his starched Wranglers and dark green western shirt. Buddy whistled and pointed to Tee's calfskin boots. "That the way accountants dress in Texas?"

Tee smiled. "You'll soon find out I ain't much of an accountant."

Tee had never been to Georgia and Buddy gave him a running monologue as they walked from the motel to the plant site. He couldn't take his eyes off the Blue Ridge Mountains as Buddy filled him with information and pelted him with questions he could not answer about Harborcraft and Snowtrack. Tee apologized when he told him he had little to reveal because he knew little.

Buddy seem surprised as he unlocked and rolled back the big receiving and shipping door to the plant. "Yeah, but you work for Jacob Locke, don't you?"

"He hired me, but I work for Harborcraft." Tee felt several pairs of eyes on him as his eyes adjusted from the bright sun. The plant floor was idle, but at least thirty workers stood in mock attention, pencils and clipboards in hand, staring at him.

Buddy laughed. "Ready to count when you say the word."

Tee opened his briefcase and withdrew the forms. "Is the auditor here yet? Can't start without him."

Buddy laughed. "You mean you can't pick him out?"

Tee scanned the faces until he saw a young man dressed in a dark suit, white shirt, and tie walking toward him. He looked about sixteen. "Jerry Minot, Arthur Andersen."

This was not Buddy's first inventory, and Tee was relieved when he took control of the process. Buddy asked him a few courtesy questions to make him feel useful. They were finished in the plant by just after noon, and Buddy sent all but ten staff members home to their families. The remaining ten went to work categorizing the finished travel trailers on the ready-for-delivery lot. That count would be easy.

"You want to break for lunch or go ahead and finish and call it a day? I'll buy you a beer at a little joint you might like."

Tee had learned enough to do the inventories in Texas. "If it's okay with Mr. Minot, let's go ahead and finish so these folks can have the rest of their weekend."

They were finished by two, and all the count sheets sat on Buddy's desk in his tiny, cluttered office. Buddy stacked the sheets and handed them to Tee. Jerry, red-faced and hot, wiped his face with a handkerchief. Tee turned to him. "Kinda hot out in that factory. You and I need to number and initial each page before we run them through the copy machine. You take one copy with you, and I'll keep the original. That suit you?"

Minot took the sheets and started the process. When they had finished, he placed his copies in his briefcase and left.

He had barely closed the door when Buddy spoke in a low voice. "You gonna count the retail lot downtown this time?"

"We own a retail lot here?"

"Yep. But we never counted it before."

"Why not?"

"Hey, I just do what I'm told. Somebody at the home office told me old Doublewide Doug actually owned the finished units on the lot personally. Said he bought 'em to solve a temporary cash problem. Did the company a favor."

Tee opened the door and called out to Minot. "We got one more count to do downtown." He turned back to Buddy. "We need all the help we can get. The higher the inventory, the better the numbers are gonna look. If they're Throckmorton's, we can always take 'em out."

They finished the retail lot count, sent Minot on his way, and went back to Buddy's office just before four. Buddy eased down into his desk chair as Tee scanned the little mobile home that had been converted to two small offices. A closet served as a file room. "Who's in the other office?"

"Used to be the purchasing agent."

"What happened to him?"

"He got fired the day after Harborcraft bought us out. They centralized all purchasing back in the home office."

"That save you any money?"

108

Buddy stared at Tee a few seconds, then looked out the partially shaded window. "Seemed to make sense, buying in bigger quantities, fewer people involved and all. But our material costs have gone through the roof. I pretty much know what everything used to cost, and we get billed a lot more now from the home office."

"Got a notepad I could use?"

Buddy tossed him one. Tee made a few notes and put the pad into his briefcase. "Folks in Georgia ever eat?"

Twenty-One

TEE FELT AT HOME IN BUDDY'S BEIGE '64 FORD PICKUP AS THEY drove a winding trail through tall pines and oaks in the Chicopee woods. Nothing but pine needles and acorns marked the trail as they drove deeper and deeper into the trees. "This a farm-to-market road?"

Buddy laughed. "This ain't no road at all. You got to recognize which trees to drive between. Don't ever come out here by yourself, especially at night."

Buddy stopped the truck in front of a long, narrow building set up high enough for tall dogs to run underneath. The porch across the front and the seclusion of tall pines made it resemble a nondescript church in the woods. There was no paint on the shiplap siding, no sign, nothing that indicated a place of business. Buddy's Ford was the fourth truck parked haphazardly around the building.

Tee leaned forward to get a closer look. "Great old building. Looks like an old honky-tonk."

Buddy stepped out. "Thought it was too early for supper and too late for dinner. This is the best place I know to give you a flavor of Georgia life. We can grab a beer and maybe some snacks in here to tide us over, then go get a steak back in Gainesville. Okay with you?"

"Sounds good." Adrenaline flowed through Tee as he followed Buddy up the steps. He felt at home here. John T and Winona would have liked this place. When he heard Hank Williams singing "Hey, Good Lookin'," his warm feeling intensified. The long narrow room they entered looked like a school cafeteria in poor country. A horseshoe-shaped bar flanked a splintery pine floor. Dilapidated tables and chairs lined the outer perimeter of the room. Staring men in overalls and fedoras like men used to wear in the Depression Era occupied three tables. A small girl with stringy, dirty, blonde hair sat alone, her feet dangling, by one of the windows.

Buddy nodded to the men and waved to the girl. She waved back. By the time Tee had settled into the chair and adjusted his eyes to the light and surroundings, a pitcher of beer sat sweating on the table. The bartender's face was full and friendly. "What brings you out so early, Buddy?"

"Dave Smith, meet Tee Jessup."

"Pleased to make your acquaintance, Tee. That sounds like a Georgia name. You from around here?"

"Texas."

"What else can I bring you fellers?"

Buddy looked toward the bar. "Got any fresh pickled eggs?"

Dave pointed to a gallon jar on the counter. "Not more'n two gallons."

"Ever had a pickled egg, Tee?"

Tee studied the boiled eggs snuggled against each other in the cloudy gray-green liquid. "Can't say as I have. I intend to keep that record intact, too."

Buddy pointed toward another jar. "They got pickled pigs' feet, too."

Tee studied the pasty pigskin and hooves. "Pass."

"Bring him a sheaf of crackers, a slice of that rat cheese, and a little of that horse radish sauce and bring me a couple of those eggs. We supposed to drink out of this pitcher or you got glasses to go with the beer?"

Dave chuckled as he pulled two tea-glasses buried in ice from a chest that sat in front of the bar. "Didn't want 'em to get warm 'fore you poured your beer."

Tee watched as Dave poured the beer. The fresh-out-of-the-ice glass looked as enticing as strawberry ice cream. "What kinda beer?" The answer did not matter.

"Pearl. Only kind they serve."

Two beers later, Tee tried a pickled egg. After a second one, the woods around the country bar were dark, and the building was full as Tee nibbled on a pig's foot. He found only a ladies' restroom inside, so he walked out and found a tree to get behind. He felt revived. A good day's work—away from home—a new friend. The sense of freedom made him almost giddy. The beer helped.

When he walked back in, two couples had taken to the dance floor, the men's overall bibs pressed tightly against the women's breasts; the brims of their soft hats folded against rouged cheeks; their brogans moved in perfect sync with the black, thick-heeled, lace-up oxfords worn by their dance partners. Tee thought of his mother as Eddy Arnold crooned "Bouquet of Roses." It was easy to see John T and Winona dancing and Jubal's face instead of Buddy's.

He felt a soft hand on his shoulder as he poured another glass from a new pitcher. A young brunette who looked no more than sixteen looked into his bleary eyes and beckoned him to the dance floor. Tee glanced at Buddy, who gave him an amused look and a slight shrug. He urged him to stand with a motion of his hand.

Arnold stopped crooning as they reached the middle of the dance floor. Tee felt like a child-molester as they held hands awkwardly and watched the jukebox pick up another record to spin. The deep soothing sound of Jim Reeves singing *He'll Have to Go* relaxed him and moved his feet across the dance floor. Tee held the girl as if she might break, careful not to brush his chest against hers. She moved with the music is if dancing was sustenance for her soul, a sustenance that had not been replenished in a long time. Her smile was full of regret as the song ended. "Thank you."

Tee smiled back. "No, *thank you*," and he meant it.

Buddy was standing when he returned to the table. "Well, I can see we need to get you something better to eat than pigs' feet and pickled eggs."

TWENTY-TWO

TEE FELT THE AFTER-EFFECTS OF THE BEER AS HE AND BUDDY walked toward the truck. He turned for a final look, wanting to keep the feeling that was connected to his family again. "What do they call this place?"

Buddy shrugged. "Everybody calls it The Pickle Palace."

Tee hung his head out the window and tried to let the cooling moist air clear away the dullness he knew would replace the pleasant buzz he had felt in the bar. But by the time they parked in front of his motel, he knew it wasn't going to work.

Buddy killed the engine in front of the outside stairway that led to Tee's room. "See that little sign over there?'

"The Red Skillet?"

"Yep. Don't look like much, but it's got the best food in Gainesville. Got a good dance floor, too. You're obviously right at home on one of those."

Tee wondered what had possessed him to nibble on a pig's foot, pickled or not. "Not too hungry, but I'll visit with you while you eat."

A young lady ushered them to a table by the dance floor. Her long dress swept the dust left by thousands of steps on the pine planks. The room was crowded and hazy with smoke. Nice enough to feel comfortable, but it lacked that welcoming, intriguing aura of the bar in the woods. Tee let his eyes adjust to the smoke and darkness as he watched couples dance.

Buddy ordered a t-bone, and Tee ordered a cheeseburger well-done. "Can't stare a steak in the face." He was staring at the untouched burger when the girl in the long dress returned.

She nodded at Buddy and put a friendly hand on Tee's shoulder. "You're gonna hurt my feelings if you don't eat that cheeseburger. Did we burn it?"

Tee leaned back and looked up. Her face was round and full, her brown eyes sheltered by long eyelashes. She didn't look old enough to be in a bar. "Nope. It's fine. Guess my eyes were bigger than my stomach."

"Buddy filled you up with pickled eggs, didn't he?"

"You could be right."

Buddy laughed. "Nadine Rodale, meet Tee Jessup. Nadine owns this joint."

She squeezed Tee's hand with both of hers. "Where you from, cowboy?"

"Texas."

"I mighta guessed. Welcome to Gainesville. Where are you staying? Hope you ain't bunking with Buddy in that worn out mobile home on the back side of nowhere."

Tee pointed his thumb to the fleabag. "Next door."

Buddy's steak was gone, and the dance floor mostly deserted when she returned. "I hear you're smooth as silk on the dance floor. I just played "Be Honest With Me." Something tells me you're a Gene Autry fan."

"One of my daddy's favorites. Who told you I could dance?"

"Honey, I can tell a good dancer by watching him go the bathroom and back. And you been more than once." She took his hand and pulled him up. Tee worried about stepping on her long dress, but Nadine responded to the slightest touch of his hand in the middle of her back. When the record had stopped playing, he returned to the table and found it cleared of dishes and Buddy's chair empty.

Tee looked around the room but found no sign of Buddy. Nadine pressed against his arm. "Buddy's like that. Just ups and leaves without a fare-thee-well. He's old-fashioned. Likes to turn in early."

"Figure up the bill, and I'll get out of your hair."

She smiled. "Already taken care of. Buddy paid me."

Tee felt the need to get outside, breathe in fresh air. "Appreciate the hospitality. Next time I come down here, I'll be ready for a steak."

Tee switched on the window unit to cool down the stuffy motel room while he showered. The air conditioner made a rattling noise when he stepped back into the bedroom in his boxer shorts, and the air was worse. He turned out the lights, cut the unit, and opened a window before sprawling face down on the bed. He was fading off to sleep when he heard a noise on the walkway outside followed by a knock on his door. The door had no peephole, so he pulled back the curtain and looked out the window. Nadine held a small sack in one hand.

He pulled on his jeans and opened the door. She handed him the sack. "Good Georgia whiskey. Home-made. Thought you might want something to remember us by."

Tee rubbed his eyes with a thumb and index finger. "Sure appreciate that. What time is it?"

"Closing time. A little after one. You gonna invite me in to sample a little of that prime stuff?"

Tee stuck his neck out the door and looked both ways on the walkway. She walked past him, sat on the edge of the bed, and opened the bottle. He stood frozen for a few seconds. "I'll get you a glass. I already had my quota for the day."

She held the glass up to the light and checked for water spots. "Just making sure the maids are keeping these clean. Guess we'll have to go to plastic before long."

"We? You own this motel, too?"

"My parents owned it and The Red Skillet."

Tee searched for conversation. "Seems like you've done pretty well for a girl as young as you look. You could pass for a teenager."

She took a tiny sip of the whiskey. "Don't kid yourself; this is not exactly a goldmine."

Tee studied the furniture and walls, wondering where this was going. Nadine looked the picture of innocence and beauty, but this was probably not going to end well. "Listen, I appreciate the visit and the whiskey, but I got some work to do at the plant early in the morning and a flight to catch right after." She put the glass on the bedside table, turned off the lamp, and started unbuttoning her blouse.

Tee felt heat and tingling nerve endings when she turned her back to him, unhooked her bra, and dropped it on the bed.

Tee knew he was in trouble. He stood and stepped toward the door. "Look, I'm flattered, but I can't be doing this. You need to get dressed."

The door opened as he reached for her bra and blouse and a man shoved him toward Nadine. She threw her arms around his neck as a second man came through the door with a camera. The flash temporarily blinded him, but Tee freed himself quickly enough to give barefoot chase as the men fled down the stairs toward an idling car. Tee banged on the hood as they backed up and drove away. When he turned, Buddy stood at the foot of the stairs.

TWENTY-THREE

TEE STRODE TOWARD HIS NEW FRIEND WITH FIRE IN HIS EYES. "What are you doing here? Who were those guys?"

"Take it easy. Look here." Buddy held up the man's camera, kicked out the film, and handed it to Tee.

Tee looked at the film cartridge in his hand. "What just happened?"

Buddy looked up the staircase and watched as Nadine closed the door to his room. She held the stair rail and took the steps sideways, one easy, cautious step at a time. Buddy stared with a half-smile of pity as she made her slow descent.

Tee looked up. "You set me up for that?"

Nadine began to cry. Buddy looked up at her, then at Tee. "Not her fault, Tee. Let her go on, and I'll tell you what happened."

She touched Buddy's shoulder as she walked away. Tee didn't want her to leave without answering his questions. "She hurt herself in the scuffle? I didn't do anything but push away from her when they busted in."

Buddy studied the bugs swirling around the weak parking lot light as

119

if they might swoop down and tell the story that needed to be told. "She leave any good whiskey up there?"

Buddy polished off what Nadine had left in her glass and started on another. Tee reluctantly sipped at the surprisingly smooth, unmarked brew. Buddy pointed his glass at Tee. "How far did you two get along on her little mission?"

"She got naked to the waist. Nothing else."

"If you had gone to step two, you would have found out she has a wooden leg."

Tee was too stunned to speak, so Buddy continued. "Didn't you wonder why she wore a dress long enough to reach the floor?"

"I noticed it, but a lot of women wear long dresses." Tee began to calm down, his anger turning to pity. "What happened?"

"Car wreck out by the Chattahoochee River about three years ago. She lost her husband, a three-year-old daughter cute as a speckled pup, and her leg."

Tee needed a minute to absorb that information, to digest it, relate it to the woman he had danced with, and to decide if he was being played the fool. He decided it was too outrageous to be a lie. "Damn. That's awful, but it still doesn't answer why she came to my room uninvited and who those guys were. And how did you get his camera so fast?"

"He gave it to me. Thinks I'm in on it. I know both those peckerwoods. I got a call Friday that you were coming. Throckmorton told me to introduce you to Nadine and leave you in The Red Skillet. Said she would take it from there."

"Why?"

"Old Doublewide likes to cover all his bases. You're an unknown quantity to him since Jacob Locke hired you. He wanted something to hold over you in case you get in his way."

"Get in his way? What does that mean?"

"Not sure."

"She seems like a nice girl. How did he get her to do it?"

"Throckmorton came down here about five or six weeks when Harborcraft was doing the deal to buy out this little plant. He stayed in this motel. She fell in with him."

"You're kidding me. That pretty girl?"

120

"Big as he is, he can be a charmer, and he ain't afraid to throw a little money around. And money was what Nadine needed. The restaurant and the motel were in deep trouble when her husband died. And there were medical and funeral bills."

"So he loaned her money, and now he's got a hold on her."

"Nadine is a sweet but very needy lady. In more ways than one."

"Who were the photographers?"

"One was the salesman who runs our retail lot. He's the one who gave me the film. He works directly for Throckmorton."

Tee shook his head. "I'm not sure what to do with all this information. Never been set up like this before."

Buddy pointed to the film. "Doublewide is likely to ask me for that. I'll send him one that's too blurred to make out."

"How much trouble will that buy you?"

"Nothing I can't handle. All I need from you is to be kept in the loop. I don't want to be kept in the dark."

TWENTY-FOUR

TEE WAS WRUNG-DRY TIRED WHEN HE STEPPED INTO HIS LIVING room late Sunday afternoon. He knew something was wrong when Jubal did not run to him. The note he had written to Sarah when he left on Friday was still on the kitchen counter, lying beside another in her handwriting. Gone to visit Daddy. Back in a few days.

Had they talked about a trip? Was there something wrong with Cutt? Why had she not called him in Georgia to tell him?

He had been looking forward to hugging his wife and son since he boarded the plane to come home. He needed someone to talk to, especially needed to see Jubal. Of course, he could not tell Sarah all that had happened in Georgia. She would probably not believe his innocence, and of course, he wasn't totally innocent. The subterfuge going on at his new job would also lead her to believe he had made another terrible decision. And it looked as if he had. The stock offering was iffy; he was dealing with a death threat to an IRS agent, and one of the owners of the company had tried to gather information and pictures to use against him. Not a good start.

123

He showered and changed but could not concentrate on television or a book. He wanted to call the ranch but decided to cool off before he did. He made his usual nighttime walk, asking for answers, searching for reasons and direction on handling his latest predicament. It was his usual bedtime when he stopped at a 7-11 to get some change. In the phone booth outside, he dialed a familiar number.

The voice on the line was groggy. Tee hesitated, thought about hanging up. "Catch you at a bad time?"

A throat clearing. "The Lord's day is always a good time to talk to one of God's children. How are you, Tee?" Father Bob's voice and words had their usual soothing effect. Tee didn't call often, and only when he was alone. He didn't know why he kept the calls secret from Sarah, but the calls were his, not hers. He felt his lost family spoke to him through Father Bob's voice. And Father Bob knew it. The priest mostly listened, letting Tee figure things out for himself.

"Just got back from a strange trip to Georgia. Got time to hear about it?"

Tee avoided eye contact with the strangers coming and going out of the 7-11 as he filled him in on the details and answered some of his questions. The priest's voice became stronger. "Are you still afraid?"

A long silence. "Not as much. Still got a lot of questions."

"Are you still worried about paying penance for the deaths of your family?"

"I know it makes no sense, but I do feel I owe somebody something, that a presence of some kind is stalking me, leaving destruction in the path behind me and in front of me. Guess it's not dying I'm afraid of, though. It's living."

"You have a beautiful wife and a lovely boy, a college education, a good job. Most men would be more satisfied. Maybe you should just give thanks to God."

"Yeah, my seventh job in less than six years and looks like I may be looking for number eight real soon."

Father Bob laughed again. "Well, you have always been clever enough to find one."

"I know it sounds like whining, but I hate what I've become. Feel like I was pushed into it. I don't want my son to know I just push around numbers for a living. And boredom scares me more than dying."

Father Bob chuckled. "Let me see. You're dealing with an IRS agent whose life was threatened, a woman in Georgia with one leg who tried to trap you in a compromising position, and a treacherous man as wide as two house trailers who has horns on his Cadillac and his picture on his license plates. And you ate pickled pigs' feet and pickled eggs. It seems that the most boring thing about your new job is the stock offering that might be cancelled."

Tee laughed. Father Bob had a way of putting things into proper perspective. "Well, thanks for your time. Appreciate the advice."

"Before you go, Tee, answer a question. Ever wonder why you accept unorthodox positions with unusual companies populated with eccentric characters?"

"Every day."

"Maybe you need the adrenaline that comes with difficulties. Even the precarious stock offering keeps you on the precipice of disaster."

Tee thought about what Jacob Locke had told him about security versus adventure. He hung up after all his quarters were gone, feeling better. Back at the house, he smoothed the covers on his son's bed, looked around the room. Ready for bed, but still restless, he patrolled the rooms, trying to see things he had little time to notice when Sarah and Jubal were there. He seemed almost a stranger in the house because he was at work so much. He brushed his teeth, leaned over the sink and looked into the mirror at a face he seldom really saw and found it looked older than his twenty-seven years. He opened the medicine cabinet to see what Sarah kept there.

Tee examined the shelves full of over-the-counter remedies. There were creams and potions to soothe the hurts of little boys, antiseptic cream for her, and one prescription bottle. He read the label. Birth control pills. The full bottle had a recent date on the label. Had she taken an older bottle with her? And why had she taken them without telling him? Why had she let him hope each month for a pregnancy that might bring him the daughter he so desired? Why did she avoid intimacy? He had still seen her nude only once and that was when he walked in on her as she stepped out of her bath.

He dialed all but the last digit of Cutt Ledbetter's number, glanced at the clock, and hung up.

Twenty-Five

TEE ARRIVED AT WORK AN HOUR EARLY MONDAY MORNING. He wanted to reconnoiter with Barry and find out which inventory he would be supervising. He walked to the east end of the building and found Barry's office empty. He stopped at Doublewide Doug's open door. Sunrays revealed the otherwise invisible spittle coming from his fat lips as the man gestured with both hands. The phone in front of Throckmorton's mouth seemed suspended as if held there by some malevolent secretary because the shoulder rest was buried out of sight in the fat of the big man's shoulder. Tee walked back to his office. Already irritated, the presence of Grady Allison's proprietary presence in his desk chair made things worse.

"Can I help you with something?"

Grady pointed to the briefcase in Tee's hand. "Came for what you got in there."

Tee dropped the briefcase on his desk with a thud. "You're in my chair."

Grady gave him a surprised look. "Well, excuse me for resting my weary body. I worked all weekend to save your hide, and that's the thanks I get."

Tee waited.

Grady reluctantly rose. "Well, I can see you're a little testy. Just give me what I came for, and I'll remove myself from your presence."

"And what's that?"

"The inventory tally sheets from Georgia, of course."

"Your guy Minot has AAs copies."

"Yes, but he's in Georgia."

"Figured he would overnight his copy to you. You guys have a fax machine, don't you?"

"You're wasting time, and time is of the essence."

"If you had your copies here, would you give them to me?"

"Of course not."

"Works both ways. What do you guys call that? Internal control? Or is it chain of possession? If AA had both copies, they could change them, and we wouldn't know it."

"Now, why would we do that?"

"You're not getting our copy."

Esther's anxious face peeked through his door as Grady left.

She sat in one of the side chairs. "You hear from Vinson?"

"I talked to him. We've got a two-week reprieve."

Esther put her hands together in a prayer position. "Thank you, thank you. When do you want to go downtown?"

Tee opened his briefcase and took out the inventory sheets. "I figure there's at least a week's worth of work right there. And still more to come from Arlington, Grand Prairie, Tulsa, and Bakersfield."

"Can I help?"

"You might."

Tee helped with both the Arlington and Grand Prairie inventories, shuffling between the three manufacturing facilities and two retail sales lots for two days. There was no message from Sarah when he arrived home late Tuesday night. He had called her at the ranch twice during the day, but nobody answered. He wanted to speak to his son, but the encounter with Nadine Rodale had left him with a strange sort of guilt he feared Sarah might hear in his voice. He also preferred to talk about the birth control pills in person, not over the phone. Guilt or not, he resolved to call her Wednesday night if she was still not home.

At seven on Wednesday evening, Tee stacked all the plant inventory sheets on his desk. His spirits fell as he thumbed through the crumpled mess. He had learned that Harborcraft had twenty-three different sizes and models of mobile homes, eleven different travel trailers, five camping trailers, and two models of motor homes. Accessories made the list add up to sixty-three different products. The only consistency was in Billy Harbor's pickup camper tops: two versions, no accessories. There were company-owned sales lots and private sales lots where Harborcraft kept both consignment and floor plan products. Tee would have cried if there had been privacy. He looked longingly at his Cougar and the welcoming dark of the parking lot, took a deep breath, and walked down the hall to Barry Steadman's office.

Barry held up a forestalling hand when he saw the look on Tee's face. "I know what you're gonna say. You need help. I've already lined up three ladies to help you price things out. They need the overtime."

"I can get 'em started, but I'll need costs numbers to price the raw materials and bills of material and labor costs for the work-in-process and finished goods. If you'll show me where those are, I'll get things ready before I go home so they can start first thing tomorrow."

Steadman's face seemed to lose a little color in the dark office. "About that. We can get the raw material costs from our purchasing agent, but there's no bill of materials or labor costs for the finished products."

Tee slumped into one of Barry's chairs. "How did you price out the earlier counts?"

"We estimated, and AA seemed to go along with the stuff we more or less made up. Now, Allison says we have to have cost figures to price it out. We don't have the records to tell us what it costs to build any of our products except for Billy's toppers."

"So you don't know if you're making or losing money on the other stuff." Tee paced behind Barry's side chairs. "Why did we bother to count? Might as well throw in the towel. That stock offering is out of the question."

Barry looked out the window at the dark trail that led to The Still. "Maybe not. I've got a crackerjack cost accountant coming in tomorrow.

He worked for Redman Industries for years. He eats, breathes, and sleeps our kind of products."

"He better be more than crackerjack. More like Superman. Did you know we're building and selling more than sixty different products?"

Lew Wallace walked in and closed the door.

TWENTY-SIX

LEW PACED THE ROOM, BOUNCING WITH EVERY STEP, WRINGING his hands. His voice was loud and authoritative, like he was admonishing schoolchildren. "I can hear you guys all the way down the hall. Keep your voices down. This is proprietary information."

Tee's face warmed at the scolding. "What are we saying that's a secret?"

Lew looked out the window as if he could see in the dark, hands clasped behind his back like a stern schoolmaster. He spoke to Barry as if Tee were not present. "I thought you explained our business plan to Tee the first day."

Barry faced Tee. "Doug sort of selected the plants we purchased based on the products they had. He says it pays off to make different models. Establishes a unique position in the industry and keeps customers from going elsewhere. We even make some custom houses to customer specs."

Lew bounced. "We intend to be the highest quality and most diversified manufacturer in America."

Tee felt he had little to lose by speaking his mind. "If those are top flight travel trailers I saw in Georgia, I'd hate to see the low quality ones."

Lew whirled so fast that he startled Tee. "Georgia has a long way to go. It was our first purchase and made before we decided to go for quality. We'll bring it into line with the other plants. Buddy Newsome knows that."

Tee nodded. "So, we're gonna build nothing but top of the line products and offer a wide variety to choose from. That about sum it up?"

Lew smiled. "Exactly. We intend to be the top consumer choice based on quality and variety."

Tee looked at Barry. "What about price?"

Lew answered. "We intend to be highly competitive on price, too. What other way could we hope to succeed?"

Tee was late and felt a sudden, urgent need to be home. Jubal might be waiting for him. He put his hand on the doorknob. "Seems like the business plans you're talking might work, but they won't matter unless we can price out the inventory, get a clean audit, and do a stock offering."

He had not called during the day, but was sure Sarah and Jubal would be waiting when he arrived an hour past Jubal's bedtime. They were not. He wondered if she had called before he got home, but it was too late to find out.

Tee arrived early on Friday morning to find a round-faced, broad man with pale, pockmarked skin sitting in one of his side chairs. The man stood and offered his hand. His face lit up with friendliness as he smiled. "Mike Clayton."

Tee took the firm handshake. "Tee Jessup. What can I do for you?"

Mike's quick chuckle made Tee like him immediately. "Thought you were expecting me. That pretty lady with green eyes stuck me in here and abandoned me. Think her name was Esther."

"You the cost accountant used to be with Redman?"

Mike leaned forward and tapped a folder lying in the middle of Tee's desk blotter. "That's me. Everything you ever wanted to know about me and more is in there."

Tee ignored the folder. "Anybody explain the problem to you?"

"I know you're looking for somebody who can take apart and reassemble your products and tell you how much each one costs in material and labor. I can do that. I worked on the assembly line for two years before I got my degree."

"Can you do it in less than thirty days?" Tee explained Harborcraft's problems in detail, and Clayton's already pale face turned grayer with each revelation.

"Nobody said anything about sixty products or the stock offering. My wife is pregnant. She left her job to prepare for the baby."

Tee nodded. "I know how you feel. I don't know for sure how much time we have to get this done, but it won't be much more than a month. You might want to re-think leaving Redman."

Mike studied his shoes. "You been honest with me, I'll be honest with you. I already quit Redman. Went to my head when I heard about this job. It fit me just right, and Redman was screwing me over, so I told them to shove it."

Tee laughed out loud and wished he hadn't. "Sorry. Guess misery loves company. You want to give it a try? Barry says I can offer in a range of eighteen to twenty thousand. Since we'll probably both be on the street in a month, let's go with the high number."

"When do you want me to start?"

"Now."

They spent the rest of the morning going over the inventory count sheets for work-in-process and finished goods. Mike checked the material prices on one sheet. "Seems way high."

The production lines were like coming home to Mike, and he wanted to show Tee his expertise as they toured the Arlington and Grand Prairie plants. He borrowed clipboards and crawlers and rolled, climbed over, under, around and through each finished and partially finished unit. His non-stop banter managed to turn what seemed a hopeless mess into a humorous one. By the time they returned to the home office, Mike had Tee convinced that they might pull it off. They were still laughing in the parking lot when Esther and Billy Harbor walked toward them. Billy looked angry and Esther appeared on the verge of tears.

Mike Clayton instantly recognized Billy Harbor and stuck out a hand. "Mike Clayton. You're Billy Harbor. Would have known your face anywhere." He turned toward Tee. "Billy Harbor stories are legendary in the trailer trash business."

Billy's mouth curved upward only a little as he tried to ignore Mike and address Tee. "Been looking for you most of the day. Vinson called. We need to talk."

Tee felt his spirits ebb at the mention of Special Agent Vinson. "What did he want?"

"Says he's getting pressure from his superiors. They want to come with guns blazing. Says he can't hold 'em off much longer."

Tee turned toward Esther. "When can we go see the guy you mentioned—the one you said would get his hands dirty?"

"I already called him. Says he can meet us after hours today. We can leave now."

Tee shook his head. "Nope. My wife and boy been gone for a few days. I need to get home tonight."

"Sarah called the office today when you and Mike were gone. Said she and Jubal would be home sometime Saturday but would be out of pocket tonight. The pink message slip is in your in-tray. That's why we set the meeting with Leftwich tonight."

TWENTY-SEVEN

TEE AND ESTHER TRUDGED ALONG ELM STREET EAST OF DOWN-town Dallas, searching addresses painted on walls, windows, and doors. The street numbers and names had faded to near oblivion and brought faded sepia visions of once proud business owners hanging or painting them, standing back to admire them and the bright future they portended in the days before the decay began. Metal numbers hung with nails during better times had all rusted. The most expensive, professionally made signs suffered the most from vandalism. They had been attacked with profanity and graffiti as if the mere suggestion of opulence was offensive. The addresses seemed to be hiding now, fading, rusting, and hanging askew, ashamed to have been abandoned by their once proud owners, anxious to sever their association with the blight that had become the area known as Deep Ellum.

Esther stopped at a stairwell and ran her finger over the faded numbers inside the darkened alcove. "This is it."

She nudged a sleeping drunk on the bottom step with her sneaker-clad foot until he moved enough to let them pass. Tee looked up and down the street again, wishing he was not wearing a suit, tie, and shoes. He felt exposed and vulnerable as he followed her up steep stairs reminiscent of an old dentist's office. He was wary of the filth in the dusty, littered stairway, but Esther seemed oblivious to the smell of urine and rotting and regurgitated food. Tee wondered if the filthy profanity written and drawn on the walls offended her.

She pushed open a door with peeling white paint and an opaque window with "Stan Leftwich, C.P.A." spelled out in faded gold leaf. A graying man looked up from a large oak desk covered with papers. Stacks of folders festooned all available shelves and flat surfaces, including the floor. Tee and Esther followed a trail to two chairs.

Tee had half-expected either a mobster type or a stereotypical accountant. Stan was neither. He stood well over six feet, though he stooped a little as he stood to greet them. His demeanor and kind expression seemed grandfatherly, but a well-tailored, expensive suit, an impressive diamond pinkie ring, and a thin gold watch said something else. It seemed as if Stan had been plucked from a downtown brokerage firm and placed in this seedy office for the first time. Tee looked around the room and saw another door, wondered if the real Stan Leftwich stood on the other side with his ear pressed against it.

Esther had insisted her father stay behind, citing the near fistfight that had almost erupted between him and Stan on their last visit. Introductions out of the way, Stan asked after Billy Harbor. Esther smiled. "Ornery as ever. Said to tell you to kiss his ass and that's the polite version."

She turned toward Tee. "Daddy has a tendency to lash out every time Stan brings up anything about cooperating with the IRS or any government agency. Just the conversation can make him apoplectic."

Stan laughed heartily as he turned toward Tee. "If Esther says you're okay, then you are. Now, who is the special agent we're dealing with?"

Tee had to rouse himself from the trance caused by the clash between Stan's appearance, demeanor, and voice versus the squalor of the office. "Name's Gene Vinson. Says Billy threatened to kill him."

The threat held no surprise for Stan. "Well, we can't have that, now can we? I believe I may have met Mr. Vinson before." He turned toward Esther. "Did you bring the files I requested?"

Stan moved several stacks of paper and folders to make room as Esther opened the large satchel Tee had mistaken for an oversized purse. Stan kept making room as Esther laid ten stacks of labeled file folders on the cleared surface. Each stack was a different color, and all the folders were new. Stan picked them up and started scanning the labels and thumbing the contents. "Good work. Couldn't find any worn out folders?" He smiled as he looked at the stacks of folders on the floor. "Then again, I expect I can find a few used ones."

Esther shook her head. "Daddy never even owned a file folder or cabinet."

Tee felt like a door stop as he watched Stan leaf through the mountain of documents and restack the folders with what appeared to be calm precision. Stan noticed his deer-in-the-headlights look. "You're probably wondering what I'm going to do to get Billy out of yet another mess."

Tee nodded. "I am curious."

Stan kept organizing the folders. "I have personally watched as Billy Harbor paid suppliers with a roll of bills he always carried in his pocket. He paid for truckloads of lumber as quickly as he paid for a bucket of screws. People loved doing business with him because he was a man of his word and always paid not just on time, but ahead of time."

Stan's chair squeaked as he leaned back, his fingers making a steeple as he told Billy's story. Tee tried to reconcile the man Stan described with the one Gene Vinson feared as a gangster, a "made man."

Stan came to the end of his story. "You see, Billy Harbor belongs to an almost extinct species. His word is his bond, his handshake his contract. He is a free man who refuses to be bound by rules he considers both unfair and onerous. In short, he has zero tolerance for any bureaucrat."

Esther enjoyed hearing the story again. "Daddy barely made it the first few years. I don't know how he managed to come up with a roll of bills to pay for things, but somehow he did. It's true he has some shady friends, and I expect they were the source of some of that money. If so, he paid it back quickly and with big interest."

Tee looked at Stan. "And there sure won't be any records of those loans or the interest paid."

Stan smiled. "That's right. When Billy got into trouble with almost every bureaucracy that can get its fangs into a small business a few years ago, one of those shady friends sent him to me."

"How did you get him out of it?"

"I reconstructed virtually all of the major transactions for the year in question. Billy took me to suppliers who provided me with backdated documents. I built financial statements, filed state, local and IRS tax returns, filed for permits, you name it. The bureaucrats loved me, but Billy never said thanks, and against all my advice about paying with checks instead of cash, he paid my bill with crisp, green folding money. Then he went right back to his old ways. But he did let me file tax returns every year."

Tee laughed softly. "Let me guess, he blames those tax returns for the trouble he's in today."

Stan snapped his fingers. "Bingo. He says if I had never put him into such a corrupt system, he might have escaped the government's oppressive hand."

"May be some truth to that." Tee glanced at his watch, thought about his son's bedtime, wondered how Sarah could be "out-of-pocket" tonight. "Makes for a good story, but that still leaves us with today's problem." He pointed at the folders.

"These are reconstructed receipts Esther gathered from vendors again, just like before. You should know there are also some documents that might not match the time period in question. But I think we can change a few dates and a few amounts and back up every line on Billy's tax return. We'll leave a couple of minor things for the IRS to find, own up to them and pay the tax and penalty."

"If everything was legit, why do we have to change dates and amounts?"

"Because some suppliers have died, some have gone out of business, and some were plain scared." He laughed softly. "And of course, a lot of them didn't report those cash payments."

"I'm sure not an expert, but in my one run-in with the Feds, the documents get a really close look."

Stan tapped the folders with a gold fountain pen. "If you run a document through a copy machine several times, we can make it look old, crumpled and authentic."

"So why do you need me?"

Stan looked at Esther and back at Tee. "The IRS can't know I am involved. They know me. And...I am not allowed to represent Billy with any of their representatives."

"I always thought CPAs could."

Stan pointed at the door sign. "That's an old sign. Nobody made me scrape it off, but I lost my certificate a few years back when I was still working for the IRS."

Tee waited silently for further explanation. None came.

Esther touched his elbow. "When Stan pulls all this together, we need you to present it to Vinson."

Stan leaned forward. "I know exactly what they have to have in the form of work papers and documentation to satisfy his superiors. All you have to do is familiarize yourself with it before you present it. I know Vinson and trust me when I tell you that Billy's threat had its intended effect. He wants nothing more than to rid himself of this project and Billy Harbor. He'll thank you for helping him to do that."

"There's one problem. I don't have a certificate either."

Stan leaned back in his chair. "Why not?"

"I hear they're pretty hard to come by. Besides, I never believed my future was in being an accountant."

"Well, Vinson came to you. I think he will let you represent Billy through your position in the company that now owns his old business. You may need an officer of the firm to sign off. Worse comes to worst, Billy may have to sit in on the meetings. But I don't think Vinson will either want or require that. Billy will have to sign, just keep them apart until you settle."

TWENTY-EIGHT

THE NIGHT HAD TURNED COOLER WHEN THEY STEPPED OUT
on the Deep Ellum sidewalk, and Tee was grateful for the unusual light,
crisp air, even if it was filled with odors of rotting garbage. He held Esther's
arm and scanned the streets for kids high on drugs as well as healthy and
sober types looking to get high on violence. Most covered doorways were
occupied by sleeping vagrants or drunks just sober enough to tilt bottles
hidden inside wrinkled paper sacks to their lips. The bums stared at the
intruders with bloodshot, wary, desperate but non-threatening eyes. He
saw a few kids dressed in dark clothes to camouflage their nocturnal movements across the street, gesturing and strutting like animals marking their
territory, staring with alley-cat eyes.

Esther tugged on his coat sleeve and pulled him toward the car. Tee
had parked his Cougar under a street lamp dimmed by the plastered bodies and waste of moths and other bugs which craved the warmth and light
enough to die to be near it. The passenger door of his black car was open,
the interior lights on. Tee pulled Esther into a run.

The eight-track tape player was gone from under the dash. Tee scanned the area for the thieves before sitting heavily behind the wheel, wondering if the burglars were near, watching from an alley, laughing. "Close the door. Need to see if we got any battery left." The engine turned slowly but did fire. He waited until he was safely out of the area before he pulled over and switched on the interior light. He let the Cougar idle as he looked in the back seat.

Esther watched his eyes as he scanned the car's interior for damage. "I'm sorry. What all did they steal?"

"Tape player and six speakers." Images of catching the thieves and dispatching them with the shortened baseball bat he kept under the seat filled his mind. He wondered what he had gotten himself into—what Sarah would think.

At home, he stared at the phone, wondering if it had rung while he was gone. He had not been home before bedtime any night since he returned from Georgia. Had Sarah called? Had Jubal asked to talk to him? If she had called, he knew that his deeply insecure wife would be angry, suspicious of his nighttime absences.

He felt he had to be at work Saturday morning because Mike would be on the factory floor in Arlington disassembling completed mobile homes and that the accounting staff would be in the office pricing inventory. He intended to lead by example. With his first cup of coffee resting precariously on an empty stomach, he looked at the stack of sheets in front of him and picked up the phone. To hell with the rules on long distance calls. Cutt answered on the first ring.

"Blind River Ranch. Cutt Ledbetter."

"Hey, Cutt. How you doing?"

"Hey, Son. Long time since I heard your voice."

"Good to talk to you, but I'm at work and in sort of a hurry. Has Sarah left yet?"

"Left about thirty minutes ago. Should get there before dark. Really gonna miss that boy of ours."

"I been missing him a little myself. He hold his own?"

"Hope you don't mind me putting him on Judson. The boy took to it like a duck to water." Tee remembered Judson, of course, short for Judge's

Son. The gelding was named for his father, the stallion they called Judge. Tee and his brother had learned to ride on him.

The thought of his son getting riding lessons without him made Tee's heart ache. "Nope. Glad to hear it. Just hate you had to do my job."

"Remember how that old horse used to run full speed from wherever he was when one of you boys came out of the house? He would run right up to you and stick his nose under your arm."

"I do. We fed him apples when we had 'em."

"Promise not to laugh, but I think that Judson kept on watching for you all these years. The first time he saw Jubal, he came running, like he thought he was you. I couldn't say no when the boy asked to ride him."

"No reason to say no, Cutt. I'm grateful for it. Can't wait to hear Jubal tell about it."

"Well, he never shuts up talking about his daddy."

"Cutt, I have to run. I'm calling on a work phone. Hope I can make the next trip."

A long pause. "Everything okay with Sarah? She acted sort of strange the whole time she was here. After what happened with her mother, I worry too much, I guess."

"As far as I know, Sarah is fine. You and I should talk more."

"I'd like that."

Mike called before five and asked about working late Saturday and all day Sunday. "I'm on a roll, Tee. I know your family is coming back, but mine is right down the road. I can go back and forth for lunch and supper from here. What do you say?"

"You forget that salaried people don't get overtime?"

"It ain't about the money. This thing is sort of turning me on. I'm weird like that, I guess."

"Go for it, but go home early on Sunday. I'll see you on Monday."

Tee's stomach complained like his throat had been cut all the way home. He had forgotten to eat lunch and felt weak. By his calculations, he should arrive in time to shower and change before they reached home. At eight, he gave up and ate a fried bologna sandwich. Tee was frantic with worry by the time Sarah's green '70 Chevy sedan pulled into the back driveway carport before ten.

The sight of his sleeping son in the front seat calmed him. He gently nudged the boy and picked him up. Jubal nestled his head against his father's neck and whispered. "I rode old Judson, Daddy."

"I heard. Your granddaddy said you took to it like a duck to water. Expect you'll be a real cowboy soon." He laid the boy down on the bed, helped him undress and get into clean pajamas, and tucked him under the covers.

Sarah stood in the doorway as he straightened. She whispered. "You putting him to bed without a bath?"

He followed her into the living room. "He seemed fine to me. I'll help him with his bath in the morning. Assume you fed him supper."

"We ate in Wichita Falls."

"I was worried sick. What took you so long?"

"What do you mean?"

"Cutt said you should be here before suppertime."

"You talked to Daddy?"

"Called him this morning."

"You called after I left but never called while I was there."

"And you never called me, never told me you were going to leave, and stayed gone for a week. Wanna talk about that?"

They stood in awkward stances, jousting mentally for the superior position. Tee spoke first. "I'll get the suitcases in."

Sarah took her time getting ready for bed while Tee sat in the middle of the front yard. He could see the moon better from the front yard, and he needed this time outside almost every night after Jubal went to bed. Without it, the house started to close in on him. He stayed until he saw the lights in the kitchen go out. He undressed in the bathroom and crawled into bed beside her. Hands behind his head, he stared at the ceiling for almost an hour, reluctant to move. "When did you start taking birth control pills?"

She stirred but did not turn to face him. "What?"

"You heard me."

"What are you talking about?"

He rolled out of the bed, went to the bathroom, returned with the pills, and held them up in the light. "These. When did you start taking them?"

Sarah looked away. "The doctor prescribed them."

"Why did you let me think month after month you might get pregnant?"

"The doctor prescribed them to regulate my periods. I'm having a few troubles I didn't want to bother you with."

This slowed Tee's racing heart a little but still did not explain the secrecy, the deception. "So when were you ever going to let your husband in on this?"

She began to cry. "I know you want another child, but I'm afraid to bring one into the world until I feel we're safe and secure. Until you keep a steady job."

Nothing but the sound of hard breathing filled the room then. Tee felt like a stranger in his own bed, in his own house. It was as if he had been living his life with a stranger for almost seven years. "Hell, I don't know why I even brought it up, why you even bother with the pills. No more often than you let me touch you, birth control pills are a waste of money, anyway." He walked across the hall to the bedroom next to Jubal.

Sunday morning, Tee quietly helped Jubal with his bath and dressed him in boots, jeans, and sweatshirt. Jubal crammed a red cap down over his thick hair as they left his room. The cap had a thoroughbred horse stitched above the bill. Tee whispered as he looked at the cap. "Nice cap. Where'd you get it?"

"Ford gave it to me." Pulling out of the driveway on their regular weekend morning trip usually made Jubal giddy with excitement, but not today. The boy seemed serious, older, quieter.

Tee headed due south and kept driving until he found a small café like the ones his father used to prefer. He felt a need to be around men like his father, brother, and himself, a necessity to cleanse himself of the life he lived on weekdays, to rid himself of that other person he had become. He wanted to see men in felt hats and boots with riding heels, men with eyes and skin that had seen too much wind and sun, hands that had done hard labor building fence, roping and doctoring cattle or driving tractors.

The little cafe beside the road looked the part, but the customers didn't. It was almost empty, and there were no cowboys, only couples dressed for church. Tee felt guilty that he and Jubal were not and made a silent pledge to change that soon. They sat in a back booth as far away from the other customers as possible. The boy was quiet, a surprising departure from the usual non-stop stream of questions that punctuated their weekend trips. Tee attributed it to being away for a week.

When they pushed away plates half-emptied of eggs, bacon, biscuits and gravy, Tee expected a complete recitation of every day's events during the Blind River visit, but he had to pull the information from his son. "Jubal, do you understand that your other grandfather, my daddy, used to be the manager of that ranch?"

Jubal looked at him with inquisitive eyes and nodded tentatively, but Tee could see that he did not. "Your grandfather John T Jessup and your grandmother Winona lived in the house where Grandpa Cutt lives now. I lived there from the time I was born until I went off to college. Then your mother and Maggie and Cutt moved in."

Jubal nodded. "Uh, huh."

Tee felt he had gone too far. It was too much for a five-year-old boy to absorb. Afraid it might lead to questions about what had happened to his other grandparents, Tee let it slide.

"Did Grandpa Cutt or your mother show you where your uncle Jubal and I carved our names on about every wall and tree on the ranch?"

"Cutt said you broke Judson when you were a little boy not much bigger than me."

"Well, I was a little older than you are when I did that. And I think it was more Judson breaking me than the other way around."

That got a laugh. "Why didn't you go out there with us, Daddy?"

"I was in Georgia when you left, son. Working. I would have liked to go, but I just couldn't."

"Coulda called. I had stuff to tell you."

Tee moved across the booth and pulled his son closer. "I should have, Jubal. I got no excuse, except I was working a lot of nights. I thought about you every day, though." He hugged him close. "In fact, I thought about you just about every minute."

Jubal's smile was tentative, forgiving. "We never went that long without talking before."

"And we won't ever again."

Jubal's return to constant conversation allowed Tee and Sarah to make it through the rest of the day. They spoke to each other through him. The boy sensed something was wrong, wondered what he had done to cause it.

146

They went on like that for two more weeks, going through the motions, acting in a play with Jubal as their audience. Tee had accepted the medicinal purpose of the pills, even the deception, but Sarah's obsession with security bothered him. He had come to believe what Jacob Locke had said about security versus adventure and challenge, and he felt Sarah should have more faith in him.

Twenty-Nine

TEE WAS BEHIND ON THE FINANCIAL DATA FOR THE STOCK
offering and had not heard from Stan Leftwich on Billy's audit when Gene
Vinson called to tell him the audit had to happen within the week. Tee
felt a headache coming on. "I'll get back to you." He hung up and walked
to Esther's office. "How does Leftwich stand on those files? Vinson is all
over me."

"I'm still calling every day. He's having a little problem with bank
statements. You know, tying in deposits and expenses to the tax return
and the documents I dug up."

"Bank accounts? Thought your daddy did all his business in cash."

"He did. That's why Stan's having a little trouble dummying up statements and checks."

The bars of a prison cell flashed across Tee's mind. "Dummy invoices
from the past are one thing, but dummy bank statements are something
else again. That sounds like fraud, tax evasion, and about a dozen other
jailhouse offenses if they call the bank."

Esther shrugged. "What choice do we have?"

Mike Clayton was waiting when he returned to his office. Said he wanted to make a progress report. Mike chuckled when he saw the distressed look on Tee's face. "You about got your plate full, don't you?"

"In over my head, I think."

"Has Jacob Locke offered any help? You even talk to him?"

"He called me once. Said to do what I could to pull off the stock offering. That's about it. I did tell him you were my last and best hope."

Mike picked up a briefcase that sat beside his chair. "We need a table to spread out some stuff."

"Lew's in California. We can use his conference table."

Tee felt a slight lessening of the weight on his shoulders as he examined the documents Mike spread on the table. Bills of material for all of the finished products, labor costs backed up with internal time and motion and other studies done at Redman Industries. All in labeled files. "You steal this labor cost data from Redman?"

Mike examined a baseball bat beside the door. "Not really. It's a long story, but we're okay to use it. I did the studies as a contractor, so they technically belong to me. Pretty much industry-wide data, anyway. I figure it's public domain. Auditors should like it."

"You may be Superman, after all. All we have to do now is apply the costs to the units. We can do that in a day or two."

Mike smiled and made a sweeping, silent gesture at the files as if making a gift to Tee.

Tee shook his hand. "My guess is there ain't two people in the whole damn country could have pulled off what it looks like you have. I'll do my best to see you're compensated if we ever get any money."

Mike grinned. "Talked to Buddy Newsome out in Georgia. He's the only factory manager we got except Billy Harbor who seems to know come here from sic 'em about building mobile homes or travel trailers."

"I like Buddy."

Mike's face grew serious. "There's just one problem."

"What's that?"

"Says he priced out both models he makes out there and the materials cost alone is almost as much as the sales price. That got me to thinking, and I looked at a few of the units made in Arlington. We're paying way more than Redman does for the same materials. They're a bigger company but not that much bigger."

"So, we've got the units priced too low or the costs too high. Which is it?"

"Looks like both."

"Lew will be back tomorrow. We need to have a meeting."

Tee dared not give voice to his thoughts. High costs, low prices, or both, they had worse trouble than he imagined. He picked up Lew's phone to call Buddy but paused as he saw a large shadow block out the sunlight coming through the window. Doublewide Dan leaned against the door frame, one hand rested on top of the half-open door. Tee worried about the hinges.

He pointed the other hand at Mike but spoke to Tee. "Been getting some complaints about your boy here."

Tee stiffened. "That so? Who's complaining?"

"Never you mind about who. We can't have you pencil-pushers getting in the way of the people who make this business work. Your boy here has been nosing around right in the middle of the production lines. He needs to stick to whatever it is you bean-counters do."

Tee glanced at Mike, who rolled his eyes. "Mike is doing exactly what we do. He may be the only hope we have of saving this stock offering."

Throckmorton's face darkened, and his fat cheeks swelled, his lips pursed. "Ain't but two things make this joint work; two things make sure your paycheck don't bounce. One is makin' 'em, the other is sellin' 'em. All you need to do is count what we make and sell. Don't get in the way of those two things." Throckmorton turned to walk back to his office, but returned. "And that damn stock offering? It's caused trouble from day one. I hope it does fail. We don't need a bunch of stock jockeys around here telling us what to do."

Grady Allison prowled the halls of Harborcraft like some malevolent dictator, supervising his junior and senior staff as they went over the books in tedious detail. The next morning, Grady stopped Tee in the hall outside Barry Steadman's door. He spoke loud enough for Barry and anyone else in the area to hear. "So where are we on the inventory? I'm getting the uneasy feeling we're wasting time. No priced inventory, no clean opinion. No clean opinion, no stock offering. Or as the Chinese laundryman said, "No tickee, no washee."

"Very funny. We're close."

Grady looked surprised. "Well now, that's more like it."

Barry walked over and closed the door in Grady's face and faced Tee. "Are you really close?"

"Mike and I have got the inventory numbers, but you need to look them over before we give them to Grady. Can you get Lew and Doug and meet with Mike and me this afternoon about three?"

"That's pretty short notice to get all three of us in the room at the same time."

Both hands on Barry's desk, Tee leaned in. "Did you not hear what Allison said?"

Barry rolled his eyes. "Grady's throwing his weight around, but I'll see what I can do."

Tee had a sick feeling in his stomach as he walked down the hall to Mike's cubbyhole. His conversation with Buddy last night had confirmed his and Mike's conclusions. Buddy was pleased to have them confirm what he had known for a few months. Mike hummed as he put the finishing touches on a spreadsheet.

Tee and Mike had spent most of the night putting the presentation together, and Tee had missed another evening with his son. The more they uncovered, the worse the future looked for Harborcraft. He wrote a resignation letter in the wee hours of the morning and put it in the folder he kept with him, the folder that spelled the possible death knell for Harborcraft and the end of Tee's seventh job.

Mike looked up and smiled. "Everybody coming to the meeting?"

Tee nodded. "Assuming the royalty around here can find the time."

"So how we gonna go about this, boss? You gonna wield the guillotine or conduct the trials?"

"I'll do it, but you may have to back me up. We want to walk in loaded for bear, like we got enough documentation to send everybody to prison."

Mike lifted his black vinyl-covered briefcase with skinned corners. "Locked and loaded. You know, prison ain't totally out of the question."

They huddled and reviewed what they had decided the night before. They were still writing and discussing when Esther dropped by before lunch with their lunches in two brown paper bags. "There's Cokes in the fridge, Mike. Make yourself useful." Mike headed toward the break room.

She whispered to Tee. "Stan called me last night. He has things ready. Can you meet with him tonight?"

Tee frowned. "Everything happens at once."

"You look terrible, Tee. Like you're about ready to keel over."

"Just be sure you get Buddy at the airport at noon. He has to be here at least an hour before the meeting."

"Anything I need to know?"

"You'll know soon enough, I imagine."

"What about Stan?"

"I'll meet him, but I may not have time to go down to Deep Ellum again."

"I'll find another place."

Tee and Mike finished by two, and Tee went back to his office to wait for Buddy to arrive. He closed the door and pulled his chair to the open window, tried to be tranquil. At five till, Tee walked with Buddy at one shoulder and Mike at the other down the hall to Lew's office.

THIRTY

TEE STUDIED LEW'S OFFICE AS THEY WAITED FOR DOUG'S LATE arrival. The walls and shelves revealed a history of Lew's career as an athlete from Little League through college. A bat and glove stood in each corner. Mounted baseballs, footballs, helmets, track shoes and trophies occupied every available surface. Photos adorned the walls: Lew hauling in a pass; Lew catching a fly ball; Lew at bat; Lew in a runner's stance. Tee wondered if he had more at home. Barry had warned about asking questions about any item, lest he be drawn into hours of nostalgic ramblings.

Today, the room seemed appropriate, like a stadium, gridiron, or baseball diamond. Gladiators were about to take the field, about to face lions in the coliseum. An hour into Tee's presentation, that field of honor pulsated with heavy breathing, heated with bodies warmed by anger, smelled of human sweat. His voice and movements had been tentative and weak at first but grew steadier and stronger as Tee saw little beads of sweat form on Doublewide Doug Throckmorton's forehead and lips. Normally uptight Lew seemed strangely calm as he stared at Doug. Barry's eyes flared open, and his lids had begun a series of upward movements as if he were trying to push them totally back so he could see more.

Doublewide Doug exploded as Mike distributed the last of six sets of handouts. He threw the stapled sheets at Tee. "You little son-of-a-bitch. I knew you were trouble when you walked in the door. Should have run you off as soon as you started sticking your nose where it don't belong. You might as well call me a damn thief."

Tee looked at Buddy, then Mike. He knew Doug had not really started paying attention until the presentation was half done. His demeanor and expression had shown complete disdain and disinterest for whatever they might impart. He had not even deigned to look at them, just stared out the window while he clipped his fingernails and let the clippings fall on the floor.

Tee paused, let Doug's remark settle. "Guess you were too busy clipping your nails to pay attention, Doublewide. We've been calling you a thief and embezzler for well over an hour and backing it up with proof." And they had. The little team had assembled an unassailable paper trail with documents showing real costs of materials compared to amounts paid by Harborcraft, cash payments made to Doug, duplicate serial numbers to mobile homes and travel trailers. A weak lawyer could have won a conviction with less evidence.

Doug stood and pointed a stubby finger at Mike, then Buddy, then Tee. "You and your asshole buddy number-crunchers are fired. Don't bother asking for severance. Just get your asses off this property. We'll mail your personal shit. And you'll all hear from my lawyer."

Buddy and Mike looked at Tee, not at Doublewide. Tee looked toward Lew. Throckmorton, unaccustomed to insubordination, rose and walked toward Tee, big half-moons of sweat under his arms, wet streaks down the front of his shirt. The heat and body odor produced by a nervous and angry four-hundred-pound giant mixed with his expensive cologne and hit Tee like a flash fire. Doug towered over him. "You not hear what I said, boy? Don't forget I got a few pictures."

Tee stepped back from the sensory onslaught, feeling heat rise in his body and flush his face. He glanced at Buddy, who winked as he stood and pulled two small marbles from his pocket. Buddy opened his fingers to let Doug see them roll in his palm. "See those, Doug? Those are your balls."

He slammed them down hard on Barry's desk. "Jack with any of us, and we'll send you to jail where you belong." He closed his fingers around the marbles, made a fist, and held it in Doug's face. "Now step back. You smell like the ass-end of a skunk."

Tee smiled with wonder at laid-back Buddy's sudden show of anger and boldness. There must be more history with Throckmorton than Buddy had shared.

Lew put his hand across his eyebrows as if his eyes could not be allowed to encounter the poison in the air. His voice was little more than a whisper. "Sit down and be quiet, Doug. You're not firing anybody. You're the one that's fired."

Doug did not sit. His voice raised an octave as his arms waved, filling the room with his smell. He turned on Lew. "You ungrateful little bastard. Who the hell do you think put this damn company together? Whose money and good credit pulled your sorry ass out of the fire more than once?"

Barry looked stunned. He said nothing, just looked longingly at the window the way a prisoner looks at stars. Lew seemed tired, drained. "You're right about that, Doug. You put it together, all right. But you did it so you could steal with both hands. Now, you've brought us down."

Everyone in the room stood and faced Throckmorton. They stared until he stalked out of the room. Lew followed him out into the hall. "Don't go into your office or remove anything from this property except that gauche, behemoth, vainglorious automobile that you drive."

Doug turned and braced himself with a hand on each side of the hall, filling a space that would hold two big men, looking like Samson holding up the Philistine columns. "Your puny ass gonna stop me from going into my own office? You forgot I own part of this piss-ant corporation?"

"We'll expect you to sign over your worthless stock in exchange for not bringing criminal charges." Lew seemed calm, his voice strong. Tee noticed the baseball bat in his hand. Lew pointed it at Throckmorton. "Call the sheriff, Barry."

They all stepped out into the hall, watched as the famous Doublewide Doug left the building; watched the horned Cadillac sway side to side as it careened away on protesting tires. Mike chuckled. "Well, I guess that went well."

157

Back in the office, Esther brought a pot of coffee and filled their cups. A strange calmness had entered the building, making the air seem lighter, purer. When Lew took a practice swing with the bat before putting it back in its customary position, embarrassment changed to laughter. Fits of giggling broke out as they took turns describing the look on Doug's face, the threats he had made. It was as if the men had spent days together in a collapsed mining shaft and had just seen their first beam of light.

Lew shook his head. "I should have known he was under-pricing so he could sell more and make big commissions." His voice dropped as he looked into each of their faces as if he might cry. "He did that right under my nose, and I let him because he was so good at sales. Never thought he would stoop this low."

Barry lit his third cigarette. "Petty larceny wasn't enough for the big man. He stole with both hands."

Doug had fired all the plant purchasing agents and recruited a central agent who cut deals with suppliers to allow Harborcraft to pay inflated prices for materials in exchange for kickbacks. Buddy described how he had recruited straw buyers to buy finished mobile homes and campers at deep discounts from Harborcraft. Throckmorton pocketed the commissions, then resold the units at full retail. He had set up a retail location to sell spare parts paid for by Harborcraft but drop-shipped to the lots. He had even begun taking finished mobile homes directly off the assembly line and selling them through sales lots he owned outright or with partners.

It was dark when Lew finally waved a dismissive hand. "I've heard enough. You men did a good job on this. How did you uncover it?"

Tee looked at Mike, then Buddy. "Buddy and Billy Harbor dropped a couple of hints. Then Mike was quick to spot the overpriced invoices because of his experience at Redman. Then he was sharp enough to devise a bill of materials. It was pretty easy after that. Doug Throckmorton was doing almost everything in broad daylight. Like he thought he was too damn smart to get caught."

Mike laughed. "Or we were too dumb to catch him."

Quietness followed. Tee noticed the door from Lew's office to Esther's little closet was cracked. He could almost feel her ear pressed against the door. "So where does that leave us?"

Lew's eyes were red. "Out on the street, I guess. The damn stock offering is caput. We can't keep this from the auditors. When we restate our financials and put real cost-of-goods-sold numbers in, all the profits will turn to losses. Nobody wants stock in a company losing money."

Tee walked to the window, watched as the moon made shadows on the little trail that led to The Still, wondered if Billy Harbor had known everything from the beginning. The meeting with Stan crossed his mind, but it didn't matter much. "Any chance we can sell the thing? Or any chance we might pull it out now that we can stop the stealing?"

Lew seemed to gain hope from the question. "There might be. I urge each of you to spend the next forty-eight hours coming up with a plan to save this company. We'll have to slash overhead, revamp our sales prices, negotiate new material prices. We might just make it work. Tee, you call Jacob Locke first thing tomorrow. He might get us short term financing."

Lew smiled an almost bashful smile. His voice was low, like he was talking to himself. "Like a trained puppy, I kept pushing for more sales, more sales. Doug must have thought me a complete idiot. It seems we were losing money on every product except camper tops. The more we sold; the more money we lost. What a joke on me."

Tee squinted in the now smoke-filled room. "Guess that's why auditors demand a physical count and pricing. That's what threw up the flags."

Barry seemed to come back to life. "At least we can tell Grady Allison and his little crew to leave the building. I hate that bastard."

Tee, Buddy and Mike locked their individual copies of the evidence in separate file cabinets and walked out together. Mike poked Buddy with his elbow and spoke loudly. "Nice touch with the marbles." Buddy and Mike laughed. Tee grinned but felt a little sick.

THIRTY-ONE

TEE COULD TELL BY THE LOOK ON ESTHER'S FACE THAT SHE KNEW most of what had happened in the meeting. She sent a message of congratulations and condolences with a smile, a thumbs up, and body language that said she was on the verge of hugging him. "Are you up to the meeting with Stan?"

The thought of meeting with Stan brought borderline nausea. He didn't need to look at his watch to know it was well past quitting time. "Not at Deep Ellum."

"Not Deep Ellum. He's due to be at my house any minute."

Tee thought of home and Jubal, still awake, listening for the sound of the Cougar pulling under the carport, watching the kitchen door. "I'm wasted, Esther. I don't know if I would understand anything he told me."

"I know you must be. But after what I heard in there, this little audit of Daddy's should be a piece of cake for you."

"Probably doesn't matter anymore, anyway. We're all going down now."

161

She looked hurt. "Doesn't matter? Daddy may be looking at losing everything or worse, going to jail. And it doesn't matter?"

"I just meant it may not matter to Harborcraft. Remember that's who I work for, not Billy Harbor." The look on her face made him regret what he had said. "Okay, okay, I'll meet with him. Where do you live?"

"Where do I live? You never asked anybody where I live? I live a few yards away from The Still. I walk to work some mornings."

Tee stopped in his office to call home, tried to explain to Sarah why he was going to be late again, but she seemed on the verge of tears when she told him she had cooked a big supper. In the days leading up to today's meeting, he had tried to explain what was about to happen, but she seemed uninterested, preoccupied with her own thoughts.

Esther waited by the front door, watching a downpour through the side window. Tee had planned on walking through the woods, but the rain killed that. She squatted and looked up at the sky. "Can I hitch a ride? I walked to work this morning."

The Cougar was deep in the lot, and Esther insisted on running beside him rather than waiting to be picked up, so her hair and clothes were wet when she slid into the bucket seat. The moisture triggered all her feminine scents. The curls in her red hair had tightened and grown darker from the rain. Her unbuttoned light coat revealed a wet blouse. She shivered from the cold. Tee cranked the Cougar and turned up the heater. The black sky and pouring rain made the car feel like a refuge from the nerve-wracking tension that had built up for days prior to the confrontation with Double-wide Doug. Tee felt all his energy leaving him. He looked at her profile as she looked expectantly out the windshield. Finally, she turned and caught him staring. She turned away and looked out the side window, ran a finger under each eye, pointed toward her house.

Her house was hidden in the back yard of another nondescript house, snuggled behind crepe myrtles, hanging vines, and shrubs. It resembled a small rundown hunting cabin with a tiny porch. Tee parked his Cougar beside her beat-up white '66 Mustang. When he killed the engine, he could hear her ragged breathing. They sat quietly for only a few minutes, long enough for the windows to fog. The fog secluded them further, made them feel alone in the world. Nobody reached for a door handle until the interior lights of a black Lincoln Town Car come on in the parking lot of

The Still. Tee looked over his shoulder and saw Stan Leftwich step out of the car, open an umbrella, and walk toward them.

It was close to midnight when they finished going over the material. Stan's worksheets were so clear and complete, his folders so organized and labeled, his summary sheet comparing every line on Billy's tax return to the documentation attached so simple that Tee was surprised he felt ready to sit down with Vinson, ready to believe Billy Harbor was completely honest. He walked to his car beside Stan, leaving Esther, arms folded against her chest, leaning against a porch post. Tee was home by one and asleep by two. Sarah tossed and turned all night.

He carried Jubal to the nursery the next morning and arrived at work an hour late. What did it matter? The resignation letter he carried with him seemed irrelevant now. Why resign from a company that is resigning from you? One swallow into his first cup, he dialed Jacob Locke's number. Tee stumbled when Locke answered his own phone. He felt clumsy as he related the details of what they had found, what had happened to Doublewide Doug. The wait for a response was tense.

"Do the auditors know?"

"I expect they do by now. If not, we'll tell them this morning."

"Excellent job, Tee. I was afraid you would find what you did."

"You knew?"

"No, I didn't know, but I suspected. When you have a company that's reporting huge profits but running out of cash, there had better be a big increase in assets or reduction in debt to show for it. Otherwise, you have an accounting or theft problem. Looks like we had both, and both were big. I expect you learned a lot more from this than you did in four years of college."

Tee knew that was true, but he felt a sense of betrayal, a sense he had been used. "With the stock offering canceled, we'll probably run completely out of money in about six months. And that's assuming nothing else goes wrong."

"That sounds about right."

"Lew and Barry seem to think you can get us a short term line of credit. Now that we can stop the stealing, we might salvage the company."

Tee could hear Jacob Locke's breathing, imagined he could hear his mind whirring. "You essentially have no salespeople; they will panic with

Doublewide gone; no purchasing people because you've exposed them as thieves. Doug Throckmorton was the heart and soul of the organization I dreamed of building. Who knew that the organs were diseased? I don't see how I can sell a sinking ship to a bank, Tee. And cancellation of the stock offering will make bad reading in the financial press."

The news came as a dull thud. "So that's it? We die a slow and painful death? Won't you lose your investment when that happens?"

"I knew I was taking a risk. You'll learn, however, never to throw good money after bad. I encourage you to help the others. Take a leadership role. It is possible it could be salvaged. It's just not a wise gamble for me or a bank."

"Any suggestions?"

"Lew and Barry will have to cut their salaries by at least half right away. If they won't do that, it's a clear signal they're not up to the task. There are a lot of other expenses and people that will have to go, too."

"Yeah, like me. Looks like my errand here is done."

"Tee, I haven't forgotten that I got you into this, though one could say you did that to yourself. I'll try to help you land on your feet. If it's any consolation, you are much more valuable today than you were when I met with you a few months ago."

"Consolation doesn't put too much food on the table."

THIRTY-TWO

GRADY ALLISON STOOD IN THE DOORWAY AS TEE PUT THE PHONE
back in its cradle. Grady pointed to a chair. "Mind if I sit down?"

Tee's dismissive wave said he did not care one way or the other, and
Grady sat down. "Just came by to say goodbye and sorry things didn't work
out."

Tee looked out the window. "Not half as sorry as I am. All that work
and expense for nothing."

"I wouldn't say that. From what I heard about that meeting, you managed to keep yourself and the others out of jail. If that stock offering had
gone public, I shudder to think of the consequences."

"Guess the Securities and Exchange Commission frowns on falsified
financials when you're offering stock to the public."

"That they do. So, what's next?"

Tee was a little wary of sharing anything with Grady. "You mean for
me or Harborcraft?"

"Both."

"I haven't had time to consider what I'll do next. Depends on if we can survive without the cash infusion the stock would have brought. Think we can?"

Grady's head went slowly back and forth. "Too late, I think. If you had found it six months ago, before you spent the money and time on the public offering, then maybe. But not now."

"You're probably right."

Grady stood to leave. "Wish I could offer some sage advice, but I never offer any advice that's not billable."

Tee stood and walked into the hall with him. "I didn't sleep much last night. I was wondering if the company reported and paid taxes on those bogus profits. If they did, they could have a tax refund coming."

"You might be on to something. Be careful you don't kick a sleeping dog, though."

"Don't know much about corporate taxes."

"You should do something about that." Grady offered his hand to Tee. "Truth be told, you and Mike probably saved our ass on this thing, too. I got a look at the worksheets this morning. They might have been good enough to fool me."

"Maybe I should have waited till the stock was sold to expose the theft."

"Then we could have all been cellmates. Well, it's been fun." Grady turned and walked down the hall but returned before Tee could sit down. "I'm older than you, Jessup. Hope you learned you can't hang your hat on anybody but yourself. Get your certificate so you will always have a job."

"Thanks for the advice, Grady. You take it easy."

Tee stood in the hall and watched four auditors with briefcases follow Grady like a herd of sheep down the hall and out the door to two waiting gray cars. Barry slowly clapped as they left. The building seemed emptier but friendlier without them. Barry motioned for Tee to follow him to Lew's office.

Lew pointed toward Esther's little office and spoke to Tee. "She find you? Seemed frantic to see you this morning."

"Nope. Haven't seen her yet. Where is she?"

"Don't know. Said she'd be back in about an hour."

Tee sat by the conference table. "So, are we going to have a big planning session? Talk about cuts and how to survive?"

Lew looked at his watch. "In about an hour. Same group as yesterday, minus Throckmorton, of course."

They were half an hour into the meeting when Tee heard Esther's desk chair roll. The meeting was not going well. Salary cuts for the top earners in the firm were not mentioned. Tee discussed the possible tax refund and hinted at layoffs in the home office. Lew and Barry pondered and rubbed their brows. Their expressions showed confusion, not confidence.

Mike broke the tension. "As many of you know, Henry Ford did invent something called the assembly line. Billy Harbor understood that, but this company has not been practicing it. We can implement standardized products, slim down the number of models we offer."

Buddy outlined changes and consolidations that could be made in the Georgia plant and in purchasing. "Hate to say it, but we should probably sell the plants on the coasts, even Oklahoma, and concentrate our efforts on the ones right here in Texas. That seems like a good way to raise money."

But Lew and Barry failed to offer any suggestions of their own or provide authorization to proceed on the suggestions made. Tee was nervous and anxious to find out why Esther was looking for him. When he heard her making excessive noise next door, he excused himself and walked into her office. She waved him away and followed him into the hall, pushed him toward his own office. Inside, she burst into tears. "The files are gone."

"What do you mean, gone?"

"Somebody took them out of my car last night."

"You left them in your car?'

"Yes, locked in the trunk."

"Somebody broke into your trunk?"

"Whoever did it used my spare key I keep under the back wheel well."

"Sounds like your daddy."

"Why?"

"Who else would know where the key was? Stan? And who else would want the files?"

"I asked him. I called Stan and got no answer, but he would have told me already."

"But who would want the files?"

Billy Harbor walked in and sat beside his daughter. "She tells me my audit files are gone missing."

Irritated, Tee nodded and waited. He had the sure sense that Billy Harbor knew something about who had taken the files and why but had not seen fit to share with Esther.

Billy rubbed the stubble on his cheek. "I heard you boys turned the big boy inside out yesterday. Sometimes it's best not to wake a sleeping giant. He's bound to be madder'n hell."

"What's that got to do with your files?"

"Doug Throckmorton knows Stan Leftwich. He introduced me to him. And he knows about the audit. Before, he needed me to get off clean to protect Harborcraft. Now, he wants us both to go down."

"What does he gain from that?"

"The big boy wants his pound of flesh from you, for one thing. Course, he may hold a little grudge because I outsmarted him when I sold my business to him and those other jerks."

Esther interrupted. "I've worked for him a long time. He's a vengeful man who has an ego to match his size. He's probably already working for the competition or starting his own company. Trust me; it will make him feel good to take Harborcraft down and you, Mike, Buddy, Lew, and Barry with it."

Tee was not convinced. "I still don't get it. Why not just wait for Harborcraft to die on its own?"

Esther felt they were wasting time. "Don't you see? He blames everything on you. In his mind, you're the one spoiled his little playground, not him."

Her tone irritated Tee. "So if he has the files and tells what he knows, the IRS can get Billy, Stan, and maybe me for tax evasion and bring enough grief to Harborcraft to end it once and for all."

Esther nodded. "And he will just sit back and enjoy the whole thing. He's a miserable, evil, person."

"So you think he stole the files himself?"

Esther shook her head. "Doug never does his own dirty work. He sent somebody. If I had to guess, it would be that sniveling purchasing agent you fired yesterday—the one with the face like a ferret."

Billy stood. "I know where the ferret lives. You two see if you can find Stan. Call me over at The Still when you get downtown."

THIRTY-THREE

IT WAS DAYLIGHT, AND THERE WAS A PARKING ATTENDANT AT
the same lot where Tee lost his sound system. He slipped the old man a five
spot to look after the Cougar, and he and Esther trotted to Stan's office
stairway. They pushed the unlocked door open, and it dragged on file folders and papers piled on the floor.

Folders were scattered everywhere, two lamps broken, all the chairs
overturned. Tee picked up one folder and saw a shoe under it—Stan's
shoe. Stan's head was one purple mass, both eyes swollen closed. The
expensive hairpiece Tee had not recognized as a wig was askew. But he
had a pulse.

Esther efficiently flipped a rolodex and phoned for an ambulance.
She dropped to her knees and pushed Tee away from Stan. "You got a
hankie?" She used it to wipe at the blood on Stan's head. The phone rang.
She motioned for Tee to answer it. "Might be the ambulance."

It wasn't. It was Billy Harbor. He asked for Esther. Tee told him what
had happened and listened for a few minutes. "Your daddy found the ferret.

Says he's in bad shape. Stan had a man watching your house and saw the ferret steal the files. Stan's man followed him home and got them back."

Esther kept up the pressure on Stan's wound. "So where are they, and who did this to Stan?"

"I expect Doublewide sent some thugs over here to steal 'em again. They probably bushwhacked him before he could call you to say he had the files."

"So Doublewide may have the files now." She looked toward the door that had made Tee curious on his first visit. She asked Tee to hold the handkerchief in place, withdrew a key from behind a bookcase, and opened the door. She dialed the combination to a wall safe, opened it, and walked back in carrying two covered boxes with "Gingerbread" scrawled on the sides and tops.

Tee felt like a sucker. "You told me you had only been here once before, but you know Stan's rolodex, where the safe is and the combination. You want to fill me in?"

"Stan had codes for all his clients. Gingerbread Man was Daddy's." She flipped through the folders inside the boxes. "These are the files. Stan must have stashed them before whoever did this got here. They tried to beat it out of him but couldn't."

"Great we got the paperwork again, but what about my question?"

She shrugged. "I didn't want you to know I had been associated with Stan. He's a sweet man, but a dark character with a lot of shady friends. He's been in trouble with the law."

"Some reason you never mentioned that before?"

"Would you accept I thought it wasn't relevant?"

"No."

"I worked for Stan for almost a year before the traffic in and out of here started making me fear for my life. Not to mention the walk to my car every night."

Tee checked Stan's pulse again and noticed a piece of wood under his slack arm. He felt a little dizzy as he gently lifted it. His initials were carved into the bat John T Jessup had cut down to eighteen inches. A vision of his father in the ranch's blacksmith shop pouring molten lead into a hole he had drilled into the end of the bat roared through his mind. *Hope you never have to use this, but don't hesitate if you do.* Tee's face went a little gray.

"What is it?"

"This is mine. I kept it under the seat of my car. They must have taken it when they broke into my car the last time we were here. They took the tape player and speakers to throw us off."

Esther eyes flicked left to right. "Okay, we're being set up here. Get a towel off the top shelf in the bathroom, wrap the bat, and hide it inside one of the boxes. Then take both boxes to your car and get out of here. Go to my house and stay there until I contact you."

Tee stood immobilized for a few seconds, trying to absorb what was happening. "I can't go off and leave you. Whoever did this may still be around."

"You have to leave. They plan to blame this on you somehow. I need to stay with Stan until the ambulance arrives. I'll call you when we get to the hospital. Key to my house is in the ceramic cat on the porch."

"How are you going to get to the hospital?"

"Dammit, Tee. Leave before they get here."

He paced three hours through her small house before she finally called. He heard the quarters drop in the pay phone. "Stan's alive and conscious, thank goodness. The cops were about to wear me down with questions when he woke up. He gave them a description of the guy who attacked him. Looks like they meant to leave him dead and hope the cops traced the ball bat back to you."

"Who did it?"

"Don't know. I'll have to get Stan alone to ask if the description was for real or not. Knowing Stan, it wasn't. He'll want to take care of this himself."

"So, you and me are off the hook?"

"No reason for anybody to even know you were there."

"Unless somebody saw me coming or going."

"Stan backed up my story about just dropping in for a visit. No reason for them to look any further. Nobody but drunks and derelicts down there to see you, anyway."

Tee still felt like a fugitive. Just before two in the morning, he arrived home to find Sarah's car gone and a note on the kitchen table. Sarah wrote a beautiful hand, but the haste and fear in this note could not have been more evident if it had been scrawled in blood.

Jubal and I are staying in a safe place until you finish whatever it is you are doing and decide to come home and stay. Don't try to find us. I need time to decide what to do. We are safe.

THIRTY-FOUR

TEE SPENT THE NIGHT TRYING TO DETERMINE WHERE SARAH might have taken their son. Two hours before daylight, he abandoned the bed and dressed. He called Cutt before daylight, pretending he called just to say hello. Cutt did not mention Sarah and Jubal, and Tee did not tell him they were missing. Tee watched from Jubal's window until the lights in Julia Cannon's house came on. He gave her a few minutes, then walked across the street and knocked on her door. Julia, a divorcee who kept a few neighborhood children, answered the door in a nightgown and robe. Her three-year-old daughter, Debbie, hid in the folds of the robe. "Hi, Tee."

"Sorry to bother you so early, but I've been out of town and seem to have lost Sarah and Jubal. You have any idea where they went?"

Julia looked across the street to their house. "No, sorry. I don't. How long have they been gone?"

"Not sure. I had to work all night and just got home."

"She didn't leave a note?"

173

Tee dared not tell her what the note said. "I keep thinking she must have, but I haven't found it."

Julia bit her lip as if to keep herself from saying more. Her eyes said she knew something she was not telling. Tee stared until she squirmed, trying to convey his urgent need to locate them. When she shrugged and looked helpless, he turned and trotted back across the street. Julia held out a hand as if she wanted to call him back, but she didn't.

Back at home, he went through all her dresser drawers, her closet shelves, unable to define what he was looking for. He did the same in Jubal's room. He could not be sure, but it looked as if a few of his clothes might be missing. He could not find his little travel bag. He wanted to hold his son, to protect him.

He made a list and started calling everyone who might know. None of their neighbors, none of their friends, none of her co-workers knew where they might be. Nobody. He finally called Cutt again. He skipped all pleasantries when his father-in-law answered. "Hate to ask this, Cutt, but have you seen Sarah and Jubal yet?"

"You mean they're missing?"

Tee read him her crumpled note.

"You two been having trouble?"

"I've got some problems at work. It's been keeping me away a lot. She resents it. Cutt, will you call me if you hear from her? You got my home and work number?"

"I do and I will. You do the same. I'll leave a hand here at the house all day, so don't wait till night to call if you find out. If you don't find her by nightfall, I'll come down there and help you look."

Tee went by the daycare center they called a nursery school and found a way to ask about Jubal without alarming the staff. He was not there. Tee did not know where else to look. He returned home and read the last words in Sarah's note again. *We are safe.* He paced the house and yard, afraid the leave the phone.

Esther called a few minutes before noon. "Where are you? Vinson and a flunky just walked in."

Sarah knew how to reach him at work, so he decided to go in. Mike and Esther met him at the door. Mike was cheerful as usual as he and Tee picked up the file boxes. "We found an empty office to deposit Vinson in. He's about to float away with coffee, though. Where have you been?"

"A few problems I'll tell you about later." Tee kept his eyes straight ahead, trying to focus as his mind searched for ways to find his wife and son. Mike and Esther led the way to Doublewide Doug's empty office. The strange mixture of the fat man's body odor and cologne still lingered in the room. Vinson stood by the window, hands clasped behind his back. A young IRS agent twirled in Doublewide's giant chair like a child on a merry-go-round.

Tee looked at the young agent as he dropped his box on a table pushed against the wall. Mike placed the second box beside it. Esther's hand was evident in the furniture rearrangement. A tray full of paper clips, pencils, pens, and pads sat on the table. She spoke as Vinson turned and showed them wary eyes. "I think I've thought of everything. If you need coffee or Cokes or snacks, just let me know. You know where the men's is."

Vinson put his hand on the lid of one of the boxes. "Thank you, but I think we'll take the files downtown and do our work there."

Tee felt as if he had been slapped. "Why?"

"We have copy machines and everything we need down there. This is likely to take a few days."

"That would mean we would have to copy everything. We can't really let you walk off with our files. We've put weeks of work into getting them organized."

Vinson's eyes grew cold. "We don't really need your permission. As I said, I can send a team of agents in here to take whatever we want."

Tee glanced at Mike. "I don't think you can take Billy's personal property or our work product without the client's permission and mine. If you can, show me the paperwork."

Vinson flinched. "It won't take long to prepare it."

Tee's face was unshaven, his eyes red from lack of sleep. "Don't know if you've heard about the problems we've got in this company, but it doesn't matter too much to me what you do anymore. I no longer have a dog in this fight. And I'm real tired of being threatened."

Mike stepped between them. "Look, we've got such an incredibly well-organized set of documents we think you can finish this in one day, two at the most. Why throw a monkey wrench into things? All three of us will help you here, and Billy's available if you need him."

Vinson seemed to soften. "You know, it's common practice for us to summon you for an appearance downtown. We're doing you a favor by even coming out here."

Tee lifted one of the box lids and saw the bloody bat inside. He had forgotten to remove it after reading Sarah's note. Angry at his carelessness, he put the lid back and lifted the box. "Okay, I'm not letting the boxes out of my sight, so we'll all go downtown. Esther, call Billy and tell him he'll have to come along."

Vinson frowned. "Billy Harbor doesn't have to be there until we do interviews."

Tee shrugged. "I can't let the boxes leave my possession. And Billy will go where the files go. He spent a lot of money getting them ready." He picked up the box with the bat and started down the hall at a brisk pace. Vinson grimaced as he slowly followed.

Tee barely had time to remove the towel-covered bat and hide it in a desk drawer before Vinson walked in. "Is Billy really in the building?"

"He's around. Available to sign anything or answer any questions. Want to see him?"

"Hell, no. I hope I never see him again."

"We figured we would keep him handy but out of sight rather than looking over your shoulder all day."

Vinson looked down the hall as if he expected Billy to come down it with a gun. "Okay. We'll try it from here." They took the boxes back to Doug's office and closed the door on the auditors.

Tee put the bat in a trash bag and took it to his car. Esther was holding the phone when he got back. "A man for you. Says his name is Ledbetter."

Tee grabbed the phone. Cutt's voice sounded tired and beleaguered. "You can rest easy, Tee. They're here."

Tee took a deep breath. "Thanks, Cutt. She tell you to call?" He put his hand over the receiver and signaled to Esther that he needed privacy. She walked down the hall to the break room.

"Asked me not to, but I knew that would be wrong."

"Has she said why she left?"

"We just had a little while to talk. I would have called right away, but I had to wait for her to get settled and out of earshot. She did say right off that she's a little afraid of you and *for* you."

"She said she was afraid of me? Cutt, I never laid a hand on her. Not ever."

"If I thought that, we would be having this conversation in person. She didn't accuse you of hitting or anything like that."

"What, then?"

"She says your bad dreams scare her. She's afraid you will hurt her or Jubal in your sleep."

Tee thought back to his last nightmare. "I have a few bad dreams about the accident once in a while, but I haven't had a real nightmare since Jubal came along."

"Maybe you have some and don't realize it."

"That's possible, I guess, but she never said a word. Why did she say she was scared *for* me."

"Maybe we do need to talk about that in person. When you got the time."

"Give it to me straight, Cutt. We can talk in person later."

"Tee, Sarah is my daughter. I can't be taking your side against her. Understood?"

"I understand that, but I need some help to figure out what I need to do to hold my family together."

"I don't pretend to know what goes on in your marriage, but I do know Sarah is a lot like her mother, and that worries me some." There was a long pause when only Cutt's ragged breathing could be heard. "Maggie left me once."

Tee sucked in a deep breath. Cutt was silent for so long that he thought the connection had been lost. "Cutt, you still there?"

"She took Sarah and went up to the mountains of New Mexico and stayed nearly a month with her sister and her crazy husband without me even knowing where she was. I lost a month's wages trying to track her down."

Tee felt a sense of trepidation. "Never knew that. Why did she leave?"

Cutt cleared his throat. "Said she didn't feel safe here, that I couldn't keep her safe. What really hurt was that her brother-in-law is nuttier than a fruitcake. Got a beard down to his knees and fancies himself some sort of holy messenger. Used religion as an excuse to beat his kids."

Tee looked both ways down the hall. "So how did you get her back?"

"She called me from a filling station in Ruidoso. Asked me to come get her and Sarah. That's why I can understand your predicament and want to help both of you."

"So why is she scared *for* me?"

"She seemed to have her story all made up when she walked in the door. Blurted it out before she even sat down. Sure you want me to tell you what she said?"

"I'm sure."

"She said she married you because you seemed solid as a rock. Stable. Then you lost or kept quitting good jobs. Said you flew off the handle and expected too much from a job. She's afraid you can't support her and Jubal and that you might even wind up a pauper yourself."

"She say anything about her own job?"

"I asked her. Said she quit. Guess she saw the contradiction then and wouldn't talk to me anymore."

Tee let the silence stretch. "Some of that's true, Cutt. But does she really think I'm not gonna provide for her and Jubal?"

"I asked Maggie the same thing. It's like they want a lifetime guarantee of support and protection. It may be a woman thing. But it's definitely more complicated than basic needs. Maggie had a deep need for something else. I don't want to discourage you, but I never found out what it was."

Tee saw Esther nursing a cup of coffee at the break room door, watching him, concern clearly on her face. "What should I do? Come out there and bring them back?"

"Give it a few days. I think there's more to this than what she's telling me. They'll be safe."

Gratitude washed over Tee. "Thanks, Cutt. I'll make it up to you."

Esther walked toward him when he hung up. "You want to talk about what's going on? You look like death warmed over."

"Home troubles, nothing I can't handle. How's it going with the feds?"

"They haven't emerged except to go to the bathroom. The kid must have a bladder the size of a peanut. He goes every fifteen minutes."

"Probably can't stand being cooped up with Mister Uptight."

It was near quitting time when Tee knocked on Doublewide Doug's door. He pulled down the big man's photo and tossed it into a trash can.

The young agent pulled on his suit coat as he opened the door. "I was just coming to find you."

Tee stepped inside. The look on Gene Vinson's face was guarded. He looked at his assistant. "Would you mind getting me something to drink?"

The young man's body language said he didn't appreciate being a servant, but he headed toward the break room. Tee sat down and looked at the stack of documents that might land Billy and himself in jail. "So, what have you found?" His voice was a little unsteady.

Gene Vinson's posture and expression matched his coiffed and stiff hair. "I expect I found just what you wanted me to find, Mr. Jessup."

Tee leaned back, surprise on his face. "And what was that?"

"One of the most organized sets of audit papers I have ever encountered. Every *i* was dotted, every *t* crossed." He held up a document. "According to my calculations, Billy Harbor will owe the Internal Revenue Service exactly three hundred and fourteen dollars and forty-two cents. That includes interest and penalties for late payment."

"What did you disallow?"

"I expect you know there were several hundred dollars of travel expenses and meals and entertainment that were obvious personal expenses rather than business. This is not my first audit, Jessup. Even the young agent I just sent for coffee suspected you were trying to turn our attention away from the real evasion we both know Billy Harbor is guilty of."

Tee tried to look hurt. "I don't know any such thing."

Vinson licked his lips. "I've already told you I want nothing more than to get this behind me, so I'm going to let it go. I don't expect there's much I could do, anyway."

Vinson slid a document in front of him. "If you can get Billy Harbor to sign this, we'll send him an invoice. When we get his check, we'll send the final closing documents and wrap this up."

Tee found Billy inside Lew's office with his feet on the desk. Billy looked over the document. "Says here I owe money. If I pay 'em, they won't ever turn loose. Keep coming back year after year if you give in just once."

"Sign the damn thing, Billy. Stan set it up so they could find what they did."

Billy stared at the form, didn't move. Tee touched it again. "Sign it. You got no choice."

Billy signed, then peeled bills off his roll and pulled change out of his pocket to come up with the payment. "You got change for a dollar?"

"They won't take cash, Billy. They said they would bill you."

"Then the deal's off. I want to be shed of 'em, here and now."

Tee called Esther on the interoffice. She glared at her father as she grabbed the cash from his hand. She went back to her desk and wrote a check to the IRS from her own account. Tee talked Vinson into taking the check and escorted them to the parking lot.

He stood in the parking lot a few minutes after they left, breathing in freedom, relishing the load off his shoulders, wondering if it was really over. Energy drained from him, and he leaned against the Cougar as if he needed it for support. He stared at the light in his office and tried to assimilate everything that had happened in the last few days. He tried to feel a sense of victory with the end of Billy Harbor's audit, but the thought of losing his family dwarfed any good feeling that might have come from that. But it did make him remember Stan Leftwich.

Esther and Mike were at the break room table when he went back inside. He sat with them. "I never asked about Stan."

Esther smiled wistfully. "I called the hospital, and he's already left. They didn't want to dismiss him, but he left anyway. So look out world, Stan is on the loose. Pity the poor guys who beat him up."

Mike looked at his watch as he stood. "Closer to bedtime than quitting time."

Their cars were parked beside each other in the parking lot. Mike drove off first, leaving Tee and Esther standing awkwardly in the moonlight. Esther got in her car and drove away. Her headlights revealed an envelope on his dash. He opened it and found four hundreds paper-clipped with a note in Billy Harbor's handwriting. "Damn fine job." Tee didn't want to go home to an empty house.

THIRTY-FIVE

CUTT ANSWERED ON THE FIRST RING AND CALLED JUBAL TO
the phone for Tee. His son sounded frightened and confused and had a lot
of questions Tee promised to answer when he came to visit. After that, Tee
called every night at eight, hoping Sarah would answer occasionally, but she
never did.

On the second weekend, he left an hour early on Friday, slept four
hours in a roadside motel on Route 66 west of Amarillo, and left before
dawn to drive out to the ranch on Saturday morning. He had tried to plan
how best to spend two days with his son, but could never get them to form
in his head. He had never just visited with Jubal, he had lived with him.
Only one thing was for sure, they would eat Saturday morning breakfast
in a cowboy café. He had promised.

The sun peeked through the back glass of the Cougar as he approached
the Denver Road crossing. The crossing brought a sense of melancholy and
dulled the hope and anticipation he had felt all week. He dared not slow to

reminiscence as he crossed the tracks. Despondency traveled behind him, and he refused to let it catch up.

He glanced at the main house, wondered if Ford and Hope were there. The sight of Cutt Ledbetter standing by the front gate of the manager's house chased away his dark pursuer. Cutt greeted him like a long-lost son, putting both hands on Tee's shoulders. "That boy warts me every day about you coming."

"Good." Tee looked toward the guest house. "Where is he?"

Cutt inclined his head toward the horse barn hall. Jubal rode out on Judson at the signal. The old palomino seemed as pleased as the boy in his saddle. Jubal was dressed like his namesake and Tee had dressed as boys: tall boots with spurs, big hat. Judson walked briskly toward them, head down and minding his manners. Jubal, eyes and ears red from the cold, held the reins loose and let the horse have his head. Tee was momentarily frozen in a torrent of emotion as his son traveled the same path, riding the same horse he had as a boy.

Tee raised both arms to take the boy down from the saddle, but Jubal grabbed the horn with his right hand and held the reins and a handful of mane with his left. He dismounted by holding on to two saddle strings, dropping his right foot toward the ground as he drew his left from the stirrup. He had to drop a little, but the strings broke his fall. Then he hugged Tee's waist. Tee's eyes filled as he looked toward Cutt, who turned his head away. He dropped to one knee so he could look his son in the eyes. "Missed you, boy."

Jubal nodded. "How long you stayin'?"

"Have to go back Sunday night, but that gives us two days. How about we go get some breakfast like we always do on Saturday mornings?"

Cutt took the reins from Jubal. "I'll put him in the barn in case you want to ride more later." He turned toward Tee. "Haul your bags into the house."

Tee stood and looked at him tentatively, then back to Jubal. "Guess your granddaddy already taught you how to tie a horse. Go put Judson up while I talk to Cutt."

Jubal led the horse to the barn, walking to the left, just beside Judson's head. Tee turned toward Cutt. "You're teaching him good."

"Rides like John T. You're too young to remember Walsh, the old man that was on this ranch before your daddy or me. He used to say John T was one of the reasons God made horses." He motioned toward Tee's car. "I'll take your bags in the house."

Tee shook his head reluctantly. "Where's Sarah staying?"

"She's staying with me now, back in your old room but left before you got here this morning. Said she would stay with friends in Amarillo so you and Jubal could have your time together. I got things all set up for you inside."

"Thought me and Jubal would spend the night up in Dalhart."

"And how you gonna entertain him up there in a little piss-ant motel? You and the boy can stay with me. He'll be more comfortable. This is where his roots are. Both sides of his family. I won't steal time away from you and your son, but I thought the three of us might hang around a little today or tomorrow. I got a few things on the ranch I want you to see."

"Anybody in the bunkhouse?"

"No full-time hands stay at headquarters anymore. Just a few day workers during spring roundup and shipping in the fall. I'd have to spend a whole day cleaning out cobwebs for you to stay there. "

"Where's Ford?"

"Still playing polo, last I heard. Most of his calls come from Dallas. He comes unannounced once or twice a year, but it's clear the Blind River is just a bad memory for him. It's his daddy's ranch, not his."

"Wish it could have been my daddy's ranch. I'd stay here all the time."

"Tom Donovan was a good man, but he might have been a little hard on Ford. And his mama spoiled him to make up for it. Father and son never got along after she died. Ford went off the rails when Tom died, if you ask me. I hear he and Hope are having trouble. People don't pay much attention to sacred vows anymore."

"Know when Sarah plans on coming home?"

"Nope. Maybe she just needs time. I push her that way every chance I get."

They both watched Jubal walk back from the horse barn, affecting a little swagger to go with the spurs and hat. Tee looked toward the house where he had grown up. "Guess it would be easier on Jubal if we stayed here."

Cutt smiled. "Sure. It'll just be the three of us. I'll cook steaks tonight."

"Let me take him to breakfast. I'll decide before we get back."

Cutt walked toward his truck, patting Jubal on the back as he passed him. "Make yourself at home. House is open. You can have your old bedroom or Jubal's."

Tee realized on the way to Dalhart that he had forgotten how to talk to his son. Guilt overwhelmed him. Their conversation seemed to be that of mere acquaintances, not father and son. When they settled in a booth at the Cowboy Café, Tee began to regale his son with the history of the famous XIT Ranch. Jubal gave him a wide-eyed stare. "Is this where I'm gonna live now?"

Tee put his fork down. "Do you like staying on the Blind River?"

Jubal shrugged. "Are you moving there?"

The question shocked Tee. "Not right away, son, but I'll be out here as often as I can until you come home again."

"You still live in our old house?" Another shocker. Jubal seemed to feel he had been gone a long time.

"Yep."

"Where will I sleep if I come visit?"

"In your old room. Or, you could sleep with me if you want to."

"Will Mother be there?"

They spent the rest of the day in similar conversations. Jubal tried to get it all straight in his mind, tried to figure out what he had done to cause his father to desert him. Tee tried to comfort him without lying to him, without telling the whole truth because he didn't know it.

Back at the ranch, they rode the dusty ranch roads with Cutt in his pickup, checked on a pregnant heifer and doctored one horse with Navicular disease and another with distemper. The steaks were excellent, the conversation and stories of old times relaxed. Tee went to bed at the same time as his son. He did not want to get into a deep conversation with his father-in-law.

In his old room and bed, he smelled Sarah on his pillow. Hand on Jubal's chest, he imagined his family together again.

On Sunday, Tee felt the pain of withdrawal as soon as he eased his arm out from under Jubal's head. He sat at the breakfast table with Cutt and watched the sun rise. Both wanted to talk about Sarah, but neither could find the right words. After a breakfast of buffalo steak and eggs, the three of them rode horses down to the river and examined Concho's burial site.

Tee stayed until dark, hoping he could outlast Jubal and the boy would go to sleep, and that Sarah would come home so they could talk. But Jubal reached up and clung to him as Tee pulled the sheets under his chin. He sat on the bed, the child's arms around his neck, and gently rocked back and forth until he returned to sleep about the time it started to snow. Cutt's expression showed sympathy as well as blame as he followed Tee into the yard. Snow accumulating on his hat brim, he watched as Tee threw his suitcase in the trunk. He leaned against the big mesquite that dominated the yard and waited for Tee to come to him.

Tee walked over and shook Cutt's hand. "Thanks for letting me stay with you, Cutt. You were right. It did make it easier all around. And thanks for taking care of my son."

"He don't want me raising him, Tee. You know that."

"I'm searching for answers. Sarah ever say a word about coming back home?"

Cutt picked up a small rock and threw it hard. "Not a word. She's about as talkative as her mother was. And I don't mind telling you I'm sick and tired of being left in the dark."

"Don't want to hurt her or you, Cutt, but this can't go on."

"Don't see how any squabble could be serious enough to break that boy's heart."

"I'll be back in two weeks."

Tee suppressed the urge to cry out as he crossed the tracks and headed east. Desperate and confused, he prayed for guidance. When he reached Amarillo, he turned toward Father Bob's church.

THIRTY-SIX

FATHER BOB COUNSELED HIM ON THE NEED TO SAVE HIS marriage until midnight, leaving Tee no time to drive home and change for work. He grabbed a few winks in the Harborcraft parking lot. As sunrise illuminated the small corporate logo, Harborcraft headquarters seemed a vestige of a bygone era, a grim reminder of a former life, a life when his family was together. Esther's face was the first he saw when he went inside, and her face filled with alarm when she saw him. Tee wondered what she saw, ran his fingers along his stubbled jaw. He was dressed in jeans, a slept-in shirt, and boots. She touched his arm as if he needed support to keep from falling, but said nothing.

Tee was trying to get his sea legs after being set adrift by losing his wife and son, to get his bearings so that he could function again on this, his turf. He found what he needed in his office—a stack of phone messages. He called Mike first, who seemed almost overcome with joy to hear his voice.

"Tee Jessup, tell me what's wrong."

187

"Over a beer. Needs to be a face-to-face conversation."

"You're on. When?"

"As soon as I return about twenty phone calls. Are there any fires to put out?"

"I can give you details over a beer, but word is somebody out there has it in for us. Suppliers tell me rumors are flying that our days are numbered. That one may be true, but a few others are just plain lies."

"I sorta got that same impression when I talked to the banks. Like they knew something I didn't." Tee had a strange feeling in the pit of his stomach again. Of course, he had not had a meal in over twenty-four hours. He had barely touched breakfast at the ranch, nothing after.

"Guess we need to do that beer about quitting time today."

"Not today. I need to sleep."

"Okay, then cookies and Cokes about three. I know Esther brought some in this morning."

"Done."

Tee returned his last phone call and made the decision it required before three. He had answered questions, started projects, made decisions, and given direction and comfort in over a dozen situations. It felt good. His adrenaline and energy were high, but he was weak from lack of food. Mike appeared with Esther in tow and a plate filled with chocolate oatmeal cookies.

Tee looked up and smiled. "Any milk in the fridge?"

They gathered around the small round table in the break room, knees touching. After four cookies and two glasses of milk, Tee closed the door. "Anybody wants coffee, they'll just have to wait." With that, he unburdened himself, telling them the whole story.

They were good, wide-eyed listeners who refrained from too much clucking or terms of sympathy. Esther seemed stunned, though her mind seemed to be churning. Mike spoke first. "So what can we do to help?"

Tee smiled. "You could tell me what to do."

At home, he called Jubal and went to bed.

Tee, Mike, and Buddy took a twenty-percent cut in pay and asked the same of all mid-level staff. Many resigned rather than suffer that. Buddy and Mike found a buyer for the California plant, and the sale netted enough to cover cash needs for a few weeks. Lew and Barry took a ten-percent cut but continued to take trips and to do extensive entertaining. Tee suspected they were using company funds to do their own job searches. He started ignoring their requests for reimbursement, claiming lack of funds. Both men seemed willing to let Mike and Buddy run the plants while Tee ran the corporate office. The two top executives offered no plans, no leadership, came in late and left early. When Lew demanded reimbursement for two months of exorbitant expense accounts, Tee called Jacob Locke.

An irritated Locke appeared at Tee's door two days later. "I fired Barry and Lew last night. A crew of professionals will be here this morning to pack up their personal stuff and change the locks. Don't let them on the property if they show up."

Tee was surprised. "And how am I going to keep 'em off? I might whip Barry, but Lew looks pretty tough."

"Not much to worry about. I agreed to pay a small pittance for their stock, which is worthless. They'll lose that if they set foot on the property."

"Have you got the authority to do that?"

"Their stock was non-voting letter stock, anyway. I hold the only voting shares now."

"What about their expense reports?"

"In the trash. Sorry it took me so long to do this. Looks like I made three errors in judgment when I threw in with those guys. I let my ego get in the way and delayed a decision that should have been made months ago."

Tee felt like a confidante of the older man. "You might have made four errors. I'm not having much luck turning this around. The canceled stock offering story is on the street. Suppliers are cutting us off or demanding cash on delivery."

"I heard. I'm promoting you to Lew's position. You can move into his office if you want to."

Tee let the rush settle over him, saw Lew's name come off the wall beside the door, saw his installed. But then he thought of the reaction of the rest of the staff. Now, he was a member of the team as well as its leader. If he took the title and moved into Lew's office, he might become the mushroom farmer Lew had been. "You said you let your ego get in the way. Moving down there would probably go to my head."

Jacob Locke smiled, and Tee knew he had passed a test. He felt good as he walked his mentor to the parking lot. The fear returned when Locke drove away.

The accounting department whittled down to Tee and Esther. She paid the bills, made the deposits,and balanced the checkbooks. Tee did the rest. For the first time, he began to understand how it all came together, how to really read the numbers, recognize problems, and see how the changes he and Mike had made were working.

It took Tee, Buddy, and Mike a month to set new prices based on real costs and honest purchasing procedures. Buddy ran purchasing from Georgia but encountered resistance from suppliers used to having their palms greased. Mike circulated among the plants, trying to streamline assembly lines and simplify the manufacturing process. He enjoyed some success, but holding on to skilled workers who smelled blood hampered things.

Billy Harbor took his twenty-percent pay cut without complaint. Tee sent him around to all the plants to do what he had done in the beginning—peel hundreds off a roll of bills and pay for truckloads of supplies. It seemed things had come full circle. Tee, Mike, and Buddy held telephone conference calls, plotted strategy, made plans, most of which were foiled due to lack of cash.

Tee presented a new business plan to their banks and renegotiated terms for all the notes that were coming due but could not secure additional working capital loans. He skirted around check kiting rules, trying to use the "float" between banks to keep checks from bouncing. A sale of the Oklahoma plant fell through, and Buddy said Georgia was too far gone to unload. They agreed to move the Georgia inventory to Texas and try to sell the real estate. They all spent their days putting out financial fires.

Three months after new prices were set, Tee, Mike, and Buddy met in Lew's office to analyze sales reports. Doublewide Doug Throckmorton had been gone almost six months, and the sales chart maintained its depressing march south.

Tee had already known the numbers were poor, but the line looked like a dove shot from the sky by the fat man himself. "Jacob Locke may have been wrong about some things, but he was right about one. Without Doublewide, there is no sales force. Hate to admit it, but the fat man was also right when he said, 'Nothing happens until a sale is made.'"

Mike studied the charts, trying to make the line head north just by looking. "It's too early, Tee. Our new product information is barely out there."

Buddy agreed. "The word will get out about how things have changed. I've had several suppliers tell me they're impressed by what we've done so far."

Tee laughed. "Yeah, but those are folks who sell what we have to buy. We need to hear it from people who will buy what we have to sell."

The southward march of expenses was encouraging, and the gap between sales and cost of sales had broadened. Everything was working according to plan. If Mike and Buddy were right about sales coming later, they might make it work.

As Mike and Buddy kept talking, Tee tuned them out, worrying about the meetings with bankers and suppliers in the week ahead, high pressure sink-or-swim occurrences. His two friends poked fingers in the air to emphasize points, marked up a new grease board with numbers and charts, laughed as they told stories of minor triumphs. He found solace in the light of enthusiasm that flickered in their eyes, the sense of accomplishment in their faces and voices. He realized he liked this job, that he might one day be good at it. He was happy at work for the first time since he stepped off his last horse, roped his last steer. He was essentially the president and controller of a small manufacturing company. He had begun to believe that he, Mike, and Buddy could pull it back from the brink.

He wanted to share those thoughts with his wife and son, but they were still gone. He had talked to Sarah only once. She told him she needed time to heal. To be patient.

THIRTY-SEVEN

CUTT'S VOICE SURPRISED TEE WHEN HE MADE HIS USUAL CALL to Jubal. "Hey, Tee. Sarah took Jubal into Amarillo to pick up a few clothes. She's late."

"Clothes? I should have brought more of his stuff when I came last time. Just hate to take it all out there. That's like saying he's never coming back home."

"I understand that. Want me to have him call when they get in?"

"Sure. Say Cutt, you do know I've been sending money, don't you? I don't want this be a financial burden on you. They're my responsibility."

Cutt chuckled. "She hasn't asked me for a cent. We're eating Blind River beef and canned vegetables from the ranch garden."

"Is Ford still okay with them being there?"

"Ford ain't been here in months. Still spending near all of his time in Dallas. He bought himself a little house close to that polo club he likes. Shuttles back and forth between there, a new cabin in the Sangre de Cristo Mountains, and Kentucky. Course, he still chases around the tracks a little to follow his racehorses but spends more time playing polo. Hardly ever see him around here."

"Hope travel with him?"

"She's been staying in the main house for quite a while. Came right after Sarah did."

"And Ford hasn't even come during all that time?"

"Nope, and that suits me. Seems to suit Hope. She's tried to make friends with Sarah, but my daughter won't give her the time of day. Hope's not what we thought she was at first. She's really just a country girl. Parents are farmers in East Texas. Figure Ford is running around on her. She seems lonesome, unhappy."

"Tell Jubal I called, will you?" Tee was about to open a novel when the doorbell rang.

Julia Cannon was a slim, willowy woman with brown hair and eyes. Tee had never seen her ex-husband, never heard him mentioned. She held out a covered dish. "Put this in the fridge and heat it up when you're hungry."

He took the plate. "You didn't have to do that, but I'm glad you did. I'm getting tired of eating out and doing grilled cheese sandwiches at home."

"Sorry to come so late, but this is about my fourth trip to bring over food. Can't seem to catch you at home any earlier. "

He looked over her shoulder at a car passing. He felt inhospitable for not inviting her in, but couldn't bring himself to do it. He wasn't in the mood for small talk. "Sorry about that. I've been working late a lot."

"I know you're having trouble, Tee, and I understand. I want you to know I'm here for you and Jubal."

Tee noticed that she didn't mention Sarah. "You remember the day I came over and asked if you knew where they were? I got the impression you were holding something back."

"Well, I'm not sure, of course. But Sarah began asking me to keep Jubal a lot more a few months ago. She would leave at strange hours, especially when you were out of town. She told me to hide Jubal if anyone but her came and asked about him."

"You ever see her go off with anybody? Ever see anybody come over here? A man, maybe?"

"No, I just know she came over a few times and asked me to keep Jubal at odd hours."

"Sarah and Jubal are staying with her dad out west. She says she needs time to heal."

The silence grew uncomfortable until Julia shrugged and left.

He sat alone on the living room couch and thought about what Julia had said. Where did shy and retiring Sarah go, and why did she tell Julia to hide Jubal? It seemed inconceivable to Tee that she would cheat on him. It just wasn't in her. He walked around, opening drawers, picking up framed photographs. He went through her closets again and realized he did not recognize most of the clothes there. He was ashamed he had never really paid much attention to her clothes. But the house was full of her, full of her things, full of her smell, full of her memories.

He ran his hand over the oak dining room table they had saved for and selected together, been so proud of. He found their paltry supply of liquor left over from a party held more than a year ago. He picked up a bottle of cheap scotch and rolled it across his palm, feeling as if he were a jilted husband in a George Jones song. Right about now, he should be on his third bourbon and water. In their bedroom, he looked at the photographs taken during happier times, sat on their bed. He had the urge to clean it all up, to erase her, but then he saw a photo of all three of them. He could not erase that.

Jubal's soap smell still filled his room. Tee picked up his pillow and pressed it to his face, held his toys, opened the drawers to the small cedar chest where his clothes were stored.

Feeling the house closing in on him, he walked down the street, walked back, surveying the only home Jubal had ever known. He had always considered it a worthless piece of dirt. The idea of actually buying a house in a crowded neighborhood surrounded by urban sprawl had entered his mind, but was quickly discarded. The thought of owning something so distasteful made him cringe. Better to save your money and buy a piece of land out in the open—land that he and Jubal could enjoy. He and Jubal. Did his dreams include Sarah? Had she suspected that they did not?

The information from Julia changed things. He felt he had to bring things to a conclusion one way or the other. But he did not want a divorce. He wanted his family back. Sarah had taken his son five-hundred miles away and had never offered any rational reason as to why. He thought about getting a lawyer to advise him, perused the telephone book, but came away confused and feeling a little dirty.

The next day, Esther came into his office and slid a card across his desk. Tee picked it up and read: Stan Leftwich, Attorney-at-Law. Wills, Divorces, Civil Suits, Personal Injury.

Esther shrugged. "He asked about you. I told him about Sarah leaving and taking Jubal. He said he would be happy to help if you needed a lawyer."

Tee waved the card. "This has got to be a fake. I thought Stan was a CPA who lost his license. Now you're telling me he's a lawyer?"

"I think he voluntarily turned in his CPA certificate to keep them from taking it. Didn't want the investigation to go public. He never talks about that, but it had something to do with his time working for the Treasury Department. But he still has a license to practice law."

"The last time I saw Stan he was laying on the floor of that rat hole he calls an office covered in blood. And my little baseball bat was beside him."

"He's all well now, but I imagine he's still plotting revenge."

"Is he any good, or just a shyster?"

Esther shrugged. "I just know he has an IQ in the stratosphere and a photographic memory. That sort of makes up for the baggage he carries. And Stan said he might be willing to barter with you."

"Even your own daddy hates him."

"Theirs is a love-hate relationship that goes back a long way. I guarantee Stan is the guy he would call if he got into trouble." She hesitated in the doorway. "Look, I'm not giving you advice. Just trying to help. He may have some ideas about how to get your wife and son back."

Mike now spent almost all of his time running the two Texas plants, and Tee usually called him first thing every morning. As usual, Mike was upbeat. "We may pull this thing out, Tee. The lines are starting to roll, and we're kicking some nice trailers out the door to the finished lots."

"How about sales?"

"That salesman you hired is cracking a few. A lot of folks knew Doug was stealing, and they credit you for bringing him down."

"Me? That was you and Buddy more than me."

"Well, the whole company is coming out of the sleaze it's been in for a long time."

"I been leaning on you quite a bit because of my personal problems. That may get worse."

"A man has got to take care of family business. We'll hold down the fort."

He knew that he should have felt grateful when Stan agreed to see him on such short notice, but he felt uneasy. *What lawyer takes an appointment on the same day a client calls?* When Tee said he could be down on Deep Ellum in half an hour, Stan told him he did not use that office anymore, that he would meet him in Mansfield at five.

Stan, dressed in a tailored dark blue suit, white shirt with onyx cufflinks, and yellow tie, drove up in a black Lincoln promptly at five. Tee met him at the door and guided him back to his office. As Stan sat in Tee's tiny office, Tee admired the razor-thin watch with gold band, the diamond pinky ring, the coiffed silky gray hairpiece that looked new.

"Ever find out who clubbed you?"

Stan adjusted a cufflink. "I believe I may know the people responsible. The police were unable to find the actual perpetrator from the description I gave them. Of course, he hit me from behind, and I only got a brief look." The discussion seemed to leave a sour taste in Stan's mouth, and his expression said the incident was distasteful and shameful, best left forgotten, and never mentioned again. "Has your wife served you with divorce papers yet?"

Tee leaned back, tossed a pencil on his desk. "No. Never been mentioned. I just wanted to know what my options are."

"Describe your ideal outcome to this unpleasantness."

"I want to get my family back together. If she won't come back, then I want to play a big part in my son's life."

"Sounds like a man who doesn't really want a divorce. Has she denied you visitation?"

"Not yet."

"I could write her a letter on your behalf. Sometimes, a letter on legal stationery will spark someone to action. Or I could begin divorce proceedings. Get the jump on things, so to speak."

Tee felt a little rushed and more than a little embarrassed. "I may have wasted your time. I'm not ready to give up yet, I guess. How much do I owe you for coming out?"

Stan looked at him earnestly. "You have something I want. I'll represent you in the event of a divorce or in any legal proceedings regarding visitation rights or custody. I will waive my standard fee if you give me what I want."

"What do I have you could possibly want?"

"It is my understanding there is thorough documentation of certain crimes committed by one Douglas Throckmorton."

"Yeah. Not sure of the legal terms, but I sure believe he belongs in jail."

"Do you still have that documentation?'

"Not here, but I can get to it." Fearing Throckmorton might send his thugs for the files, he had rented a safe deposit drawer for his copy.

"I want access to it. I'll copy and return everything if you want it back."

"When?"

"As soon as you can get it. Call me and I'll pick it up."

"I can't think of any reason you shouldn't have it. I'll pick it up tomorrow and give you a shout."

Esther appeared at his door a few minutes after Stan left. He turned toward her. "Do you ever go home?"

"I did go home. Long enough to cook you supper and bring it back."

Tee was taken aback. "Well thanks, Esther. A man could never ask for better friends than you and Mike." He reached out for a hug of gratitude, the plate still in one hand. Her response was tentative, awkward, one-armed. Her touch, the feel of her, the femininity he missed, flooded his senses, flushed his face, worried him.

She brushed his cheek as she pushed him back. "Enough of that. I need to get back."

THIRTY-EIGHT

MIKE'S REPORTS PLEASED TEE, AND THE FINANCIALS SHOWED a small net income for the month, even a growing positive cash flow. He sent a copy to Jacob Locke.

Exactly four days to the hour after he left, Stan's Lincoln pulled into the parking lot. Tee and Esther watched from Tee's office as the tall man unfolded from the black car. "Where does he office now that he's not down in Deep Ellum?"

She smiled. "In that town car. You wouldn't believe all the stuff he has in there. There's even something he says is equivalent to a telephone."

"My lawyer works out of a car and talks on a CB radio."

Esther laughed. "It really is a telephone, not a CB. Laugh if you want to, but you would be surprised at the business he conducts out of that car. Sells life insurance for estate plans, too."

Stan appeared at the door before Tee could respond. He nodded at Tee and Esther. "Good afternoon. I came to pick up the documentation we discussed. My sources tell me that events unfolding now make my need for the files more urgent."

Tee dropped the last box of the Doug Throckmorton folders into the Lincoln's truck and slammed the lid. "Mind if I ask what you're gonna do with those?"

"Stan smiled. "I'm not at liberty to say right now, but I expect you'll find out soon. I guarantee no harm will come to you as a result of granting me access. And I will return them if you wish."

"Glad to be rid of 'em." Tee tried to see inside the Lincoln as Stan sat behind the wheel. "This your office now?"

"For the time being."

"None of my business, but is it true you sell life insurance, too?"

Stan smiled patiently. "I do a lot of estate planning. I sell insurance to wealthy clients to allow liquidity for paying their estate taxes."

Tee's gaze locked on the phone attached to the hump in the floor-board. Stan chuckled. "Yes, that is a car phone. The technology is still pretty weak, but it functions. I am in your debt. Call on me for any legal service now or in the future. If not a divorce, perhaps a will."

Tee smiled. "Thanks. I'll call you if I need you."

Esther followed him to the coffee pot the next morning, and he poured them each a cup. Tee lifted his cup in a toasting gesture. "Clear something up that's bothering me a little."

She sipped. "If I can."

"What the heck did Stan want with the Doublewide files?"

"One never knows what Stan is up to. You remember I told you some-body would pay for that beating he took? I still figure Doug Throckmorton had something to do with it."

"I still don't get why Doug wouldn't go away and Stan just forget about it. Why rattle each other's cage?"

She patted him on the shoulder. "You'll probably never understand a man like Throckmorton. Or Stan, for that matter." She started counting using her fingers. "One, he wants to get back at Daddy because he bested him when they paid too much for Harborcraft. Doug thought Daddy was a rube, and Daddy let him think it. Stealing the files that saved Daddy from big IRS fines or worse would have exacted a little payback. Doublewide felt like a knock on his head would be clear warning for Stan to stay out of his affairs. Two, Stan and Doublewide go back quite a long time. I think Doublewide may be the reason he lost his CPA license. And three, he left the bat there so you might get charged with assault. You already know why he has it in for you."

"So Stan figures to get his own revenge with the dirt on Doublewide. How?"

"You remember that old radio program where Orson Welles booming voice said, 'Only the Shadow Knows'? I used to call Stan the shadow. He's a complicated character. My guess is we haven't seen the last of Doug Throckmorton around here, and Doug hasn't seen the last of Stan."

"You think Doug might come back here for some kind of payback? What could he do?"

"Don't know. I just know he holds grudges. I've seen him do vengeful things. My guess is he's probably mad at everyone associated with Harbor-craft. This little company was his own private bank, and he hates having it taken away." She held up four fingers. "Also, number four, Jacob Locke never came to Doug's defense when Lew fired him, and it was Locke and Throckmorton that worked together to buy out Daddy and the other com-panies. Doug feels betrayed by Locke, Lew, and Barry."

Tee had thought his problems with the fat man were over. "Just what a company hanging by its fingernails needs—powerful enemies." He forced a smile. "On a brighter note, we might actually pull this thing up by its bootstraps. Make it hum again. Now that...that would be the ultimate revenge against Doublewide Doug."

THIRTY-NINE

TEE'S WEEKEND TRIPS TO VISIT JUBAL HAD SETTLED INTO A routine Tee found disconcerting—leave Friday at quitting time, arrive in Amarillo at midnight, take Jubal to breakfast Saturday morning, spend the rest of Saturday and most of Sunday fielding questions he could not answer from Jubal, leave at his bedtime on Sunday, work Monday with two hours sleep in the parking lot or no sleep if he went home to shower and change. His spirits were always low when he left on Sunday, but they cratered as he crossed the railroad tracks on this particular Sunday. He needed renewal, so he headed toward Father Bob's church.

He saw a light behind the etched glass of the rectory. A shadow told him someone was inside and awake. He had not talked to the priest in a long time, and the thought crossed his mind that he might not be alive, that the movement behind the glass might be a complete stranger. It was bedtime. If he left now, he would barely get home in time to dress for work. He knocked on the priest's door.

Father Bob's striped flannel pajama legs protruded from his black robe far enough to cover his bedroom slippers and drag the floor. When he lifted them to keep from stepping on them, Tee got a glimpse of skin around his ankles. He had never seen the priest dressed in anything other than priestly vestments that seemed to cover him from head to foot. He seemed less powerful, almost ordinary. "Sorry to bother you so late, Father."

The old priest's eyebrows were longer now, whiter, the lines in his face deeper. He looked sleepy as he ran a hand through mussed hair. "I'm afraid I dozed off while I was saying my evening prayers. I will ask God's forgiveness, and he will grant it to an old man. What a pleasant surprise to see you. Come inside, and I'll fix us some tea."

Tee sipped Father Bob's strange-tasting brew. Winona had been fond of it, the priest had said. The old man drew him out as he always did, skirting around the edges with conversation as boring as the weather, gradually delving into his personal trials and tribulations. Tee spilled his guts, feeling cleansed with each revelation about work, Sarah, and Jubal.

Father Bob expressed his disappointment and disapproval of divorce, urged him to continue his attempts to reconcile. Tee stared into his tea. "I never figured I would be a divorced man, never figured I would have to visit my son at another home. But I can't do much when she won't talk to me."

"Sometimes we have to sacrifice a little happiness for our children. Sometimes, we have to sacrifice everything for them."

"I understand that you know the Bible and mean well, but I really need hard advice." Tee stood and walked to a stained glass window. He pretended to study the etching.

"That's Christ in the Garden of Gethsemane."

Tee spoke without taking his eyes off the glass impression. "Sorry, I don't mean to be rude, but I've thought about it till my head hurts. I can't hogtie her and drag her back."

"Do you still love her?"

"I'm ashamed to admit I probably almost never showed it when we lived together, but now that she's gone, I realize I do love her. Her daddy has explained a lot of things I didn't really understand before. I think I could give her what she needs if she would give me a chance."

"Can you give her the security you say she seems to require?"

"Well, you know the doubtful outcome of my current job. That's sort of held me back from going to her on my knees." Tee dropped back into the soft chair in Father Bob's living room. "Look, you mentioned sacrifice. I am willing to sacrifice my life for my son, but what can I do now to keep him whole, keep him happy, and keep myself as his father from five-hundred miles away?"

Father Bob smiled. "You must pray." He held up both hands in a prayerful pose. "I know you want answers. Pray for them."

"I tried that. Look where it got me."

"It got you here, didn't it?'

Tee smiled. "Maybe it did." He leaned forward. "I hate to admit it, but I guess I don't know how to pray."

"Now we're getting to the problem. Tee, you have to give God permission to come closer. Try this mantra: Let go and let God."

"Let go and let God. But what if God doesn't?"

"You have to give Him your trust. Look, I know you well enough to know you have an organized mind—everything in its place, everything happening when it should. Am I right?"

"Never thought about it that way, but I suppose."

"Try to think of God's Universe as a well organized dynamic. Ask him to guide you to where He knows you need to be, and trust He will start work on helping you get there immediately."

"So, is he going to bring that about or am I?"

"You are. Think of yourself as a partner with God. When you sincerely ask, ideas and solutions, and people will start to come to you. You may not recognize it, but that will be God's Voice, His Hand directing."

"I wish I could believe as strongly as you do."

"Were you praying when you decided to stop by here?"

"I guess I might have been asking for guidance."

"And where are you? Can't you accept the possibility that God put you where you needed to be?"

"Did he put me into this terrible situation at Harborcraft?"

The priest chuckled. "The bonds of partnership between man and God cannot possibly explain why bad things happen. Our test is to examine them, pray, forgive, and move on."

Father Bob picked up his Bible. "Have you heard of the parable of the talents in the New Testament?"

"No."

"Read it. It's in Matthew twenty-five. The message in this story is that everything comes from God, and when God gives us gifts, we have a responsibility to use those gifts and make them multiply."

"What gifts?"

"Not everyone gets the same gifts. Learn how to recognize yours. Don't let them go to waste. Invest them. Invest in yourself. Don't bury them as one fellow did in the parable."

Tee stood and shook the old man's hand. "I'll read it. Like always, I feel better after talking to you. Confused, but better."

Father Bob laughed. "It will become clearer with time."

Tee looked at his watch as they walked to the door together, the priest's hand on his shoulder. It was after midnight. Father Bob turned the knob but did not open the door. "I have something that has helped me in prayerful meditation. Maybe it will help you, too."

He walked back to his desk, rummaged through two drawers, and returned with an eight-track tape. "It's old and much used. There may not be much life left, but it's yours if you want it."

Tee took the tape. The label was worn off. "What is it?"

"A beautiful rendition of "The Lord's Prayer." I seldom hear it without my own voice interfering. I can't resist singing along. It transports me to God's presence."

Tee was pleased he had replaced the Cougar's tape player. "Thanks. Can I buy it from you?"

"Think of it as a loan."

He seemed to be transported from the living quarters to the parking lot without any physical effort on his part. He stood there alone, doubting his ability to forgive, saw the light in Father Bob's quarters go out.

FORTY

HE WATCHED FROM HIS COUGAR AS EMPLOYEES FILED INTO the offices of Harborcraft. He had parked in the farthest corner beside some shrubs, under the shade of trees, hoping not to be seen. The catnap he had planned for a half hour had stretched too long, and now it was too late to shave and clean up in the office restroom before anyone arrived. He had driven all night and still smelled of horses from Sunday's ride. An hour of shut-eye had only made him groggy. He looked in his suitcase for his toiletry bag and realized he had left it at Cutt's. He wondered what had possessed him to stop here for a few minutes rest instead of going home, taking a shower, and changing clothes, wondered about Father Bob's advice about letting God put you where you needed to be. Had God put him here to keep him from falling asleep on the road? When he saw Esther walk past his office window, he went inside.

He grinned sheepishly as he stepped into the break room. Esther's hand paused in mid-air with a tablespoon of coffee grounds, her face registering surprise. "What happened to you?"

"Rode hard and put up wet."

"Lew would not approve of your appearance. Drive all night again?"

"Yeah. And Lew ain't here anymore."

"You look like you could use a cup of coffee."

Tee opened the refrigerator and found it wanting. "Suppose I could bum a piece of bread and make me some toast?"

"No, but I'll make you some. Got some jelly, too, if you'll share what happened this weekend."

Tee shared what he wanted her to know, leaving out any mention of Father Bob. He had never told anyone about the priest. He offered no details about Sarah, and Esther did not ask. He appreciated that. "Now, if I just had a toothbrush. Left my toiletry bag out there."

"How did you know I had one?"

"You keep a toothbrush at work?"

"Of course, I brush my teeth after lunch."

"Thanks, but I wouldn't do that to you."

"You afraid I have germs?"

"It's not that. Just don't want to ruin your toothbrush."

"When a person offers something as personal as her toothbrush, you don't turn it away."

He knew it was silly, an overreaction, but he felt a flood of tenderness. "Yes ma'am. I would be honored and grateful if you would loan me your toothbrush and a little toothpaste. I'll wash it with hot water when I'm finished."

"That's better. I'll get it."

"Don't suppose you got a razor and shaving cream?" Tee brushed his teeth, combed his hair, and made himself as presentable as possible before starting to work. Probably sent by Mike or Esther, a steady parade stopped at his door to kid him about his unshaven face, dusty boots, and jeans. Everyone seemed to know about his bi-weekly trips to the Panhandle and seemed sympathetic. His troubles and his willingness to come to work dressed so casually seemed to endear him to them. The stream of comments and laughter lifted his spirits, made him forget he had lost a night's sleep.

The latest financials were coming together, and he wanted to turn them over to Esther for typing before the day's end. If Jacob Locke approved, he planned on making a company-wide announcement of a reinstatement of all voluntary salary cuts. He was fading at four when he handed the financials and supporting schedules to Esther. Mike met him in the parking lot as he headed for his car and home.

"Hello, Cowboy. Leaving early, are we?"

"No sleep last night and not much the night before. You coming to see me?"

"Nothing that can't wait."

"You look like it can't wait."

"You talk to Buddy?'

"Yep. Said he was leaving this morning, trailing the trucks carrying what little inventory was left in Georgia."

"Well, he just called. Probably nothing, but he said the trucks were pulled over not more than fifty miles away from the plant. He figured it was a permit issue, but they're still hung up."

"Why didn't he call me?"

"Figured I knew more about permits and moving mobile homes, I guess. Plus, he figured you needed sleep, not problems."

"I guess everybody knows my personal business. So, what do we need to do?"

"You need to go home and get rid of those bloodshot eyes. I'll make some inquiries and update you in the morning."

His empty house seemed welcoming, somehow. Fatigue, he guessed. A shower was first on his mind, then food and bed. The doorbell rang when he stepped out of the shower, a surprising intrusion he found unwelcome. Still wet, he pulled on some clean jeans and ran to answer. Julia smiled when he opened the door, his hair and upper body still wet. Debbie stood next to her mother, examining the droplets running down Tee's chest. Tee dropped to one knee and took her hand. "Hey, beautiful. Guess who I saw this weekend." Tee really liked Debbie.

She clasped her small hands. "Jubal. When's he coming home?"

"Soon, I hope."

Julia handed over a covered rectangular aluminum foil pan. "Sarah told me you liked stuffed bell peppers."

Tee took the pan. "I sure do. I need to take you and Debbie out to eat to make up for this."

She nodded toward his nipples. "I can see you're losing weight. And you were already pretty skinny."

Embarrassed, Tee looked down at his upper body. "You think?"

"I can put that on a plate for you. Heat it up if it needs it. You have iced tea?"

"Not made. Been drinking Cokes."

She stepped around him and took the pan back, placed it in the oven. Things were awkward while she pulled out a plate and utensils and opened cabinet doors. "Napkins?"

Tee pointed toward a roll of paper towels. She pulled the dish from the oven and scraped the contents onto the plate. "Go ahead with your supper."

He was reluctant to eat while they were there but sat down and took a forkful. Julia kept up light banter while he ate.

He smiled when he put his fork down. "That was delicious. Sorry about the mess around here. I come and go at all hours. Just haven't had time."

More awkward quiet. Julia took Debbie's hand and led her to the patio door. "Mind if she plays out there a minute or two? She and Jubal used to really like playing in your back yard."

"Sure, but it's pretty cold out there." He flipped on the patio light.

"She's dressed for it." Julia closed the door and turned to face Tee. "I owe you an apology, I think."

"What for?"

"I thought something unhealthy was happening with Sarah. I should have told you."

"Do you know more than you've told me?"

"I know that she's frightened of something. When she brought Jubal to me at odd times, she was always extremely agitated, like someone was after her. I thought she was having an affair, but now I don't know."

The phone rang before he could answer her. Buddy's voice was strained. "Sorry to contact you at home, Tee, but you said to call anytime."

"Sure. What's up?"

"They confiscated all the trailers at the state line. Said we couldn't leave the state with any travel trailers because they got liens against 'em. Threatened to throw me in jail when I protested. Bank sent 'em. Said we were trying to sell out of trust."

"We don't owe the Georgia bank a damn cent. I consolidated everything with banks here."

"That's what I told them. But it appears Doublewide had duplicate paperwork on all the trailers and went down and mortgaged them again without us knowing it. Then he told the banks we were moving their collateral."

Tee made his signature clicking sound. "How did the bastard get that done?"

"He's fully capable of switching the ID plates and double mortgaging."

"Have they taken the trailers yet?"

"Just about to leave. They're forcing our truckers to take them back to some yard close to the old plant. Dollar against a doughnut it belongs to Throckmorton."

Tee sighed. "All I know to tell you is to follow them and see if you can find out. Sounds like we need a lawyer we can't afford."

Julia was still in the same spot when he hung up. Tee took her hand. "Listen, Julia, if you think of anything or hear anything, please let me know. I can't thank you enough, but I just got some bad news at work that I have to take care of."

FORTY-ONE

IN SPITE OF THE BAD NEWS FROM BUDDY, TEE COULD DO nothing at night, and he needed rest for the very bad day coming. Pure exhaustion closed his eyes for a few hours. Still not used to eating breakfast alone, Tee was at his desk an hour early the next morning. He was spilling coffee grounds on the counter when Esther and Mike walked in. Tee handed her the spoon. "My hands seem to be shaking this morning. You didn't know better, you'd think I had a hangover."

Tee turned to Mike. "You hear anything more from Buddy?"

Mike shook his head. "Same thing he told you last night."

Tee watched Esther put the filter in. "You think you could get in touch with Stan Leftwich for me? We may need him on this thing with Georgia."

She started the coffee percolating. "I called him last night after Mike told me. Says Doublewide Doug is making his move earlier than he expected. He's doing everything he can to stop him, but we may have to let Georgia play itself out."

"Play itself out? What does that mean?"

"I took it to mean Stan doesn't have all the ammo he needs yet to stop him."

Tee was on the phone with the highway patrol when Esther came in to tell him that Jacob Locke was on the other line. He hung up on the rude and useless law enforcement clerk and punched the button to talk to the company's owner. "Glad you called, Mr. Locke. We got trouble with the Georgia inventory we were moving."

"I know, but I'm afraid we have more troubles than that, Tee."

Tee braced himself. "What now?"

"Know anything about bankruptcies?"

"Never had any direct experience, but I left a couple of companies who were close to filing."

"I got a call this morning that a petition has been filed to force Harborcraft into involuntary bankruptcy."

Tee clicked. "Who filed it?"

Jacob named three companies who supplied Harborcraft with raw materials. "I thought you had negotiated deals with everybody."

"I did. But the three you mentioned were caught with their hands in our pockets. They paid kickbacks to Throckmorton. When I sat down with them, they readily agreed to be last in line for payments and to write down what we owed them by half. We have six months before we have to pay them a damn cent."

"You get that in writing?"

Tee sighed deeply. "No. They said putting it in writing might subject them to criminal charges. I agreed to forego a written agreement if they would write off half of what we owed. I thought I cut a great deal." Tee waited for the rebuke. None came. "I figured if they reneged, I could bring charges."

"I've pulled out all the stops to get to the bottom of this, Tee. Looks like Throckmorton has finagled a couple of director positions for himself. He's on the board of one of these creditors. He also turned a big deposit into a seat on the board of one of our banks."

"Three creditors. That's all it takes to force bankruptcy?"

"If a debtor owes them a lot and is seriously behind, three's all it takes."

"What can we do to fight it?"

"We have twenty days to appeal."

"What happens then?"

"Chapter Seven, involuntary liquidation."

"Can we go ahead and file for Chapter Eleven? Won't that give us a chance to reorganize?"

"Too late for that once this involuntary thing started."

"Mr. Locke, we're almost out of the woods here. I sent you financials this morning. This company is really above water."

"Yes, and your team has done a hell of a job. Those financials might help us beat this, but my attorney says not to get our hopes up. Most Chapter Sevens go full steam ahead."

"So, we give up?"

"No, document all the agreements you made with the banks and the criminal stuff on those three creditors. I'll let you know more in the next day or so."

"Will do."

"And Tee, you can't let anybody there know. They'll leave like rats from a sinking ship."

Tee spent the rest of the morning pulling together and organizing what Locke had asked for. Esther gave him strange looks but complied with each request for data without questions. By late afternoon, Tee decided Locke's admonition to keep things secret did not include Esther and Mike. And he didn't really care if it did. He needed their help and their moral support. He called them into Lew's office and told them.

The three of them huddled for the rest of the day in a misery-loves-company meeting. Recriminations were plentiful: Why did we not catch this sooner? How did Locke allow himself to be deceived by an obvious con artist like Doublewide Doug? Why did they not press charges against Throckmorton? Why did the CPAs not recognize the firm was selling products at below cost right away? Those things seemed obvious in hindsight. Wallowing in self-pity, Tee called Buddy. He usually gave him a lift when he needed it. But Buddy took the news even harder than they had.

At closing time, Mike brought in a bottle of scotch and poured a jigger in three coffee cups. Esther made a face when she downed hers, Mike savored his. Tee did not pick his up. "Never drink to feel good when you feel sad, only to feel better when you feel good."

Mike smiled. "I don't need an excuse to drink good scotch. I like the taste." He stood, poured himself another jigger, raised the cup. "To Harborcraft. May she rest in peace."

Tee leaned back in Lew's chair. "Yogi said it ain't over till it's over."

Mike raised his empty cup. "Tomorrow, then, the battle begins. I'm going home to my lovely wife." He took a few steps and turned back. "Sorry, Tee. That was insensitive of me."

Esther and Tee stared at the emptying parking lot, heard the footfalls of departing employees, wondered aloud and silently how many of them had already heard. When the sounds of silence filled the building, Esther reached for the bottle. "How are things going with Sarah?"

She wished she could take the question back when she saw Tee's expression change from smiling to gloomy. He shook his head. "Nothing's changed."

FORTY-TWO

WHEN TEE WALKED IN THE NEXT MORNING, THE SENSE OF gloom was pervasive. Bankruptcy proceedings have a way of getting out on the street through court clerks. He had to violate Locke's instructions. In a standing-room-only meeting in Lew's office, he told the corporate staff and all the plant managers and supervisors the truth and instructed them to relay the information to their personnel. "Anyone with questions can call me. We are in this to the end. A fight to the finish."

The reaction surprised him. Their initial despair and fear quickly turned to aggressive anger. The employees wanted to fight. Fist-shaking, back-pounding enthusiasm erupted. They wanted to save their company and their jobs. Tee was rejuvenated.

They worked double shifts seven days a week for fourteen days, pulling together all the supporting documents that seemed to prove conclusively that Harborcraft was a viable enterprise and that the three companies forcing bankruptcy were corrupt. The data were undeniable. Even with conservative sales forecasts, the cost-cutting, improvements in manufacturing, and adjustments to sales prices were going to result in positive cash flows and profits as far as the thirteen column pads they used for analysis would reach. The company would be completely out of debt in four years and ready to expand with more plants, people, equipment, and products. The entire company gathered in The Still to celebrate what they saw as a bright future after all the documents were delivered to Jacob Locke and the attorney representing them in the forced bankruptcy proceedings in Fort Worth.

Tee sounded and felt upbeat as he announced the findings and forecasts that had been presented to support their case. "I think we have a really good shot at saving this company. But just in case, I'm going to hand out checks that get everybody paid through the day of the hearing, including accumulated vacation time. I am asking you to hold them until we find out the results of the hearing. If things go well, I'll ask for them back."

On the day of the hearing, they gathered at The Still again. Tee had expected a wake-like atmosphere, but it was celebratory. They brought in pizzas and beer at noon, figuring the longer the hearing lasted, the better their chances. Everyone expected it to be over my mid-morning. After lunch, the mood turned somber. At two, the loud shop buzzer reported a phone call. Tee answered a wall phone covered in sawdust. He found a box to stand on after he hung up.

He held up his hands, palms down, to get them quiet. He tried to look in as many eyes as he could before he spoke. His voice came out squeaky, and he cleared his throat. "That was Jacob Locke on the phone. He said to thank you all for the effort you put forth. It was exemplary."

Mike shouted from the front, smiling. "Exemplary's a big word, Tee."

"Big word for a big-hearted group of people. I am proud to work with all of you, to be part of a tremendous team." Quiet then. Everyone knew what was coming. It was all over Tee's face. "They ruled against us, folks." The roar was instantaneous, shouted questions as to why, curses.

Tee held up his hands again, begged for quiet. "I wish we could commiserate, regroup, fight back, but we have about an hour to get our personal possessions off the property. Constables and officers of the courts are on the way now. You're not supposed to know this, not supposed to be warned, but you deserve to know. They're afraid you'll start taking company property, and I can't say I'd blame you if you did."

Tee paused to steady his voice. "But I'm asking you not to. Get your personal stuff, put it in your cars, and move off the property. Jacob Locke said that when the padlocks go on, getting your personal stuff, even your cars, might be delayed."

The crowd began to stir after a minute or two of stunned silence. Many stopped and asked Tee if they could cash their vacation checks and thanked him for writing them. He told them to take them directly to the bank. In ten minutes, everyone except Esther and Mike had dispersed. They studied him, waiting to see how he would react, what he would say. Tee sat down on the box and looked up at both of them. "Something bad wrong with a world that lets a bunch of crooks shut down a viable, going concern full of hard-working people."

Billy Harbor walked through the open shop door. Tee waved him over. "Didn't see you in the crowd. If you got any personal property here, better get it."

"I heard. I got all my stuff when I sold this outfit. Nothing I got here is worth taking home."

Mike watched as a few employees parked and came inside to load up their personal belongings. "What now?"

Tee pointed toward corporate. "Now, we've got less than an hour to get our own stuff and move our cars. We can park over here after that since there's no gate to lock."

Tee and Esther walked down the hall, passing tearful employees carrying boxes. Tee looked in his office, opened his briefcase, and threw in everything that belonged to him. The only thing of value was a small portable calculator that seemed to fit him better than any he had ever used. He was pleased he had hung nothing personal on the walls.

He passed Esther with her two boxes on his way out and took one. "Where did everybody come up with boxes so quick?"

"From the grocery store dumpster half a block away."

"You drive today or walk?"

"Walked, unfortunately."

"Okay, throw your stuff in my car, and I'll park in your driveway."

Mike watched them from The Still and walked over. "Okay, we got our stuff. What now? Tell us exactly what Locke said."

"About the only thing he said was what I told everybody. He sounded shocked himself. Said he would call me at home tonight after he meets with the attorney. "

Mike looked at him as if he expected more. "So, we're just S.O.L.? We're screwed after all we put into this business?"

Esther shrugged. "Looks like it."

Mike flailed both arms. "I need to take a swing at somebody."

Tee smiled. "I know the feeling. Want to go over to Doublewide's house and drown him in his own swimming pool? I understand he can't swim."

They sat around Esther's table and wallowed in self-pity and recriminations for an hour. She fried some eggs and ham. When they finished eating, there seemed to be nothing left to say. Mike clinked his fork against his empty plate. "For the first time since I can remember, I got nowhere to go in the morning."

Esther rested her chin in her hand. "I'll miss seeing both of you. You made working here fun. I hated it before you both came."

The gravity of what happened had dawned on Tee. He had no income to support his family and could last only a few months. He rose suddenly. "I have to get home in case Locke calls. I don't expect a thing to change, but I want to hear what he has to say."

FORTY-THREE

LOCKE'S VOICE WAS STRAINED. "THE FIX WAS IN, TEE. DOUG Throckmorton is better connected in Dallas and Tarrant counties than I ever imagined. This would never have happened on my turf. As you know, our case was strong. But the judge's mind was clearly made up before we walked in."

"What about the three crooked suppliers? How did he get them to file?"

"Fellow outside the courtroom told me Throckmorton convinced them it was the only way they could get their money. Said he would see to it they were first in line when they start liquidating."

"I read up on this a little. Don't they have to show we were misappropriating assets or squandering money before they can force bankruptcy?"

"Their attorney represented that we were stealing travel trailers and other inventory with both hands. They cited the Georgia debacle, saying we were moving stolen inventory across state lines. They had pictures of trailers parked in front of employee houses but offered no proof they were stolen. At least one of them was not even a Harborcraft product."

"Was Throckmorton there?"

"No, but you could feel him behind the scenes. Probably waited in the judge's chambers. I'm sure he arranged the whole thing."

"Is there an appeal or are we done?"

Tee thought he heard a light moan. "He outsmarted me, Tee. I owe you and all your fellow employees an apology. I never botched anything this badly before."

"Apology accepted, but I don't know if I will ever see those other folks to pass that on. Are we kaput or not?"

"We are. It would be sending good money after bad to go against a stacked deck. What are your plans?"

"I got no plans now."

"I advise you to spend this time doing a lot of soul-searching. Decide your purpose in life."

"Time? What time? I have a wife and son to support. I have to have a job. And I'm afraid this wonderful experience working for drowning companies is wearing a little thin."

"Trust me, you'll appreciate it later. As for time, I did get one concession out of today's hearing."

"What was that?"

"I got you a job working for the bankruptcy court."

Tee was angry and miserable as he waited in his car by the padlocked gates an hour before normal office hours the next morning. He was there out of curiosity more than anything else. And he wanted to sit down with Esther and find out her plans. Locke had arranged for Tee to work during bankruptcy proceedings until all assets were liquidated and the proceeds distributed to creditors. That could take six months, maybe a year. His salary was scaled back to what he had made at Wellstone. He felt like a traitor, like he was sliding back in time, but decided he had to take it until he could find a real job. He called Mike and Esther to get their opinion. Both approved, but he thought he heard a little resentment in their voices.

He watched as the constable wordlessly opened the padlock on the parking lot gate, then the one to the building's main entrance. He handed Tee two duplicate keys and left. Inside, Tee was overcome with despondency. The offices already smelled like an abandoned building. He picked up the phone and got a dial tone, then walked the eerily silent halls. Wind whistled down the halls; the doors and walls creaked as if the building were dying not from loneliness, but from a heart attack. It made sounds as if it were trying to fill its lungs with air, to take a decent breath. In Barry's office, he found Bo, the mouse that Barry had regularly fed bread crumbs, lying dead on the floor. Tee took Bo outside, dug a hole with his pocket knife, and buried him. It seemed as if he was burying his last job and all the people he had worked with.

The phones were ringing when he walked back in. Most calls were from friends and family members of employees who didn't know Harborcraft was no more. Tee explained the situation at least a dozen times before he started telling them to call home numbers. He fielded calls from angry creditors that he had negotiated deals with, made promises to. He decided to call the others instead of waiting for them to hear the news from the court. Some understood and accepted his apology; others felt he had betrayed them; one offered him a job interview in Chicago. Most accepted the inevitable with resignation, as if they knew Harborcraft had been circling the drain for quite some time, that vultures had been hovering. The company and everyone who worked there were now part of the distant past, an unpleasant memory. There was no time for a funeral, or even a eulogy, only a trip to the landfill of failed ventures.

Tee was having some cheese crackers and a Coke at his desk when an angry short man built like a fire hydrant with bushy red eyebrows and steel wool red hair appeared in the hall outside Tee's office. "You Jessup?"

Tee nodded warily. All doors had been locked behind him, even the parking lot gate. "And who are you?"

"I been trying to call here all day. You ain't supposed to be on the phone, and you been on it all day. Supposed to wait for a call from me."

"Like I said, who the hell are you?"

"I represent Bryan Ketchum. He represents all parties to this bankruptcy. They call him a referee. All you need to know is, he's the one signs your paychecks." He pointed to the phone in Tee's office. "That phone will stop ringing tomorrow. We cancelled the number and installed a new line. It's to be used for court business only. We'll be calling regularly to see if you're here. You need to answer."

The man's manner was not exactly rude, just matter-of-fact. If he had been in a better mood, Tee might have found it amusing. "And if I'm not? Am I allowed to leave for lunch, for example?"

"Lunch is twelve to one. We won't call during that time."

"Can I go to the bathroom? What if I'm out in the lot?"

Fireplug ignored the question. Tee pressed. "And what am I supposed to do, exactly?"

The man handed Tee a folder. "All the instructions are in there." He turned on his heel and left.

Locke had told him he would be working with a bankruptcy referee. The legal forms said it would be Tee's job to keep records of the orderly liquidation of all Harborcraft assets. The court would decide who bought what and when, and for what price. Tee's job was to prepare monthly reports on forms that would be provided and submit them to the court. He would not be paying any creditors or handling any money. The logistics of how he would perform these duties were not made clear, only that most of the finished trailers, homes and campers would be brought to the corporate parking lot and lot beside The Still. Raw materials, furniture, and other assets would be auctioned onsite at a later date.

Tee spoke to himself. "So my job is to sit by the phone and wait for instructions." He left a few minutes after two, allowing enough time to get to the bank with his paycheck. The teller told him that all of Harborcraft's bank accounts had been frozen within minutes of the court ruling. All the checks he had written to the employees had bounced. He folded his and put it in his shirt pocket, a souvenir to remind him to never be so naïve again.

He stood at the door with the padlock in one hand, the key in the other at quitting time. He could not wait to get to Esther's, to hear a friendly voice. But she didn't answer his knock on her door and her car was gone. Tee drove home to an empty house.

The next day, he wandered the halls again, found coffee still in cups, some with little chunks of curdled milk floating, half-eaten sandwiches and donuts being attacked by ants. He emptied all the trash cans that had begun to smell, sat at every desk.

At lunch, he picked up a copy of the *Dallas Times Herald* and *Fort Worth Star Telegram* for his job search. He tried to concentrate on the want ads, but couldn't. He made a call to the *Amarillo Globe* and had them send him a subscription form. If he had to change jobs, he might as well find one close to his son.

Half a day in, he knew that working for the court would drive him crazy. Finally, he heard a familiar voice when he picked up the phone. "Hey, I know where a man might get hooked up with a good lookin', one-legged woman if he's of a mind."

Buddy's voice lifted Tee. "How did you get this number?"

"I have my sources. What's it like working in a graveyard?"

"This is worse than a graveyard. It's a damn mausoleum. Never had an experience like this. You?"

Buddy sighed. "I can only imagine what it's like to be totally alone in a dead business."

"Ghosts are walking around. Seriously, I'm having a hard time keeping my head up. What are you gonna do?"

"Been helping the one-legged woman run her restaurant and motel. I helped get Throckmorton out of the picture, and we're partners. I got my eyes on a second motel."

"You're kidding. You and Nadine?"

"Yep. I guess you could tell I was always kinda fond of her. When she heard I was out of a job, she proposed it."

"Marriage?"

"No, just a partnership, but who knows?"

As they hung up, Tee wondered if he would ever see his good friend again. He dialed Esther's number. No answer. The day lasted at least a week. Tee locked up at five minutes before five and went home to an empty house again. He dialed Esther. Her hello sounded tired, and Tee was tongue-tied so long that she almost hung up. "Just checking in to see if you're okay."

"That's nice. I've been interviewing for jobs all day. And I'm working part-time for Stan again until I can find one."

"Where? I thought he let his office go."

"He rented me a car. I picked it up today and will drive it to Georgia. There's a chance I might go to some other states, too. I never traveled much, so it sounds like fun."

"Doing what?"

"I'm sworn to secrecy."

"Where in Georgia? And why not fly?"

"You know the Shadow. He's got funny ideas. I may be bringing back some stuff he doesn't want to check to baggage on an airplane. Says I have to keep it my sight at all times."

"Dangerous stuff or illegal?"

"No, just important." Her voice softened. "But it's nice of you to ask. Enough about me. I feel sorry for you over in that empty building. Don't think I could stand it."

"Are you sure you're okay with me working for the enemy?"

"Of course. You have a son to support. I'll call you when I get back from Georgia. I'm not coming over there, but maybe we can have lunch one day when I'm home."

"When will that be?"

"I truly don't know. If I see Buddy down there, I'll say hello. Listen, I've got to pack and get to bed. Talk later."

FORTY-FOUR

TEE TRAVELED TO SEE JUBAL AGAIN OVER THE WEEKEND, BUT
Sarah left the ranch before he arrived. Cutt was jubilant because Tee was
there and because it was raining for the first time in almost two months.
Any rainfall in that part of the country was always welcome, but it left
Tee and his son confined. They had their breakfast and drove around
aimlessly. Tee bought Jubal a new pair of boots in Amarillo. They treated
Cutt to an early supper in Dalhart.

Back at the ranch, Cutt and Tee sat on the porch and watched the
rain slow to a drizzle. They talked about old times while Jubal ran back and
forth, acting two years younger than his age. It seemed to Tee that he had
regressed, changed, and not for the better. He made coyote noises at the
end of the porch as Tee turned to Cutt. "What's got into him?"

"He's acting out. Sarah's spoiling him, letting him get away with stuff.
And he doesn't understand what happened."

Tee walked the length of the porch and back. "This can't go on, Cutt.

The boy needs both parents, but Sarah won't even speak to me. Hides. Won't take my calls. I'm at the end of my rope."

"I still can't take your side against my own daughter, but I'm beginning to believe he would be better off with you. Sarah's in some strange frame of mind now. Course, you might have a tough time without a job."

"I'm still drawing a paycheck from the court." Tee wanted to change the subject. "Been seeing a light on at the main house. Ford over there by any chance? Maybe he might change his mind and give me a job taking care of his racehorses or something. I could be close to Jubal that way."

"Ford's still in Dallas last I heard, but his wife is there. She's been here almost as long as Sarah has, but Sarah won't make friends with her."

Tee frowned. "I can't get used to a woman living over in that big house all by herself. I'm not too surprised that Ford is neglecting the ranch, but leaving his wife here is strange."

"Well, I'd rather have her any day than him. She's actually trying to learn how the ranch works."

Tee grinned. "If I didn't know better, I'd say you were kinda sweet on her."

Cutt shook his head slowly but did not smile. "If I were ten years younger, I might be. Somebody needs to take her away from her worthless husband. Somebody about your age."

Tee gave him a quizzical look. "She's at least five years older than me."

"I didn't mean you. Hell, you're married to my own daughter."

The phone rang inside, and Cutt trotted to answer. In a few minutes, he stepped back outside. "Speak of the devil. She wants to talk to you."

Tee felt a surge of hope. "Sarah?"

"No. Hope Donovan."

"Mr. Jessup?"

"Yes."

"Hope Donovan, Ford's wife." He heard something akin to fear in her voice.

"What can I do for you?"

A long silence, a deep breath that sounded like she was gathering courage. "I guess Cutt told you I'm on the ranch. I need to talk to you before you go back."

"Okay. Shoot."

"Do you mind if we talk in person? It's not something that should be discussed over the phone."

Tee was wary, but curious. "Okay. Where and when?"

"I can meet you in the yard over here when you're ready."

He would not have recognized her if he had seen her anyplace else. Hope sat at a wrought iron table in a wrought iron chair under an outdoor umbrella that was no longer needed. Two steaming cups of coffee sat on the table.

A few pounds heavier than when he last saw her, she was dressed in Wrangler jeans and matching jacket, both worn threadbare. The long blonde hair he had admired at his wedding was pulled back in a ponytail. She wore no makeup, at least none he could detect, but she was still attractive. Her eyes were red and her chin quivered as Tee sat beside her.

Cutt had told him she was not what they thought, but Tee still suspected she had married Ford for his money. "So what's this about? Is Ford okay?"

She wrapped one delicate hand over a wrist and squeezed. "Ford is fine. I don't know where to start."

"How about at the beginning? You're starting to worry me some."

"Suppose Cutt told you I've spending a lot of time on the ranch without my husband."

"He mentioned it."

"I don't want to burden you with my own problems, but I can't help but notice that you and Sarah are also living apart."

"That's right."

"What I am about to share with you is very private information. It's going to be hard for you to believe. I ask that you hear me out before judging me."

Tee took his first sip of coffee. It was still hot. "Fair enough."

Hope's hand shook a little when she set her cup down. "Let's begin with Maggie Ledbetter, Sarah's mother and Cutt's wife."

Tee's shock showed. "What about her?"

"I believe Ford is responsible for her death."

Tee leaned back relieved, thinking he had a hell-hath-no-fury-like-a-woman-scorned lady on his hands. "You're mistaken. Maggie died in her sleep at home."

"Cutt said she died from sadness. Did you know there is a condition called broken heart syndrome that can really cause heart problems? Ford caused Maggie to die just as sure as if he strangled her."

"What are you talking about?"

"Ford is a very sick man."

"I thought you said he was fine."

"Physically, he's never been in better shape. But he's mentally ill."

Tee discerned the reason for the meeting. Hope and Ford were divorcing, and she needed Tee to help separate him from a share of the Donovan fortune. Someone to corroborate her story, someone also scorned. "Look, I can't get dragged into your marital problems. I got enough troubles of my own."

"Please hear me out."

Tee readied himself to hear some type of bizarre tale, her way of getting revenge on Ford for infidelity. "Go ahead."

"Ford first raped Maggie when he was eighteen and she was forty."

Tee let that soak in as he stared into the black liquid in his cup. He tried to remember what Ford looked like at eighteen and what Maggie looked like at forty. The vision came of a middle-aged woman and a small boy. "First? You mean there was more than once?"

"There's no way to tell how many times but certainly more than once. He's got some sick attraction to meek and needy women. Makes him feel powerful. He thought he saw that in me, but I am not like Maggie."

"Cutt would have killed Ford with his bare hands if that were true."

"Cutt didn't know. He still doesn't."

Tee was incredulous and didn't try to hide it. "Maggie would have told him right away. And how do you know this if Cutt doesn't?"

Hope's expression turned ominous. "Your mother told me before I married Ford. She took me aside the first time I met her and warned me about Ford. I'm sorry, but I thought it was some sort of devious scheme to keep me away from the Donovan fortune. I thought Winona saw me as a gold digger."

"No reason for her to do that. She had no claim to the Donovan fortune."

"But I didn't know that back then. After we married and I found out some things about Ford, I asked Maggie."

"You came right out and asked her? And what did she say?"

"I tried to be delicate, but she knew what I was suggesting right away. She stared at me with the wildest eyes I have ever seen. She started to hyperventilate. I thought she was going to faint. I hastened to apologize, tried to calm her down. I finally had to go outside and leave her alone."

"She never answered?"

"No. But I thought she might have a heart attack and die. The desperate look in her eyes told me the answer."

"So, how does that prove what you're saying? I still can't believe Maggie would have kept this a secret from Cutt. I also don't believe my mother would have told you her friend's secret."

"Your mother was a fine, strong woman who was simply trying to protect me without hurting Maggie. She swore me to secrecy and never imagined I would tell Maggie."

"None of this makes any sense, but let's say you're telling the truth. Mother might not have told Cutt, but she would have certainly told Daddy, and Daddy would have told his best friend. He would probably have even told Earl Donovan. They would have seen to it that Maggie was protected and that Ford got what he deserved."

"See, that's what I thought. That's why I didn't believe Winona. But consider this: if Cutt knew, he would have probably killed Ford and gone to jail. From what little I know of your daddy, he would have helped Cutt kill him, and they might have both gone to prison. Either way, Ford's daddy wouldn't have believed it and would have fired them both."

Tee moved the handle to his cup, but left it where it was. He remembered John T saying that Earl had a blind spot when it came to his son. "But still, Mother would have told somebody, even if it was the sheriff, just to protect Maggie."

"Would she? I thought so then, but I don't think so now. Your mother knew Maggie better than anyone, and she knew that having this revealed would have been devastating to a deeply insecure woman like Maggie. Plus, she would never have admitted it and certainly never testified to it in court. That would have left your mother out in the cold and your daddy out of a job."

"So what made you decide it was true? Ford brag about it or something?"

Her face flushed. "Believe it or not, I was pure when we married. Ford made me swear to it, and I told the truth. I thought it was sort of sweet of him."

"Don't see what you're getting at."

"On our wedding night, Ford couldn't . . . you know."

Tee saw her face flush, nodded to indicate he understood.

"He blamed me, said I wasn't a virgin. But I was."

"So, you never. . . ."

"On the last day of our two-week so-called honeymoon, I was in a public cabana on the beach by our hotel changing out of my swimsuit. He came inside the women's bathhouse, ripped off my clothes, and took me by force. Anyone could have walked in."

Tee's eyebrows shot up. "Maybe he was just trying to make it exciting."

She shook her head almost violently. "I tried to think that at first, but I knew better. Rape is rape. In all this time, we've never had sex any other way. He has to hurt me, dominate me."

"I never heard of anything like that."

"I don't know if you know this, but I'm a registered nurse. I don't claim to be a psychiatrist, but I made it my business to find out who I had married. I think Ford is a sadist or something akin to that. As for Maggie keeping it a secret, some people have an obsessive need for security. They will sacrifice everything for it. Maggie would not dare risk Cutt's job by telling on Ford."

Tee felt a chink in his armor of doubt, but it was still too incredulous to accept. "I just can't believe that anybody could keep something like that to herself."

One hand on top of the other on the wrought iron table, she leaned forward. "Ever heard of traumatic bonding? Sigmund Freud?"

"I've heard of Freud."

"He says a victim may identify with her attacker. It's a way for the ego to defend itself. There was an incident in Stockholm where people were kidnapped and kept in a bank vault. They began to identify with their captors. Same thing sometimes happens with battered women. They keep coming back for more."

"Maggie might have been shy and retiring, but you're basically saying she was insane. Not to mention what you're saying about Ford."

"Maggie was deeply disturbed. But Ford is the most insecure man I have ever met. He has everything going for him, but he cannot handle any relationship where the other party might be as strong as him. He has to dominate. From things he's said, I think his father was cruel to him."

"So why tell me all this?"

She made a tent with her fingers. "I filed for divorce. There's not much you can do for me, but I think I might help you."

"How's that?"

"By telling you to protect your wife and Jubal. He's such a sweet little boy."

Tee stiffened. "What does that mean?"

"Ford had a deep obsession with Maggie until she died. Sarah is a lot like her mother, so it's possible he may have an obsession with her."

Tee leaned forward and put his arms on the table, shook the coffee cups enough for some to spill. "What exactly are you saying?"

"He spends most of his time these days in Dallas. I know he went to see Sarah a few times while she was there. I don't know if they ever really got together. I suspect Sarah is fighting to stay away from him, to keep him away from Jubal, and to keep you from finding out."

Tee thought about what Cutt had said about Ford staying in Dallas, had a vision of Sarah leaving Jubal with Julia in a state of panic. He stood. "She would have told me."

Hope's face showed doubt. "Remember Maggie. She never told."

Tee stood and shivered slightly as if he could shake off the filth. "Thanks for the warning."

They walked toward the yard gate together. "I didn't mean to upset you, but I have held this inside until it's eating at me like a cancer. There are several reasons why I'm staying at the ranch, but Sarah is one of them. Ford won't come here as long as I'm here."

"How can you be sure?"

"I've got a restraining order against him. The judge allowed me to elect this house as my primary domicile. And just in case, I have a private detective watching his movements. If he heads this way, I will know. Your wife and son could not be in a safer place. They were not safe in Dallas."

He extended his hand to her in a gesture of partnership. She took it. "I should tell you one more thing for your own protection and because I think you need to know. I want you to try and stay calm because this is going to upset you. Can you do that?"

Tee made no such promise.

"Ford wants a child, a boy, someone to pass his legacy to. He has this perverted idea that he can be a better father than Earl was to him. When I didn't conceive, we were both tested. He's essentially sterile but won't accept it. Blamed me."

"So he can't have a child?"

She nodded. "The news devastated him, so he refused to accept it. Please don't take this the wrong way, but he says Jubal is proof the tests were wrong."

Tee felt the blood run to his face, warm his entire body. "You mean he's saying that Jubal is his? That he attacked Maggie and Sarah, mother and daughter?"

"Not in so many words. But he said if he had a son, he would look exactly like Jubal. He wanted me to think Jubal was his son. It sickened me to hear another perverted attempt to shore up his shattered virility. If it wasn't so evil, it would be pathetic."

"So how do I get in touch with Ford in Dallas?"

Hope reacted as if he had slapped her. "I can't tell you that. I didn't tell you this so you could go look him up and get yourself arrested for attacking him."

"I just want to talk to him. See what his side of the story is."

She shook her head. "Sorry. I do promise to let you know if he comes anywhere near Sarah."

"That's assuming your private eye is watching him around the clock."

Tee tried to calm his anger as he walked back to Cutt's house. Hope's tale was hard to believe, and he still suspected her motives, especially after she refused to tell him how to contact Ford. He broke into a trot as he returned to Cutt's house, feeling an urgent need to see his son. He passed Cutt, still sitting on the porch, and found Jubal in the barn. He watched Jubal carry on a conversation with Judson. He examined every feature. He was a duplicate of his namesake. But he still had to confront Ford.

Back on the porch, he sat beside Cutt in silence for a few minutes until Cutt finally leaned forward. "Well, how long you gonna keep me in the dark?"

Tee looked across the prairie, gathering a lie. "She said you told her I was good with numbers. So she wants me to go over all of Ford's holdings and figure out what she's got coming to her."

"Seriously?" Never meant to get you mixed up in a mess like that."

"Cutt, I need to talk to Sarah. She won't take my calls and goes off to hide somewhere when I come out here. I know you know how to get in touch with her. Please tell her I need to talk to her. I think we can work things out."

"You know she sold her car?"

"She sold her car? What's she driving?"

"Been driving my truck."

"Why would she do that?"

"Said she needed the cash. She's sort of a hoarder, like her mother."

"That makes no sense."

Tee experienced conflicting feelings toward Sarah as he drove home Sunday night. Perhaps she had been frightened all this time. That would explain some of her erratic behavior. Maybe she moved away to protect her son and herself, not because she wanted to end their marriage. But where had she gone when she left Jubal with Julia?

His feelings toward Ford were not conflicted. He began to plan for the confrontation.

FORTY-FIVE

TEE CALLED FORD'S POLO CLUB THE NEXT MORNING FROM
Harborcraft but got no answer. He found a Plano phone book but there was
no listing for Ford Donovan. When he called the club again after ten, the
receptionist refused to acknowledge that Ford was or ever had been a member until Tee manufactured an emergency. She took him through a litany of
what seemed to be scripted questions designed to protect members' privacy.
Tee was able to prove he knew enough about Ford for the receptionist to put
him on hold. After a long wait, she told him that Ford was out of the country
on a hunting trip and was not expected to return for several days. She refused
to give a private number or address. But Tee knew someone who could find it.

He noticed the Mustang in Esther's driveway as he returned from
lunch. He had just picked up the phone to call her and ask for Stan's help
in locating Ford when the first mobile homes arrived in the parking lot.
Tee spent the rest of the morning logging as inventory arrived in a steady
stream. He filled in the serial numbers on the court forms he had been
supplied and compared them to his inventory records.

He was still logging when Esther walked on the lot. "Been trying to call you. I see now why you didn't answer."

"Yeah. Sorry. Looks like this is gonna go on all day. Are you busy tonight?"

"No. Come on over after work."

The homes and trailers stopped their steady stream an hour before quitting time. There was barely enough room to walk in the lot. Billy Harbor's camper tops, some warped and bent from abuse, were stacked haphazardly on top of each other. He didn't want to seem eager, but there was no place to go, no reason to stall, after he locked the gates. He wanted to freshen up, but the round trip home and the shower would take almost two hours. Fireplug had asked Tee to park his car on The Still's lot to make room for another travel trailer, so he walked to Esther's house.

He saw her through the screen door, the first time he had ever seen her in jeans. A black, loose-fitting sweatshirt complemented her skin and eyes. He knew that long deprivation from the touch of a woman was affecting his thinking, and she might as well have been dressed in a revealing nightgown. He could smell hamburger steak smothered in onions before he opened the screen door and knocked on the door casing. Hot meals were another deprivation he had suffered from far too long. She stayed by her skillet when she saw him and waved him in with one hand. Inside, he stood awkwardly, unsure what to do with his hands.

She took no pity on him, just gestured toward a small kitchen table big enough for two. He sat down, feeling a little woozy from missing lunch. She lifted the steak and onions onto a platter and spoke without looking up from her work. "You feel good and want to feel better?"

Tee didn't understand the question.

She opened the small refrigerator. "I remember what you said about drinking. You know, never drink to feel good when you feel bad, only to feel better when you already feel good. I picked up some beer this afternoon in case you feel good."

Tee felt dangerously close to losing control of his emotions and didn't want alcohol to make things worse. "Rather have iced tea if you have it."

She set two glasses on the table filled from bottom to top with ice cubes drenched in iced tea. A sprig of mint floated on the ice and tea, a lemon slice carefully split across the rim. She had to reach across him to set down her own glass. Her hair smelled like shampoo and supper. Their knees occasionally touched under the tiny table as they ate.

He borrowed her phone to call Jubal and she heard snippets of their conversation while she cleared away the dishes. It was awkward when he returned. They have never been at a loss for words when Harborcraft had been alive, but now, the conversation seemed shallow. She said she couldn't talk about her work with Stan, and she didn't want to hear about Harborcraft. That was in the past, and it made her both mad and sad to remember.

He declined her offer of coffee, asked to stay where he was when she beckoned him into the living room. "I like sitting here." He had developed a rational story to explain why he needed Stan's help to find Ford and was about to begin when she sat down beside him. "We have to have a serious talk."

Her look disturbed Tee. He was not prepared for more bad news. "Sure, what about?"

She sat stiffly, hands clasped, and seemed reluctant to move her hands or body. "Circumstances sort of changed our relationship, Tee. Would we even be having supper if Sarah had not left you? Would we still just be co-workers if Harborcraft was still alive?"

"I'm not sure I understand the questions."

She moved the lemon wedge around the rim of her glass. Her eyes were shining with the beginnings of tears but did not overflow. "I looked forward to seeing you every day. Our relationship was sort of developing at a natural pace...a comfortable pace. We were becoming good friends. Nothing more. Then, all of a sudden, you're separated. Right after, the company goes down. Now, we seem to be pushed along by circumstances."

"So that worries you?"

"I don't know. I can't explain it, but I wanted it to flow along naturally, like a gentle stream." Her face colored a little.

Tee chuckled softly. "So what would have happened if that little stream had turned into roaring rapids before Sarah left me?"

"I thought about that, too. See, I can never be a home breaker. I would never have stayed in the stream if it came to that. Been there, done that. I wanted us to row our own boat. Now it seems like somebody else has the oars."

She ran water over an ice tray, pulled the lever, and filled their glasses with fresh cubes. "I know that makes absolutely no sense."

Tee liked her fingers touching his ice cubes, enjoyed the depth of the conversation. "I think I see what you mean. You wanted our relationship to bloom naturally, not be driven by events that threw us together."

"Exactly. Yes, and I wanted it to be, I hate to say the word, but pure. But I'm not so dreamy-eyed that I see stars. I know you're vulnerable now, that you have needs that are probably not being met. I don't want us to be pushed along."

"You feel like I'm rushing you into something?"

"Not at all. I sense that you want your family back more than anything, that you're miserable without them, that you still love your wife. I want you to know I can't and won't interfere with that, but I also don't want to get hurt in the process."

"Understood."

"There are some things about me that I feel the need to tell you. I don't have any really close women friends, and I need somebody to talk to. I have to warn you that you may not want me for a friend after I tell you."

"Then maybe you ought not to tell me."

They talked till midnight at the kitchen table, then moved to the living room couch. By four in the morning, Esther had revealed her life story. Pregnant at sixteen, she had lost the child at five months and could never have children again. She had never married the father. Shook was a made-up name; she was still Esther Harbor. The pregnancy caused the end of her parents' marriage and her mother to leave home in shame. She had not seen her since. She occasionally dabbed at tears but told the whole story without breaking into sobs.

"So, I'm damaged goods not only in the moral sense, but I also can't have children."

He had remained silent while she told her tale, listening carefully, avoiding any expression that might seem negative. "I don't see you as damaged goods. And I am grateful you honored our friendship by sharing this with me."

"I messed up early on when I was a kid and could never un-ring that bell." She brushed her arm against his. "Nobody can undo what's been done. It robbed me of my childhood. I know I'll never get that back, but I want a chance to do it right."

"Is that why a pretty girl like you never married?"

She flinched slightly. "I dated some men, but I never got close enough to a single one to tell them my story. Guess I was afraid they would run, not walk, away from me. And I was not strong enough to deal with that rejection."

She stood and stretched. "So you see we're both wounded soldiers in the war of love."

"I have a little darkness in my own past to share with you, too, but we'll save it for another time."

FORTY-SIX

TEE GOT STAN'S PHONE NUMBER FROM ESTHER THE NEXT morning and called him. Within hours, Stan confirmed that Ford was in Australia looking at ranches to buy. He also provided a private number. Tee called every day but got no answer. He spent most of his time at work writing letters and sending out resumes. Almost all of them went to Amarillo and the few towns within a hundred miles of it. Leaving out Dallas and Fort Worth narrowed the potential employer list dramatically. When the response was tepid, he feared his job-hopping history had caught up with him. His one defense against Sarah's complaints had been that he had always been aggressive enough to find a job. He was reading another thanks-but-no-thanks reply when he saw Grady Allison tapping on his window. Tee waved him toward the main door and went down the hall to open it. Grady handed him one box and reached for another on the ground.

"So what's in the boxes? Thought I had seen the last of audit files."

"You still got any conference tables?"

"Same as always. Head toward Lew's office."

They unloaded twelve hardbound books, six ring binders, and twelve spiral-bound books. Grady stepped back to admire the stacks. "I heard you were out here minding the bone yard. This is something that can make your time useful and keep you from pulling your hair out."

Tee picked up one of the hardbound books. "CPA exam for 1970—Practice Portion." Just holding it made Tee's stomach turn. "Must be a few hundred dollars in materials here, Grady. You selling?"

"It's a long story, but I don't have a crying dime in this stuff. Could be worth thousands to you, though."

Tee was touched, but suspicious. "You really think I could pass that thing?"

"About eighty percent don't pass all four parts the first time, but that doesn't mean you can't. There's practice, law, audit, and theory here. Practice is the long one. Two parts and tough."

He picked up one of the law books, and Winona's voice brushed past his ear. He could not make out what she said. "Mother always said I could be a lawyer, but she didn't want me to because she didn't like lawyers. When's the next exam?"

"Three months, but you need to apply right away. I can help with that."

Tee's eyes widened. "Listen, Grady, I can't thank you enough, but I sure hate for this stuff to be wasted on me."

Grady opened one of the ring binders and withdrew an application. "Fill this out and follow the instructions. I've already filled in the experience requirements. I'll help if they question it."

"I don't want to sound ungrateful, but why?"

"You can thank Jacob Locke. Well, gotta go." He stuck out his hand. "Call me if you need any help with that application. There's some good tricks about studying in that ring binder. How to use mnemonics and acronyms, for example."

"I don't even know what those are."

"You will soon. It's a way of taking the first letters of the words in a list and making a common sounding name or word with them. Helps you remember a long list of rules."

They shook hands. Tee awkwardly patted him on the back as he left. "I'll be sure and thank Mr. Locke, but I appreciate your help, too. You sure I can't pay you at least something?"

"You can pay us all back by using it."

Tee was grateful, but could not keep from feeling he had been given a tough assignment, a challenge he did not want. He spent the rest of the day thumbing through the past exams, looking at the terrible questions. He knew few answers. By the end of the week, he walked the halls, carrying a book, sounding out acronyms. He concentrated on law first because he figured it would be easiest. He was talking to himself, reciting statistics and facts when he heard a knock on his window. He looked out to see the smiling face of Mike Clayton.

Tee met him at the front door with two folding chairs. "Let's sit outside. It's too damn depressing in there." Tee didn't want Mike to come inside and find out he was studying for the CPA exam.

"It's warm enough, I guess. Looks like you went back to your cowboy roots."

Tee wore boots and jeans and had not had on a tie since the second day. "Don't see any sense in dressing up when you never see anybody."

Mike handed him a bottle of Johnny Walker Red. "I know you don't drink much, but I thought you could use this on special occasions. I work for a liquor and wine distributor now, so you need to take up drinking. I need the business."

"No kidding. You're a traveling salesman. Well, you'll be good at that." He held up the bottle and let the sun sift through the amber. "Thanks, Mike. I may have to turn this thing up if things keep going downhill."

"What are your plans?"

"Looking for a job close to where my wife took my son. Not having any luck."

"Figured you to be gone by now."

"Me, too."

Mike made a half circle with one arm to indicate the inventory on the lot. "You know I still have a few contacts in the industry. They tell me the vultures are circling this bone yard. They say you need to get out."

"What does that mean?"

"You missing any houses or trailers yet?"

"Hell, I don't know. I don't bother to count 'em every day. Lot seems still full. What do they mean about vultures?"

"The boys who forced us into bankruptcy. They plan on getting first choice beforex everything gets auctioned. They want all their money back, not twenty cents on the dollar."

"How?"

"One old boy I used to work with said bankruptcies are usually corrupt, nasty proceedings when you have a bunch of inventory like Harborcraft. The lawyers involved, the judges, and referees take their picks of the good stuff. Then whoever greases their palms gets second choice. The honest creditors get what's left."

"Locke told me Doublewide organized the forced liquidation. Did your friends say anything about him?"

"His name came up. You still got those files on him?"

"Stan does. You still have your copy?"

"My wife put the box out with the garbage. Better hope Stan has your copy in a safe place. And you better watch your back around here. I wouldn't show up at all at night."

"You really think they'll come in here at night and start taking stuff?"

"I heard it had already started." Mike pointed to a silver trailer parked less than a hundred feet away from where they sat. "Where did that Airstream come from?"

"I never even noticed it. Wasn't here two days ago."

"Looks like the swaps and stealing have already started. Course, I'd rather have that used Airstream than most of the new trailers here. This old stuff made before we took charge is mostly junk."

Tee grabbed his inventory and a clipboard, and they walked the lot. They found two empty spots. Mike pointed. "See how they moved things around to make it look like nothing had been disturbed. They'll get more flagrant as time goes by."

Tee found the missing units on his sheet. "They got good taste. Two top-of-the-line travel trailers."

"And they'll be handing out those camper tops like Crackerjacks. No way to trace 'em."

Tee was embarrassed to have been so naïve. "Not sure what I can do about it unless I start being a night watchman."

"I'd file a written inventory at least once a week with the referee to cover your ass. He's probably supervising the handouts, but at least you'll have cover."

"It's really no skin off my nose if they steal the whole damn lot full, but I hate to see the suppliers who stayed with us get screwed."

"I don't want to cry wolf, but I'd get that little .22 pistol you showed me and keep it handy. Throckmorton may be worse than we thought. I hear he's dangerous."

"You serious?"

Mike shrugged as he brushed off his black slacks. "Here's my card. Next time I'm in town, I'll drop by and take you to lunch. Got an expense account now."

Forty-Seven

ESTHER FOUND A JOB AS A TELLER IN A LOCAL BANK AFTER SHE
tired of the subterfuge and travel involved in working for Stan. She and
Tee talked a lot, laughed a lot. It helped cool his rage at Ford and abate
his impatience to confront him. Tee truly enjoyed her companionship, and
he tried his best to think of her only as a friend, his best friend. When he
found things getting out of sequence, he always tried to imagine Sarah's
face, what it would be like when she returned. He was building a relationship with a woman his son did not know, hundreds of miles away from
where he lived. He felt he had no right to be happy apart from Jubal. And
he still loved Sarah.

Tee's nights at home alone became almost unbearable after spending
his days alone in an empty office building. His calls to Jubal every other
night had become difficult. He could hear doubt and frustration creeping
in. Sarah spoke to him only when she had to discuss something about their
son. When she did, she seemed frightened and cut him off when he tried
to discuss their future together. Frustrated, he demanded to know when he

could bring Jubal back home for an extended stay. She panicked and could not speak. Cutt took the phone from her and told Tee he was concerned she was about to suffer a nervous breakdown.

Tee was two weeks into studying the theory portion of the exam, walking the halls and reciting answers to sample questions that might appear on the exam when he felt, rather than saw, someone in the building. He turned and saw Fireplug coming up the hall toward him. Then he felt the mobile home move, the floor creak, as Doublewide Doug filled the hall.

Fireplug stepped into the small room that had been Esther's office and leaned against the door frame as Doublewide advanced. "I see the pencil jockey still can't find a decent job. Still hanging on like a parasite."

Tee thought of the pistol in his desk. He folded his arms and leaned against the hall wall, tried to look casual. "Looks like I'm not the only parasite in the building. One's just a lot fatter than the other one. Is it true that elephants throw peanuts to you at the zoo?"

Doug's lip twitched slightly. "You got two boxes with my name on 'em around here. Where are they?"

"Don't know what you're talking about."

Doug made a slight signal to Fireplug, who started going through the offices. Tee went to his office, opened a drawer, and slipped the pistol into his waistband at the small of his back. He pulled his shirt tail over the pistol and followed Fireplug room to room. Fireplug found two boxes hidden behind the doors of Lew's built-in bookshelves. The boxes were covered with garbage sacks. Fireplug withdrew one and carried it to Doug. Product Cost and Price Analysis was written on all four sides and the top of each box. Throckmorton and Tee had the markings stamped into their memories. Doug looked at the box, smiled at Tee. "Thought you didn't know what I was talking about."

"You said boxes with your name on them. Don't see your name anywhere on those."

"Pretty stupid of you to keep this stuff around here. Course, it don't matter much now, anyway. Does it?"

Tee smiled back. "Not to me. I already proved you're a thief and took this company down. Taking the evidence doesn't change a thing."

"How did that work out for you, kid? Look around you. You're a caretaker at a graveyard, and all those people are out of a job. My guess is a loser like you is having trouble finding work. Else he wouldn't be hanging around here suckin' on a dry tit."

Tee felt adrenaline and rising anger and walked a little closer, keeping one eye on Fireplug. "Is it true that those horns on your Cadillac belonged to your mother?"

Doug stopped smiling and took a step toward Tee. Tee fingered the pistol. Fireplug's snigger broke the tension. Doug laughed out loud, piled the second box on top of the first one that Fireplug was holding and they both walked out. Tee watched through the window as they dropped the boxes into the Cadillac's trunk and drove away.

Esther got Stan on the phone for Tee that night. "Doublewide came for the boxes today, just like you predicted."

"Good. He'll feel safe now and start to come out from behind the curtain. Our rather large friend has an almost irrational fear of tight spaces, and the prospect of spending even a day in a jail cell terrifies him."

Tee felt better. "What if he looks inside the boxes?"

"You credit him with too much intelligence. He's cunning like a jackal and ruthless, but not very smart. Even if he does look, he won't know what he's looking at."

Stan paid Esther to take regular walks beside the bone yard at night, always carrying a flashlight, a small .38, and a camera Stan had loaned her. Her vigilance was rewarded after a week of such walks. From dark shadows, she saw and captured on film Fireplug and two men in suits examining the motor homes and travel trailers, concentrating on the most expensive models. Stan had provided a picture of the bankruptcy referee and two of his lieutenants, and Esther recognized one of the men when he stepped inside a motor home and turned on the interior light. The home was missing the next morning. Tee mailed a written report of the missing motor home and put a copy of the report along with the photos of Fireplug and his friends in his Cougar.

FORTY-EIGHT

TEE SAT IN THE CAR AND LOOKED AT THE ENTRANCE TO THE Dallas Convention Center. He had spent the better part of three days inside the round building, almost twenty hours, answering exam questions. He was mostly numb, unsure of what he should be feeling. It was in the mid-thirties, and the light mist coating his windshield threatened to freeze. He had told nobody he was taking the CPA exam, not even Esther. Grady Allison might know he had applied to take it but not that he had actually followed through. He couldn't believe it himself. He knew he had nailed the law part and felt good about theory, not so much about audit and practice. He would get no credit for passing just one part. Applicants had to pass at least two or retake the whole thing. He pushed against the steering wheel, easing the tension from his shoulders. Nothing to do now but wait. Results would come in the mail in about two months.

His self-imposed isolation for a week before the exam and for the three days taking it had felt almost liberating. He had told Esther he was traveling on job interviews and had told Fireplug nothing. He expected to feel relief, like celebrating, but he didn't feel either of those things. Celebrate what? He might have failed. Tee needed Friday night and the weekend alone to shore up the energy required for a return to the mausoleum, time to contemplate what had happened and what it might mean. He knew Saturday would bring sadness, just as it always did on the weekends away from his son.

Monday morning, he found little changed at Harborcraft, but he had changed. He had to push his legs to move down the lonely hall. The old building's stale smell had gotten worse, and it seemed as if the ghosts of former employees and dead mice were haunting the place. His job search had come up empty. He punched in Jacob Locke's number and waited, wondering what Fireplug and his bosses would say about the unauthorized long distance call. Locke's voice was weak. Tee was hesitant. "Mr. Locke, this is Tee Jessup."

"I think we have known each other long enough for you to call me Jacob, Tee. How did the exam turn out?"

Tee knew it would be a waste of time to ask how he knew about the exam. "Guess I'll know in about two months. I think I passed law." The silence was awkward, and Tee felt a need to fill it. "Learning the tax rules sure turns you against the government, doesn't it? What an unfair, corrupt mess."

"You don't know the half of it. Wait until you're really victimized by the byzantine tax laws and corrupt bureaucrats."

"I need a job, and I'm having trouble finding one. This court work has about run its course." Tee told him about the theft and corruption of the process.

Jacob was not surprised. "Document everything. As for a new job, I have had my feelers out but nothing so far. You should know I am sort of out of the loop. My influence has waned."

"Because of Harborcraft?"

"No, because my kidneys are failing me. I am not expected to live out the year."

Tee could think of no satisfactory reply. "I'm really sorry to hear that. And I'm sorry to have bothered you with my troubles." When they said goodbye, Tee sensed their connection had been severed forever.

Tee called Esther at the bank to let her know he was back. She seemed distracted, distant. They met at El Chico's for supper. Taking her out to eat was Tee's clumsy attempt at an apology for his absence and lack of contact. Few words passed during the meal. At her house, the chill continued. Tee knew he had to do something to warm things up. "Okay, I've been out of pocket for over a week. Should have told you beforehand. Friends don't do that sort of thing to friends."

"Where were you?"

"I told you I was looking for work."

"That doesn't hold water and you know it, Tee, and it's not the first time you've been untruthful with me."

"What are you talking about?"

"I poured out my heart to you. Told you about my sordid past, everything. I left out nothing. You didn't reciprocate."

"I don't know what you mean."

"So you're telling me there are no major events in your life that you didn't feel comfortable sharing with me?"

Tee didn't answer, and Esther knew there was no turning back. "I know, Tee. Did you forget I worked for Stan part-time? He checks out everybody he has serious dealings with. I know what happened to your family, to you. Why couldn't you have shared that with me? I gave you plenty of time."

Tee stood and put on his coat. "I never told much of anybody about what happened. It's my cross to bear. I don't want pity, and most of all, I don't want people analyzing everything I do or don't do based on something that happened when I was barely out of high school."

Esther's eyes were wet. "You think I would do that? After all this time, are we not close enough for you to trust me? I trusted you."

He removed his coat, sat down and told her the whole story, leaving out his continuing contact with Father Bob. When he finished, he felt restored. "Guess that's why I can act a little strange sometimes, why I'm drawn to the sounds of trains. The singing of the rails, the rattling of trestles, the whistle. It's all like a song. Like my family calling me for help."

"Do you have bad dreams about it?"

"The nightmares slowed when Jubal was born. One spook still occasionally follows me."

"Thank you for telling me. It helps me understand a few things."

Forty-Nine

THE PHONE WOKE TEE ON FRIDAY MORNING BEFORE DAYBREAK. Her voice quivered with urgency. "This is Hope Donovan. I think you need to come out here."

He sat up in bed. "What's wrong?"

"How soon can you be here?"

"Damn it, Hope, tell me what's wrong. Is Jubal hurt?"

"No. Jubal is fine. But I got a call yesterday from my detective. He lost contact with Ford when he left the country and thinks he may be headed this way. I had him served with some papers Tuesday that probably upset him."

"You think Sarah and Jubal are in danger?"

"He's probably coming to try and throw me out of his house. But you need to come anyway. Something has gone south between Cutt and Sarah."

"What went south?"

"I went over yesterday to warn Cutt that Ford might be coming and there might be trouble between him and me. Asked him to stay close. I

257

can't really describe what was going on, but that house was frigid. You could cut the tension with a knife, and Cutt had been drinking. Sarah seemed too despondent to carry on a conversation. She's jaundiced, and she's down to skin and bones."

"Did you tell Cutt so he knows to keep them both close?"

"I can't really get over to him the urgency of things without telling him what I told you. He's out tending to some first-calf heifers he doesn't want caught in this storm."

"Could you go over and stay with Sarah and Jubal till I can get there?"

"Be better to bring them over here. I don't think Ford will break the restraining order by forcing his way in."

"I'm on my way." Tee hung up and tried to call Cutt or Sarah, but there was no answer.

He called the airport to book a flight to Amarillo. All were delayed due to an approaching winter storm. He threw some clothes into a bag and left in the Cougar at daybreak. Late winter rain and drizzle hit his windshield as he left Grand Prairie. It turned into sleet outside of Wichita Falls, then to blowing snow and near blizzard conditions at Quanah. He pulled under the canopy of a closed service station when he could no longer see the road. Snow and ice had started to accumulate under the Cougar's chassis that he knew might strand him. He coaxed some hot water out of a bathroom faucet and dislodged as much as he could with a tire tool. He knew the roads might be impassable if the snow continued to fly. When he pulled out, Johnny Rodriguez crooned from the tape deck, "We're over, but we still can't say goodbye." He didn't want it to be over.

———————

Maggie had left her diary in an old cedar chest, inside a concealed pocket of a ragged quilt, a place she knew Cutt would never look. Sarah discovered it a day after moving in with Cutt when she took the quilts out to a clothesline to work them over with a quilt beater. She felt the hardness of the diary with the second blow to the ragged quilt. She unhooked the tabs and removed it, assuming it was something left from Maggie's childhood, something she might read to Jubal when he was old enough to understand the thoughts of a little girl. It was a cheap little thing, covered in brittle, cracked red plastic, the edges worn down to the cardboard underneath. She put it on a table beside her bed to read on a rainy or snowy day.

Jubal cajoled her into letting him go out on the porch to watch the first sprinklings of snow. She bundled him head to foot and let him outside on the condition that he stay on the porch. The weather made her think of the diary as she brewed a fresh pot of coffee. She retrieved it from the cedar chest. It wasn't a little girl's diary; it was a mother's diary, and Sarah shivered more with each page, became more nauseous with each word. She felt unfit to use the inside commode, so she ran outside in the snow to cleanse herself, to expel the bile and poison in her system. She had known of her own horrors but not of her mother's.

Jubal watched as she retched. "You sick, Mama?"

Sarah scooped a handful of snow from the porch rail to wash out her mouth. "Must have been something I ate. You about ready to come in?"

"Nope. Can I go out to the horse barn and check on Judson?"

"You know better. This could turn into a blizzard before you know it. You might not find your way back." It was not an exaggeration. John T had strung a line between the barn and house years ago after getting lost in just such weather.

She made him come back inside, gave him a biscuit and jelly left from breakfast, and coaxed him into watching television from the couch. She went back into the bedroom that had been Tee's and opened the diary again. Her mother's writings became more and more rambling as the date of her impending death drew nearer. Sarah was near that time in her reading when a knock startled her. A knock on the door of an isolated ranch house in the middle of desolate country in bad weather is a rare thing, and it seemed to Sarah that it was the grim reaper himself, come to exact the punishment she had coming. She looked through the kitchen window and saw Hope standing at her door in a hooded wool jacket and down coat, stomping one foot and then the other.

Sarah was almost glad to see her and managed a smile when she opened the door. She closed the living room door to filter out the sounds of the television and the two women sat together at the small kitchen table, sipping coffee, the diary between them. Hope reached across and covered Sarah's hand with her own. "It's none of my business, but I couldn't help but notice you and Cutt weren't getting along the other day."

"He's been after me to go back to Tee. Says I have to at least talk to him or Tee will give up on me. I think Daddy loves him more than me."

"I see. Well, as someone in the middle of a divorce, I can't very well give advice, but I think Cutt may be right about at least talking to Tee."

"You don't understand. Talk would make it worse."

Hope gave her a sympathetic nod. "I don't know Tee that well, but maybe you're misjudging him. Give him a chance."

Sarah filled their cups. "You don't know how bad my situation is, the unforgivable things I've done."

Hope put her hand on the diary and Sarah pulled the diary close to her chest mumbling, "My mother's diary from when she was young."

"I see. Look, Sarah, I didn't come here to scare you, but you need to know that Ford may be on his way out here."

Sarah's eyes immediately filled. She pressed the diary to her chest and tried to screw up courage that had eluded her all of her life. "Daddy might need to know that, but I don't see what that has to do with me."

Hope scooted her chair closer and put her arm around Sarah. "Sarah, I know what's probably in that diary. It's all right."

Sarah's eyes widened. "What is it you think you know?"

"I know that my husband has been harassing you for years. I know that he has some type of perverted attachment to you. I found out more than a year ago. I don't blame you for it. Ford is a sick man."

Sarah began to sob. "I wanted to be faithful to Tee. Ford said it would be just the one time. I said no. Then he threatened to tell Tee that Jubal was his son." She stopped and held up a hand as if giving sworn testimony. "God as my witness, I never broke my vows until after Jubal was born."

"I never met Tee's brother, but I'm told that the boy is his spitting image. I know for a fact that Jubal doesn't belong to Ford."

"I know that, too. Ford does, too, but he seemed to develop some sort of unnatural connection to Jubal. Brought gifts by the school, came to our house at all hours. I had a hard time keeping it from Tee. Ford promised to leave Jubal out of it and not tell Tee about our past if I did what he asked."

"So you did?"

Sarah's voice broke. "Yes."

"Did he keep his promise?"

"After the first time, he stayed away for a while. When he came back, he threatened to take Jubal and go to another country. Australia, he said.

Asked me to go with him. Said we could take care of him better than Tee and I could. Someone with as much money as Ford might actually take him and we would never see him again."

"Did he rape you every time?"

Sarah's face flushed as if she had been struck. "He was always violent. I will never tell anyone about all the things he made me do. But we always began with a pretend kidnapping. He made me walk along some street in a bad part of town and would drive by and force me into his car. You can imagine the rest."

Hope nodded. "You don't need to give me details. Believe me, I know." She took both of Sarah's hands in hers. "I want us to be friends. You can help me, and maybe I can help you, but right now, we need to prepare in case he comes."

"You think he will really come in a snowstorm?"

"He has a new four-wheel drive pickup. This weather will be a good chance for him to try it out. I expect he's like a child with a new toy."

Sarah put the diary on the table, patted it repeatedly, began to sob. "He called me yesterday. Told me you served him with papers. Said he was a free man and I could be a free woman."

"What did you say?"

"Nothing. I just listened. What should I do now?"

"You have a gun around here?"

"Several."

"You know how to shoot?"

"Daddy tried to teach me and Mother, but neither one of us did very well. I don't know that I could actually shoot anybody even if I could use a gun." She looked toward the door where Jubal watched television. "I'm really worried about Jubal until Daddy gets back. Then we'll be all right."

"Why not come to the big house until Cutt comes in?"

"Won't Ford come there first?"

"Maybe, but I have a restraining order against him, and he knows I can shoot him and get away with it. And he knows I will."

"I think I may take Jubal and go to the Holiday Inn in Amarillo. That's where I go when Tee comes."

"That's crazy in this weather. You'll be safer with me. Knowing Ford, he might find you there, and you'd have nobody to protect you."

"Let me think about it. If I decide to, I'll bundle Jubal up again, and we'll come over."

"Don't wait too long. He may be close."

Sarah's newfound courage dissolved as soon as Hope left. The thought of Ford invading her safe haven combined with the images in the diary and made her feel as if she might have another panic attack. She packed an overnight bag for herself and one for Jubal, dressed him for the cold. The day had turned dark as night, and the snow was ankle deep as they stepped out on the porch.

Cutt's personal truck wouldn't crank, so she tried the International Scout the ranch kept for hunting parties. The Scout struggled with the cold but finally started. She followed the tracks that Hope's ranch pickup had left.

Hope met them at the door with toys and books she had found in the house. She hugged them both and led them to the kitchen for hot chocolate and tea. Sarah sat close to the window so she could watch the road. The conversation between Hope and Jubal relaxed her momentarily. Then she remembered. Her face turned pale as she stood so quickly her chair fell back. "I've got to go back to the house for a minute. I left Mother's diary on the table. Daddy must never see it."

"Can't it wait? This could get worse any minute, and you might get caught out in it."

"If Daddy ever reads that diary, our lives will all change forever." Sarah headed back in the Scout. The snow concealed the headlight beams from a white pickup approaching from the east until she was almost in her yard. The pickup paused at the Donovan's house and then started toward hers. She cut her lights and kept going.

When Sarah did not return, Hope called. No answer. She made sure all the newly-changed locks were secure before cuddling up with Jubal on the couch. She read to Jubal from a child's book that Ford's mother had once read to Ford.

FIFTY

CUTT ARRIVED BACK AT HEADQUARTERS ON FOOT, HALF
frozen. His Blind River truck had thrown a rod about twenty miles away,
but he kept driving until the engine locked up about a mile from home. He
left a new-born calf wrapped in blankets on the front seat of the truck and
trudged through the boot-top-high snow. The calf's mother had stayed
alive long enough to let the calf nurse his vital supply of colostrum, so it
had a chance of survival if bottle-fed. He saw the light on in his house,
yearned for a cup of coffee, but there was the calf to think of first.

When his pickup would not start, he headed for the Scout, but it was
gone. He figured Sarah had seen the storm coming, gone into Kiowa to
stock up in case they were snowed in. The Scout was reliable in the snow,
and Sarah was a fair driver, but he still worried. They had parted angry,
and he wanted to put things right.

He went inside for dry, lined gloves, rubber boots, and a slicker. A
man's boot prints had left a snow and mud trail inside the kitchen and living room and down the hall toward the bedrooms. Cutt figured the tracks

263

must belong to one of the ranch hands or a neighbor, probably come to ask for supplies or help of some sort. He noticed the red book on the table, the orange light glowing on the percolator. He called for Sarah and Jubal. Outside, he saw more tire tracks. The Scout tracks, now partially covered with snow, appeared to head both toward the highway and toward the Chinook. Maybe Sarah had taken some supplies to the new young family that had recently moved in up there. The pickup tracks could signal a visit by a neighbor or one of the hands. But Cutt knew he had a calf that was certain to die unless he went back for it. Nothing to do but saddle a horse.

Judson stuck his head out of his stall as if volunteering for service. But the old horse's ribs showed, his withers seemed higher, and his back was beginning to sway. He deserved to stay out of this storm. A three-year-old mare that stood a little over fourteen hands with breeding prospects so low she had not been registered or even named looked like his best option. He saddled her and headed back south for the calf.

He was back in less than an hour, covered in snow, calf across the saddle gullet. The little bull's squirming gave him a warm feeling. He put the calf in a horse stall still wrapped in a blanket with plenty of shavings, left the mare saddled in a stall with a flake of alfalfa and a serving of sweet feed. He went inside to look for a note from Sarah but was irritated when he found none. She knew better than to go out in this weather, and it was time for her to be back. The storm was getting worse.

He found a bottle and nipple, filled it with milk, and returned to the barn. A sense of serenity washed over him as he fed the calf and bedded him down. He piled shavings and hay around the baby bull. "If you make it through the night, you got a fighting chance."

He wanted to shed his wet clothes and settle in but needed to find Sarah first. He called Kiowa's only grocery store and got no answer. He called Hope and nobody answered. He realized he might have to ride the mare to Hope's and hope that the old pickup Ford kept in the garage there would start. Tired and weak and stranded, he knew he needed fuel before facing the storm again.

He poured out used grounds and put in new, started the percolator, searched the cabinets for something to tide him over. He made a peanut butter sandwich, opened the diary while the coffee percolated. He was a few pages in when he heard the shotgun blast.

Cutt mounted the little mare and urged her through the snow toward the big house. The wrought iron gate was open and swung gently in the breeze. He stopped the mare outside the open gate to clear his head and get a feel for what might have happened. He thought rage had blinded him, driven him out of his mind, because there in the front yard, stood long-dead Earl Donovan. He was dressed in the same big hat and floor length leather duster he wore when important guests were at the ranch. Guests wanted to see their conception of a real cowboy, and Earl Donovan was not a man to disappoint.

The sight immobilized Cutt for a few seconds. Then he heard Ford's voice coming from under Earl's five-inch brim hat. Blood dripped from his wrist onto the snow. Hope pointed her double barrel shotgun at his other arm. "Get in your truck and get out of here. Leave this boy and his mother alone."

Cutt unwound the latigo string that held his rope, shook out a loop, took one swing, and threw. There was a soft whoosh of air as the rope sailed past Ford's right ear, a thump as the back of the loop and the honda hit Ford shoulder high in the back. The loop circled perfectly, made a figure eight behind him, and dropped down around his knees. The loop scraped denim as it dropped around Ford's ankles. Cutt jerked his slack, dallied, and pulled Ford's legs out from under him. He pushed the little mare toward the river, dragging Ford, one of his arms dangling like a useless appendage. His body left a wide, bloody trail a blind man could follow.

FIFTY-ONE

TEE HAD TO STOP SEVERAL TIMES TO DISLODGE ICE AND snow from his chassis, but he finally turned off the highway onto the Blind River Headquarters road. As he crossed the Denver Road tracks, the familiar feeling of passing through a time tunnel returned. John T, Winona, and brother Jubal were always inside the tunnel, alive. He felt his usual urge to pause, but his son and wife were on the other side.

He saw the white truck in front of the Donovan house as he drove past but did not recognize it. The front door of Cutt's house was left ajar. Snow had drifted into the entryway, settled atop the freezer closest to the door. The house looked ransacked with snowy footprints and mud throughout, a small red book on the floor, a wet coat he recognized as Cutt's hanging in the mudroom. He called for Sarah and Jubal but got no answer.

Outside, he saw the bloody trail that looked like a deer carcass had been dragged through the snow. He drove back to the Donovan house. A few feet inside the wrought iron gate, a big hat lay in the snow. He ran down the rock path to the front door and knocked.

Holding a shotgun, Hope pulled him inside and locked the door behind him. She leaned the shotgun in the corner beside the door. The look on her face terrified him. "What's wrong? Where's my family?"

"Jubal is here. He's asleep in the back and safe. Sarah was here, but she went back to Cutt's to get something."

"That Ford's truck outside? Did he go down to Cutt's?"

"I can't be sure. He got here just after Sarah left. I think he may have cut off her return, so she is either hiding or took off in another direction. She may have left the ranch while I was fighting with Ford."

"You fought with Ford?"

"I shot the son-of-a-bitch. The coward let his truck idle out there for close to an hour. Then he got up the nerve to come knocking, demanding to be let into his own house. He was all dressed up like something out of an old shoot-em-up."

"You really shot him? Where is he?"

"Cutt came when he heard the shotgun, I guess. He roped him and dragged him off."

"That explains the bloody trail. Did Cutt say what he was gonna do?"

Hope took a deep breath. "I think Cutt may know about what Ford did to Maggie."

Tee shook his head. "Damn. He'll kill him." Tee looked toward his Cougar and the white truck. "Sarah in the Scout?"

"Yes."

"And you have no idea where she might have gone?"

"The only place I could think of is the Holiday Inn in Amarillo. I called. She's not registered there, and I think she's had time. I hope she's not stranded in this storm."

Tee paced. "I don't know where to start looking for her. Only thing I know to do is follow Cutt's trail. Maybe he knows where she is. Either way, I need to stop him from killing Ford. The Scout's good in the snow, so Sarah's probably safe."

"She could have gone to one of the sub-ranches if she was afraid to pass by here to get to Amarillo."

"Are the keys in Ford's truck?"

She dangled a set of keys. "He left it running, and I went out and turned it off. Hope it's got gas."

FIFTY-TWO

CUTT SLOWED THE MARE TO A WALK BARELY FAST ENOUGH to keep the rope tight around Ford's ankles. When Ford stopped struggling to free himself, Cutt wondered if he was dead. Hoped he was. The rage that had burned his guts since he read his wife's diary had changed him. He no longer felt like Cutt Ledbetter. He was a stranger who was dead inside.

He knew where he was going. The highest mesa on the Blind River was called Rattler Ridge for good reason. A man trying to climb to the top afoot was likely to encounter a rattler or two on the way up. A rider could see and be seen for miles. Rattler Ridge was less than a mile from headquarters.

Cutt, like John T before him, rode to the ridge every spring and fall to supervise the big roundups at ranch headquarters. He felt peaceful, almost majestic, during those roundups, like there was no better job on earth and no better man to fill it. A gnarled scrub oak they called Sentinel seemed to have sprouted out of rock and survived on pebbles and sand stood as a monument to perseverance. Cutt had always considered the tree an old friend, a testament to his own determination to survive in harsh circumstances. He always kept a coffee pot and two tin cups tied to a limb with barbed wire.

Cutt released his dally and threw the end of the rope across a limb, caught it and tied it hard and fast to his saddle horn. Ford groaned a little as Cutt stepped off the horse. He walked back to watch as Ford used his one good hand and arm to struggle with the loop around his ankles. Earl's old duster spread behind him like batwings. The leather coat he wore underneath was reduced to a few wispy strings. Blood and mud and icicles picked up when he was dragged across the river plastered the threads of his undershirt to a back scraped raw by the harsh terrain. The snow and the coat had probably kept him alive.

Cutt made a kissing sound to the mare. The horse stepped forward until Ford swung in the air. "Whoa." Cutt bent and propped one elbow on a knee so that he could look into Ford's terror-filled eyes. "You've got yourself and me in a terrible fix, Ford. We got to find us a way out of it."

Ford looked at the mare. Teeth chattering, he struggled to find his voice. "That horse spooks, she'll drag me over that limb and won't stop till she reaches the gates of hell."

Cutt rubbed his chin. "You could be right. She's barely three. Anything could spook her. Doubt you'd make it over the limb, though." He spoke to the horse. "Back up, girl." She stepped back a few feet and Ford propped on his good shoulder.

He took several halting breaths that sounded like sobs and spit out a wad of mud and blood. "You damn near killed me."

Cutt made clicking and kissing sounds, and the mare moved until Ford swung again. "Whoa." He bent over to speak directly into Ford's upside down face. "See, that's how it works, Ford. The mare backs up and you get to rest; she walks forward and you get to hang by your ankles and let the blood rush to your head. We all clear on that?"

Ford was so cold he could barely form the words. "Clear. I need some water."

"Back up, girl." The horse backed up enough to allow Ford to rest his upper body on the ground. Cutt gave him a coffee cup filled with snow.

FIFTY-THREE

TEE FOLLOWED THE TRAIL LEFT BY FORD'S BODY. HE STOPPED
Ford's truck when his headlights cut through the lessening snowfall to
reveal a man and a horse on Rattler Ridge. Something that resembled a
deer carcass hung from the Sentinel. He stopped the truck a few feet from
them, kept the lights on the carcass. Cutt's red-eyed stare sliced through
the headlights' glare and chilled Tee to the bone. He left the lights on,
the engine idling, stepped out of the truck, and waited for Cutt to speak.
When he did not, Tee walked over and looked down at Ford's face.

Ford squinted up. He shook so much that Tee could barely understand
him. "I'm gonna die if you don't help me."

Tee's face was blank. "You know where my wife is?"

"I have not seen her. I swear."

Tee looked up at Cutt, who seemed to have aged a decade since his
last trip. "You know where she is?"

"Figured she went for groceries and supplies. She's not back yet?"

"No. What you got planned here, Cutt?"

271

Cutt studied the look on Tee's face as if trying to determine if he was an enemy or cohort. "Did you know this bastard raped my wife and yours? He killed Maggie just as sure as if he shot her."

"He raped both of them? How do you know that?"

"He raped Maggie when he was about twenty and she was forty. Raped her several more times over the years. She wrote about it in a little diary she kept."

"And Sarah?"

Cutt had trouble forming the words. "The damn pedophile took Sarah the first time when she was twelve, kept doing it right up till the time you took her away from here, I guess. Maggie wrote it all down. She knew it was going on but never told me."

Cutt looked away, his voice breaking. "Kept it from me all those years."

Tee groaned. "When did you find out?"

"Not more than an hour ago. Sarah left Maggie's diary on the kitchen table. Guess she wanted me to see it." Cutt sat in the snow and leaned against the tree; put his face in his hands. His voice was ragged. "I saw Maggie once or twice with that little red book, but she kept it to herself. I figured it was full of female stuff I didn't really need to know about."

"Did she say in there why she didn't tell you?"

Cutt rubbed the stubble on his cheeks. "I'm ashamed, Tee. Ashamed I didn't figure it out and ashamed of why she didn't tell me."

"Just tell me why."

"She was afraid I would lose my damn job. Can you believe that? Maggie, my own wife, was willing to sacrifice our daughter to this predator bastard for the sake of my monthly paycheck. You know as well as I do either your daddy or me could find work on any ranch in three or four states."

Cutt looked at Tee, waited for a reply. None came. "That makes my whole life meaningless, Tee."

"I expect it was more than the job. You would have killed him if you had known, Cutt. Hard to find a job when you got a warrant for murder hanging over you. And you might have had to kill Earl, too."

"Don't see how anybody could blame a man for protecting his family. All those doctors. All they did was prescribe pills. Said it was depression. She wouldn't tell 'em. Couldn't reveal this terrible thing to anyone, and it ate away at her till it killed her."

"That explains Maggie. Why didn't Sarah tell you?"

Cutt nodded toward Ford. "Maggie told her I would kill Ford if I found out. That I would go to prison. Guess she didn't want to lose her daddy."

Tee stared at Ford for several minutes. "I know it's hard to understand, but when you think about it, they endured torture for several years to protect you and somehow hold the family together."

Cutt looked over Tee's head toward headquarters. "Maybe, but that still leaves me with the job at hand. You go on back and find Sarah. I'll handle this."

Tee kneeled again and looked in Ford's eyes. "If I ever saw a perverted mental case that deserved to die, it would be you."

Cutt flinched as Tee walked toward him. "Go on. You need to find Sarah."

"You gonna do the one thing your wife and daughter spent all those years trying to keep you from doing?"

"You don't understand. This bastard took away my reason to live. He's made everything I ever did seem worthless. I was no good as a father or a husband. Couldn't protect my wife or my daughter."

Tee walked over and nudged Ford's leg with a boot. "I felt the same way when I found out Sarah had been protecting Jubal from the predator son-of-a-bitch. But, is he worth it? Will we feel better if we kill him?"

"You got no part in this. You were never here. Just get away."

"Too late for that. You know that. They'll know I was here."

Cutt put his boot toe against Ford's cheek. "We got the boy to think about. He can't lose his daddy. Anyway, there ain't much left to kill."

"I'm afraid he's gonna freeze to death. He's lost a lot of blood. Let's throw him in the truck and head back. I need your help to find Sarah."

FIFTY-FOUR

THEY THREW FORD INTO THE BED OF THE PICKUP LIKE A BAG of feed. Cutt mounted the mare and coiled his rope as Tee headed back in the truck. He drove past the Ledbetter house and went straight to the Donovan's. Still no sign of the Scout. Hope answered his knock. "Did you find them?"

"I've got Ford in the pickup. Any word from Sarah?"

"No. Is he alive?"

"Barely, I think. Can I leave him here while I search for Sarah?"

Hope hesitated but finally nodded.

"Better get something on the floor. He's pretty bloody." Tee put down the tailgate and dragged Ford out by the collar of his leather coat, about the only article of clothing that might hold. Ford's feet hit the ground, and Tee kept dragging until he was on the living room floor.

He looked down at Ford and then at Hope. "I think he's pretty used up, but if he tries anything, shoot the other arm. Jubal still asleep?"

"Out like a light. He didn't even stir with the shotgun blast. This is a tight, almost soundproof house."

275

"I don't know what else to do, so I'm going to start with Chinook. Call the Highway Patrol and see if she might be stranded on the highway. If she shows up, try shooting off the shotgun or a rifle. I might be close enough to hear."

Hope nodded toward her husband. "What am I supposed to do with him?"

"You're a nurse, aren't you? Call an ambulance or patch him up yourself. You'll have to explain the shotgun pellets if you call an ambulance."

He found the remnants of the Scout's tracks on the way to Chinook. He was relieved enough to begin forming words of reconciliation as he slowly trekked the ranch road. He would start with an apology for not paying better attention. Looking back, he should have known; all the signs were there. The birth control pills; her unnatural fear of intimacy; never letting him see her nude; her urgent desire to leave Blind River, followed by a strange desire to return. He probably would have noticed if he had not been so focused on his own self-pity after losing his family. He had spent most of his waking hours thinking of his parents, his brother, his son, and work. Little thought was given to Sarah. He would find a way to make it up to her.

He was within sight of the Chinook cabin when he saw where the Scout's tracks left the road at a spot where the road slanted from west to east, causing a snowdrift. The tracks led around the snowdrift. Tee stopped. Sarah knew this road as well as he did, knew about the steep incline on the right side. He started to follow the tracks, then saw the limb by the side of the drift. One tree stood between headquarters and Chinook. They called the big mesquite Lone Tree. Accumulated snow had caused a limb to fall. The Scout's passenger side tires had crossed the big limb. Tee got out and followed the tracks. The Scout lay on its driver side a few yards down the incline toward a gulley. The passenger door was open.

Tee climbed on top and looked down into the cab of the Scout. It was almost filled with snow. He threw handfuls out until he knew for sure Sarah was not inside. Snow had covered her tracks, but he was sure she would have headed for the cabin. He returned to the truck, drove through the bank of snow and crept toward Chinook headquarters. He found her a hundred yards from the wreck, leaned against a large rock by the side of the road. Snow and ice covered the blood that had oozed from a gash in her forehead; her hair, eyebrows, and eyelashes were white with snow and ice. A bone had broken the skin on one ankle.

Tee put his thumb on one cheek, his index finger on the other, and gently moved her face back and forth. When he picked her up, he was struck by how light she was. He had carried her only once, and that was across the threshold at the Holiday Inn. He carried her to the pickup, placed her in the seat. He turned around in the Chinook headquarters yard and headed back to Blind River headquarters. Weeping, he apologized all the way to the Ledbetter house, begged her to speak. From the yard, he could see Cutt at the small kitchen table, reading the diary. He considered going past, taking Sarah to Hope, but he could not take the chance that Jubal might be awake and see his mother like this.

Cutt stood as Tee carried Sarah inside and laid her on the couch. "Please, God, no." He talked to her, pleaded with her, as he used warm cloths to wash the blood and snow away, but Sarah did not answer.

FIFTY-FIVE

HOPE WIPED AWAY FORD'S BLOOD, GAVE HIM ORANGE JUICE
and water, and helped him into a chair by the roaring fireplace. She brought
his mother's Smith-Corona into the room and began typing. After several
starts and stops and revisions, she handed him a confession that detailed
the rapes of Maggie and Sarah and violation of his restraining order. "Sign
this and I'll doctor those wounds and feed you. Otherwise, you'll likely die
from blood poisoning and exposure."

Ford scribbled his signature, and Hope began pulling out the shotgun
pellets with tweezers soaked in alcohol. She bandaged the worst of the
wound. When she was finished, she pointed to the phone. "Call one of
your henchmen to come and get you."

He made the call, then sat back in the chair and relaxed after coaxing
a double shot of whiskey from Hope. As the pain subsided and he began to
doze off, he figured the statute of limitations had probably run on the rapes.
If not, he would say he signed with a shotgun against his head. Who would
take a distraught woman's word over a respected rancher's? Three hours later,

two men and a chauffeur arrived in a stretch limousine. They put Ford on a stretcher and put him in the back of the limo, drove him and his pickup away.

An autopsy was required. The medical examiner in Amarillo told Tee and Cutt that a healthy woman should have survived the crash and exposure to the elements, but Sarah had been emaciated, her liver irreparably damaged from near starvation.

They buried her beside her mother. Tee and Cutt agreed on a graveside service like Maggie's. Father Bob Messenger presided. Jubal held his father's hand as he stared at his mother's coffin. When Father Bob completed his message and after Tee and Cutt accepted condolences, Tee led Jubal to John T, Winona, and Jubal's graves. Jubal seemed to understand for the first time how he came by his name.

Tee was surprised there was so little to pack. He closed the trunk on the Cougar and stood looking at his stricken father-in-law.

Cutt stared at his boots until he could find his voice. "What about Ford?"

Tee looked toward the main house. "What about him?"

"The man belongs in prison or in a grave."

Tee nodded. "Yes, he does. But we can't kill him, and we can't carry him around on our backs and in our heads the rest of our lives. He wins if we do that. Besides, we got a boy to raise."

"You're just willing to let it go?"

"Don't know if I can, but Father Bob says it takes courage to forgive. Said only a coward carries a grudge."

"Told me the same thing. I said God may forgive Ford, but I never will. He said I wouldn't get into heaven unless I did." Cutt chuckled softly. "I told him to ask me again when he's reading me last rites."

"We still kin?"

"You bet. You two the only family I got left."

"What do you aim to do?"

Cutt shook his head. "You remember what I told you about not really ever owning anything? Well, this is what it looks like." He made a sweeping motion of the manager's house and all the barns. "I'll stay here long enough to sell what few cows and horses I own. Ford tries to run me off before then, I'll finish what I started."

280

"What then? You want to go with us?"

He handed Tee a business card. "That feedlot in Dalhart made me a standing job offer more than a year ago. If it's still good, I'll do that for a few months. If it don't work out, I'll maybe go to another ranch. What about you?"

"Got no idea. Can't keep working in a tomb for a bunch of crooks. Me and Jubal may head out and see which way the wind blows. I'll call you when we get settled."

Tee stopped at the Donovan house and let Jubal honor his promise to give Hope a goodbye hug. Tee got one, too. With tears in her eyes, Hope whispered in his ear. "You know that whatever she did, she did to protect your son and you."

He stopped the car at the railroad crossing, rolled down the window, and listened. It seemed a lifetime had passed since he came to answer Hope's call. He tried to connect, to hear a message, heard nothing but the wind. He said goodbye to his wife, parents, and brother and drove away.

Tee smiled at the sight of John T's old pickup sitting under the church parking lot light. It had not been there for several visits, so he assumed the old priest had given it away or sold it. The black '57 shouted John Theodore Jessup. The restoration showed the touch of a patient expert, an expert who knew how to make the truck look new while retaining its original character. Tee smiled as he looked through the windows at the refurbished interior. He could not remember the seats and dash ever looking so good. The tailgate opened and closed with ease and the bumper was straight.

The light was reliably on in the rectory. Tee knocked on the door. Father Bob appeared in a crisp white T-shirt, black slacks badly worn at the knees, and a pair of hiking boots.

"Sorry to bother you so late again, Father."

"No bother at all, Tee. Come in."

Tee pointed toward his car. "Could I ask you to come out here? I don't have long, and Jubal is asleep in the car."

The priest pulled a black pea-coat from a hook on the door and walked past Tee toward the Cougar.

Tee leaned against the Cougar's hood. "It's a long story, but I'm gonna need a pickup with a trailer hitch, and I don't have time to trade."

Father Bob stared into his eyes for a long time as if he were reading his mind, searching for the truth. He finally nodded and walked over to John T's '57 Chevy. "Well, you have a fine one right here. No need to trade."

"I always figured the truck belonged to you or the church, especially after you restored it. But I do need it right now. I'll bring it back."

"It is now and always has been your truck. Truth be told, your mother left me the money to fix the bumper and tailgate, and I just didn't have time before you took it that first day."

"I'll leave my Cougar here."

Father Bob looked through the Cougar passenger window at Jubal in the back seat; then his gaze rested on the front seat. "Is that the tape I loaned you?"

Tee softly opened the door and handed the tape to Father Bob. "Sure is. Appreciate the loan. Afraid I about wore it out." He was surprised and a little disappointed when Father Bob did not hand it back.

"I have always admired this year model of Cougar. Prettier than a Mustang that year, I think, especially in black." He smiled at Tee's surprised look. "It's perfectly acceptable for a priest to like automobiles, Tee. Music and cars have always been my hobbies."

They moved the suitcases from the Cougar to the pickup bed and exchanged titles and registrations. The noise woke Jubal. He looked around to get his bearings and looked as if he might cry, but he managed a handshake. The priest gave him a peppermint while Tee made him a bed in the front seat of the pickup. He used the distraction to move the baseball bat and his pistol from the Cougar to the Chevy.

Tee felt good when Father Bob cajoled a hug from Jubal. The priest touched his arm as he put his hand on the driver's door handle. "Call me when you get where you're going. I still see deep trouble in your eyes. Don't let the anger reside in your head. Purge it."

The pickup had a calming effect as they headed east. The feel of the steering wheel, changing gears, even the smell, reminded him of John T and Winona. When Jubal went back to sleep, loneliness set in. Tee reflexively reached for the tape he was used to playing in such quiet times, but it was gone. He made a mental note to buy one, but did not know the name of the Italian tenor on the tape that Father Bob had lent him and taken back. When he turned the radio on, he noticed something different. A small cassette tape sat halfway in a slot that had not been there before. He pushed it in and the soothing, inspiring strains of *The Lord's Prayer* filled the cab. The surround sound came from the dash, the kick panels, and behind the seat. Tee smiled and said a silent thank you to Father Robert Messenger and to God.

Outside Vernon, he saw a lighted arena and pulled over to the shoulder. Two young boys and an older man were mounted in the arena. A young Mexican in a sombrero worked the chutes. Dust hovered over and around the riders, the Mexican and the cattle, giving them all a ghostly aura, as if the scene were being played out in another place or time, in another dimension. The lights illuminated the dust particles.

One of the boys took practice swings as the Mexican boy reloaded the chutes. His father raised his empty right hand and pointed to his elbow with the other hand as he made roping motions to show the boy. The boy stood in the stirrups, leaned forward, and swung his loop just over his horse's ears. He backed into the box and took another practice swing before nodding. The Mexican released the steer, and it exploded out of the chute, the boy and his horse close behind. The loop was perfect, the dismount quick and smooth, the flanking effortless, and the tie quick. The boy raised his hands in the air as his father dropped his flag and pushed a stopwatch at the same time. The man rode over to the boy, stepped down, and slapped him on the arm. The other boy rode beside the older man. Tee could see their white teeth as they grinned.

His eyes filled as he turned to look at his sleeping son. Jubal grunted as if he knew his sleep was being observed. A wagon wheel neon sign blinked vacancy a few yards in front of them, reflecting off the Chevy's hood. He registered and paid a friendly night clerk with cash and parked a few feet away from the front door.

He carried Jubal into the dreary room, pulled back the top sheet and blanket, and laid him fully clothed on the bed. Jubal opened one eye as Tee stripped him down to his underwear and put him under the covers. He brought in their suitcases and double-checked the door's lock before taking a shower. Something told him he needed to be extra cautious, like someone was chasing them. Out of the shower with a towel wrapped around his waist, he peeked through the dusty curtains. The arena lights went out two at a time. The two boys and their father turned the steers loose. Tee went to bed and snuggled his son.

Jubal was looking out the window when Tee awoke. He watched his son's back as the boy stood in his underwear, studying his strange surroundings like a small puppy begging to be let outside. "What do you see out there?"

Jubal turned, his eyes still swollen from sleep. "Where are we?"

"Vernon, Texas. Headed home."

Jubal's face clouded up like he was going to cry. Tee stepped out of the bed and put his arm around him. "Know what? It's Saturday. We're gonna have our usual weekend breakfast. Let's get you cleaned up and your teeth brushed."

They had bacon and eggs at the café next to the motel before heading toward Dallas. Tee spent the first few miles explaining the pickup and whose it used to be. Jubal leaned forward in the seat, trying to see over the dashboard, looking for something familiar, something to cling to. He did not mention his mother or grandfather and neither did Tee.

They arrived at Harborcraft in Mansfield at sunset. Tee had spent most of the trip trying to work out a plan in his mind. He killed the engine by the front gate and stared at the bone yard. Jubal stared with him at first, then turned to him. "Are we going back to our old house?"

"Do you want to?"

The boy shrugged. "What about Cutt? Will I ever see Judson again?"

"Cutt will be fine. We'll see him soon. As for Judson, I can't promise. I know he will be fine. I left him a long time ago, and then he found you."

"Are you going to work? This is still Saturday."

"No, son. I just stopped here to pick up something that belongs to me."

The details of how to collect that something would not come to him. He pulled away and went to a nearby Dairy Queen and bought them both a cone. He parked in the parking lot of The Still and went to work on his cone, Tee licking and swallowing as if he were infusing needed information, not ice cream. The night was not terribly cold, so they bundled up in Jubal's blanket and sat on the dropped tailgate. Esther stepped out into her yard as Tee took the last bite of cone. Hands on her hips, she waited for some type of acknowledgement from Tee. He waved and she walked over.

She went directly to Jubal, ignoring Tee. "You must be Jubal. I'm Esther. I've heard a lot about you."

Jubal nodded without speaking. Esther carried the weight of the conversation for a few minutes, but she gradually got Jubal to open up. Tee tried to make eye contact, and she occasionally glanced his way when Jubal said something interesting, but she quickly averted her eyes. Only when she asked a question that Jubal could not answer did she look his way. Jubal pointed to Tee. "You'll have to ask him."

Tee was deep in thought and had not heard the question. "What?"

"You're feeding your son ice cream at suppertime. I asked where you were having supper."

"Glad you brought that up. That's why we stopped here. To ask if you would care to join us for supper."

They walked in cool, moist air, their breaths trailing behind in smoky funnels, each holding one of Jubal's hands. Her presence seemed to make Tee feel safer, happier. It was near closing time in the small café, and the food was warmed over, but Esther kept Jubal laughing. He devoured his hamburger and Tee realized the boy had not had lunch. Tee learned more about his school and wondered why he had not asked the questions that seemed to come natural to Esther.

At Esther's house, she sent Tee for Jubal's pajamas without asking his opinion, put him in her bathtub. He was asleep on the couch an hour later. Tee told her everything he could, but some things could not be given voice. He spoke in low tones, regularly glancing at his son to make sure he was not listening. She sat by Jubal's feet, shook her head, cried a little, and patted his feet. "Did he see any of this?"

"No."

Esther picked up Jubal and carried him to her bed. "Do you know how close you came to doing something that might have sent you to jail for the rest of your life?"

The question surprised him. "Being a father to this boy was always uppermost in my mind. I never intended to kill Ford. I probably saved Cutt from killing him."

"What if he files charges?"

"Then we release the diary and his signed confession. Hope will back us up. He might not go to jail, but believe me, Ford will not want that kind of publicity."

"Should I call Stan?"

285

"No. But you might tell him what happened the next time you see him."

"Speaking of Stan, I have something to show you."

Esther went into her bedroom and came back with a group of photos fanned out in her hand like playing cards. She spread them on her coffee table in front of the couch, a big grin on her face. "Pick them up in order, this end first."

Tee picked up the first one, taken in the dark of the bone yard. Doublewide Doug, Fireplug and the two attorneys were featured in their full glory examining a trailer. The second showed them inside a mobile home. The third showed them pulling the trailer away. All were date-stamped beginning on the day Tee isolated himself to prepare for and take the CPA exam and each successive day until the day he left for the Blind River. The next to last photo showed the arrival of Gene Vinson and three Special Agents, badges shown and guns drawn. The last photo was a close-up of Doublewide Doug Throckmorton in cuffs, being led to a waiting car by Gene Vinson.

"Who took these?"

"Stan and I. He's got a fancy camera with a telescopic lens."

Tee felt strangely empty. A month or even a week ago, the photos would have brought a shout of glee. Now, he was ambivalent. "I knew Stan was planning something but couldn't figure it out. Throckmorton and the lawyers played right into his hands by stealing the trailers, didn't they?"

"Yes, but it was more complicated than that. He's been working with Vinson for a long time on Throckmorton. He took your box of evidence to Vinson at the IRS and waited for the chance to get the photos to back it up. Of course, Stan had already done Vinson's work. The evidence box alone was enough to get him for tax evasion. Catching the dirty lawyers was a big bonus for Vinson. Sets him up for a nice promotion."

"And, of course, it ensures his everlasting gratitude to Stan."

"Stan can be beautiful at times. He also told me that Doublewide's trophy wife had already filed for divorce."

"Did they arrest the bankruptcy lawyers? The referee? Fireplug?"

"No, but they may seek indictments. These crooks apparently have a lot of stroke at the Tarrant County Courthouse. Stan was out to get even with Throckmorton. He said stealing from a bankrupt firm with assets like travel trailers and campers is sort of accepted. Said it's like blood in the water to sharks."

"They all deserve to go down."

"What about you? What now?"

"Well, the thought of going back to that graveyard over there makes me sick to my stomach. I know that, no matter what, I won't be working for the court anymore."

"Have you found another job?"

"No. I can last about a month, maybe two if I'm careful."

"Then what?"

"I don't know. I feel pulled to get away from here."

"Well, you have a house rented, and you can expand your search into this area. That should land you something pretty quick."

"Right now, I need to go over to the bone yard and collect a few things. Can you watch him while I do?"

"Sure."

Tee drove the pickup over to the bone yard, cut his lights, opened the gate, and backed up to the Airstream.

FIFTY-SIX

TEE BACKED THE TRAVEL TRAILER INTO THE PARKING LOT OF The Still, hoping it would draw less attention alongside the battered camper tops, and walked across the street to Esther's. She waited just inside the screen door. "What do you think you're doing, Tee? Haven't you been through enough trouble? Now you want to get arrested for robbery?"

"It's either steal it myself or wait and let the lawyers steal it."

"I can't believe you even said that. This makes you no better than them."

It was not the reaction Tee had expected. "They owe me almost three weeks' pay. Harborcraft owed me two weeks of vacation pay and two weeks' salary when it went down."

"Not enough to buy that trailer." She looked through the window at the Airstream, bit her jaw as if she were trying to digest his rationale. "Why the Airstream and not one of the new Harborcraft trailers?"

"It belonged to one of the lawyers who stole a new one. It's not on any inventory. He needed a place to park it so he could sell it."

"You're making that up."

Tee crossed his heart. "I showed the Airstream to a potential buyer a few days ago. The guy had a copy of an ad for it out of the Dallas paper with the lawyer's phone number. Fireplug called me and told me to let the guy in the lot."

"But I don't see why you would take such a big chance. What are you going to do with it? You can't sell it."

"Actually, I can. I think I've got their scheme figured out. This trailer, for example, doesn't even really belong to the lawyer who left it here. He got it from a client who couldn't pay his bill. He never changed it to his name after taking it from the guy. Probably so he could avoid paying taxes on the fee."

"Maybe so, but those guys are practicing, expert crooks. If you try it, you'll get caught."

"Maybe, but I don't intend to sell it, I intend to live in it."

Esther's face showed her shock. "What about your house?"

"Been paying rent monthly since the lease expired."

"Where are you planning on living in this trailer? What are you not telling me?"

"Before this happened, I planned on taking it out west so I could be close to Jubal. Now, I don't know for sure."

"You don't know?"

"My plans are not clear, Esther. Not even to me. I need to get this boy someplace safe and get him started on a new life. I have some ideas, mostly about getting us a horse or two to ride and being out in the country. That was gonna happen out west; now it looks like east. West has a bad taste now."

"This is crazy."

"I'm following this little voice in my head and trying to heed advice from someone who helped me when I needed it most."

"And what about us? Our friendship, I mean."

"You said it yourself. We need to let things develop. If they're meant to, they will." He saw a look on her face that said betrayal. "Look, my wife is barely gone. I have a kid who has had everything he thought was permanent taken away from him twice. He needs stability, and right now, and I'm the only one who can give him that."

"What about food on the table, clothes on his back, and other silly things like that?"

"I've never failed to feed and clothe him yet. Don't intend to start now."

"He needs a mother."

"Yes, he does, but he just lost his."

She crossed her arms. "You've really thought this through, haven't you?"

"Honestly, no. Just taking it one step at a time, trying not to make a mistake that hurts him."

She dabbed at unwanted tears. "When are you going?"

"Has to be now. I can't let this trailer sit here all night, and I need to drop by and pick up my clothes and what few possessions we have."

"You do know you'll have to have it serviced before you can actually live in it, don't you?"

"Fireplug told me to take it to one of our old dealers and get it filled with propane, water, battery charged, the works. I had it done the day after he brought it in."

"Jubal is all tucked in and cozy. Wait until morning."

But Tee was adamant. Something told him he needed to move, get farther away from the Blind River and far away from Harborcraft. Esther followed him into the house and watched as he picked up his son and carried him back to the pickup. She helped cover him with the blanket Tee had brought from Cutt's. They turned and faced each other then, Esther succumbing, openly sobbing. Tee hugged her and pulled away. Esther stood in the yard of The Still and watched moonlight flicker off the silver Airstream as it pulled away.

———◦•◦———

The house in Grand Prairie seemed foreign to him as he pulled under the carport. He gently shook Jubal awake. The boy rubbed his eyes and stared as if he had never seen the house before. Tee put a hand on his shoulder. "We're gonna load up our stuff and your bed, then bunk down here for the night. I want to leave in the morning before first light. Okay?"

Jubal nodded. He walked directly into his room and examined his new trundle bed. "Who's been sleeping here?"

"Nobody. That's your bed. I've been waiting on you to come back so you could sleep in it first. Tonight, though, I'm gonna take it apart and put it in the travel trailer. We'll camp out together in the living room."

Most of Tee's folding clothes were stored in cardboard boxes. He grabbed both duffel bags and footlockers and a suitcase and started stuffing them with everything on closet shelves, in kitchen cabinets, and the bathroom. He carried his best hanging clothes to the travel trailer and hung them in its tiny closet, left the rest. By the time he had disassembled Jubal's bed, the boy was asleep on Tee's bedroll. Tee slid the chest, saddle and stand, and all his tack and tools into the pickup bed and placed his .22 magnum rifle behind the seat. He crawled in beside Jubal around midnight.

He slept fitfully, replaying the night of Sarah's death. In the dream, Jubal watched his grandfather drag Ford away from headquarters and across the river. The boy's pleading cry awakened him. Tee steadied his hand before touching his son's chest. Jubal's breathing was steady, his body warm. It calmed Tee. He dressed himself and then the boy in boots, jeans, and hats. The comfortable, familiar clothes made them feel more confident and energized. He put a loaf of bread and the contents of the refrigerator into an ice chest and said goodbye to the other furniture. They pulled out of the driveway for the last time at dawn.

Over a quick breakfast at a truck stop east of Dallas, Tee still felt watched, like a man on the run from a possible murder and now a stolen trailer. On the road again, Jubal sat forward in the seat, his head just high enough to see over the dash. Tee felt unusually affectionate and proud of his son because he had not questioned, had not complained about an unknown destination. He stopped at a small store and gas station for ice and groceries. An hour later, he pulled into a roadside park. Tee needed to get his bearings. Up until this point, it had seemed as if someone else had been driving the truck. Now, he could feel control return to him and he did not know what to do with it.

He and Jubal stepped outside and sat on a concrete bench, covered in Jubal's blanket. Jubal looked up at his father. "How far are we from the Blind River?"

"About five-hundred miles, I would guess."

"Are we going a thousand miles away?"

"I think not much farther." Tee looked up as a skein of geese honked encouragement and directions to each other, changing positions in the V formation. Tee had the distinct feeling they were calling him, that the V was an arrow. He stood and folded the blanket. "Those geese seem to be flying in the wrong direction. What say we follow them?"

The geese seemed in no hurry, flew out of sight a few times, only to appear again. When they swooped down past a wooded area, Tee figured he had lost them for good. But he was on a path now, a winding dirt road that seemed to be leading away from civilization. He could not turn the truck and trailer around now, even if he wanted to. The road seemed to cut deeper and deeper into the soil, as if time and the flow of many years of water had cut nature's path and allowed man to use it.

A sparrow sat in the middle of the sandy road, and he straddled it. In his side mirror, he saw the bird flop helplessly behind him. It had probably flown up as he crossed over it and injured itself on a tailpipe or muffler. *Just a sparrow. A pretty useless bird. Millions more like it.* But he stopped, walked back, and picked up the bird. He cradled it in both hands and brought it to Jubal's door. The boy took the bird from his father without a word passing between them. He held it and one lost feather gently in both palms as they pulled away.

A mile farther down the road, Tee stopped in the middle of a rattling bridge with high banisters. The bridge sat at the end of a sharp curve and spanned a creek wider and deeper than some rivers. He rolled down his window and the smell of creek water entered the cab. The sound of gently rolling water seemed more like a song, bringing with it the echo of a train whistle, the rattling of a trestle.

FIFTY-SEVEN

TEE FELT HIS WAY IN THE PREDAWN DARKNESS OF THE UNFA-
miliar trailer as he made coffee, trying not to wake Jubal. He found the
sparrow on the fold-down kitchen table, half buried in the blanket, still
alive. He carefully opened drawers and cabinet doors in the tiny kitchen
and found an unexpected treasure of eating and cooking utensils. He
pulled a tin tray and shallow saucer from a shelf and poured water in the
saucer. Using the faint light that seemed to be climbing the tree line in
the east, he pulled some seeds from dead weeds growing outside the trailer
door, mixed them with some bread crumbs, and sprinkled the mixture on
the tray beside the saucer of water. When he carefully placed the sparrow
next to the feast, the bird took no notice.

Tee stepped outside, plastic coffee cup in hand, and stood under the
window where Jubal slept. The air was moist and heavy with the smells
of early spring as sunlight topped the trees and revealed a sloping valley
filled with the smoky mist of rising dew. The valley seemed familiar, but
he could not be sure. He seemed to have parked on the lip of a bowl, with

the raised rail bed, earthen embankments that followed the creek he had crossed the night before, and a tree line at the bottom of a hill making up the sides of the bowl. The embankments followed the creek and were obviously manmade to prevent flooding. As two coyotes retreated into the trees to escape the sunlight, he knew why it seemed familiar. Winona had described this little valley to her sons, boasting how her father and grand-father had helped build the embankments with Fresno scrapers and mules. Bottomland, she had called it. He could see why.

He went back inside to finish dressing and wake Jubal. The sparrow had still not touched the seeds but did flinch a little at the loud knocking on the trailer door. The little camper seemed to rock with each hard rap. Tee snapped a couple of snaps, tucked his shirt into his jeans, and opened the door, prepared to face an angry landowner. A tall, thin man with a handlebar mustache and a felt hat with a four-inch brim that looked firm enough and thin enough to be high quality beaver looked up at Tee. He wore boots with tall slanted riding heels, his Wranglers stuffed inside tops that reached almost to his knees, the initials JHL imprinted on mule-ear pulls. He held the reins to the tallest saddle horse Tee had ever seen with one hand. His other hand hung between the folds of a long, red wild rag draped over a blue denim shirt.

The tall, skinny man studied Tee, nodded toward his pickup. "I see a saddle in that pickup that's seen a lot of use. You own it?"

The man with the mustache seemed low on patience as his face con-torted with either pain or anger. "Well, do you or don't you?"

Tee stepped out of the trailer and stood face to face with the man, who stood a good four inches taller than his own five-eleven but easily ten pounds lighter than Tee's one-sixty. "It's mine. Has been for a good long time. Sorry about parking here without asking. Seemed like a good, out of the way spot. We'll move on and get out of your way."

The man shifted his hand under the neckerchief and grimaced from pain. "Name's Joe Henry Leathers. You can call me Joe Henry. I ain't ask-ing you to leave. Hate to ask a stranger on short notice, but I need some quick help if you can handle yourself on a horse. Saw you parked here when we came in before dawn and noticed the saddle. Wouldn't bother you if I had time to get into town for help."

Jubal, dressed like Tee, appeared in the doorway. Joe Henry's expression softened. "Well, looks like there may be two cowboys in this little trailer. Sorry to wake you, son."

Tee felt a rush of pride as Jubal stepped beside him. "This is Jubal and I'm Tee Jessup. How can we help?"

Joe Henry pointed south. "There's a rise a little piece up this road where an old farm family used to live. I have one of my best mares in a ten-acre pasture with my favorite gelding. When we got here this morning, a roaming, sorry stud was in the pasture with them. The mare's in heat, and I don't want him to get to her. The gelding has kept him off so far, but the stud's cut him up pretty bad."

"So you want me to help get him out of there?"

Joe Henry nodded. "Can you use a rope?"

"I could a long time ago."

"If you could once, you still can."

"How do I get up there? Is there room to turn around with this trailer?"

The man handed the motley gray's reins to Tee. "No time for all that. Take Paladin here. The boy can ride with you and I'll run along behind. It ain't far. No time to waste. I got a man up there can help out till I get there."

Joe Henry sat down on the ground and pointed toward his spurs. "You'll need these with Paladin. If you can help me get these off, I'll loan you my pair."

"I got my own. Give me a minute." Tee rummaged in a duffel bag until he found his spurs and strapped them on for the first time since college. He nodded toward the improvised sling. "What happened to your arm?"

"That damned stud bit me and then ran over me. He's a mean, worthless, son-of-a-bitch." He looked toward Jubal. "Excuse my language, son."

"You got a gun? Could be the only choice."

"The man I left down there has a .410, but I told him to use it only if he had to. That little shotgun might just make him mad or put out an eye. You don't have a rifle in that trailer, do you?"

"Got a .22 magnum in the pickup. Might do if you can get close enough." Tee pulled the rifle from behind the pickup seat and handed it to the man. Jubal seemed to sense trouble but said nothing as his father examined Paladin. Tee had to jump into the stirrup. He pulled himself up and swung Jubal up behind him.

They rode in an awkward lope to the hill. Tee, with one hand reaching behind him to be sure Jubal stayed on, tried to make sense of his surroundings. The heavy timber made him feel unsure. When they arrived, he dropped Jubal to the ground with one arm, dismounted, and quickly shortened the stirrups one notch. He winked at Jubal. "Joe Henry's got some sure 'nough long legs."

A second mounted man waited beside a porcelain, clawfoot bathtub converted to a water trough that sat under the spigot of an old well hand pump. Tee knew by the way the man slumped in his saddle and leaned to one side that riding was not his strong suit. His face was deeply pockmarked; his very black, bushy eyebrows matched his eyes. The striped railroad cap he wore made him look even more out of place on the horse. The mounted man had at least a hundred pounds on Tee. The big man urged his horse forward by an awkward move of his hips and put out a ham hock hand toward Tee. "Tecumseh Blaisdell. Folks call me Blaze. Since you're riding Joe Henry's horse, I guess you came to help. I ain't much good with a rope."

Tee nodded as he tried to acclimate himself to the hill. There was an old board and batten house still standing with a deep porch all the way across the front, what looked like a tool shed, and a covered shed with an open front probably used for storing hay. Joe Henry arrived out of breath before Tee saw the horses. When he adjusted his sling, Tee got a look at the deep bite marks. "Break any bones?"

"I think maybe two fingers, maybe my wrist, but I think it's just sprained. You see the horses yet?"

Joe Henry pointed. "The gelding and mare are in that little bunch of trees over there. The stud is over in that corner a few feet away. So far, the gelding has protected her. But he won't be able to much longer."

Tee found the horses in the shade. "Okay. What's the plan?"

"The plan is to get a rope and halter on the stud and haul him home. We got a trailer."

"Why not catch the mare and move her and the gelding out? Be easier."

Joe Henry moved his hand under the sling. "That's how I got my fingers broke. Besides, we'd still have to deal with the stud. He don't belong here."

Tee looked around for a loading pen or chute. There was none. "Ever think about running him out and on down the road?"

"We ran him out yesterday. You see where it got us."

"Has he ever had a halter on him?"

"He belongs to a widow woman a mile or so down the road. She can lead him like a pup. She's got some notion he's gonna draw big stud fees."

Tee had roped more than a few horses but not in this type of country. Joe Henry saw the doubt in his expression. "The pasture slopes off down to bottomland toward those flood levies over there, a plain rectangle. The fence is none too good, but it's up all the way around."

"Looks like a lot of trees."

"There's a lot better and a lot worse places to rope."

"Even if I can get him in the open to rope, he's likely to go through that fence like it's not even there and cut himself up."

"If he does, keep chasing him till you get a shot with the rope. I want him caught. I aim to take him to the widow woman."

Blaze opened the barbed wire gate for Tee and pointed east down a slight incline. "There's a dead stump down there might work for tying him up if you catch him. I ain't much good with horses, but I'll help if I can."

Tee nodded. "Much obliged, but let me try it first." He shook out a loop in the rope Joe Henry handed him, swung it over his head a few times to see if he could still feed the loop both ways. It felt familiar, good, like an old friend.

Joe Henry pointed to the stud. "Don't get yourself or Paladin messed up like my gelding."

Tee stopped when he got close enough to examine the horses. The gelding backed his ears and circled the mare in case Tee represented another threat. A loose flap of skin on his cheek bounced as the gelding waltzed around her. Tee could see other bite marks on his back, hoof cuts from kicks on both hips and shoulders. He felt a surge of admiration for the gelding's courage, pity for his injuries, and anger toward the stud. The mare was frightened, but unhurt. The stud looked to be a coming-two-year-old, a deep sorrel with blaze face, driven only by hormones mixed with adrenaline and testosterone, no brains or training. He seemed well-fed, but his dull coat made him look wormy. His eyes were red and full of hellfire as he stared at Tee and the big gray.

Tee tied four knots in the tail of his rope as close together as he could get them and rode toward the stud. The stud backed his ears, showed his teeth, gave a slight squeal and charged. Tee hit him in the jaw with the knotted tail and spurred out of his way. When the stud turned to charge again, Tee rode toward him and was surprised as Paladin hit him hard enough with his chest to knock the stud off balance. Before he could charge again, Tee hit him hard between his ears with the knotted tail. When he turned his back to kick, Tee spurred his horse to the side and swung the tail hard against the stud's hips and kept swinging and hitting until the stud trotted east toward the creek levies. Tee followed and kept up the punishment until the stud broke into a dead run, trying to escape the rope.

Tee dropped the rope's tail and shook out a loop, rode close to the stud's hip, and threw it around his neck. He left the slack loose and rode alongside, occasionally slapping the stud with the knots to let him know who was in charge. He wanted the horse to believe he was caught and get used to it before taking up the slack. As they neared the east fence line, he tightened the slack and let the stud feel the loop around his neck, gently, then firmly tugging, hoping to get him to gradually slow and turn away from the fence. Tee wanted to get close enough to the stump to wrap the rope around it. But the stud did not slow and would not be herded toward the stump. Tee took a single dally and moved a little farther to the left, jerking the horse's head a little, but not enough to show him who was boss. There was not enough power with the neck loop. They made two trips around the perimeter of the pasture this way, the stud weaving in and out of trees, trying to elude his pursuers and drag Tee off his horse with a tree limb. Both horses were lathered with sweat and the stud was starting to blow, but Joe Henry's huge Paladin was barely breathing hard.

As they started the third trip, Tee was tiring and felt tied to something he could not get away from. The stud seemed to know the stump spelled the end of his adventure and stubbornly stayed away. The situation could be dangerous if the stud figured out a neck loop would not control him and decided to turn and charge. Just as Tee wondered what John T would do, it came to him. He un-dallied, tossed his slack over the horse's hip to the right side, let it drop to the stud's back knees, re-dallied, and turned hard left. Paladin's tremendous power turned the stud's neck as the rope took his knees out from under him and he fell on his side. Paladin seemed to take satisfaction in dragging him a few feet before Tee turned him back. He opened his pocketknife in case he needed to cut the rope, stood in his stirrups, and waved for Joe Henry and Blaze. Paladin had obviously held calves before and backed enough to keep the line taut.

FIFTY-EIGHT

JUBAL SAT IN THE PICKUP SEAT BETWEEN TWO STRANGERS as if he had known them all his life as Blaze drove the pickup and trailer down the hill. Joe Henry was first out of the pickup, rifle in hand. Jubal followed his new friends as they walked toward the downed stud. He knelt from a safe distance and looked into the stud's wide eyes, then at the rifle. The horse's mouth foamed as he lay panting.

Tee worried Jubal might cry. "No sign of anything broke. Expect nothing's hurt but his pride." He knelt to look directly into Jubal's eyes. "This had to be done, son. Now we won't have to shoot him." Jubal breathed a deep sigh.

Tee began to feel sorry for the horse when he kept sharp hooves still as Blaze tied rope hobbles around his front ankles. He seemed almost obliging, as if apologizing for rude behavior. Blaze slipped a halter and lead rope onto his head.

No longer downwind from the mare, the stud loaded like a gentleman, and Joe Henry turned toward Tee as he closed the gate on the trailer. "I am much obliged to you, sir. What can I do to repay you?"

"Well, we owe you for a night's stay on your place. Call it even. But I am looking for work. You know anybody needs a hand around here?"

Joe Henry looked at Blaze. "Could you get by with part time if I threw in a little dirt to park that trailer on and a beef to eat every once in a while?"

Tee looked at his son. "That might work till I can find something steady."

"Fair enough. Come see me in town tomorrow morning. We'll work out details. My office is on the southwest corner of the square."

Tee was embarrassed to ask, but had to. "Which town are we talking about?"

Joe Henry looked at him, his expression amused, as he used his good hand to point north. "Riverby is about three miles down that road you're camped by."

"Riverby doesn't ring a bell."

"Not many know about our little town. Took its name because it's by the Red River. Get it?"

"Makes sense. By the river, Riverby. The west end of the Red runs out to the Panhandle."

"Yep. Same body of water."

Tee looked at his son. "Mind if I ask where the living quarters are?"

"You're standing in the yard now. Needs the water and electricity hooked back up, but Blaze can get the old house livable in a week or two. You can park your trailer here and live in it till he does. That old hand pump works for drinking water till he can get the other one working for inside water. There's an outhouse."

Tee looked back down into the bottom land. The terrain did not rival the high plains, but something drew him to this hilltop and the small house.

Joe Henry noticed the distant look in Tee's eyes. "They call this place Redheart Hill. Indian family lived here once. You're not afraid of ghosts, are you?"

"Never met one. Why?"

Joe Henry pointed to a patch of ground a few yards south of the well pump. Stones had been loosely arranged around a rectangle about four by eight feet. "That's a grave. They say the Choctaw man who lived here was

304

pretty high up in the tribe, a shaman. The tribal council thought he had turned to the dark side, maybe a witch or some such thing. They sent two of their own down here to kill him."

Joe Henry pointed toward the grave. "They shot him right there while his wife and son stood on the porch. The wife went into the house and came back with a Winchester rifle. Dropped one before he could move and got the other one between the shoulder blades when he bolted toward the bottom."

Tee walked over and examined the grave. "So who's buried in the grave? Her husband or his killers?"

Joe Henry's voice took on a staccato quality as a woman's voice began to overshadow his, reminding Tee of the static that used to drown out the sound when he and Jubal listened to *The Lone Ranger* on the family's old radio. "A little of both. The story goes they believed a man's spirit resides in his heart, so the old woman and her son cut out both killers' hearts, then burned their bodies. It came a young flood that night and the creek got out and stayed out for several days. They finally had to bury their man in the yard. The woman buried both the killers' hearts under his body."

Tee saw wavy black and white images like the ones that appeared on the screen of the first television in their ranch home as the story was told. As the blurry images grew clearer, he saw a woman standing by the grave, each hand resting on the shoulder of a young boy. One son was waist high, the other a tad shorter. The woman wept. The boys stared up at their young mother, concerned not about the story, but about her weeping.

He rubbed his eyes with thumb and forefinger. Where had he buried this memory until now? "So there's two hearts and a body buried here?"

"No, just two hearts. The boy came back for his daddy years later. They say he buried him on Choctaw land in Oklahoma."

"So that's why they call it Redheart Hill. Who's the ghost?"

"Some say it's the two killers. Some say it was the man who didn't take kindly to his grave being disturbed. Wanted to stay here where his wife lived. The little wife lived for fifty more years. Could be her. Could be all four."

Tee looked toward the railroad. "Can you hear the train coming through here?"

"Hear it? Hell, you can feel it. This whole hill vibrates. The light will come through the bedroom window when it rounds that curve, rattle the walls of the house when it crosses the trestle. Makes for good sleeping. I like the sound of trains."

Leathers pointed to Blaze, who was loosening the cinch on his saddle. "Blaze there won't stay around here after dark. Says the train drives him crazy."

Tee wanted to change the subject. "Your ranch, does it have a name?"

"Two Hearts. What else?"

FIFTY-NINE

TEE HAD EXPECTED A LITTLE TROUBLE FROM JUBAL WITH school, but the boy seemed almost excited when the teacher took his hand and led him away. Tee was on the southwest corner of the square before nine. The corner office was built of native red and gray stone with an oversized Mexican door, had windows on the west and north filled with wooden shutters that appeared to have rifle ports. Tee liked it a lot. Reminded him of the Alamo.

He tried the door and found it locked, walked south down the street and stopped in front of a crumbling façade that still had a fading sign that said blacksmith and livery, saddle and harness. He sat on the bench outside the office and scanned the square. Buildings that appeared to have been built in the mid-nineteenth century blended well with a few newer ones. A library on the northeast corner, a small museum on the northwest. A hardware store, grocery store, a propane and butane supplier, a five and ten, a café, city hall, the phone company office, TP&L office, and a small bank hunkered in with other typical small businesses. Tee liked it all.

307

Joe Henry appeared without notice, nodded to Tee and, arm still in a sling, unlocked the door. A tear in his jeans above the knee was the only thing that had changed about his appearance from the day before. He flipped on the lights and invited Tee in. "Catch those shutters for me, will you?"

Tee unfolded the hinged pine boards and let light in to expose an oak antique sheriff's desk and two side chairs with horns for backs and arms and cowhide with the hair still on for seats. The outside walls were stucco, and the inside walls were antique bricks. Log beams crisscrossed the ceiling. Everything in the room was rustic and western, most of it antique. "Those rifle ports in those shutters?"

"Yep. Can't be too careful. Never know when Indians might attack. I have a picture of how this old building used to look. I tried to restore it." Joe Henry sat in his desk chair, also made of horns and hide, and motioned for Tee to take a seat. "Have any trouble getting the boy in school?"

"Nope." Tee ran his hands over the smooth horn chair arms. "Mind if I ask why a rancher needs an office in town?"

"Ranching is who I am; I do a few other things to eat. Tell me about what you do besides being a fair hand with a horse and rope."

Tee was caught off guard by the question. He had come to get details on the ranch job.

Joe Henry smiled and leaned forward. "What was the job you ran away from?"

"What makes you think I ran away from anything?"

"Don't mean to pry, but a man shows up here in a barely used travel trailer, a little boy trailing along behind him, wearing Panhandle cowboy gear, out of work, and don't know where he's at; it makes me think he left somewhere in a hurry. None of my business, you understand, but I like to know who I got working for me."

"How did you know I was from the Panhandle?"

"I'm out there quite a bit. I've seen cowboys all over the country. They all got a certain style, but Texas is one of the few places where the east cowboys dress different than the ones in the middle of the state, and the ones in the Panhandle are different than both." He pointed toward Tee's hat and boots. "Now, you I expect you worked in the Panhandle about a decade ago. Styles haven't changed much, but they have changed some."

Tee felt uncomfortable. "Okay. You got me. I grew up on the Blind River Ranch in the top of the Panhandle."

"Guess that explains how you learned to handle a horse and rope."

"My last job was as an accountant. Haven't done cowboy work since college."

Joe Henry laughed out loud. "You're a damned accountant? Who did you work for?"

"Last job I had was working for a lot of low-bred lawyers. A pack of thieves that bankrupted the company I worked for, then went after what was left like a flock of buzzards."

"Sounds like you got a low opinion of lawyers. What if I was to tell you I was a lawyer?"

Tee had the feeling Joe Henry expected him to, so he resisted the urge to look around the walls for evidence of a law degree. His shrug was almost imperceptible. "Guess I would just say congratulations."

Joe Henry slapped the table and laughed again. "You're all right, Tee Jessup. I think I might help you out with a full-time job if you agree to stay and help me on the ranch."

"You really a lawyer?"

"A man does what he has to do. My lot in life is to swim around in the cesspool the practice of law has come to in this country. Sounds like you don't feel much better about bookkeeping." He stood and put on his hat. "Come with me."

They walked one door east and stepped into a building that looked abandoned. Joe Henry's office was everything this one was not. Cheap metal desk cluttered with paper and folders, a ten-key adding machine with the numbers worn off, curtains that looked better suited to a bathroom shower, black desk chair and two mismatched metal side chairs, and file cabinets with broken drawers. The brick walls facing the street were clumsily covered with sheetrock without taping and bedding. Floors along the length of the inside walls were covered with brick dust and bits of mortar and sand from walls of crumbling bricks and mortar. The ceiling was high; Tee figured at least eighteen feet, and covered with stamped metal squares. Most of the white paint on the tin ceiling had been beaten back by rust and time. A few squares hung loosely, exposing pine beams in advanced stages of rot from leaks. The building reeked of dust, rat urine, and mildewed paper. Tee thought he heard bursts of static and words from a short-wave radio coming from behind the back wall.

Joe Henry picked up a file folder from a pile and dropped it. Dust particles swirled, visible even in the dim light. "This little business belonged to Wesley Simpson. He had a stroke nearly a year ago, and I bought it from him before he died. Need somebody to run it."

Tee tried to take in more of the room, looking for some clue as to what kind of business it was. "What is it?"

Joe Henry opened a closet and pointed to a bookcase inside. Tee groaned when he saw one shelf of binders labeled Internal Revenue Code, and a second, bigger shelf with seven Commerce Clearing House binders labeled Income Tax Regulations. "That's depressing."

"When old Wes died, he left a lot of people, including me, in the lurch. We're about six months behind on things now. Reports have to be filed. Plus, it's tax season. There's some quick money to be made."

"I don't think so. This is exactly what I'm running from."

"We all have to do things we don't like. I practice law to make a living, not because I like it. It's a disgusting job most of the time. Tell you what, you keep ninety percent of all your fees; send me ten until I'm paid back my fifteen thousand. Then it's all yours."

Tee made a sweeping gesture and turned a half circle. "Fifteen thousand? You paid fifteen thousand for this?"

"That's just the practice. I already owned the building." He laughed. "Trust me. There's more here than meets the eye. Old Wes did all right for himself."

Tee shook his head. "I appreciate the offer, but this is really not for me. I never really did any tax returns. My experience is with corporate accounting."

"You got your certificate?"

"Nope. Did Wes?"

"No CPA, but he was an Enrolled Agent. You know, a guy who can represent clients with the IRS without being a CPA."

Tee nodded. He knew what an Enrolled Agent was. He thought about Jubal in school, about Blaze getting things ready on Redheart Hill, about the train. "Guess I don't have much choice. I'll stay long enough to get things caught up. No promises after that, though."

Joe Henry extended a hand. "Fair enough. Ninety-ten split. But if you leave before I'm paid in full, it all comes back to me."

Tee shook the hand and nodded toward the back wall. "What's that noise coming from back there?"

"That's Verda's police radio."

"Who's Verda?"

Joe Henry motioned for Tee to follow as he opened a door in the back corner. Tee followed him into a dark hall. Joe opened the first door on the left. "Bathroom. You share it with Verda and her customers."

The overpowering smell in the hall was familiar, but Tee could not identify it until they walked into a bright beauty shop filled with the chemical smell of a permanent wave. One woman peeked out shyly from a hair drier, another sat in the single beauty chair, her hair festooned with rods and paper ends, Verda puttering with one curler and a paper end. The police radio belched static and the occasional word or two from the sheriff or a deputy, a small radio played George Jones singing "The Grand Tour."

Verda turned and smiled as they entered. Soft gray hair draped across her shoulders. Her smile and easy manner reminded him of Winona. The women smiled coquettishly at Joe Henry and more primly at Tee. Joe Henry told them a little about Tee as he introduced Verda and her customers. Verda took Tee's hand firmly in her own and spoke to Joe Henry. "So this young man is going to be my new roommate?"

Tee read the backward sign on the window. The Four Forces. "Like the name of your shop. What does it mean?"

Verda laughed. "That sign has been there for more than ten years, and nobody ever asked. Wind, cold, rain, and sunshine, the four forces of weather."

SIXTY

TEE PICKED UP AN EXCITED JUBAL AFTER SCHOOL AND TOOK
him to his new office. The boy seemed not to notice the things that
depressed Tee. He looked at the room with wonder. "I can walk down here
after school." Tee began to think this might work.

At home, they finished putting up Jubal's new bed in the old house.
He had still not slept in it and would not for a few days until Blaze got
the well pump working, and they could find some used furniture, but it
represented permanence. The sparrow died on Saturday morning. They
buried it above the two hearts. Blaze helped, taking off his railroad cap
and patting Jubal's shoulder as they laid the small bird to rest.

Tee and Jubal gathered and stacked flat rocks in a ring for an outdoor
fire, and Tee prepared to fry some eggs and bacon for supper. Blaze was
walking toward his truck to leave when Tee came out of the trailer with a
carton of eggs. "We got plenty, Blaze. Stay and eat with us."

Blaze turned and walked back. "Maybe some other time. The wife is
waiting."

Tee looked up as he broke the eggs in a cast iron skillet and started to scramble them. "Sure. Say, did that widow woman let Joe Henry cut her stud?"

Blaze looked confused, as if he had forgotten about the stud. "No. Says she can't bear to do that to her pet. Promised to keep him up, though." He turned toward his truck, then came back. "Joe Henry tell you why I quit the railroad? Why I don't stay around here long after dark?"

"Said the train noise bothered you, but I didn't know you worked for the railroad. Except for the cap, I guess."

Blaze nodded. "Engineer for almost twenty years. Now, I can't abide the noises from the train." He looked around to be sure Jubal was out of earshot. The boy was by the fence, petting the wounded gelding. "See here, it's like this. A few years back, I ran over a couple right over there." He struggled to keep his voice from breaking. "They stepped out from behind the trestle in the dark. No time to stop. I just didn't see them soon enough. Why do you reckon they did that?"

Tee kept his eyes on the scrambled eggs until the odor of them burning reached his nose. He shook them, turned them, and slid them on two tin plates Jubal had placed on the rocks. He swallowed hard, looked toward the trestle, then up at his new friend. "Not your fault, I'm sure. Who knows why people do things that don't make sense."

Blaze nodded, shuffled his feet, turned to leave. With his back to them, he mumbled something Tee could not make out. "What was that?"

Blaze turned, embarrassed. "Said I lead the singing at a little country church a few miles from here. You and Jubal would be welcome if you're of a mind."

The church was just as Blaze had described. Tiny, in need of paint, but nestled among giant post and red oaks. Blaze seemed to be expecting them when they entered. He looked directly at Jubal as he led the small congregation in the first hymn, *His Eye is on the Sparrow.* "I sing because I'm happy, I sing because I'm free, His eye is on the sparrow, and I know He watches over me."

<hr />

Weeks passed before Tee walked across the square to a phone booth in front of the Gulf States United Telephone office. He knew his fear was irrational, but he still felt pursued and didn't want to make the long distance call on his new office phone, didn't want to establish a direct link between his old life and this fragile new one. Besides, every word spoken in the old office seemed to echo and possibly travel over walls and through the attic to who knew where. Maybe Verda's beauty shop. He closed the folding door of the phone booth, pulled the crumpled business card Cutt had given him out of his billfold, got his quarters ready, and dialed the number.

"Feedlot." Cutt's brisk voice surprised Tee. He had expected the call to be a blind alley.

Tee told him where they were and that he had enrolled Jubal in school, told him about the job at the Two Hearts Ranch and the bookkeeping practice where he was suddenly part owner. It sounded better than it was, but Tee did not embellish it. Cutt sighed heavily on the other end. "I miss that boy. If you're settled, let me have your number and address. I'll come to see him when I can if that's all right with you."

Tee provided his office phone number and address. "You know you're always welcome wherever I am, Cutt." Tee wanted to ask about Ford, but didn't. "Your new job working out okay?"

Cutt hesitated a few seconds. "Better than expected. It's steady, and I usually get home by six. First time in my life I could say that. Even get off every other Saturday."

"Come see us first chance you get." Tee hung up and walked a few steps toward his new office before turning back. He checked the change in his pocket, then pushed open the screen door to a small grocery store to get more. Father Bob's number came to him easily. The old man's voice seemed fainter. Tee used as few words as possible to tell him where he was and how life had changed for him. He did not mention the railroad.

Father Bob cleared his throat. "You have been in my thoughts since you left your car here. You'll be surprised when you come to pick it up, by the way."

Tee laughed. "I'm sure I would be, but the car is yours. You have more than earned it."

"I'll leave it to you in my will. By the way, where can I reach you?"

Tee squinted to see the street signs across the square. "I'm at the corner of Texas and Oklahoma streets in Riverby, Texas. Looks like my office number is 200 Texas Street."

The wait was uncomfortably long as Tee imagined that the priest was writing it all down. "I hear something reassuring in your voice. Have you forgiven yourself and the others who harmed you and your family?"

Tee was surprised. "I do feel a little better, but not there yet."

"I told you God would bring you through the dark tunnel and into the light. Have you opened the door for Him, given thanks, extended your hand, asked for His help?"

"I try."

"Then you are being guided. We can't expect to see our ultimate destinations. We just keep walking, keep asking to be guided. I expect you are where He wants you to be for now. And I expect you are using your gifts."

Tee felt lighter as he walked back. Over a period of several nights in the dark of the woods at Redheart Hill, he had gradually let go of his resentment toward his father and mother, had even thanked them for the sacrifice they thought was right, though he could not accept that it was.

SIXTY-ONE

JUBAL ADJUSTED TO SCHOOL QUICKLY, MADE LOTS OF FRIENDS.
Tee could almost tell when the boy was thinking of Sarah and Cutt and
life on the Blind River, but he seldom gave voice to his thoughts. He had
become a loner of sorts at home, keeping company only with a dog and
cat he called Rivers and Flo. The tail-wagging, tongue-lolling, speckled
pup had shown up at the screen door one morning with his traveling companion, a black tuxedo cat. Tee suspected Blaze, a childless man, who
seemed to have adopted Jubal as his grandchild. Tee had tried to shoo
them away before Jubal woke. He worried about the boy growing fond of
them, and then losing them to one of the many coyotes or other varmints
that roamed the bottomlands. But they would not shoo. They seemed to
know they had found a home.

Jubal walked down to the creek and into the surrounding woods with
Rivers and Flo whenever Tee let him. His lonesome forays seemed to nur-
ture him. Blaze called him a woods child. They had nursed the mare and
gelding back to health, and Joe Henry encouraged them to ride both. Jubal

changed the gelding's name to Judson and rode him almost every day, whether Tee went along or not. He named the mare Sweetness. Tee worried about him but wanted the boy to live free on the land, free to roam. It gave him pleasure to complement what Cutt had taught the boy about horses. Jubal was a natural.

By the middle of April, Tee knew most of Simpson's bookkeeping clients and was almost caught up on all the accounting. He had learned enough from studying for the CPA exam to bluff his way through tax season by using the code and regulations left behind by Wes Simpson. He liked not having to take orders from anyone but his clients and felt himself emerging from the ten-year tunnel Father Bob had mentioned. The friendship between himself and Joe Henry was developing. The lawyer's extra decade of experience made him too young to be a father figure but old enough to be a good mentor.

As Joe Henry shared more and more of his own past, Tee revealed details and told stories about all the companies that had either fired him or gone under, about the protocol at the bank, about a giant named Doublewide. He had considered such stories tragic until Joe Henry laughed at each one. His laughter made the stories seem less like failures and more like learning experiences that were, yes, pretty humorous when considered from the perspective of a rearview mirror. He did not reveal too many details about his personal life, only mentioning that his family and later his wife had been killed in car wrecks.

Joe Henry showed up at closing time on April 15 carrying two glasses and a bottle of Jack Daniel's Old No. 7. He sat the bottle, the glasses, and his hat on Tee's desk. "Me and Wes always had a little celebration on tax day."

Tee smiled as he watched Joe Henry pour. "My daddy always liked his whiskey to come from Tennessee. Guess a little celebration won't hurt. Just one, though. Tired as I am, two would probably put me out."

Verda appeared in the hallway door. "Well, if the two of you ain't two throwbacks, I never seen one. Who ever heard of a cowboy lawyer and a cowboy accountant."

Joe Henry held up the bottle. Verda shook off the invitation. "Long day. I'm headin' home."

Joe Henry poured himself a second. "I hear good things on the street about you. Seems like you took right to it."

"Looks are deceiving. This is so far from anything I ever imagined for myself, I can't believe I'm doing it. Seems like I'm sort of working for the government, helping these people file taxes."

"Never saw a man so intent on denying his calling. Did you know that I'm a licensed paramedic? I quit law school to follow that career. Then Daddy got sick and Mama begged me to pass the bar so I could take over his law practice. So here I am, but I'm still not cut out for the law."

Tee felt a sense of camaraderie. "That's still better than a bookkeeper."

Joe Henry put a tall boot top across the corner of Tee's desk. "Tell me something. What was the primary problem with all those companies that went under while you worked for them?"

Tee was so surprised by the question he couldn't come up with a quick answer.

Joe Henry answered his own question. "I'll tell you what it was—piss-poor bookkeeping. They didn't know how to keep books. Even that big bank was still in the Stone Age with its accounting."

"You're part right, I guess, but I didn't exactly come to the rescue."

"You didn't know enough. But now you do. That's a skill to be proud of, a useful skill. You got clients now who count on you. It's not about working for the IRS or government; it's about working for these good folks trying to keep the government off their backs and out of their lives as much as possible."

Tee was standing on a ladder on the sidewalk outside his office door the next day when he felt someone watching him. He turned and saw her, the sinking sun outlining her as a dark shadow, making her hair look dark auburn. She was smiling underneath a baseball cap. "Whatcha doing, cowboy?"

Tee balanced the ladder to keep from falling. "Well, I was putting up this sign."

She read it. "Apollo Accounting. That you?"

He sat down on the top step of the ladder, studied everything about her from above. "Might be. What do you think?"

"I like it. Why Apollo?"

"It's a long story, but let's just say it's something my mother would like."

He stayed seated on the ladder, reluctant to step down. He was pleased

319

to see Esther again, but he wanted to be more pleased. He had sealed off his past life and felt a little resentful that she had opened the seal. He stepped down and hugged her. "How did you find me?"

She sensed his reticence. "You gave my address for your mail, but you never gave me yours to forward it."

"I intended to. I was going to call as soon as I got really settled and had good news."

She studied his expression, looking for the real explanation.

Tee's smile seemed forced. "As you well know, I left behind a lot of unfinished business. I had to be sure it wasn't following me. So, how did you find me?"

"You forget who I used to work for?"

Tee nodded. "Stan, of course. I figured he could locate me in case of emergency."

She held out an envelope. "Don't know if this qualifies as an emergency. I have some utility refund checks in my car that need to be cashed, but I figured this couldn't wait."

Tee frowned as he stared at the envelope, imagining a warrant for his arrest, a newspaper clipping of Ford's death, a subpoena. "What is it?"

"Look at the address."

The letter was addressed to John Tee Jessup, CPA. Tee read it twice and tapped it against his palm. "Can't believe it."

He ripped it open and read. "I passed. All four parts."

"Looks like you may need a new sign."

He wanted to shake both fists in the air and shout but kept the euphoria inside. "We have to celebrate. Can you spend the night?"

"Is there a motel in this metropolis?"

"There's a bed and breakfast out at a place called Redheart Hill."

She looked doubtful.

Tee pointed toward home. "It so happens we have a house with two beds and a trailer with one bed. You can have the trailer." Her scent brought to mind cinnamon and cloves, freshly turned earth, and the first flowers of spring.

He introduced her to Joe Henry first, hoping his gift for gab would give him time to analyze his own feelings. She was captivated when they returned to sit in Tee's clean and orderly, though still dull, office. They were still sitting there when Jubal walked in from school. Esther smiled brightly but let Jubal make the move into her arms. His bashful hug seemed to be nourishment for her.

They bought steaks and went home then, home to Redheart Hill. The butane stove in the old house worked now, but Tee had acquired a grate wide enough to rest across the rocks that surrounded his campfire. A storm had obligingly felled a hickory tree in the front yard, and Tee was gradually cooking away the wood. A few feet away from his hickory fire, Esther sat leaned against a big post oak, and Jubal, deep down in his cowboy hat, squatted on his heels in front of her. Flo was curled in her lap, and Rivers leaned against Jubal's leg. Tee wished for a camera.

Steaks sizzling and potatoes baking in the coals, he strained to hear their conversation. Jubal pointed in all directions, telling a different tale with each point of the compass. The boy had become part of Two Hearts Hill. The wind shifted enough to bring sound but not the words. He moved the steaks away from the blaze so he could hear better. Esther asked Jubal about his favorite place in the woods. "The trestle," he said without hesitation.

She smiled. "Why? Is it the sound of the train?"

He shrugged. "I like the train, but mostly I like it because they seem to like having me there, like they wait for me to come back."

"Who's they?"

Jubal's face reddened. "Birds. Squirrels. Rabbits. Even had a coyote come close once. It's like they talk to me."

They talked and laughed during supper and after until it was Jubal's bedtime. He objected but not much. Esther had the fire going again when Tee returned after bedding him down. "He's not afraid all alone in that old house?"

"He was at first but not now. Expect he's already asleep." He sat on the blanket beside her and they listened to the bottomland sounds of whippoorwills and an owl.

She stared into the fire. "I sense you are still grieving over Sarah."

The question surprised Tee. "Raising a son alone worries me a little. Somebody told me once that a boy needs a mother."

"I didn't mean to imply...."

"I know."

"And the grief?"

"You don't miss much." Tee warmed his hands by the fire. "Truth is, I can move on from the grief, but it's the guilt that bothers me."

"Guilt?"

"I should have seen what was happening. It was right there in front of me, but I was just too absorbed in my own self-pity to see how afraid she was. I could have stopped it, kept her from leaving, kept her from dying."

"I think you're being too hard on yourself. You're making a new life for you and your son. You have to move on."

"I will." He looked toward the old house and the outbuildings. "This place is not much, and it doesn't even belong to us, but it's a start toward a normal life. I crave normal."

Her eyes glistened as she nodded.

"It's a compromise, I know. No big ranch. No racehorses. But for the first time, I feel like I'm captain of my own ship." He laughed. "Joe Henry likes to quote poetry. Says he is master of his fate, the captain of his soul. I like that."

The next morning, Tee made coffee and went out on the porch before sunrise. He loved the sounds of morning in the woods. An owl that roosted nearby called, a rooster answered, a roadrunner ran across the yard. Tee waited for the Airstream lights to come on. As the sun crept around the corners of the house, he heard her car start, watched her drive away.

———

At camp meetings throughout the Choctaw Nation in the 1820s, people began having visions of their newfound sacred power. One man told a group that he had seen himself born and raised in a dark wilderness. While pushing through brambles and bushes, he came upon a candle's light the power of Christianity. He made his way to the light to seize the new source of power. Another man described swimming up from a muddy river to see the light.

—James Taylor Carson
*Shamanism: An Encyclopedia
of World Beliefs, Practices, and Cultures*

www.ingramcontent.com/pod-product-compliance
Lightning Source LLC
Chambersburg PA
CBHW030637020726
47493CB00006B/1761